After Black

Lynne Fisher

After Black

ISBN-13: 978-1086991208
Copyright © Lynne Fisher 2019

All rights reserved. No part of this publication may be reproduced, stored in or introduced into a retrieval system, or transmitted in any form or by any means without the prior written permission of the copyright holder.

This is a work of fiction. Names, characters and incidents are the products of the author's imagination. Locales, public names or business names are used for atmospheric realism purposes only. Any resemblance to actual people, living or dead, or to businesses, companies, events and locations is completely coincidental.
Any resemblance to published or unpublished work is entirely coincidental.

The moral right of the author has been asserted.

Edition 2019

Cover design by DRF
Images courtesy of Pixabay.

After Black

'One does not become enlightened by imagining figures of light, but by making the darkness conscious.'

Carl Jung

PART ONE

Chapter 1

Christmas was over and she was glad to see the back of it. It was now Monday morning and a fresh start in the new year of 1990. An early January drizzle was spitting onto the kitchen window, a mirror of blackness intensified by the harsh electric light blazing from inside. The outer darkness shrouded the grizzled winter garden and fields beyond. Janet always used to find January a raw kind of month, feeling exposed to the glassy edges of another year ahead. Any hopes she dared to foster always seemed to be swatted like flies. But today, she didn't particularly mind the gloom of winter or the chill in the air. She had some hopes again, and this time they were like butterflies, bursting with colour. And this time, no one could swat them dead because her life had changed for good.

It wasn't that she felt happy exactly, that would be going too far. She couldn't even remember what happy felt like. Smiles and laughs were just for show, she'd learned those tricks at work – good for serving the customers, putting a face on. The self-help books were wrong; acting happy didn't make you feel happy. No. All she wanted was some inner peace for her fresh start, but that still felt elusive as something specific was on her mind. Something that had been disturbing her sleep for the last few nights, something beyond her control. And being out of control was something she found unacceptable, like a pile of dirty dishes, a floor that needed vacuuming, an unmade bed, a loose thread on the back of her cross stitch. And that *something* was the reason why she was up so early for work this morning, and why she was washing up her breakfast dishes so slowly, to use up the time, glancing at her reflection in the window now and again, all the while trying to restrain herself from probing her problem from every angle with her dissecting scalpel. She tried to distract herself by contemplating the withered poinsettia on the windowsill in front of her.

She'd been marking its slow decline for two weeks now, deliberately not having watered it, with those automatic glances you give anything in line of sight of the washing up bowl, dragging your eyes from the tedious to the just as infuriatingly familiar. Susan, her daughter-in-law, had insisted it would brighten up her kitchen as she'd plonked it firmly down onto the kitchen windowsill. And Janet was forced to keep it there as the family kept popping round over the holiday – 'just to make sure you're not too lonely,' her son, Scott, kept saying. Janet knew he meant well, but wished he'd rein his wife in. Susan was like a flighty mare careering around a meadow, neighing and snorting, knocking the jumps over, kicking up the buttercups, refusing to be put in harness. She'd bored holes into Janet's new Chinese rug with the pronged hooves of her red stilettos perched on the ends of her leg-of-mutton calves, as she airily recounted her new year's resolution to lose some weight. Janet had cringed, watching those heels grind into the pile. So, she'd felt perfectly justified in asking Susan to remove her shoes.

Susan had been incensed. 'You know, you can be a bit obsessive, Janet,' she said, as she flung them towards the front door. She'd looked angrily at Scott for support, but he'd remained neutral by shrugging his shoulders.

Wise boy, thought Janet, and she smiled at her doppelgänger in the window before she began drying the dishes with her linen tea towel.

Just then, the phone rang. It made her start as she'd not had any calls since New Year's Day. Peeling off her rubber gloves, she hurried into the hall and tentatively picked up the receiver.

It was Ann Waters, her friend from Masons, the department store where she worked.

'Just checking you're okay this morning, Janet,' Ann said. 'We'll have our lunch break together at two, okay? Ron says that's fine. And we're both down to finish at six. I'm looking forward to seeing you. There's a few changes and some gossip, maybe some news, but it's too early to say. How are you bearing up?'

Janet found it a relief to hear Ann's voice, harmless in its familiarity, harmless in her very nature. Ann was positively biddable.

'Oh, I'm alright, I suppose, Ann,' she replied. 'Just looking forward to getting back into a routine. You know. It'll do me good.' She tried to make her voice sound just a little pensive, with some heavy-toned acceptance to convey the cruel hand of fate, and certainly not to sound as if she could possibly be interested in any news. After all, Janet reminded herself, I *am* supposed to be the grieving widow.

Going back into the kitchen, she was itching to know what the news was. Whether it had anything to do with the problem she'd been trying to dissect for nights in a row. She felt the hackles rise on the back of her neck, as fiercely as an angry she-wolf protecting her young. I've got to get myself under control, she said to herself. This is ridiculous. I'll find a way of handling it somehow. As she marched towards the sink, the red poinsettia flashed at her again, like a traffic stop light making her break hard and halt. She hated these plants. She hated the way they infested supermarkets just before Christmas, like a December virus, catering for the masses, those easily led. It was so predictable the way people planted them on top of their trolleys piled high with gluttonous quantities of Christmas food and booze, people who wouldn't normally take any interest in houseplants, people who wouldn't even know how to look after them. And poinsettias looked so unnatural anyway, like badly folded origami trying to look like flowers.

Well, Janet said to herself, Christmas is over. It's a new year, a new start for a new me.

And for once, these words really meant something to her, as if they'd been fashioned just for her.

And thinking of this, she grasped hold of the poinsettia,

balled the fading red bracts tightly into her fist, and lifted the plant in its pot off the windowsill, like a toddler picking up a doll by the hair. She turned and flung the whole plant into the gaping mouth of her kitchen bin. A heavy thud echoed through the house like a bullet shot and Janet's lips curled into a thin smirk. That was the last of the Christmas tat. She had already taken down the tinsel and baubles, having decided to abort the Twelfth Night tradition this year – she wasn't afraid of any more bad luck now.

Thomas, her tabby cat, was sitting by the bin. Unflinching, he eyed her rubbish disposal act like a wise Buddha, his yellow eyes slanted in understanding. He knew all manner of things and he'd witnessed and personally experienced a lot worse in this house. A lot of bad karma.

'Sorry, Thomas,' she said, putting down a dish of his favourite tinned sardines and giving him a pat on the head. Thomas opened and closed his mouth in a silent response, reserving his audible miaows strictly for emergencies only.

Tidying the dishes away, Janet made herself a cup of instant coffee and took it into the living room. She set it down on a glass-topped side table by her winged armchair near the regency-style marble fireplace. This was her favourite chair for her favourite view of the room. But before sitting, she sidled to the front bay window and twitched aside the frilly edge of her net curtain to look out onto Willow Lane. This was a well-practised habit, and with the aid of the street lighting she could make out that all was more or less in order. There were no parked cars blocking her drive entrance; no wheelie bin belonging to her nosy next-door neighbour, *just a quick chat*, Winnie Parsons, encroaching upon her territory as was frequently the case; and not too many cars parked at the Reynolds's opposite, who had a habit of inviting all and sundry to any festive or celebratory family occasion, such dedicated followers of convention which they were. Simply any excuse for a boozy party. And their silly outdoor illuminations were still brazenly advertising their crass taste.

She sat down and checked her watch. It was still a little early to leave for work so she leaned back in her chair, just lightly, so as not to crush her cross stitch cushion, and sipped her coffee. As she tried to relax, her mind was tugged straight back to the problem she'd been trying to distract herself from, that *something* beyond her control, and the only real remaining hindrance to her happiness as far as she could work out. And that something was actually a *someone* – by the name of Marian Johnson, who was employed by Berkeley Fabrics to run a concession within Masons soft furnishing department where Janet was employed as a sales consultant. Marian Johnson, who was in Janet's opinion, nothing but a jumped-up little trollop, a flirt in a tight skirt and tight blouse, buttoned low to show off her cleavage for the male customers to ogle, with a tight walk and a calculated wiggle to keep their eyes glued to her backside. And this jumped-up little trollop was keen for more power. Janet not only sensed it, she could smell it on her, floating in the wake of the clouds of her cheap scent.

Janet felt her heart pounding and a rising heat pumped through her body – just thinking of Marian could do this to her. But this time Janet was more disturbed than usual, because she had heard rumours about Ron, her department manager, most specifically, that he might be deciding to retire early due to stress. Nothing confirmed, nothing in writing, nothing to work with or act upon, but she knew that Marian may have heard the rumours too, and the thought made her stomach flutter with nerves, and nerves were not acceptable in Janet's world. Something would have to be done.

To once more divert herself, she ended up unconsciously directing her eyes to another source of conflict. To where Susan had stood in her stilettos on the Chinese rug. She thought she could still see the two indentations about eight inches apart, so she got down on her knees to examine them. They were right in the centre of a rose and scroll motif by the edge of the fireplace. She had already brushed the pile soon after the assault was perpetrated, but still, there seemed to be flattened wool fibres. She tutted as she stroked the pile back on itself to fluff it up, cursing Susan once again. Something would have to be done about her too. She was a bad influence on her son, far too demanding, and she felt truly mortified that Susan had to be the mother of her beloved grandson, Daniel. But this problem would have to wait, she had to get back to work first.

As Janet got to her feet and put her left hand out onto the mantelpiece to steady herself, she stiffened. A sense of déjà vu unexpectedly hit her in the gut and her stomach turned over. The pose she held was familiar, all too familiar. It was how she had stood when Frank, her husband, was dying – right there, in front of her, lying on the floor by the sofa, looking straight at her. He'd got himself all worked up, which wasn't a good idea when he suffered from angina and had suffered two heart attacks already, but it was a regular occurrence as he was so very prone to stress.

She thought it was just an ordinary attack at first. He was standing explaining something he felt passionate about, then he groaned and grimaced, and the words he was uttering were blown apart by his wheezing breaths. She'd seen him having this kind of angina attack before.

But this time was different. His knees buckled under his tall frame and he fell in front of her as if he was making a proposal of marriage. Sweat beaded into droplets on his shiny bald pate. He groaned and fell to one side in front of the sofa, one folded arm now clutching the other, eyes wide, pale blue irises pinning her to the spot like a bug under a microscope. Time swelled as Janet stood there, unable to move, as she held onto the marble fireplace. Frank's nostrils flared, his neck muscles were as corded as a stick of celery, and he kept grunting, trying to say something to her in-between his gasps for breath.

What was it?

Finally, fear loosened its hold on her. She broke her petrified pose and sank to her knees in front of him. He clutched hold of her hand and tightened his grip. He squeezed so hard that the gold ring he always wore bit into her fingers. She cried out in pain, but he held on, keeping her close.

'Janet –'

He drew her closer, his bicep muscle bulging through the cotton of his shirtsleeve. She wanted to scream, but couldn't make a sound.

Then, looking hard into her face, Frank said what were to be his last words, and he spat them at her.

'You fucking bitch!'

Adrenalin now crashed through her and she wrenched her hand away. Springing to her feet, she grasped the marble mantelpiece once more, but was unable to break eye contact with Frank.

Her husband of 34 years lay before her – as motionless as she. Not only not moving, but now he didn't seem to be breathing either.

'Frank?'

No response.

'Frank!'

Still no response. Just that glare in his eyes that would later turn into a dull glaze.

And finally, she came to her senses and dashed for the phone.

That had been on the evening of the 5th December, just gone. The emergency services had been unable to resuscitate Frank and he was declared dead at the scene. He was 65 years of age. The cause of his demise written on the death certificate by the couple's GP, and cleared by the coroner, was cardiac arrest due to coronary artery atherosclerosis. Frank Brewer was buried a week later, where his loved ones paid respects. Janet had taken compassionate leave from Masons and extended it into Christmas and New Year.

Today was the 3rd January. And now, still standing in this pose, remembering Frank and their life together, Janet felt tears smarting in her eyes. But she wiped them away. She must get over this, she simply must. She'd done so well, she'd got through the funeral, she'd visited the grave with Scott, she'd even sorted out Frank's clothes. And she'd replied to all the condolence cards and letters and reviewed her finances. Very soon she'd be in receipt of Frank's pension, and there was some life insurance to come through. But Scott had thought it was far too soon for her to return to work.

'You're shutting away your feelings, Mum,' he'd said.

'Keeping busy is what will get me through,' she'd argued several times, wanting to arrange a return date, so he'd relented and given his blessing.

Now she was ready to go back to work. The work she loved doing, at Masons where she truly belonged.

Looking at her watch again, she gulped down the rest of her coffee, stalked into the kitchen to rinse out her cup, then headed back through the living room to the front door, snapping off the lights.

'See you later, Thomas,' she called over her shoulder to the cat.

Stepping in front of the full-length mirror, strategically placed next to the coat stand behind the front door, she slipped on the black patent leather court shoes which were waiting for her, and surveyed herself from top to toe in the mirror. This was an important ritual before leaving for work which she'd so missed lately.

She was dressed in a black work suit, the jacket coming down to her upper thighs, with padded shoulders to rival Alexis Carrington's attire at a business meeting in *Dynasty*. The pencil skirt just covered her knees, showing off her shapely calves, which were encased in sleek charcoal-tinted 20 denier tights. A white blouse with a scalloped collar gave her a concessionary touch of softness. She was a smart looking woman for the age of 54, and she'd held onto her figure remarkably well, which Frank had always appreciated.

Janet's facial features were bold. Strongly arched

eyebrows for good expression, clear green eyes and a well-formed mouth. Her nose was a tad Roman and a little too prominent making her profile rather pointed. Adding to this severity was the fact that her hair was coloured rook black, cut into a streamlined bob, and for work she brushed it back tightly into a tortoiseshell clip. She always ensured to dye her hair regularly and just yesterday had retouched her roots.

Happy with her appearance, she moved closer and examined her face, not to check her immaculate makeup, with the tiny scar on her left cheek well-concealed as usual, but as if to stare into her soul, to ensure all was well there. To make sure that although returning to work meant having to suffer that strutting strumpet, Marian, Masons was truly where she belonged, and Marian, despite her ambitions, was going to be nothing more than an occasional irritation.

She removed her shoes and slid her calves into some sleek black leather boots which were more appropriate for the winter weather, and shrugged herself into her long black woollen coat. Carefully placing her court shoes into her black leather handbag, she shouldered it and reached for her car keys. Just before she opened the door and clicked off the last light, she took once last look into the living room and through into the kitchen, with a swift running glance up the staircase. She smiled. The house was all hers now and it would look exactly the same on her return from work. There would be no tension on approaching the front door, no mess to clear up, no awkward conversations, no Frank, sitting slumped in his chair watching quiz shows or the news, to cater for. Just order, peace and a new life at last.

Chapter 2

After driving into central Cheltenham, Janet parked her indigo Volkswagen Polo in a residential side street, ten minutes walk from Masons on the Promenade. The drizzle had thickened into porridgy sleet, so Janet shielded herself with her umbrella. Marching along with her characteristic poker-backed walk, her boot heels striking the greasy wet pavement with a military rhythm, she suddenly halted and gazed back at her car. She loved looking at it parked up like this. It was all hers and she was proud of having bought it herself on instalments when she had first began working at Masons around five years ago, just after Frank had retired. Frank had not approved of her new job and had refused to let her borrow his Volvo, so she had got the bus into town until acquiring her own car. This new independence was an elixir to her spirit, that once in her system, she'd fiercely protected. And she'd found it addictive. And now Frank's 'precious' had already been driven from her life, sold by Scott at her own request to a local dealership. She had relished the sight of the Volvo's grey hulking body disappearing down the road, then parking her own car in the garage instead.

Now, as she turned into Pilgrim Street, she felt a current of warmth tingle through her body at the sight of other sales consultants disappearing into the narrow shadowed doorway set halfway along the rear of Masons. It was 8.40am and they all had to be standing to attention at their posts with their floats in their tills waiting for the buzzer to mark the start of their trading day at 9am. They were all part of a vital team, like soldier ants entering the nest of the queen to do their duty and serve, trained to the highest standards for a store that was known in the town for its excellent customer service. In fact Masons was viewed by the local populace as the Harrods of Cheltenham, far superior to House of Fraser and John Lewis. It was the original flagship store of what was now a whole fleet, trading their wares throughout England and Scotland. And as Janet entered through the staff entrance of this queen bee of the retail world, her heart thumped with anticipation at the prospect of her day.

Down the creaky, recycled fire escape steps into the bowels of the nineteenth-century building she went, her footsteps clattering on the open fretwork, with more feet urging her on from behind. Down she went, well below ground level, then along a dimly-lit concrete corridor and into a locker room, where rows of olive green metal 'cubicles' were lined up for assisting in the transformation of the individual into a member of the collective. Janet squeezed past the thrusting bottom of a bulky woman with a stiffly starched hairdo, bending over as she changed her shoes, then she headed straight for her own locker, number 149. She opened it and glanced inside – just one accusing hanger still there after she'd brought it from home five years ago. It looked desolate in such lonely isolation and she felt a sense of triumph as she hung her coat upon it once more. Changing into her high heeled court shoes, she thrust her boots towards the back of the locker.

Now there were just two more things to do before going up to her department. Reaching into her bag she pulled out her name badge, burnished gold, with Masons etched at the top, and with a princess crown above the 'a', then her name centrally placed – Janet Brewer. Staring at her surname she felt a tightening in her chest. She always hated her married name, and she'd already considered changing it back to her maiden name, but 'Turner' wouldn't sound so different to most people, and what would Scott think? She stabbed the pin into the lapel of her jacket and snapped it shut. Taking a deep breath, she picked up a bottle of her favourite Obsession perfume from the top shelf of her locker and spotted some scent onto her wrists and behind her ears in true Hollywood fashion, just like she'd seen Hedy Lamarr do it, one of her favourite actresses. She didn't care that its potent spices made people cough a little as she passed by.

Snatching a glance at her watch, she quickly left the locker room, and paced down two more creepy crepuscular corridors, then shouldered open a swing door on her left. Here was a staircase, one of many, placed all along the length of the building. These irregular offshoots, just like a rooting system, led up from the building's dark victorian underbelly, up and up, to the ground floor light and polish and the domain of the customers, customers who were privileged in gaining access to the store through stately revolving front door entrances just off the Promenade. Doors which once had men in livery to assist with the slightest whim, who helped ladies with full skirts and parasols from their carriages, intent on buying the latest lace, to approach the swagged and garlanded exterior, to enter the potted palm palace, to ponder their purchases.

But today, well-oiled escalators and lifts carried the customers higher to more floors because the sky's the limit in the world of commercial trading.

As Janet began climbing the first of three staircases, she remembered what it had felt like when she first started working here. How she had kept getting lost in the bedrock of this building. How with all the corridors and stairways turning this way and that, with a few blind alleys, it had felt like she was inside one of those Escher drawings that Scott had been fascinated by as a teenager. All those buildings with impossible pathways, stairways, paradoxical geometries and perspectives leading nowhere, with anonymous marching figures who seemed to know exactly where they were going – just like all the staff of Masons seemed at that time, all certain of their own pathways to their own departments.

Or, how getting lost in this architectural nightmare was also like trying to find your way through a labyrinth. And without the benefit that Theseus possessed, of Ariadne's thread, you could end up being eaten by a monster and vanishing from the world forever, or maybe die of starvation, slowly shrivelling, desiccating and collapsing into a pile of bones, to perhaps one day awaken the piercing screams of another lost soul.

Janet grinned as she recalled these feelings. A couple of months after these nervous beginnings she'd made it her quest to master the puzzle of the maze and had swiftly worked out a few alternative routes for herself, depending on exactly where she wanted to emerge. Then she'd stepped smartly onto the back of a slinky metallic snake or two, to ride to her desired destination. She'd finally felt like a bona fide member of staff – staff number 7788, department number 15. Rate of pay £3.30 an hour, unless you were employed by a concession, which was considerably higher.

But the feature that set Janet apart, and it was one she was proud of, was the fact that she worked on the soft furnishing department, where the mostly female staff earned 1% commission on their individual sales. Why? Because they had to train on the job and learn a great deal, they had to do calculations and quotes, as well as pack up fabric lengths and linings with making instructions enclosed, to be despatched to Masons curtain makers in nearby Cirencester. So they had to apply themselves well and certainly earned every penny of their commission. They were sales *consultants* on the soft furnishing department, not just 'lowly' sales *assistants*, like the adjacent bedding department. This distinction was very important to Janet. Of course, when she'd found out the men on carpets earned 5% commission on *their* sales, she felt justifiable indignation. Outright sexism at work here, she'd exclaimed to Ann, who'd helped her learn the ropes. Yes, of course, they also had maths to do, but surely their own training in soft furnishing was just as complex, arguably more, seeing as the carpets staff only had to work out surface areas of floors to get a square metreage for a quote and put an order in, whereas soft furnishing might have to calculate anything from Austrian blind cord metreage to rolls of wallpaper for a room. I mean! It just wasn't fair. And what would Maggie Thatcher think of that! Ann had nodded in agreement like a winded-up automaton nearing the end of its current energy capacity.

Right now, just as Janet turned the corner of her second staircase, her eyes darted to a jagged hole in the wall on her left. In a wall, in dire need of some plaster filling and repainting, there was the black hole she could never ignore, a black hole just bigger than the size a fist could make. When she'd first started, she'd felt a dreadful aura of violence and despair coming from it, as if someone had punched a hole into it from the outside in, or the inside out…but who could work out which, why or when? Later, when she was going through the stressful first few weeks of training, she saw it as a black hole of escape…to remind herself that escape was still possible, and of course leaving the job would've suited Frank down to the ground. But that had been five years ago, when she'd been determined to prove Frank wrong, to prove herself more than capable of this work, and more recently, she'd had a far more effective use for this black hole that she passed every time she went up this staircase to work. Marian Johnson. That trumped-up little tart, with her tight skirt, tight blouse and her permed hair, dyed red from a bottle. With her red lipstick mouth, and her thick eyeliner, her cheap bangle earrings swinging back and forth as she flicked her hair around, with her trashy nail extensions poised around her tawdry biro to scrawl out some indecipherable curtain order…Janet could always feel her gorge rising in anticipation of having to work in proximity to Marian for the day as she manned her desk in the Berkeley Fabrics concession. And she even had to stomach catching sight of her now and again at the local Sainsbury's after work, though what someone like *her* was doing shopping at Sainsbury's she had no idea.

But Janet had a defence to come to her aid. She'd come up with a visualisation trick that she'd creatively adapted from a self-help book on how to take control of one's life. And instead of visualising a peaceful place of one's own choosing to go to for stress alleviation, Janet visualised hurling Marian Johnson, shrunken to the size of a doll (and her resemblance to a Sindy doll was quite remarkable), right through that hole in the wall, coming to rest at the bottom of an abyss with a thud and a whimper, never to be seen again. What a sweet image. And as Janet imagined this once more, flinging Marian through the hole, she smiled once more. It would hopefully serve her well today.

And so after another dingy corridor and another pair of battered wing doors, she emerged into the light of the public space of the first floor. A sleek shiny escalator escorted her to the second floor where the soft furnishing, bedding, carpets and furniture departments were all located, together with the cash office. Home. She was home.

And there was such a welcome.

A spangled ocean of red and white sale banners filled her senses, all flagged around the departments. Banners hanging at regular intervals from the ceiling. Standing frames heralding the way. And the merchandise emblazoned with A4 sale frames on gleaming glass displays, sale bins, all tidy to start the day. Sale tickets slapped onto goods to grant the public their Christmas wishes, to hear the tills ring out the January Sale cheer. Red, green and gold baubles and stars slowly rotating in celestial mobiles seduced to induce that 'treat yourself' sparkle, while bugle-calls of percentage reductions rang out loud their greetings of the season: 20% off! 25% off all orders! And of course there was 50% off! – even better.

For one moment it was just too much for Janet. The fluttering butterflies in her stomach went into a flying frenzy and she felt her heart thudding against her ribcage. All the visual delights seemed to waver before her eyes as if she was seeing a bountiful oasis through the intense heat of the Sahara. But she took two deep breaths and her vision slowly stabilised and she forced herself to get a grip. By the time she strode onto the soft furnishing department she had resumed her customary poise – only to be further challenged by Ann running up to her from the till. Ann halted in front of her, then with obvious hesitation placed her arms around Janet's shoulders and squeezed her into a hug.

'Good to have you back!' she gushed into her ear, while Janet went rigid with horror, her arms stiffly pinned to her sides in the very antithesis of reciprocation. Surely Ann knew she didn't go in for this kind of thing?

Ann sensed her feelings and pulled away hastily, a look of guilt flitting across her face. 'Sorry, Janet, but it really has seemed like such a long time without you. It's been chaos here!'

'Why? What's been happening?' Janet asked sharply.

'Oh, we'll talk about it later…it's just there are so many orders to get out, and Gemma's still learning. And we're still an assistant down, and we still don't have an assistant manager to help Ron. I've been run off my feet!'

Janet wasn't in the least surprised to hear this. Gemma Smithson was a 21 year old, who'd worked on the department for around four months. Why they had allocated this drippy youngster to soft furnishing was a mystery as complete as that of the lost city of Atlantis, and in Janet's view, quite outrageous. Not only that, but her whole demeanour and dress was inappropriate for Masons. Gemma had proudly informed Janet, when she'd questioned Gemma's appearance for her notably thick eyeliner and long black hair, that she happened to be a Goth. That she didn't wear her piercings at work and kept her makeup to a minimum, and that was fine with the personnel manager. And she'd even gone as far as to suggest that Janet had leanings towards the Goth look herself. For once, Janet had been rendered speechless. But after Gemma realised that to get on in the department and thereby keep her job, she needed to learn the ropes from the skilful Janet, she'd swallowed her principles and had been very accommodating ever since. Clever girl after all, Janet thought, with some grudging admiration, as she now glanced at Gemma, who was slouched over one of the serving benches studying an order, though her posture left a lot to be desired. God knew what the next one they lined up would be like!

Then her gaze scanned the far reaches of the department and the adjacent concession of Berkeley Fabrics towards the cash office. There was no Marian. Instead, a frumpy looking woman was sitting behind the serving desk, her ample bosom ballooning onto the edge of the desk, and…what was that she was wearing? A *cardigan*? Well, really! Gemma could get away with it, but not someone so obviously middle-aged!

'Who is *she*?' she asked Ann, her eyebrows hitched up to maximum altitude like a scarily on-the-edge Joan Crawford.

'Well, that's one of the changes. It's Marian's part-timer. She started a few weeks ago to help cover the opening hours. She's doing the morning shift, Marian's coming in at one, same time as Ron. They'll be doing until eight together with Gemma.'

'Yes, but who is she?' repeated Janet, glaring into Ann's gentle eyes.

'Milly, her name's Milly Carter. She's from Gloucester.'

'Milly?' Janet felt an instant repugnance to the name. It just so happened to be what her father had called her mother, Mildred. It was an affectionate term for a mother who Janet hadn't been close to, so Janet was forced to disparage it. 'Milly, as in Milly-Molly-Mandy?' Janet's tone was distinctly sarcastic.

Ann clamped her hand over her mouth, stifling a giggle. 'Janet!' She paused. 'It's short for Emily. I asked her. She's quite nice, actually. Do you want to say hello?'

Janet shook her head. 'I'll see her later on.' Then she looked closely at Ann.

Reassuringly, she looked just the same. The same silver hair, set by curlers and sprayed into position, brushed well back from her ivory complexioned face. The same delicate makeup and powder, the same navy suit, the same navy high heeled court shoes, the same rather meaty calves – but then whose wouldn't be wearing such shoes for work for 25 years or so? After all, Ann was a veteran of Masons. And it was for this reason, and for the fact that she was 'old school', that Janet had grown fond of her, despite her lacking backbone at times. Ron liked to call herself and Ann the two doyens of the department.

It was a quiet first hour to the first trading day of the new year. Ann updated Janet on what was going on with the customer orders for the makers, Clothworks, in Cirencester, and talked her through the various sale discounts that were currently running. Even Gemma chipped in, and seemed in her own way genuinely pleased to see Janet back.

'Where've you been, Mrs B?' asked Gemma.

Janet knew it was a rhetorical question, but she smiled to herself as she quite liked being called this by Gemma.

She shot Gemma a sideways look. 'How about wearing a proper jacket for the new year?' she commented, her eyes glancing over Gemma's long cardigan.

Gemma slowly shook her head, considering. 'No...not really me, you know that. I'm not into power dressing. I like to preserve just a smidgeon of individuality.'

Janet tutted, then strode across to introduce herself to a visibly nervous Milly, who, she was able to observe, had stuffed the ripples of flesh below her waist into an ill-fitting sausage skin of a pencil skirt. And wonder of wonders, she turned out to be recently widowed herself.

'What a coincidence!' Milly breathed, twisting her biro around in her fat-fingered hand, on which was squeezed a large ruby ring, of distinctly vulgar proportions, Janet felt. But she smiled back at Milly...keep your enemies close, she decided. And Milly-Molly-Mandy who obviously ate too much candy, could come in quite handy – as a source of information with respect to Marian.

While Ann and Gemma took it in turns to go for their customary earlier tea breaks on this strangely quiet morning of the season, Janet settled into measuring out fabric for a curtain order at one of the serving counters – namely 27.5

metres of Sanderson's 'Golden Lily Minor', colour 'sage' stock fabric, currently reduced from £9.99 per metre to £7.50. She noticed the music playing over the tannoy was no longer choked with sickeningly syrupy Christmas songs about roasting chestnuts or Mommies kissing Santa Clauses. Thank God for that!

She'd already suffered the slings and arrows of the usual *Happy New Year* greetings, chanted like jarring musical notes for quite unnecessary emphasis by passing bedding department staff. But today she felt more equanimity than in the past, where she'd had to disguise her sneers at the sheer folly of thinking such a greeting could make any difference to anyone's life. But this time, she found the refrain a little more tolerable. After all, maybe there wouldn't be the usual outrageous fortune to come with *this* new year? And there was still no sign of Marian. Even better without her around – though yet to be achieved permanently, which was Janet's new year's resolution. And of course, there had been *I'm sorry for your loss*, tacked on to the end of the new year greetings, kind of muttered dully, with distinct overtones of apology. And she found herself marvelling at the convenience of black for mourning just happening to be her favoured work colour – talk about killing two birds with one stone.

By the time she hauled out another roll of fabric from the stands, swung it nimbly onto her shoulder, then thumped it down onto the counter for unrolling and measuring, she was feeling that familiar pleasure once again. This was home, this was what she loved doing. She had so missed pulling the fabric out into a pile-up of waves, then feeding the selvage through one hand to the other marking out the metres on the brass ruler set into the counter. Then the sharp satisfying bite of the scissors into the fabric, the slicing through, keeping a straight line, the cutting to the grain. She was always complimented on this by customers who were intent on making their own drapes. *You cut so straight!* they would exclaim. Then the picking up of the selvage once again, section by section, to gather the folds of the whole length evenly in her hands and against her chest, before laying the heavy weight of it down for the final folding and sliding it into a generous carrier with the Masons crown logo stamped onto it to give the contents the royal seal of approval. Or sometimes the customer wanted it rolling, not folding (and they were of course always asked which they'd prefer). Even better for Janet. She'd measure out, pick up the leading edge and toss the bulk of the whole over the opposite side of the square bench where it would plop to the floor, much to the temporary confusion of the customer. Then Janet would fetch a spare inner cardboard tube, align it horizontally in front of her on the bench, parallel to the flat cut edge of the fabric, before rolling the cut edge on to the tube, carefully keeping it straight. Then there would be an against gravity feed as she pulled and rolled, pulled and rolled, adjusting both selvages, left and right, all the while to ensure a good alignment. Then two large carriers would be slit open and used to wrap each half of the roll, with parcel tape delivered swiftly and squealingly from a tape dispenser around the overlap, along the whole length, and then sealing in the ends. Janet did all this with consummate choreographic skill, her arms and legs moving in a calculated and practiced rhythm, her feet changing position in a courtly dance. And she loved this display and she loved being watched. She'd heard there were new measuring machines designed to automate this procedure. She was repulsed by the very idea, but knew John Lewis was still doing it this traditional way, and since they were Masons main competitors she wasn't worried.

Masons soft furnishing department was a testament to the building's traditional heritage. On the perimeter alongside the buffed shiny vinyl walkway which divided soft furnishing from bedding, were glass display cases of packed ready-mades and a multitude of cushions – braided, fringed or plain-piped. Also some hefty A frames, with five rolls of stock fabric slotted into each side on metal poles. And numerous sale bins were stuffed with discontinued ready-mades, and heaps of remnants – decent lengths of up to 5 metres, not the slim pickings you found elsewhere. And the display staff usually had some stock fabrics draped into ruches on tall metal stands on wide plinths, where the fabrics cascaded down like waterfalls and opulently puddled at the base. At the back of the department, streamlining the walls, were the manufacturers' sample curtain displays for the custom-mades, coordinated by colour, where each sample curtain had a price card for the various widths and drops, orders to be undertaken by the manufacturers themselves. These were easy orders for the staff to process, and made up for the more time-consuming orders for Masons own curtain makers. A higgle-piggle of pattern books hung from the manufacturers stands, forever looking like a battle ground of willpowers jostling for available hook spaces.

But in the central area of the department, and in truth its very beating heart, were two massive square serving benches, where the staff were usually working on their feet, day after day, serving customers with fabrics, linings and tapes, for those enterprising souls who made their own drapes and saved a lot of money, or taking orders for those who were far too busy and far too well off. In all cases, customer window measurements had to interpreted carefully and adjusted accordingly, fabric and lining quantities calculated, taking into consideration pattern repeats, and then making up costs applied. In this department the customer was certainly *not* always right, which suited Janet perfectly.

This beating heart's life blood was supplied by three large square frame stands, three shelves deep, laden with rolls and rolls of stock fabrics to choose from. This is where the value for money really was. Glazed chintzes, cotton satins, dupions, moirés, damasks, plains for trimming, velvets… and massive rolls of heat-resistant table felt for those posh Cheltenham dinner parties, where no doubt guests would *wow!* at the new drapes of their hosts. The fabrics were supplied from the manufacturers at discounted 'on the roll' prices, rather than by the metre prices, so the saving could be passed on to the customer. And there were some beautiful designs for making up into a bounty of creative possibilities, and florals and velvets were *in*. Velvets to be made with the pile up or the pile down? That was the question. These were the times of frills and fancy in plainly designed suburban homes. These were the times of pencil pleats, pinch pleats, stuffed goblet headings, interlined pomp and pageantry, tiebacks (piped, frilled, or both), valances (frilled or plain contrast trimmed), swags and tails and jabots, austrian blinds, festoon blinds, roman blinds, fringed leading edges, tassel tie backs...roller blinds, vertical blinds, venetian blinds, and all manner of net curtains sold by the 'drop'...from plain voiles with envelope hems or lead-weighted edges, to lacy café nets and flounced jardinières – you get the picture. And it was the very hey day of manufacturers such as Crowson, Rectella, Today Interiors, G.P. & J. Baker, Romo, Sanderson, Blendworth and Montgomery, to name but a few, as they say in marketing.

And the staff of this department kept this heart pumping. Janet and Ann were experienced, skilled and quick. Gemma was catching up. And there was to be a new member of staff who would be trained up appropriately and perhaps an assistant manager for Ron.

But this positive thinking, which Janet allowed herself to indulge in this morning, just for a little while, as she measured out some ecru lining to go with some Rectella 'Papillon' colour 3 stock fabric to go to the makers, was soon to be in serious doubt – the fizz was to turn quite flat.

At 1pm, Ronald Richardson, manager of the soft furnishing department of Masons in Cheltenham since the year of 1978, strolled onto the department with his usual lolloping stride. He brushed his floppy ginger fringe out of his eyes as usual, but as he approached Janet, Ann and Gemma, processing orders at the serving benches, Janet noticed something distinctly different about his bearing and she felt an icy finger stroke up her spine. Something had changed. He was less stooped over, and for once, he was smiling, in fact he was grinning like an idiot, so widely that he looked to Janet like a maniac. Her breath hitched in her throat and she completely lost count of the lining she was measuring.

'Good to have you back, Janet! Happy New Year to you!' Ron said, thrusting his hands into the deep pockets of his oversized trousers.

'Thank you, Ron. I really needed to get back to work.'

'Yes, yes, indeed,' he said, continuing to beam and nod as if broadcasting a signal upon which the fate of planet Earth depended.

Gemma, Janet and Ann glanced at one another with their eyebrows knitted together.

Ron looked around, his head twitching like a nervous bird checking for prey – the prey being potential customers, which he characteristically hated serving.

'Just while it's quiet,' he muttered, 'I'd better give you my news.'

Gemma and Ann scrutinised Ron's pasty white face, and his grin slowly departed like the sun moving behind a raincloud.

Janet directed her eyes to the floor, noting the salmon pink carpet by the bench needed a dammed good clean. It was so grubby. Why hadn't it been done? It was ridiculous the way no one did anything to –

'I'm leaving. Early retirement.' Ron said, breaking in on her thoughts like a pneumatic drill.

Resistance was futile.

He looked down at his scuffed leather shoes. 'You may have suspected something…' he tailed off.

'No!' Janet said. 'You can't!' She moved closer to Ron, her eyes now riveted to his face. He stepped back, but was forced to return her gaze and his cheeks reddened. He yanked his hands from his pockets and flung them out wide.

'I'm sorry, Janet! I know how much you like it here, and the way things are. But I've just had enough and I need to get out. It's as simple as that.'

'But why?' Janet fired the question at him.

After a stunned silence, Ron went on to explain, shifting from foot to foot, while Ann and Gemma gave him kind and sympathetic nods and glances, and while Janet mustered together an arsenal of emotional weapons to launch at him – anger, betrayal, despair – twisting her face into endless permutations, while in the close heat of the store, despite the sleety winter outside, beads of sweat started to run into Ron's eyes and wet his forelock into rat's tails.

He was so tired all the time, he said. Could hardly sleep these days. There was so much pressure from upper management. Things had changed too much over the last few years, with central buying taking over the stock ordering, with the sales targets set so high, with him having to justify any changes he wanted to make, with everything becoming more and more impersonal...it was time to leave, it was the right time. His wife was happy about it, he'd been hard to live with over the last couple of years, and he owed it to her too, and the kids, and their grandkids. He'd just handed in his notice. He was to leave at the end of February. There was nothing else to say. There really wasn't.

As the three women and Ron stood rooted to the spot like a frozen tableau in a classical painting, the women's attention wholly transfixed upon Ron, a voice broke in and shattered the silence like a rock hurled through a window.

'So who will get your job, then?'

Janet flinched at the sound of this voice. This aggressively blunt, yet chirpy voice, with a very faint trace of North Devon burr. Her head swivelled inexorably to its source, like a iron bolt drawn to a magnet. And there she was. Marian Johnson, standing just behind Ron. The trumped up little tart of Berkeley Fabrics. The Sindy doll had clawed her way from the black hole, with not even a broken fingernail to show for it, right back into Janet's life.

And asking Ron *the* question before they'd even had a chance to think about it. Before it was even seemly to do so. And it was not even Marian's place to ask. But there she stood, in her navy skirt and tight blouse, so thin you could see her lacy white bra underneath, with a bolero style jacket open to show off her cleavage. There she stood, with her arched eyebrows, pouting red lips, one hand on her hip, with a rudely direct expression on her face. Just who the hell did she think she was?

'It's none of your business!' Janet said, her mouth set hard into a line.

'Glad to have you back, Janet,' Marian said. 'Happy New Year to you too.'

She sidled up to Ron, who turned to face her. 'So who will get your job, Ron?'

'I'm sorry, Marian. It's very early days and it's nothing really to do with Berkeley Fabrics.'

'Well, it is really! It's still all one department.'

'Nevertheless, you have your own area manager…'

Marian sniffed and flicked her hair over her shoulder. She turned away abruptly. 'Oh, never mind, I'll find out about it. I might just apply myself.'

Her words trailed behind in her wake, stirring up the already tense atmosphere, and their eyes followed the source of this disturbance.

They watched Marian strut over to Milly to do the shift handover, bending over the desk like an angle poise lamp and assuming what Janet felt to be a deliberately sexually provocative position. Yet since there were no male customers in sight, on this occasion, she decided, it was probably intended as a snub to themselves.

'She can't apply, can she?' Janet asked Ron, just managing to control her tone of rising panic. But inside raw fear crashed through her, making her want to rush to the ladies.

Ron shook his head, still staring at Marian. He rubbed his bottom lip with a pondering finger. 'I hardly think so. I've never known it to happen before.'

'But who will be likely to get your job?' Janet asked.

'I've no idea. Someone experienced, hopefully. Someone far more experienced than Marian. The idea of her is preposterous. But I suppose I really don't…' He stopped and twitched his head around again, seeing with a look of alarm that a few customers were beginning to flock on the perimeter of the department like crows getting ready to take their pickings. 'Er…I'll leave you to it,' he mumbled, 'I've got some paperwork to do in the office. Just give me a shout when you and Ann go for lunch.'

And with that he sidled away, snaking around the fixtures and fittings to avoid the predations of the crows. After a few struttings around, the crows settled themselves at the benches as customary, and Janet, Ann and Gemma had no time to even consider their fallback positions after Ron had dropped his bomb, too busy did they become with unrolling fabric, selling off sale stock, and doing their extensive maths for some curtain orders – though Janet found concentration now as elusive as trying to catch hold of a dandelion seed fluttering its way to the ground, all fluff and whimsical fancy – just like Marian.

Chapter 3

It was only when Janet and Ann pushed their way through the swing doors of the staff canteen that they could begin to discuss the predicament of Ron's retirement. Rushing through the department managers' eating area, with the pungent smell of boiled cabbage enveloping them despite it hardly ever being on the menu, they joined the straggling queue at the counter to choose today's lunch, a choice of sausage, beans and mash, or lasagne and salad. The fact that it was the latest designated lunch break of 2pm meant that the hot favourite of the day – fish, chips and peas – had already gone down the gullets of a hungry workforce.

Janet and Ann made their way carefully with their loaded trays of lasagne and salad and cups of coffee, to the very end of the general staff eating area, choosing a table next to a window looking down on Pilgrim Street at the rear of the store. Usually they got into discussion with a gaggle of ladies from perfumery at the adjacent table, but it was too late for that today and they were glad of it. A private talk was in order.

'So the rumours were true,' Janet said grimly, as she looked down at the tops of umbrellas floating along the oil-slicked pavements of Pilgrim Street.

'I can't believe he's going,' Ann whispered. 'He's been the nicest manager I've ever known on the department. What will we do?'

Janet frowned at her, the lines deepening like knife cuts between her dark drawn brows.

'I don't know. But do you think our little floozy is really interested?'

'What? Ann sat back, thrusting down her knife and fork with a clatter. 'No, she can't be! She's only been here five minutes and she doesn't work for Masons anyway!' She shook her head like a victim in a horror film being advanced upon by an avenging ghoul, unable to stop the shaking, taking too many breaths in, as if building to emit a piercing scream. Then, as if realising she wasn't actually in a horror film, she sighed deeply instead. 'It'll just be all talk, trying to wind us up. She wouldn't stand a chance.'

Janet looked hard at Ann. 'But she might,' she said flatly. 'You know what it's like these days. We've seen it before. In they come. Too young to know any job well, straight from university or college. Hired externally without us even knowing or having any say in it. And our department needs some speciality, and I bet the management couldn't care less about that. And even if the new manager learns the ropes, they'll soon leave for another promotion, like they do, and we'll have to begin all over again training another manager…it's just a joke!'

She'd barely touched her plate of food, but now she stabbed a fork into the glue of her cooling pasta. 'We *can't* let that happen, and we *can't* let Marian become *our* manager.'

'She wouldn't dare apply,' Ann said, looking worriedly at Janet.

'I think she would. I think she'd dare do anything. And I can't have it, Ann, I just can't.' Tears began to prick in the corner of Janet's eyes and stung like acid.

Ann reached out and touched her hand. 'Don't upset yourself. You're vulnerable just now with losing Frank.'

Janet flinched at the mention of her late husband and pulled her hand away. She could see him in her mind's eye looking down at her and smiling that smile of his. This image came quite frequently, especially at night. Goosebumps prickled her skin and she shook away the feeling, just like she shook out her sheets before fitting them tightly and smoothly to the bed she now slept in alone.

But she decided it was time for a show of vulnerability. 'I know, you're right, Ann. I'm far from back to normal yet.' She did her best to produce a pained look. 'But don't you see? I can't get back to normal with Marian becoming our manager.'

'But, Janet, how can she? She's only been here a year! It's just impossible.'

'That one can talk her way into anything. That flirt in a skirt. It's alright for you, you can retire if you want to. I can't afford to do that, and I don't want to, I love it here.'

'But I'll stay as long as you do!'

'Oh, Ann. Will you?'

'Of course!'

And here the conversation had to end, as Janet insisted they should still go and scour the sales racks in Eastex and Jacques Vert together as planned. Despite their worries they couldn't possibly miss out on the opportunity of 50% off sale goods, with an additional 20% off with their staff discount cards. What more could be said or done right now, anyway?

The rest of the afternoon passed in a flurry and flounce of fabric orders, made to measure orders, and a miscellanea of sales, sending the takings to a record level for this first trading day of the new year. Berkeley Fabrics were also inundated, with knots of people clustered around the desk. Janet was annoyed to see that Marian seemed unphased by the pressure of being on her own. In fact she became more vivacious, and it seemed to Janet that her lipstick became redder, her skirt even tighter, her giggles more shrill, even her repeated leg crossings seemed to accelerate in speed.

It was all Janet and Ann could do to get away at 6pm, leaving Gemma and Ron to work the last couple of hours. As they descended by the customer lift (and yes, surprisingly this was allowed), then trudged their way through successive lower floors into the corridor leading to the staff lockers, down into the very pit of this high class store, Janet felt a shadow wrapping around her heart like a shroud. Her inner she-wolf sensed it. After all, it had known plenty of practice.

As she and Ann paused outside the staff entrance under

the spotlight of a streetlamp, with the rain darting around them in playful gusts, and in the standoffish gaze of some anorexic window mannequins, Ann tried to placate Janet.

'Try not to worry. It might work out alright.'

Janet felt Ann searching her face for some visual sign of agreement, but despite her newly found artifice since Frank had died, she found herself unable to deliver.

Shivering in the winter cold after the warmth inside the cocoon of the store, she now needed to get away and be by herself. 'Better get home,' she said sharply. 'You mustn't miss your bus.'

'Okay, well have a good evening, won't you?'

'Yes, yes,' she said. 'You too.'

Inside her Polo, while the windscreen wipers tried to thrash away the rain to help her see the road ahead more clearly, her thoughts thrashed back and forth like clothes in an old fashioned washing machine. As she followed the blurring tail lights of those in front, as she braked hard at pulsing stop lights and pedestrian crossings, impatient to get home, she felt everything she had worked for was hanging in the balance. She gripped the steering wheel hard as she swung the car into Willow Lane in Charlton Kings, then jerked it to a halt in the drive of number 9.

After ramming her key into the lock and shoving open the front door she was met with a cold black silence for the first time since Frank died. Logically, she knew this would be the case and had tried to forestall it by resetting the heating timer the day before, but she'd been overly efficient and hadn't allowed for the hour it took for the house to heat up. 'Damm it,' she said to herself, shaking off her coat and hanging it up.

Making her way into the kitchen, a hairy snake brushed around her leg. Her heart leaped into her throat and she quickly snapped on the light to discover it was Thomas now sitting by his feeding bowl and fastening his inscrutable gaze upon her with his message quite clear. She tutted to herself for being so jumpy.

'Okay, Thomas, just give me five minutes,' she muttered.

Quickly putting the kettle on, she switched on the heating and turned on the oven for a ready-meal, a habit she'd begun recently after a lifetime of having to make home-cooked meals for Frank. She switched on some lamps in the living room to cosy it up… and only then did she put some cat food out for Thomas. He obediently bent his head to the task; a priority he knew he was not, because he knew his mistress well, but he also knew he was far more important in Janet's life than she could ever imagine and this knowledge sustained him.

Trudging through the hall, Janet noticed the answer phone flashing. It turned out to be Scott who'd left a message checking to see how she was. She dutifully phoned him back, reporting she was fine, keeping it short and sweet, not wanting to tell him about the pending departmental changes, because she simply hadn't had time to reflect rationally on it yet. And rationality was key when you had an escalating conflict situation. You had to relax and mull things over before deciding on your next move. She went upstairs to get changed, resolving to try to enjoy the evening as she had planned and imagined so many times over the last couple of weeks. The very first proper evening of her new life.

Now stripped down to her underwear she enveloped herself in what she designated as her housecoat. It was a printed floral, full length, crossover-style, dressing gown, with belt and leading edge frills (usually reserved for Sunday evenings), which helped her enter the world of those glamorous black and white films set in country houses, with roaring log fires and polished mahogany tables adorned with bowls of roses and boxes of chocolates. Tonight however, the fantasy wasn't running smoothly, in fact one might say the projector needed tweaking. But Janet was determined to try hard to get it to work. She would not let the impending changes wreck her special evening.

Back downstairs in the living room she put on the electric fire in the grate of the fireplace, turning on all three bars, and sitting in her favourite armchair, she began to rub her calves and feet which were aching after being on her feet all day. Having been out of training for quite a few weeks, she'd been expecting this lapse in physical stamina, but it was a reassuring kind of pain which she actually relished. Her shepherd's pie was now in the oven and she had a glass of red wine by her side. She flicked to the 3rd January in the television guide, her mouth twisting into a sneer at seeing that the festive programs were still dominating, but her mouth softened when she saw *Coronation Street* was just about to start. She heard the familiar bash of the cat flap in the kitchen which meant Thomas had just gone out for *his* evening entertainment.

Waiting for the oven timer to ping, she sipped her wine and settled herself back in her armchair to watch her second favourite soap, the first place being reserved for *Dynasty*, which was a mid-week Thursday treat. Ken and Deirdre's marriage was in trouble again. Deirdre has found out Ken has been unfaithful to her with Wendy, who works on his paper with him. Ken is torn between the two women, but Deirdre throws him out to help him decide. Quite right too, thinks Janet. And poor Emily is duly suffering from that special kind of pained Christian distress, which only she knows how to express, while the aftershocks rumble through the Rovers and down the street that the Barlow's marriage is over.

This kept Janet distracted for a while as she ate her meal with small and tidy bites, but thoughts of Marian applying to be department manager kept attacking her like arrows trying to find their most deep and tender target. And while she tried to concentrate on an episode of *Poirot*, having a particular fondness for David Suchet, with the remainder of her shepherd's pie clotting and congealing on her Denby plate from Masons, while she sipped more wine than usual, the arrows kept up their assault. It was unthinkable that

Marian would be accepted for the job, wasn't it? And yet, what if she was? After all, she did have this knack for influencing people. She would be impossible to work with, and even worse to work *for*…and she'd boss Janet around until she couldn't stand it anymore and would be forced to leave, to leave her beloved Masons. Then Janet would have nothing in her life. Nothing. Marian would flaunt the rules too. She was always giving unauthorised discounts on her Berkeley Fabrics orders. She was flighty, flirty and flagrant. Janet's hand tightened its grip around her wine glass like a vice, while her heart thumped irregularly, missing beats. She was a jumped-up little trollop. She was a little *bitch*!

And an arrow pierced her deeply where she felt all her hurts piled up inside – into that very place she tried so hard not to go to, which she usually managed to keep walled up.

Gasping, she crashed the wine glass down hard onto her glass-topped side table. The high pitched splintering noise vibrated through her taut nerves like a scream, while splotches of wine spilled like blood. Turning her head to inspect the damage, she moaned when she saw a tiny crack in the thick glass of her lovely table top – and of course there was only one person she could blame for that! Grimacing, as she set about tidying up the shards of glass and mopping up the wine, she was thankful that her housecoat at least had been saved the stain of Marian.

That night, as she lay in the centre of her double bed trying to sleep, she was grateful for the orange glow of the street lights picking out the edges of the furniture in the front room and forcing back the shadows. Frank had always insisted on them using the back bedroom which faced over the garden and fields beyond, but she'd felt so smothered by the suffocating blackness, that after he died she'd swapped rooms. After all, she'd reflected, there were no fond memories for her in the bed she had shared with Frank. And this room was where she had always kept most of the things that were important to her: her cross stitch and embroideries

– all beautifully stretched and framed, her porcelain thimble collection, and her magazine and shopping catalogues for bedtime reading. There were some other things that were important too, but they were locked in a battered and bruised wartime suitcase that her father had given her before she married, now secreted in a corner of the attic where Frank had never ventured.

As she lay in the pathway of a filtered band of orange light, she found the thoughts fluttering around in her skull, like starlings in a locked room, begin to tire. Just a few more flaps of wings, then a stillness settled. Groping around for a solution to the 'Marian Johnson as potential manager problem' had been fruitless. Normally, when she had a problem to solve, a good idea would take seed. Then she would water it. She would feed it. The plant would grow leaves and the roots would firmly embed themselves in nutritious ground, and her idea would bear ripe fruit to solve her problem. Just as she had eventually done with Frank. But this time there was nothing. Why?

And then she realised, because this was simply beyond her control, wasn't it?

Sighing, she flicked on the bedside light, grabbed hold of the January issue of *House Beautiful* and propped herself up on her pillow. Glancing through patchwork quilts on country pine beds, her mind emptied enough to have a sudden spontaneous thought, which rose to the surface of her mind like a bubble.

And it popped.

It was so simple.

If Marian did apply for the department manager's job, then she would do the same. After all, if they happened to consider Marian, they might just consider her too. She'd work on Milly-Molly-Mandy so she'd find out straight away if Marian did apply, she'd get Ron on her side, and get him to show her exactly what he did, to give herself every fighting chance.

Half an hour later, she lay in semi-darkness again, more

comfortably now, just drifting on the edge of consciousness. But then Frank's face appeared. Her dead husband, hovering over her, hooked nose, ice-blue eyes, heavy jowls, smiling that smile of his, just before he made his point. Janet shuddered. This had been happening since he died and she hated it. Sometimes he said things too. Tonight was one of those occasions.

Apply to be the manager? Frank grinned. *As if you could do a job like that!*

Janet stiffened. 'Go to hell, Frank. Where you belong.'

Then she turned onto her side and managed just a few hours of precious oblivion.

Chapter 4

The next few days at Masons were tense for Janet as she waited to find out whether or not Marian was indeed going to apply. Ron could tell her nothing and stayed in his office adjacent to the cash office most of the time, studying sales figures, he said, but Janet knew it was more a case of avoiding both customers and questions. Janet also knew that Marian would never tell her personally and the two of them were avoiding contact with each other like spies set on their respective secret missions, no pot-shots, no verbal assaults, not even any underhand sniping. So, Janet decided to work on Marian's colleague, Milly-Molly-Mandy, when she was covering for Marian, by accompanying Milly on a few lunches in the staff canteen beginning on the Tuesday.

Of course, she explained the reasons for this odd deviation into the enemy's camp to Ann, poor Ann who was so easily confused it was almost laughable, but after Janet had finished appraising her of the situation, Ann had understood perfectly and said she'd back her up to the hilt. And what else indeed? Gemma had merely cast her ghoulishly gothic eyes up to heaven, stating, 'Whatever, Mrs B'.

If only Milly had been so easy to handle. Instead, Janet had to endure listening to Milly twittering on in the canteen about what a wonderful husband her Archie had been, before being able to dig for the information she wanted. Not only that, but she wore a very common brand of perfume, Anais Anais, the same her daughter-in-law, Susan, wore, which she had to suffer for its chokingly high floral notes.

'He was the love of my life!' Milly said, as Janet sat opposite her, trying not to breathe in, while she watched Milly gobble toad-in-the-hole down her gullet, to further inflate the pouches of her well-rounded figure. What's one more lump of dough to such a Rubenesque scented beauty, anyway? Janet thought. 'I miss him all the time,' Milly carried on. 'It's been a year and it feels just like yesterday. I ache for him, don't you ache for your Frank?'

With her fork poised in mid air, Milly stared at Janet with her red-rimmed big brown eyes that always seemed to be leaking tears. The look was searching, pleading...and Janet could see she was desperate for some empathy. This was her chance, she decided.

'It hurts, yes, Milly,' she tried to look downcast, gazing into her coffee cup.

'It's so recent for you!' Milly grasped Janet's hand with her own, with the fat ruby ring winking up at her. 'But you will get through it. You will. Just like me.'

Janet suffered the feel of Milly's podgy flesh without pulling away, as every nerve in her body was screaming at her to do.

They re-enacted the same pose on the Wednesday, and on the Thursday it was third time lucky for Janet. She sensed it was time for her to make her move. 'Yes, it's so recent. And I came back to work thinking it would help. But these uncertainties are really bothering me. They're making it so much harder. So stressful. I need to know what's happening, Milly. Who is going to be our manager?' She tried to wail in desperation, and it was easier than she anticipated.

Milly said nothing. Her eyes darted around the canteen and she twitched like a nervous bird, still clutching Janet's hand.

Janet continued to wail. 'Is it going to be an insider or an outsider? Marian said she might apply and she just doesn't like me! You've seen that for yourself. If I knew, I could prepare myself...I don't know what to do!'

Milly broke hand contact with her and her eyes swam with tears. 'Oh, dear. I...I...I'm not supposed to say anything!'

'What? Please tell me what you know. Please, Milly?'

'But…but I promised, you see! I promised her!'

Aah, Janet thought, so that's it. She's just given the game away. Marian is applying, otherwise there is nothing to have to hide.

Marian was wringing her sweaty hands together in her distress. Janet enjoyed the sight for a few moments, then decided to put Milly-Molly-Mandy out of her misery.

'It's alright, Milly,' she said with a resigned tone. 'I can't ask you to break a confidence.'

'I want to help, I really do…but…it's my job as well…I need the money…'

How stupid can she be? Janet thought. She doesn't even realise she's practically told me.

'It's quite all right,' she said, patting the back of Milly's hand while noticing the bumpy balls of fibres on Milly's woollen cardigan for the umpteenth time. And she could resist no longer.

'You know, you can get a gadget to get rid of those pilling bobbles. They're called clothes shavers. I bet you can get one from haberdashery.'

Milly stared at her, wide eyed. Her mouth hung open. Then she looked down at her sleeves and cardigan front.

'See what I mean?' Janet remarked.

Milly's chin wobbled and a flushing of scarlet rose into her sun-weathered cheeks. Her eyes swam with tears again, but she managed a response. 'I've got one of those at home, thank you, I just haven't gotten around to using it yet.'

Janet arched her eyebrows. 'Well, it's about time, don't you think?'

That afternoon, Janet paid Ron a visit in the soft furnishing manager's office. She cut right to the chase, while he absently fiddled with the woolly worn edges of some green cardboard files on his desk. It was relatively quiet on the shop floor and Ann and Gemma had agreed to hold the fort while Janet spoke to Ron.

'I have been given to believe that Marian is applying for

your job,' said Janet. 'Do you know anything about it, Ron? Has she said anything to you?'

Ron gaped at her. 'No. Not at all! How do you know?'

Janet smiled. 'Let's just say, a little bird told me.' A very fat bird actually, thought Janet.

Ron flopped down into his chair and brushed his hand through his forelock. 'Well, I never!'

'You said before, you didn't think she stood a chance. Well, I can't afford to chance it, Ron. So I want to apply too.'

Ron jerked his head back and his eyes bulged out at her like a tree frog's. 'You!'

'Yes, me. What's so unbelievable about that? I can't stay here if she gets the job, so I might as well apply myself.'

Janet explained her feelings to him and her position, and that surely personnel might consider her under the depleted staff circumstances that were now threatening the efficient running of the department. As she talked and Ron listened, he began to nod and Janet could see she was winning him over with her reminding him of her five years work experience on the department and her commitment to the job and Masons itself.

'Well, one thing I do know, Janet, is that if you were to leave after me, this department would certainly suffer, and any new manager wouldn't have a clue how to run it, that's for sure! It'll go down the pan and I don't want that.'

Janet felt her legs become watery as if the determination to convince Ron had been all that was propping her up, without her actually knowing what her next move would be. She sank into a chair by Ron's. And she quickly felt assailed by doubts. Could she really go through with this? And Frank intruded again, *Just who do you think you are, Janet?* And she helped him out with her own put-downs, thinking, They'll never give the job to me at *my* age. I may feel like a thirty year old, but I'm fifty four! And I get hot flushes. They want students, they want graduates, who think the job will be easy, beneath them almost, or they want over-confident trumped up little upstarts like Marian.

'Do you think I stand a chance at my age?' she asked Ron, tightening her laced-together fingers in her lap.

'You just might, Janet. They can't be seen to be ageist. And I think under the circumstances internal applications would be considered first. I'd rather see you get it than Marian, so I'll do what I can.'

'But what about the stress? After all, you're leaving because of it.'

Ron laughed. 'Oh, Janet. You'll be fine. You're made of sterner stuff than me, a bit like our Maggie Thatcher of the department, you are, our very own iron lady.'

Then his cheeks reddened as Janet stared at him, wide eyed, uncertain of what to make of his comparison. Stuffing his hands into his pockets, Ron turned on his heels and rushed out through the door of the office, muttering over his shoulder, 'Wait here. I won't be long.'

Alone in the cramped office, Janet felt disorientated by the rare motivation she'd ever witnessed before in Ron. She sat still listening to the drone of a computer she didn't know how to use, and the tuneful strains of innocent prattle drifting into the room from the cash office women. But slowly their prattle became, in Janet's mind, disparate voices saying disapproving things: *Who does she think she is? Just who does she think she is?* And even her own long-dead mother, Mildred, joined in the chorus, addressing her directly now: *You've got ideas above your station, my girl! I want, never gets. So put up or shut up!* And then there a particular favourite of her mother's, *You've made your bed, you lie in it,* which wasn't actually applicable on this occasion, but which Janet felt the force of nonetheless, since her mother had spat it out at her over and over again whenever Janet had tried to suggest her marriage to Frank was less than ideal. And finally came *You're as hard as nails, you are,* which must be what Ron was alluding to when he said she'd be fine in the job, a veritable Maggie Thatcher. In response to this saying of Mildred's, which Janet had found out from her one day was actually a twisted kind of compliment, she'd always fought back, thinking – it takes one, to know one, Mother.

While Janet's mind was still flinching from these destructive voices from the past, Ron bounced back in, clutching an A4 envelope. He thrust it at Janet and plonked himself in his chair.

'It's all in there. Application form, job description, everything. Have a go at filling it in, then you can pass it by me before you hand it in. Probably best to hand it in on Monday.'

Janet looked at him, eyes narrowed. 'You mean, it really is feasible?'

Ron grinned. 'Yes, Janet, it's feasible. I spoke to the personnel manager and recommended you. And Marian *has* already asked him if she can apply. He can't stop her, but he's not keen. So if you can make a decent application and argue your case, you stand a good chance – a far better one than Marian, I should think. Okay?'

Janet slowly rose to her feet. She felt as if she didn't know where to take them next, so she paused and placed them at an angle to one another, in her characteristic first position ballet pose. She'd adopted this as a child after watching some girls in their ballet class after school – her mother had refused to let her attend, so Janet used to study the poses through a window into the gymnasium.

Right now, the position calmed her racing heart and centred her, as it always had.

'Thank you, Ron.' She tried to smile. Not one of her false smiles, but a genuine one, where it would reach her eyes. But it wouldn't come, not after so many years, so she just turned her mouth up at the corners as usual.

'Just come and see me if you have any questions about the job.'

'Thanks, Ron. I will.'

Then she turned and marched out of the office, gripping the envelope, past the twittering voices of the ladies behind the glass in the cash office, and back onto the department to tell Ann and Gemma her news.

That night, sleety rain sputtered on the living room window as Janet sat in her winged chair. Thomas lay curled up in the overstuffed easy chair Frank had used, opposite Janet, with the sagging in the seat a visible reminder of the very space Frank had taken up in the house, this chair being frequently where his force had been most felt. Indeed Thomas had felt it too, having been thrown off it on numerous occasions by Frank. But now Thomas had sole occupancy, as undeterred at breaking rules as cats can be, and Janet didn't have a problem with him sitting on the rose and peony linen union furniture she had cared for over the last three years – a sale buy from Masons. The cat was welcome to Frank's chair now. He could even scratch it if he felt so inclined.

Thomas cast a curious glance at Janet now and again, as she read the job description of departmental manager. She was taking a few notes and jotting down some questions to ask Ron. It was mostly the terminology she had problems with: *account analysis, forecasting, profit protection*...she put question marks by these, but she was able to tick her understanding of *merchandising, stock availability, sales profitability, targets, central buying*. Her *maths* was fine, her *keyboard skills* were dubious, though she'd done a secretarial course many years ago, and Scott might be able to help her out –

Thinking of Scott, she poised her pen in mid air like a surgeon holding a scalpel briefly aloft before making another calculated incision – what would Scott think about this application? He was already doubtful about her returning to work so soon, what would he make of her wanting to be a full time manager? He'll be shocked, she thought, he'll think it will be too much stress, he'll try to put me off. She cocked her head to one side. But there again, he's always been supportive of my working at Masons, he used to stick up for me with Frank over it. Maybe, when I explain...

Her pen resumed its ticking...yes to having *excellent*

customer service skills, a talent for motivating others, ability to remain calm under pressure, being able to adapt to challenging situations (a lifetime with Frank had prepared her well), yes to *confident, with a sense of responsibility, helping with promotions and advertising campaigns.* She had to question mark *analysing sales figures* and an *understanding of retail law*…but it did look promising, it really did. So she began pencilling in the application form which she resolved to get to the personnel manager first thing on Monday morning.

To fend off the disapproving voices which had plagued her earlier, she poured herself a glass of wine and turned to her current favourite self-help book by Dale Carnegie, *How to Win Friends and Influence People*. As she reminded herself of the principles of handling people, winning people to one's own way of thinking and ways to make people like you, using the egos of others to one's own advantage, she realised just how much of this she had actually been putting into practice – and this was oh so good for the future! And as her mother immediately tried to undermine her again with *I want, never gets!*, she found her father retaliating, which he had rarely done in real life – *Life is what you make it, Janie.* And yes, he really had said this once, when her mother was out of the room.

And it seemed these voices from the past had more to say as she remembered her Auntie Vi, her mother's pretty younger sister, who'd *done very well for herself* her mother used to say bitterly, by marrying a grocer called Ted, with his very own shop, his very own family business, namely T.E. Granger. Not like Janet's mother, who'd married a lowly poorly-paid office worker, by her own account, in Janet's father, Albert. And it had been her Auntie Vi who'd encouraged Janet to apply to the Coop after she'd left school, where Janet had her very first taste of customer service in the ladieswear department of the Coop store in Castle Street, Bristol. And this department had been a cut above housewares, and many more cuts above working in a grocers, or, God forbid, a factory, where a lot of the girls her age had ended up. Shop work in fashion had been a very good job for a smart young lady in those days, and it hadn't been long before Janet had been assistant manager too.

Janet paused here in the shifting sludgy river of her memory, damming it up before it could flow on, but dredging the very last fact into the present to see if it had any relevance to her job application. After all, it was experience of management of some sort, even if it had been over thirty years ago. She decided to describe it a little in her previous employment history. Auntie Vi would have approved, and then Janet found herself drifting again. She'd just adored being with her Auntie Vi, while she watched her serve the customers in Granger's on a Saturday, while the rich smells of scoops of loose tea and coffee wafted past Janet's nose and into paper packets, while she kept her aunt company behind the counter. This had usually been when she'd been getting under her mother's feet, or when her mother had her hands full with her younger brother, Norman. And at these times, Auntie Vi would try to cheer Janet up.

You're a looker you know, our Janet. You'll soon be having the boys running after you. Janet had appreciated this because her mother had never passed comment on her looks. All her mother had said, when Janet developed breasts and hips, was *Don't you ever bring any trouble to this door.* But her Auntie Vi had said something else, something Janet had never forgotten. Something she had tried to do, but had let go of when it just seemed impossible after her marriage to Frank – *To thine own self be true.* Her auntie told her it came from the Bible, but she'd later found out it was Shakespeare. Never mind, it seemed just perfect now. She would indeed be true to herself by going for what she wanted out of her life, now that Frank was gone. She was going to prove a worthy adversary for Marian. And fortified by this and a little more wine she carried on filling in the form. And she wouldn't forget Dale Carnegie's advice either, to be charming and appreciative to get what she wanted. She would up her game.

Chapter 5

The next day was unusually busy for a Friday. Janet, Ann and Gemma were preparing a stack of curtain orders to go to Clothworks in Cirencester the very next day, with customers taking advantage of the free making per width for unlined curtains on all stock fabrics over £7.99 per metre, with half price making for lined ones. So the ladies were frantically working at the serving benches during any small lulls between customers, by unrolling and measuring, then rerolling quantities of fabric and lining for each order and bagging them up with hand-written instructions.

Janet observed that Berkeley Fabrics seemed to be ticking along as usual in a rather more orderly fashion, thanks to the luxury of a desk for customers to sit down at to place their orders – currently there was 20% off all custom-mades. And it was a far simpler system, just form filling alone, and hence not very taxing in Janet's opinion. That's how the flirt in a skirt gets away with the job, she reflected with regard to Marian. As if she could ever have the brains to take on the main department. Janet bent over the serving bench and perched herself on her elbows to write out the maker's instructions, then she slowly shifted her gaze as stealthily as a praying mantis to check out Marian a few yards to the left at her desk.

She looked more or less the same. But Janet noted that her wavy red hair looked a little more Farah Fawcett than usual, all big blousy waves, as if she'd spent more time with her curling tongs and hair drier this morning. And why would that be? Who was she trying to impress? She couldn't possible have handed in her application yet. Surely there was no connection? But there she was sucking the tip of her cheap biro and pouting at the husband of the married couple placing an order with her, her cleavage pressed up against the edge of the table, just as brazen as that girl washing the car in *Cool Hand Luke*, driving the chain gang crazy with their low lust. And that girl had known *exactly* what she was doing. Oh yes, Marian knew it was the man who usually had to agree on big household expenses, which custom-made curtains most certainly were. So if she got them on side...leading them by the you know what, then more commission for her. As Janet turned her attention back to her writing, she heard Marian giggle and the sound of the high-pitched tittering forced her to grind her teeth together. Tarty little piece, she thought. It would be so wonderful to get rid of the little whore somehow.

During Janet's coffee break, Ron managed to find time to look over her application form with her in his office. She asked about profit protection and he explained that it just meant things like preventing shoplifting, ensuring correct pricing of goods (in the department's case, correct quoting and estimating for curtain orders), properly training staff, and making sure that merchandising procedures were adhered to.

'It's not much of a problem on this department, Janet,' he said, 'but relevant if the department takes on a new member of staff to replace you if you get the job, because they would need training up well.'

Janet nodded. 'Right, and what about my computer skills, they're not that great.'

'Oh, don't worry about that,' Ron said. 'If you get the job, I'll run through the basics with you, show you the systems.'

Janet flinched and touched her throat. She felt taken aback. She was simply unused to people offering to help her. A rush of gratitude flooded through her, but she simply didn't know what to do with it, unaccustomed as she was to handling it. All she could hear herself saying in a strangely alien voice was, 'Thanks.'

Ron continued his reassurances. He had no doubt if she

got the job she would pick it up on a need to know basis and he urged her not let the job description jargon put her off. He told her to put him down as a reference and if she should get an interview to emphasise her experience on the department and her commitment to Masons.

'And if you can come up with any ideas on increasing takings, then all the better,' he said, grinning. 'That's the way to play it.'

In the afternoon there was more unrolling and rolling of fabric and a far more relaxed Janet found herself remembering an old Enid Blyton story she'd read as a girl, namely 'Pinkerty and Old Mother Ribbony Rose.' Poor little gnome, Pinkerty (who was, in Janet's current view, a very silly little gnome who let himself be pushed around), worked for the nasty witch, Ribbony Rose, in her ribbons shop where the fairies came to buy her wares. Pinkerty had the job of rerolling all the ribbons the witch unrolled to show the fairies. He did it well with little appreciation, and the old witch was very unkind to him and all the fairies felt so sorry for him. But of course there was a happy ending – he was invited into fairyland to roll up the new baby fern fronds to protect them from the frost, and all the fairies loved him. A real *aaw* moment. Sentimental slush, reflected Janet. But remembering it bothered her. What was the matter with her? She was done with the past. It was dead and gone. Like her former family, apart from her brother, Norman, who she'd lost contact with, so why had the past been pushing its nose into her present business lately? She bristled and tensed her spine, deciding to turn her attention back to the here and now. And that meant her adversary, her nemesis, her arch enemy, Marian. If she'd been a mere irritation before, she'd now earned a significant promotion in Janet's life.

As she looked to the left, she saw Marian strutting up to the perimeter of the department where some glass cabinets were over-stuffed with discounted cushions to attract attention from the walkway which divided soft furnishing from the bedding department. And onto the top of one cabinet, she plonked down an A3 frame. Janet inserted a pin into the selvedge of the fabric she was measuring and jotted down her metreage, then she strolled over to see what Marian had done, because meddling with *their* departmental display outside of Berkeley's concessionary area was simply not allowed. The red and white sign read '20% off all custom-made curtains with Berkeley Fabrics' and Janet saw red in more ways than one. She snatched it up and stalked over to Marian who was now seated behind her desk.

'You can't do that,' Janet said, thumping down the sign in front of her, and she cast her eyes up at the ceiling where a chained Berkeley Fabrics sale banner hung. That,' she said, pointing up at it, 'is surely adequate!'

Marian shoved back her chair and stood up. She narrowed her eyes at Janet and swished her hair over her shoulder. 'Keep your hair on, Janet. You're not in charge of this department. You can't tell me what to do.'

'It doesn't matter whether I'm in charge or not, you can't meddle with our business or our space!'

'But we need more footfall back here. I have targets to make!' Marian said, changing her tone into a whine, which was, as far as Janet was concerned, simply one of Marian's repertoire of strategies she had witnessed her pull on Ron many times. Too many times.

'We've all got targets to make!' she replied.

'Well, I'll have to talk to my area manager, then,' Marian said sulkily, 'to see if she can negotiate more advertising. That will do it, I expect. I'm supposed to report any hindrances to my job. I really don't know who you think you are, Janet.' She tilted her chin up at Janet, stuck her hand on her hip, thrust her chest out, and curled her lip.

As Janet stared back at her, at the little bitch saying out loud that very phrase that Frank had been so fond of, she felt a burning fury rise in her blood. Her muscles clenched and she could feel her pulse pounding in her ears. Just for a moment she saw herself leaping at Marian, grabbing her around her throat, making her bangle earrings shake, and throttling her. But although she restrained herself, her resolution to proceed with caution deserted her.

'Well, things just might change around here after Ron's left,' Janet said. 'With a new manager, you never know what might happen to Berkeley Fabrics in this store. A new manager could have a very different kind of influence.'

Marian sniffed and wrinkled her nose. 'What do you mean? A new soft furnishing manager can't possibly have any say over this concession!'

Janet smiled. Marian suddenly looked older, with hard living evident in her weathering tan and the crows feet around her eyes.

'Maybe not any say over this concession being here,' she replied, ' but a new manager *can* have a say on the layout of the whole department, including Berkeley Fabrics. And anyone loyal to this department will make sure of it.'

Janet smiled again, this time openly at Marian.

Marian stared back at her, her eyes widening. 'What are you getting at, exactly?'

'Nothing. I'm just saying things might change around here in ways *you* might not like.'

Smugness oozed out of Janet, premature smugness she knew full well, but she was so enjoying wrong-footing Marian. She crossed her arms and jutted out her chin.

Marian stepped back from her, a spark of understanding firing in her eyes. 'Oh my God, you're applying, aren't you?'

Janet bit her lip, she hadn't meant things to go this far. She hadn't wanted Marian knowing, and so have a potential advantage. But now the scratching cat was out of the bag.

'You are, aren't you?' Marian repeated.

'Well, so what if I am? If *you* can, I certainly can!'

'What? Marian's jaw dropped to the floor. 'How do you know? How did you find out?' Her eyes bulged in surprise then slowly narrowed as she stitched her thoughts together. Then she scowled. 'Milly must have told you. She promised me she'd keep it to herself. But you've been pretending to be her friend, haven't you? And she's so flipping soft, you probably wormed it out of her. You're a nasty piece of work, Janet.' She hesitated, then turned on her heels and sat back down at her desk. 'Anyway, you don't stand a chance – not at your age.'

Janet recoiled as if being flicked by a whip. *Her* a nasty piece of work! And what about the comment about her age? The one thing that might really be against her. Bubbling fury boiled up inside her, threatening once again to overspill.

'Janet!' Ann called over from a serving bench. 'I need your help with this, I want you to look over my calculations.'

Janet just managed to check herself and she looked hard at Marian. 'Well, we'll see how things turn out, won't we? I've got more experience and know the department inside out, which you don't, not to mention the fact that you've only been here five minutes.' She spat the words out.

Marian spat hers out too. 'Well, we'll see, won't we!'

Ann began to hurry over, but Janet waved her back. She marched to the bench and grabbed hold of the selvedge of the roll she was measuring.

Ann leaned in close beside her. 'She's not worth the bother,' she said, in hushed tones.

Gemma, who was bent over a calculator with her obsidian hair falling straight around her face, looked up and rolled her gothic eyes. 'Seriously, Mrs B, she *really* isn't.'

Janet took silent note that Gemma and Ann happened to be right, and stealth was now in order.

Saturday was too busy to think. Sunday, the store was closed and she tweaked her application. And on the Monday morning she handed it in. For that whole week she kept a low profile, staying away from both Marian and Milly, determined to let the dust settle if she and Marian ended up going for the job head to head.

The dust didn't settle for long. On the next Monday, on the third week in January, she found herself being summoned to the personnel manager's office at 3pm, to be interviewed for the post of departmental manager. They were considering internal applications in the first instance, as Ron had suspected. There had been no sign of Marian so far today, but that didn't mean she wouldn't suddenly turn up. In fact, Janet thought, as she quickly used the ladies powder room on the second floor, she could be being interviewed right now. She could just see her flicking her hair around and pouting her lips. All, lip, leg and tit. After washing her hands and checking her appearance in the mirror, Janet took the stairs down to the first floor and weaved her way through ladieswear, then fine china, her nerves beginning to tighten and vibrate, jingling and jangling inside her.

Seated outside the personnel office, at least dressed for the part, Janet reflected, in her customary black suit, white blouse and black patent leather court shoes, she waited for a few minutes, straining to hear what was being said by the cotton wool voices coming through the wall. It was easier to do this than let the silence in the waiting area swell and swallow her.

As she was just about to get up and begin pacing to ease the jangling, the door handle turned and Marian strutted out of the office. She was wearing a demure dark green and navy checked suit, the skirt well below the knee, with her blouse buttoned up beneath her jacket. Janet's mouth sagged open, she could swear it was an Eastex design. What was the likes of Marian doing buying Eastex? The little minx had certainly pulled out all the stops.

'May the best woman win,' Marian said tersely, snapping a glance over her shoulder at Janet. Then she disappeared down the corridor, her stiletto heels rat-a-tat-tatting on the polished floor.

In the next few moments, before Janet could gather herself together and tidy up her fraying edges, she was ushered into the office by Kenneth Brown, the personnel manager. But much to her dismay, Patrick King, the store manager himself, was there too – a corpulent, imposing figure, his facial contours carved by a hatchet, his flinty eyes boring into her like drills to find her weak spots. All dressed up in a grey silk suit and a bright red tie. For a moment she could swear he was ballooning up and out, all around, like a bad guy in a Disney cartoon, arms crossed, leaning towards her, eyebrows hoisted into question marks, his stockade of teeth bared. So she wrenched her gaze away and concentrated her attention instead upon the mild-mannered, good guy, Kenneth Brown, in his nondescript dark grey suit.

And Kenneth got the interview up and running, much to her relief.

After going over her application, asking a few routine questions and noting her very early responsibility from the Coop days, much to Janet's delight, he went on to explain what they were looking for, that some training would be given over the systems, and then finally he asked *the* question.

'Can you tell us why we should employ you for this post, Janet?'

And Janet had rehearsed her answer, but needed to swallow hard first. 'Well, I'm very loyal to Masons, and I've grown to love working in the soft furnishing department. It runs really well, meeting its targets, thanks to Ron's superb management, and I really applied for the job to ensure that we can carry on delivering what Masons customers have come to expect – namely a high level of customer service, efficiency, and the best quality products. I feel it's so important for a new manager to have a few years of experience in soft furnishing, which students straight from university won't have. I know the departmental workings inside out. And maturity is important in soft furnishings as it can be quite demanding at times.'

The store manager interjected. 'In what way, demanding?'

Janet faltered. Wrong word, she thought. Negative word. Now there's a problem. Oh, God. Her hands, laced together in her lap, now clamped tighter together and shook slightly. Come on, she urged herself, come on! Turn it around to positive changes needed for the better. Turn it around!

She coughed and cleared her throat to form a smooth

channel for her words to flow through – come hell or high water.

'Well,' she said, 'demanding in the sense that we don't have a service desk for customers to sit and relax at while we assess their needs and give them quotes.'

'But surely it doesn't need that much time?' Patrick King observed, his frown lines deepening, like acid biting into the score marks of a steel engraving plate.

She looked back at him steadily. Tell him how it is, she reminded herself. 'Well, actually it does. We have to work out customers' curtain measurements from their window measurements and they often need help in deciding what designs they want, what accessories, like pelmets, tiebacks…that kind of thing. Then we frequently have to work out all the fabric allowances on the spot to give them a quote – that's for the custom-made service with Masons own makers in Cirencester. It's the most popular choice due to the stock fabrics being good value for money. So, it can take anything from half an hour for a couple of pairs of curtains, to two hours for a whole house. And they do want to do it there and then. It requires good concentration and I think they trust a mature person more.'

Patrick King's eyebrows shot up and he looked at Kenneth Brown. 'I wasn't aware of this time issue,' he remarked.

Janet continued. 'Berkeley Fabrics has a service desk, and the carpets department and the furniture department have desks, and all their orders are simpler and quicker to process. So, if we had a desk too, we could serve the customers placing the large time-consuming orders at the desk, and keep the big benches, which are *vital* for order processing, for the quicker-serving customers, instead of them all queuing together. Plus a desk looks more professional and is far more comfortable for people than standing by the benches for long periods, getting irritable and tired.'

'Of course!'

'That's just one suggestion I can make to increase takings

with a simple, low cost change.'

'Absolutely, Mrs Brewer, you have my full support. I have no idea why this hasn't been brought up before!' He cast a furious glance at Kenneth Brown, whose cheeks flushed red.

Then Patrick King leaned back in his chair, and muttered to Kenneth Brown, 'We'd better bring up the other matter.'

'Yes, yes, of course.' Kenneth Brown hesitated. 'Er…this is a rather more personal question, Janet, but…we were wondering if you were ready for this level of responsibility, seeing as it's only effectively a few weeks since your husband died.'

Janet suddenly felt numb. A granite rock settled in her stomach, weighing her right down. Dismally aware of her silence stretching out in the room, she realised she hadn't even considered they might bring up her bereavement. And yet, it was so obvious that they would. It would be a big issue for them, if not for her. What was she supposed to say? Begin to babble that it was quite all right? And would they believe her? She was meant to be all vulnerable and weak like Milly, all wilting with sorrow and mourning, work merely serving as a distraction from protracted grief, a sobbing and wailing grief. But this was so far from the truth. The truth…and she thought of Frank. Frank saying, *Just who do you think you are?*

And she fought back. The truth, she thought. Risk the truth. Fine. They might as well have it. Some of it, anyway.

She steadied her gaze and made sure she looked at them both directly in turn rather than evasively – a Dale Carnegie tip. 'Well, if I may be perfectly honest, my husband didn't really approve of my working. It was an issue between us, you see.'

Patrick King nodded. 'Hmm, quite common of his generation, I expect. But times are changing, as my wife keeps reminding me.' He tried to wink at Janet, but could only produce a spasm in his muscle-bound jowl.

Janet tried not to flinch. 'Yes, exactly. Well, now I feel

able to go for what I want, a proper career of a kind. I realise it may seem a little unusual, but my son is grown up and I really am free to pursue what I want out of my life.' She paused. 'And as for it not being long since my husband died, well I couldn't possibly have any control over the timing of Ron deciding to retire.' She sighed. 'I suppose it's a case of now or never for me.'

The two managers glanced at each other and Janet could read nothing from their expressions. It was a little daunting, but she'd had more than enough. She felt like a squeezed-out sponge with nothing more to give. Being honest had battered her defences and she needed to recover. She could do no more.

And it seemed the managers agreed.

'Well, thank you, Janet,' Kenneth Brown said. 'We'll let you know. You've obviously got the stamina for it as you've been full time for five years and Ron has given an excellent reference and his is really all that is necessary given your employment history. We can hardly go to the Coop now, can we?'

Cue moment for polite laughter all around, a shaking of hands, and a hasty retreat for Janet.

After she closed the door quietly behind her, she let her body sag as she slowly made her way down the corridor, touching the wall now and again to make sure she wasn't in a dream. To connect herself to reality, she checked her watch. It was around 4pm. Thank God there was only an hour left until closing time.

When she dragged her weary body back to the department, she found Ron had left early, but Ann and Gemma wanted to hear all about it. They clamoured around her, quacking like ducks seeking scraps, but Janet was resolutely unforthcoming and set about the cashing up.

'But how do you think you did, Mrs B?' Gemma was insistent, draping herself over the top of the till like a siren and searing her ebony eyes into Janet's face.

'Give her some room,' said Ann, fluttering her hands at

Gemma.

As Janet lost count of the five pence pieces for the third time, she looked up at Gemma. 'I don't know,' she said. 'I really don't.'

And the truth was, she didn't — not one inkling.

But she didn't have to endure this state of limbo for long — a limbo between winning and losing, succeeding or failing, between living or dying inside. Just the next morning she was summoned again, and this time Kenneth Brown was alone in his office. He was smiling and he offered her a seat.

'Okay, Janet, I won't beat around the bush, the job's yours if you want it — but maybe a trial period is best, say six months? And to begin immediately after Ron leaves, so that's Monday the 3rd of March. And Mr King was most insistent that we sort out that desk for you.'

Janet's mouth felt dry and she ran her tongue around the inside of her mouth. Wasn't there some mistake? Was this really happening? But as she held Kenneth Brown's gaze, she could see it was real. His steady eyes, his look of enquiry, awaiting her confirmation. She had got the job of departmental manager of soft furnishing. She had done it, against all the odds, against Frank, and against Marian.

'You've not had second thoughts, have you? Kenneth Brown's eyes narrowed with concern.

'Oh, no…not at all,' Janet stammered. A surge of tingling pulsed through her, the kind you get when you feel a response to something wonderful, or equally, when a ghost walks over your grave. But Janet's tingling made its mind up. It was to be joy rather than fear, and a warmth crept through her body, right into her heart, and it finally reached her face. She smiled. And this time, the smile did reach her eyes.

Chapter 6

Standing by Frank's graveside on the following Sunday beneath a bruised sky, Janet shivered in her thick black wool coat. It was a frosty morning and the cold pinched her nose. The short blades of grass in the Charlton Kings cemetery were crispy-sharp underfoot, and the top of Frank's polished granite headstone was veiled in a white crystalline mould. The last time she had been here was on the day of his funeral, on the 12th December, and the inscription, in its Old English silver font, still made her shudder.

> In Loving Memory Of
> Frank Ernest Brewer
> A Dear Husband,
> Father, and Grandfather
> Died 5th December 1989 Aged 65 Years
> Rest in Peace

And most of it was a lie.

There were no loving memories, he had been far from 'dear' in any respect, and she certainly wished him no peace – no soft, fluffy cotton wool clouds of tranquillity for Frank to float around on, no shining palaces in a celestial city to wander through. Just the opposite in fact. He belonged in a Bosch painting of hell, being tortured by highly inventive demons with tailor-made tools. And yet perhaps this was a little too vivid, too active, maybe she just wanted to think of him as absolutely nothing, a vapourised, dematerialised Frank. But of course, he hadn't been cremated, his will had stipulated burial, so she hadn't been able to hurl his dust into a force ten gale and be done with him. No. He was right here, under the earth in front of her, beginning to decay and become food for worms. And she pictured him down there inside his coffin – had anything got in yet? And just how long would it take for the flesh to be consumed and fall away? And even then, the bones of him would last. And she hated the very bones of him. She shivered again. The soil hadn't been seeded over yet, and the clotted clumps of earth looked as if they were infected with a musty white blight. There was supposed to be one more space for her in this burial plot. But that was taking irony too far. She had no intention of keeping him company. She dragged her eyes back to the headstone's inscription.

And it had been an agony of irony letting these words be carved into his stone. But how could she do otherwise? There was Scott, their son, and her lovely grandson, Daniel, to think of, and she'd wanted to shelter them from the biting acid of her corrosive marriage. She hoped she'd protected Scott as he was growing up, but she wasn't sure, and they'd certainly never discussed it. She had shielded him like a she-wolf, always making sure he was out of the way when Frank had yet another point to make.

With her gloved hand she touched the tiny scar on her left cheek. She couldn't remember what point he'd been making when he made that mark. He made so many points. He'd slapped her, of course, as he always did, hard and stinging with heat, but this way there was usually no physical evidence of bruising – a calculated ploy from a former member of the Gloucestershire Constabulary, respected by his favoured colleagues for being a hard-liner. And he'd taken to wearing a gold ring on the little finger of his right hand, a ring she'd never seen before, which he maintained was a signet ring inherited from his father. The cast carving was of a spread eagle grasping a sword in its talons, the symbolism of which remained obscure to Janet, but she wondered if it had anything to do with freemasonry. And somehow, when he slapped her, the ring had caught her and cut into her cheek, just by the side of her left eye. She'd had to go to accident and emergency, telling them some story or other, she couldn't remember what she'd said now. Only two tiny stitches had been needed and it had healed well, but the scar had gone on to become a daily visible reminder of Frank, every time she used her touch-up stick on it when applying her makeup – year in, year out.

And what had she done with the ring after his death? It hadn't been a difficult decision to make when the undertakers had handed it to her after preparing Frank's body, and she'd reluctantly let them drop it in her open palm. She hadn't wanted Frank to wear it. Why should he get to do that? Scott hadn't wanted the ring. She didn't want it. There were two brothers of Frank's, but there'd been no contact for years and they hadn't come to the funeral, which had been a very poorly attended affair.

After the funeral, and after a few more days of the ring burning and smoking inside her as she carried it around in her handbag, she'd suddenly felt the urge to get rid of it while she was shopping on the Promenade in town. Pausing by a drain hole, she had the ring clenched in her hand and almost uncurled her fingers to let it drop into the dark abyss, to quench its fire, and to be washed down to flow with all the human detritus; that seemed so fitting. But three golden spheres rolled into her thoughts, the kind of spheres that hung over a certain type of shop she'd been in several times as a girl in the forties – and she had the idea to pawn the ring. Dispose of it the old-fashioned way, with no intention of redeeming it, like she'd seen her mother do countless times when the family was struggling during those lean post-war years. Pawning had a grubby, used, and degrading feel to the process, which she decided was most appropriate. And of course if Frank's spirit was hanging around somewhere, he'd be spitting with anger. So that would be even better. It would be like one apocalyptic tit for 34 years of tat – the length of their marriage. She found a pawn shop called Money Spinners in the high street and got around £100 for Frank's ring. Then she'd gone straight up to Montpellier and spent the money by having her hair done, a full manicure, and after that a pot of tea and a slice of Victoria sponge at Betty's Tiffin regency-style restaurant, under the approving gaze of its carved caryatids. She'd ended her excursion back down on the Promenade, buying three porcelain thimbles from an antique shop to add to her collection. It was literally an afternoon well spent.

Now accustomed to the cold, she smirked down at Frank's headstone, smelling a meat-pasty aroma puffing from a nearby bakery. Nourishing food and welcome warmth. Life went on. But not for Frank. And that was why she was here. It was to be her only visit. A visit to celebrate her victory. Over him, and her own personal one.

He'd been quiet lately, ever since she got the job. No spectral visions of him leering over her and robbing her of sleep, no tormenting voice prodding into her mind. And good riddance. There would be no laying of flowers for Frank, no paying of respects. Just this address at his graveside, with the wreath of holly she had laid at his funeral now withering against the ice-cold granite, its berries shrivelled and sucked of life.

She glanced around to make sure there was no one within hearing distance, then her eyes bore down upon his headstone in the manner of an avenging angel. She was now to make *her point,* and her sword blows would find their mark.

'I got it, Frank,' she said. 'I got the job. And I know *just* who I am – I'm the new manager of soft furnishing for Masons, and I'll be making £12,000 a year.' And in increasingly powerful vitriolic tones she continued. 'This is my time now. You can't stop me. You're dead and buried and I hope you rot in hell.'

A hunched passer-by, just beyond the perimeter railings of the cemetery a few yards away, stopped in his tracks. He pushed his spectacles back onto the bridge of his nose with his index finger and stared at her – the woman in black, who was blasting apart the idealised stereotype of the grieving widow. His mouth sagged open like a gate on a broken hinge. She saw his shock, became hot with embarrassment, then fought back by giving him one of her flat stares, like a reptile on a rock – knowing and defiant. The man fixed his mouth, turned, and hurried away.

Janet decided it was time she did the same.

That Sunday afternoon Janet relaxed at home wearing her floral, frilly housecoat slightly ahead of schedule. Sitting in front of the telly with a box of Thorntons chocolates by her side, she'd decided to watch the Sunday matinee, *Wuthering Heights*, with Merle Oberon and Lawrence Olivier, a true black and white classic from 1939. Tucking her legs underneath her in her easy chair, with Thomas in the sag of Frank's seat opposite, she settled down, with a little time to reflect, just before the film started, that her week had gone very well indeed.

She'd told Scott about the job with some trepidation when he called around on the Tuesday evening to see how she was getting on. After looking stunned, then sitting down with a bottle of Carlsberg, his favourite lager which she kept a small supply of in the fridge, he'd asked an awful lot of questions and she answered them as rapidly as he fired them at her: yes, she was serious; yes, the offer was serious too; yes, she was fit enough; yes, she knew there'd be a lot of responsibility; yes, she was up for it; and yes, she'd give it up if it got too much for her. She was struck by the fact that she didn't have to answer no to anything, but of course she'd never told him about how she felt about a certain working acquaintance. *That* might have generated some conflict.

'Oh well, Mum,' he said finally, 'I suppose you might as well give it your best shot. I know how much you love Masons, and you need to keep busy right now. I'm sure Susan will be pleased for you too. It's a real achievement, a woman of your age getting a management position.'

Susan, she thought. Well, the flighty mare had better not pester me at work, thinking I can use my influence in some way to aid her shopping sprees, or top up her pile of stilettos.

The very next day Janet had signed her job contract, and while reading it afterwards had spotted the salary, which she'd never even noticed before. She was stunned to see that it was double her present pay as a sales assistant, and with the 50% management discount she'd get with her staff store card, she'd be able to do a lot more spending if she wished. Of course, money wasn't exactly a problem. Frank had been a traditionalist and had named her as his main beneficiary. After all, he was estranged from his surviving brothers, and Janet was the mother of his only son. But she'd still been surprised not to find smatterings of posthumous spite here; it had been many years since she'd seen any signs that he cared for her. But no matter. Now the house was hers, the mortgage having been finally paid off a few years back, and she'd shortly be in receipt of Frank's retirement police pension. She didn't expect much from his life insurance payment because of his smoking, drinking, and angina being on record. But who knew what might happen?

And as for her work, well Ron, Ann and Gemma had been so pleased for her, it was almost touching.

Ron had shook her hand, pumping his arm up and down like a piston. 'Good going, Janet! I'm so pleased I can leave this behind in your very capable hands.'

Ann had stretched her mouth so wide, the resulting smile, if that's what you could call it, looked like something out of *The Muppet Show*. It was most disconcerting.

'I'll be able to retire with peace of mind, now,' she breathed. Then she frowned and looked at Janet. 'You'll let me off my promise, won't you? Remember I said I'd stay as long as you did, but now that you're going to be the manager...' she tailed off.

'Yes, but you won't retire straightaway, will you?' Janet asked, alarm bells clanging as she remembered Ann was already working beyond her retirement age.

'No, no, not right away. Just when you've got it mastered,

Janet.'

Gemma had been, well, Gemma. Hoisting her gothic eyebrows and rolling her eyes like marbles, she said, 'Thank God, Mrs B.' Then she hesitated. 'I can still call you Mrs B, can't I?'

Janet considered it. Just how would it sound to others? Disrespectful? Over-familiar? But then she looked at Gemma and saw the ploughed furrows in her forehead. She decided to be magnanimous and smooth them out. Everything, right now, had to be clean and tidy. 'Why, not?' she said.

'Cool,' replied Gemma.

'But I'm counting on you to help train up the new girl when we get her.'

'Or him,' commented Ron.

'Sure, Mrs B,' Emma smiled, once more appearing to be serenely on the other planet she far preferred to this one.

Milly had been in for a couple of afternoons and had tried to ignore Janet, but of course she just didn't have the backbone for it, did Milly-Molly-Mandy, and she'd glanced over at Janet a few times looking as frightened as a rabbit, in fact her nose was practically twitching with fear. Janet had so enjoyed going over to her desk for a chat.

'No hard feelings, I hope,' she said, noticing the bobbles on Milly's cardigan were conspicuous by their absence. Well, well, she mused.

But Milly had been primed by Marian. 'Of course not,' she said, her bosom swelling and her voice fluttering. 'But I'm not an employee of Masons, we have our own management.'

'Of course,' Janet purred. 'Of course you do. But we can all get along, can't we?'

Milly had clamped her eyes to her paperwork, one of Marian's cheap, chewed tip biros shaking in her grasp. She'd drawn her mouth into a crooked line and made no reply.

And as for Marian herself. Well, that had been something to behold.

'I suppose congratulations are in order, Janet, but you're not getting any from me,' she said, looking up at Janet from the Berkeley Fabrics desk.

As she locked her gaze upon Janet, Marian's glittering dark brown eyes drilled venom into her and Janet was taken aback.

'It's a simple case of nepotism,' Marian continued, 'and we all know it. I suggest we steer well clear from each other from now on. I've got my job to do and you will have yours.'

Marian curled her lip at Janet.

Janet mirrored her in response.

Then Marian jerked back her chair and stood up in a snug spandex skirt, whilst showcasing her nipples in a tight muslin blouse. 'I'm going for my coffee break now, not that I need to report to you. Just you remember that, because I won't be! You hear me? I won't!'

Janet had been left standing there, her heart pumping hard, her fists opening and closing, wondering just how on earth she was going to handle this jumped-up little tart. It wouldn't look good to management if there were tensions right from the start in the department, and naturally, she'd not disclosed her issues with Marian during the interview. If they'd got a whiff of interpersonal conflict they'd have cast their net far wider afield.

But wonder of wonders, Janet had been most surprised that by Saturday, Marian was simply doing her job and keeping out of Janet's way, and had obviously instructed Milly to do the same. So maybe things would turn out alright after all, and she wouldn't have to find a way of getting rid of Marian. But there again, she'd never had much luck with 'maybes'.

Wuthering Heights began, and Janet, thawed by the electric fire in the grate, and nurtured by the taste of her chocolate truffles, which she usually ate by biting off the tops then nibbling around the sides, found herself drifting and floating into the fictive space of another world.

And when Heathcliff held the dying Cathy in his arms, Janet felt a sharp stinging tear squeeze its way out of the corner of her left eye. It dribbled down her cheek. Thomas looked at her with his wide green eyes, his head cocked at an angle.

She was thinking now of another love from a long time ago, in a different life. Why she was thinking of the past now, she had no idea. It was dead and buried like Frank. And yet…as both Cathy and Heathcliff embraced in death on a wind-whipped Peniston Crag, as they were finally reunited in their passionate love for one another, finally together in each other's arms, she shivered from head to foot. The shivering tingles tugged at her heart, making it throb painfully in a way she remembered experiencing before – just once before in her life, for a protracted length of time – and that had been so very bad. And as Ellen, the housekeeper, finished the story of *Wuthering Heights* by telling the good Doctor that Heathcliff was now with Cathy – 'He's with her. They've only just begun to live,' she said, Janet felt sobs rising and ballooning inside her, creating a terrible pressure she couldn't contain. Gut-wrenching sobs building and pressing. She needed to let them out lest she burst. So she wept in convulsing spasms, crying into the chocolate box on her lap, onto the roses of her housecoat, making blossoms of wetness bloom there. Sobbing harder still. Streams of mucous trailing from her nose. And she found it hard to breathe, and she heard herself making these gasping sounds, so alien, not her, it wasn't her, it couldn't be her, her hands clenching into fists on the arms of her chair, while the credits rolled…while Thomas broke his mesmerised pose and ran for the cat flap.

His action broke in upon her, bringing her back to herself. Shoving the chocolates from her lap, and scattering them on her Chinese rug, she got to her feet, squashing some of the truffles underfoot. She staggered into the kitchen, her vision blurring in and out of focus, while she blinked away hot tears. She tore down sheets of kitchen roll from the dispenser and began to mop her face, feeling a terrifying urgency to wipe away her shameful mess of emotion.

That evening, after clearing up and making herself a ham salad, she tried some rationalisation. It had simply been the film — that was all. She had been taken in, hook, line and sinker, by the wailing music, the simpering syrupy sentiment, the pure plaintive slush. She'd been stressed lately, her sleep had been terrible, so her nerves were frayed. She was also at a vulnerable age, 54, and not quite through the menopause yet. Mood swings were a primary feature. She should let herself off the hook, be kind to herself like the books said. Now everything had changed, she'd be fine. She was in control now, for the first time in her life.

But although her mood improved, still, she couldn't bring herself to listen to some of her favourite records from the fifties from her days at the Coop, as she'd planned to this evening. Frank had always objected to her playing them, but now he wasn't here, she could do as she liked. There was Frank Sinatra's 'I've Got the World on a String', old blue eyes himself, the ultimate crooner, and yes, the irony over the name had bothered her for years, and of course, Frank the husband had hated Frank the singer. There was Dean Martin's 'That's Amore' — the girls she went to the local dances with had loved singing along to that one. There was Tony Bennet's 'Stranger in Paradise', Frankie Laine's 'I Believe', and Nat King Cole's 'Unforgettable'. What good times she had then. She had enjoyed dancing then. She had dreams then, with a man she loved — then. She'd planned to listen and move to the music, to invite the butterflies back into her life after such a long absence. She had her victory. She'd won. She deserved some fun. But perhaps, she reflected now, feeling wrung out of any emotion, it was just a little too soon. She had to learn the ropes of her new job first and prove her worth. So Janet picked up her cross stitch instead and gathered her threads together, making sure there were no loose ends, but little knowing what she had set in motion by applying for her new job to thwart Marian, and that she'd be reacquainted with heartache once again.

PART TWO

Chapter 7

Janet stood by the window that looked down into Pilgrim Street at the rear of Masons, a composed black figure framed in a regency window. Fat pigeons waddled on the parapets of the three storey roofs opposite, stalking the shifting beams of spring sunshine flashing through the gaps between scudding clouds in this early June, and flapping down onto the pavements to conduct searches for food by the bins. Janet watched them for a moment, heads bobbing and nodding, then turned to conduct her own inspection of the soft furnishing department – now she was the queen of all she surveyed. And it felt so right, she could have bobbed her own head in approval.

She'd been manager for three months now and it had been a time of many changes, educations, transformations and modifications, whilst she put Dale Carnegie's advice on best practice leadership skills to the test. Good leaders arouse enthusiasm in others, praise rather than criticise, and see things from each other's individual viewpoints (particularly useful for Gemma, she found). A remarkably more cheerful Ron, lighter in step and straighter in body from having cast off his wearisome burden, enjoyed coming in on an informal basis to train Janet on the key areas she was lacking in. And thanks to him, she was now familiar with spreadsheets and databases, she could analyse sales figures and make sales projections, she could lay her hands on all the supplier information. In short, although she knew she still had a lot to learn, she felt confident that she could handle the job. And what a great feeling it was – with a tiny touch, as light as the flutter of a lacewing, of familiarity. A tiny touch of memory from her Coop days. So one could go as far as to say that the climate inside Janet had changed favourably with the seasons.

She'd been out a few times with the Steadmans, the married couple who Masons employed to deliver the department's measuring and fitting service, to see how they operated. And she'd found someone local who could make up loose covers for customers as an extra benefit. There was also a new secretary, who'd been employed to help soft furnishing, carpets, and furniture with store administration. But perhaps, for Janet, the best thing of all, was simply the new desk for the department, just a few metres away from the window where she now stood, where Ann was sitting taking a curtain order from an elderly couple who couldn't decide on whether they wanted their velvets made with the pile going up or down.

'It's a richer colour, pile up, and doesn't show finger marks,' Ann was saying patiently, with her immaculately coiffed nimbus of silver hair, 'but it's sleeker to the touch, pile down. See?'

The couple fingered the swatch wonderingly, staring at the powder blue velvet, their faces drawn into cavities and crevasses of concentration.

Yes, the desk was just perfect, Janet mused.

And there was Gemma. Over by one of the serving benches, trying not to slouch, in a long navy skirt and tucked-in, shapeless white blouse, with her cardigan shrugged off, because the temperatures within the victorian building of Masons had recently soared, with no air conditioning practically possible in this grand emporium of Cheltenham to ease the greenhouse effect. Still, it was by no means unbearable – not yet. Gemma was showing the new lady how to do fabric calculations, while the department was quiet, and as instructed to do so by Janet.

The new lady had been with them since the beginning of April. She had no previous experience, which just typically demonstrated how management *still* viewed this department as not being on the same level as carpets or furniture. Well, Janet intended to do her utmost to change this faulty perception. However, Claire Bennet was doing quite well, with an interest in interior design and plenty of enthusiasm. She was a housewife, with two older boys, and had wanted to return to formal employment. She'd agreed to be full time until they got someone else for the department as promised by Kenneth Brown, but ideally she wanted three days a week. She was smart, petite and personable, but did have difficulty sometimes lifting heavy rolls of fabric off the racks, especially the Bulgomme heat-resistant table felt which they sold by the metre, though she'd said her son was giving her some weight training to help with this. Janet had been suitably impressed by this dedication. From her conversation, it was also clear that she had a far from ideal relationship with her husband, which pleased Janet even more.

The made-to-measure curtain displays dressing the rear walls of the department from top to bottom were beautifully colour-coordinated, with patterns broken by occasional plains. This was one of Claire's first tasks which Janet had deemed entirely satisfactory, much to Gemma's nose wrinkling annoyance. But this was a little sign of healthy competition which warmed Janet's heart. Janet had made sure the department's carpet had been cleaned thoroughly throughout, and the swing doors, situated between the two serving benches at the rear, leading to the goods lift and down to the loading bay, had been given a fresh coat of white paint. And what a difference, Janet reflected now, congratulating herself. Just marvellous. Her eyes roamed further.

New stock fabric displays lined the front perimeter of the department on the A frames – 'Spring specials' bought at whole roll, wholesale prices from Crowson, which Janet had elbowed into the department, with the store manager, Mr King's, approval, despite central buying restrictions. After all, she'd argued, she knew Cheltenham's tastes, and Mr King had applauded her enterprising attitude.

Then finally, her eyes travelled on to the far corner of the department, in front of the cash office, and her own office, to Berkeley Fabrics, where her eyes came to rest. And everything here was exactly the same. The same Milly-Molly-Mandy, still eating too much candy, judging from her swelling figure, keeping her head down and her ample chest and muffin tops well-trussed. The same Marian who had barely spoken a word to Janet since their previous altercation, and that was just how Janet liked it, bearing in mind that Dale Carnegie also advised avoiding arguments, a more challenging concept, but suitable for a manager. And there was Marian, right now, talking to Milly, flicking her out-of-a-bottle red hair around as usual.

There was just one thing though. And it was so highly vexing, Janet was sure Marian was doing it on purpose. Just a few days ago, Marian had begun wearing suits, starting with the one she had worn for her interview – the Eastex one with the green and navy checks. And it had already caused *some* customers to think that *she* was the departmental manager, instead of Janet.

Janet had mulled this problem over for a couple of days, turning it around, looking at it from all angles, instead of firing off wildly like a badly loaded and poorly aimed pistol, using her new leadership practice of avoiding confrontation. But she'd come up with a solution using one of her favourite aphorisms of dear Dale's, which was 'to bait the hook to suit the fish'. And her approach decided, just ten minutes ago, she had finished putting her plan into action in her office. She'd obtained the telephone number of Gillian Makepeace, Marian's area manager, from personnel, and had rung her up for a chat. She began with the usual pleasantries, to soften her up, then she got to the point, expressing her concern over Marian's new dress code. Her argument was that whilst Marian looked quite lovely, she was concerned because the in-house protocol of Masons allowed Masons management to wear coloured suits, but otherwise all other staff had to wear navy or black. Therefore by wearing a coloured suit, Marian was appearing to be a Masons manager rather than a

Berkeley Fabrics employee, so in a way she was misrepresenting the company. And Janet's ploy worked beautifully.

'I see your point, Mrs Brewer. I'll have a word with her straightaway.'

'Oh, *do* call me Janet. And I look forward to your next visit.'

Janet had put the phone down and grinned. Her new behaviours were succeeding, and talking to the woman had been most enlightening. She'd sounded just like another fluffy floozy, and she knew how to handle *them*.

Right now, she was due her lunch break. She took the 2pm shift. This had always been her preference, but she now had the added benefit of it actually showing consideration to her girls, in that she could cover for them at the busier times, like a good manager should.

'I'm off to lunch, Ann,' she said, strolling past the desk.

Ann looked up, nodded and smiled.

Janet missed Ann. Now she was a manager, she had to sit in the management end of the canteen. It was a rule that staff and managers shouldn't sit together – far too familiar if respect and discipline had to be maintained. She fully agreed in principle, but wished she could make Ann an exception. They'd always done their chatting in their break times or a little on the shop floor, but now, unless they met up out of hours, as Ann had immediately (and rather brazenly to Janet's mind) suggested, Janet never got a chance to find out what the latest in-store gossip was. What was happening with that young lad who was popular with the girls, who was newly promoted to security from the loading bay, who was always a bit cheeky when they checked out through the staff entrance? Was the firmly married Kenneth Brown really having an affair with his secretary? What was it about bosses and secretaries? Was it the power and the subservience? The being at close quarters registering every frown, sigh or smile? The conducive close working environment in which to project those inner wishes, sorrows or desires? How unoriginally and thoroughly depressing it was! And who was it who said the secretary might be pregnant after they found a positive result test kit in the ladies powder room bin? And since management would get into trouble participating in this unsavoury dark side of human interest, and although Janet was just itching to grasp the threads of this gossip like a lifeline, she found herself left behind, floundering on the surface, while the petty-minded shameless folk dived down to these depths without her. Oh, it was *so* hard.

The other annoying thing was she found she had little to talk about with the other managers in their area of the canteen. The ones she was most familiar with naturally came from the second floor. The carpet department manager, Niall Walsh, was a lanky, stooped, question mark of a young man, whose grey suit hung from his frame, and who gave his belt a regular hitch as if to stop his trousers falling down. He had an overgrown hedge of moustache and a prematurely receding hairline, as if the former was making amends for the latter. Janet found him shifty and uncommunicative, shunning small talk and seemingly determined to be evasive on all counts. He bolted down his food, racing against the clock, so that he could then shift himself to be with his cronies for as long as possible, sitting in a hazed rank miasma, pensively puckering his mouth around his roll-ups. How he'd become a manager, Janet just couldn't imagine. The furniture manager, however, was a different prospect.

Hugh Boatman was a well-muscled man with a large frame and a kind, avuncular demeanour, which Janet quite liked. He'd made her welcome, and talked about his family a good deal, together with the stresses and strains of management. But he had asked her an awful lot of questions about her private life, and trying to pry the answers out of Janet was like trying to extract individual stones from a roughcast cemented wall, and even if you got one or two little pebbles loosened, there were the blocks of stone underneath to fortify the whole structure. So these days he muttered on about the weather or moaned about Patrick King putting too much pressure on furniture for sales.

Then there was Shirley Appleton, the bedding and linens department manageress, who Janet had spoke to reasonably frequently as they managed adjacent departments. A sugary boiled sweet of a woman, Janet had decided, in a shiny cellophane wrap, probably a pastel-coloured pear drop, who was always well made up with her sprayed blonde hair never out of place. Shirley rated Clarins anti-wrinkle day and night moisturising creams as the secret to her successfully youthful complexion, together with treating herself to a 50ml pot of Icone occasionally, after Janet had tried a little Carnegie-inspired sucking up to her, saying how smooth her skin was and asking – what was her secret? Would she mind sharing? And yet, Janet sensed Shirley's charm was indeed skin deep. How perfectly fitting. And as for her being steely beneath the saccharine, well that was to be expected with a boiled sweet – but of course, boiled sweets could always be cracked wide open.

And as Janet sat now in the canteen by the window overlooking Pilgrim Street once again, with her modest portion of fish pie, it was Shirley who joined her. Shirley, who Janet knew wouldn't have a clue how to run a soft furnishing department, when all she ever had to do was manage the stocking of shelves with ready-made bed-linens, accessories, pillows and duvets – all point of sale merchandise. But they did have *something* in common – they both had a concession within their department. Shirley had Dorma Bedding to contend with, and had aired her frustrations with Janet from time to time. So today, Janet had something to report on this subject, and welcomed Shirley to sit down.

'And how are you today?' she asked Janet, as she placed her knife and fork by her plate of salad, smiling with her simpering pink lipstick lips to presumably coordinate with her sickly sweet salmon pink suit. She had a white chiffon blouse underneath, with a waterfall of a tied bow cascading from her neckline, as if to stress, if further insistence was needed, her extreme femininity and sensibility.

Janet responded in kind, then decided to run her recent victory over Berkeley Fabrics past Shirley. She contrived to describe it impartially, careful not to suggest a shred of professional animosity towards Marian.

'I should think so too,' Shirley commented, taking a sip of tea, then touching the corner of her mouth with a napkin. 'That was well-handled. So all you have to do is check she does what she's told.'

'Oh, I will.'

Then Shirley looked at her closely, in a searching way, with her pencilled brows arched in a parody of enquiry. Janet pulled an inch or two backwards, feeling a strong sense of dis-ease. What was coming next?

'Have you considered, though, that maybe you should wear some colour yourself?'

And her gaze felt like a torch beam prying through the keyhole of Janet's locked door of privacy. How dare she become personal? How dare she?

Janet felt her eyes shifting, she just couldn't keep them still. How dare the woman? She focused once again down into Pilgrim street, then brought herself back to the window box display of brightly blotched pansies right outside the canteen window. Maybe she was over reacting? After all, the woman was obviously into fashion. She decided to find out where the question was going, but she wouldn't make it easy.

'I've always preferred black. It's serious. It's professional.'

'Yes, I know. But the general staff can also wear black, as well as navy, and the managers are allowed more freedom and can wear colour. So colour distinguishes management from general staff to the public. That's the reason why the strategy the lady from Berkeley Fabrics adopted, actually worked. So why don't you take advantage of it yourself, Janet? Why don't you get yourself some coloured suits?'

Janet thrust herself back into her seat, eyes slowly widening in understanding.

'I see the penny has dropped.' Shirley smiled demurely, then began to pick at her salad – pick – nibble – nibble – pick, like a curious squirrel checking its nuts.

Janet looked hard at her. She saw the sarcasm in a peanut brittle layer beneath the surface sweetness of Shirley. The sheer cliff of her façade, with the ruthlessness that no doubt lurked behind it.

And Janet wanted to get away, before she tumbled down before that smarmy slick mask of a face.

'I'll think about it,' she said, as she grabbed hold of her handbag to leave.

'Yes, you should. You really should.'

And when she told Ann back on the department what Shirley had said, Ann dumbfounded her by agreeing.

'Black can be off-putting to the customer, Janet. It might be okay for us, but managers shouldn't come across as too aloof, for when they have to deal with complaints and such like. Would a coloured suit really be so bad?'

'Well…I don't know…'

'Why don't you go and have a look right now. It's quiet enough here.'

And so, Janet found herself working through the stock of suits in Austin Reed, Jaeger, Viyella, Jacques Vert and Windsmoor (determined not to touch Eastex with a barge pole) feeling a distinct sense of the surreal, and scowling at the staff of these concessions to leave her be. She tutted to herself, thinking that buying new suits was a totally unnecessary and extravagant expense. But then she remembered Frank's moderate life insurance policy had recently paid out, and of course she wouldn't be paying the full amount on the tickets using her store card, so she continued her search.

And seeing this stern woman in her black suit and her severely scraped back bob, the concession staff left her to it.

She rejected the beiges, too easy to mark; she eschewed the bright reds, the vivid blues, because she would simply feel disturbed in the head if she wore these colours; she felt sickened by the mustards and pinks; she squirmed over the browns; and slowly through a military and methodical process of elimination, she ended up by choosing two suits, both size twelve.

One was a dark purple cotton and wool blend from Viyella, with a faint cream check, the jacket hem resting on her hips, and so showing off her fine figure. The other was from Windsmoor, in plain bottle green, which matched her eyes, and the jacket was longer, with pockets. Both jackets had the prerequisite shoulder pads, and her patent leather court shoes accessorised well. She paid around £150, after 50% discount with her staff card, and duly marched down to security by the staff entrance on Pilgrim Street, to hand in her shopping and to receive a numbered disc for her 'deposit'. This was to be handed back over to redeem her goods as she left the building at the end of the day. A daily ritual for all, where those who had to collect their shopping at the security hatch often had to queue up the internal fire escape, whether they be managers or not. And those thin card discs, with their felt-tipped numbers, became greasy thin and grubby with time, picking up the sweat from thousands of sticky fingers through which they'd passed, picking up the imprints of the worker bees. Year in, year out.

The very next day she forced herself to wear the purple suit, rather than the bottle green which she favoured. But she felt a statement had to be made, and this was the suit to do it. Just before she left the house, she could have sworn Thomas stared at her in marble-eyed wonder, but cats were so hard to read it was impossible to tell. At first, she'd felt distinctly unreal to herself putting it on, as if trying to turn herself into someone else for which she had no planned model to work from. And what if she simply couldn't endure it? What then?

But things improved for her throughout the day. Her colleagues were most supportive. And she found, much to her surprise, while looking down at her smartly fitted sleeves, that the suit began to take on an air of glowing sophistication. And they all admired it so. Ann, Gemma, Claire and Shirley. Only it was the first three she took notice of. She'd decided the previous evening, after rolling the problem of Shirley around in her mind like a multi-faceted gemstone purporting to be the genuine article, and considering her from all angles, that Shirley was a fake, that she had flawed duplicitous tendencies. Not only that, but she sensed Shirley thought she was better than Janet, that she was a cut-above. Well, she'd be keeping up a facade of her own from now on. She could do the condescendingly agreeable act too if she tried. These days she could do just about anything.

And in this frame of mind, with the purple suit settling on her bones and moving forward with her, rather than against her, she stalked through the department on the way to her office, right past the Berkeley Fabrics desk. It was 8.55am and Marian was just arriving, dressed in her customary navy spandex skirt and tight blouse and jacket. The Eastex suit had left the building.

As they caught sight of each other they stopped in their tracks, Marian on her way to her desk, Janet just passing it, with about four feet between them. Marian gasped. Her mouth fell open, then snapped shut. She looked Janet up and down, opening her mouth again to say something, but nothing came out. She shook her head numbly.

Janet smirked and tilted her chin up.

'You bitch,' Marian said, her mouth hardening into a thin slash, and her eyes glittering like gimlets.

'Careful,' Janet replied. 'You don't want to get into any more trouble, do you?'

'It was *you*. She wouldn't say, but I know it was you. And now look at you. What's the matter, Janet, frightened the customers won't know you're the very important manager?'

Marian's sarcastic little girl's high-pitched tone sliced sharply through Janet's defences. Her breath hitched in her throat and her heart began hammering.

'You're the one who's playing games,' she managed to spit out. 'You stay out of my way, or I'll find a way of getting you out of here altogether.'

Marian flounced around her desk and stood behind it. They both stared at each other like two cats, each poised to strike to defend their territory, daring each other to cross the line. Mouths twitching with anger, hands clenched, nails at the ready for ripping and slashing, eyes cutting into each other – eyes full of hate. Dale would have thrown his hands up in horror.

But Janet broke her pose first and strode off to her office. After all, she thought, I've won for now. And I plan to keep on winning, and I'll find a way of getting rid of her somehow.

Chapter 8

Marian behaved herself for the next two months, while Janet, who was getting much closer to the end of her own six month trial period, kept a close eye on her. Whether or not this watchfulness was actually influential in the apparent truce, or because her regular practice of hurling Marian's Sindy doll effigy (now wearing the Eastex suit) through the hole in the stairwell wall was proving efficacious, Janet had no idea, but it seemed good protocol, so she carried on, with a steel band of determination clamped around her heart. She was thoroughly enjoying the job now, and she'd found a new kind of strong assertiveness in herself which made her feel she'd done just the right thing in becoming manager of the soft furnishing department. Indeed, who else was there who could have done it in her place?

Sales targets had been exceeded and Mr King had congratulated her with his characteristic pumping up and down handshake. 'Excellent, Janet. Tip, top! Keep up the good work!'

They had reached their target for newly contracted store card customers, these sales drives being generated by percentage off incentives with the first sale, which could be a considerable saving on a curtain order. The department was well stocked and in good order. Gemma was training a new young man, who was sticking it out, despite initially appearing about as much use as a chocolate teacup – though Janet suspected Gemma's smouldering charcoal-eyed attractions had something to do with his increased efforts – and of course he helped out with the heavy lifting. There had still been no entirely suitable candidates for the job, so Kevin Jones would have to do for the foreseeable future. And the present and the future were Janet's life now. With a widow's pension from the police force and a moderate life insurance payout for Frank's timely demise, with prying fingers from the past trying to clutch hold of her having retreated into the shadows, Janet's life filled with financial security and light.

It was the middle of August now, and a record-breaking heat wave for this year was simmering in the Cotswolds with highs of 37 degrees centigrade. This meant the temperature inside the staunch elderly building of Masons was even higher, turning it into a steaming botanic garden hothouse. Customers had to be prepared to wilt and swoon in the heat in order to browse the new exotic early autumn trends, or buy bargain summer fashions in the full flowering bloom of the summer sale. And because heat rises, the second floor, where soft furnishing was located, was the hottest floor of all. And the intrepid shoppers, who, despite the lure of the sun shining approval upon the attractions of the nearby hills, or the brightly flowered Cheltenham parks in which to push babies in prams, were instead hell-bent on entering the store to spend their money to increase their property. And the heat hit them like a thick fog bank, dimming their senses. When they regained some speech, as they always managed to do, this is what the staff had to listen to, over and over again:

'How do you stand it in here?'

'Isn't there any air conditioning?

'Surely the store could have some air conditioning.'

'The fans don't seem to be doing anything!'

'It's unbearable!'

'But, honestly, *how do you* stand it in here?'

And the staff had been instructed by upper management never to complain, never to agree that the heat was indeed unbearable, but on the contrary it was quite alright, thank you, that one simply got used to it. Well, whoever would have believed that quite contrary to popular belief the customer could be wrong and not always right? That the heat *was* bearable. Look at us, cry the staff, we're fine! Never mind that the women must wear stockings or tights and under no circumstances go bare-legged. Why? It's not seemly. Really? Never mind that our feet are slipping around in our wet shoes as we stand still or walk the thick carpets in the heat of our very own saunas. Never mind that the underarms of our blouses and shirts are wringing wet, not to mention our 'down below', you know…and if you're unfortunate enough to be female and over fifty and going through *the change*. Well, hush now! We don't want to talk about that. No one wants us talking about that. But with all these hot flushes? Well, God help us! And who needs night sweats when we can have day sweats in here? But seriously, we'll be lucky if we survive in here!

But Janet and Ann were the doyens of the soft furnishing department and they obeyed the rules and disseminated them just like good superior officers in Masons army. They led by example, they led from the front. No admission of discomfort to the public, no complaining even to each other, because customers just might overhear, and complaining leads to a negative environment. And no slacking at all costs; appearances are everything. And all of this was despite the two women's foreheads beading drops of condensation, despite the air shimmering like a mirage in the desert, despite feeling swimmy in their jungle heat, despite feeling wrung out of all their essence, like over-used floorcloths used day in and day out by overworked maids for the benefit and comfort of the superiors who employed them in their service.

And into this distinctly tropical milieu, this Saturday afternoon in the middle of August, arrived Scott, Janet's son, with his wife, Susan, and their little son, Daniel. They moved along the aisle separating bedding from soft furnishing, just visible as bobbing heads and shoulders, with Susan trailing behind and looking at everything in sight. Then they turned right onto the department, making a beeline for Janet standing next to Gemma at a serving bench.

Janet was not expecting them.

And as she was talking to Gemma, checking that Kevin had been taught how to work out pattern repeats, when she spotted the familiar figures, her words trickled to a halt like the last few water drops of a spent stream evaporating in the heat, and she became rooted to the spot, her joints stiffly held in a fast-drying glue. Gemma followed her gaze.

'Hi, Mum. Sorry to just descend on you like this.' Scott wiped his forehead with the back of his hand. 'How do you stand it in here?'

Janet's tongue was stuck fast to the roof of her mouth which felt rough and dry like sandpaper.

Gemma looked closely at Janet, revealing nothing of her wonderings with her gothic dour demeanour.

'Grandma!' Daniel piped up. 'Mummy's come to get some curtains. She says she wants lots and lots of frills! But we don't like frills, do we Daddy?' He turned to look at Scott, who grinned, then he turned back to Janet, his face tilted up expectantly.

And it was Daniel who came to her rescue. His little cheerful face, his mop of dark glossy hair, his shining blue eyes of excitement. Her seven year old grandson, Daniel. Her sluggish affection was stirred, something Daniel always managed to do. It was his innocence, his delight in the simple things, and his love. Love that was so remote and almost alien to her. A feeling which, if it wasn't for Daniel, she knew she'd have lost altogether and would have considered herself better off without it. And it was this love which moved her into action now.

She forced her tongue free and swallowed to moisten her mouth. 'Hello, Danny! Well, does she now? We'll have to see what we can do, won't we?'

'Thanks, Mum,' Scott said. 'And don't worry, we have a budget so that should help. Susan insisted we come here, and I thought it would be good for Danny.'

She managed to crack open a smile. 'Yes, of course, that's fine. Let's go over to the desk.'

She decided that if she had an order to concentrate on, things should be fine, that she could tolerate her work life and private life colliding head on in this sliding reality. But when she looked around for Susan, her heart lurched and sank at what she saw.

Over to her left, Susan was sat at Marian's desk, chatting. Chatting and laughing, giggling and tittering as if they knew each other well, as if they were the best of friends. They'd be getting their knitting out next, if either of them was capable of following a pattern. And as Scott muttered that he'd go and get his wayward wife, she barely heard him, as she watched their respective mouths. Marian's full red lips were gabbing away at Susan's fat flapping mouth, opening and closing in rapid fire, at such close range. It was monstrous.

And Janet felt her legs start to give way like strands of spaghetti. She flopped into her chair, unable to speak, heart crashing in her chest, forcing down a rising urge to scream out loud at the horror she was witnessing. Every cell in her body was crying *This cannot be!* How did these two women, both of whom were a real issue for her, come to know each other? And just how well did they know each other? Had they discussed her? Did they snicker behind her back, exchanging Janet-focused anecdotes? Exchanging their opinions of her? Her hand trembled as she picked up her pen to hold onto something she knew, something she could control. Meanwhile Daniel was giving her sideways looks as he fiddled with the pen pot. She opened a drawer and gave him a colouring book and some felt pens, essentials aids to making sure parents had no distractions from spending their hard-earned cash to embellish their homes.

Scott hurried back over, with a visibly reluctant Susan in his wake.

'Hello, Janet! Sorry, I just had to stop to chat to Marian,' Susan explained. She sat down opposite her.

'How do you know her?' Janet snapped.

'Well…well,' Susan stammered, flinching away from Janet's hard look. Then she drew herself up. 'I really don't see that it matters, but we go to the same aerobics class at the leisure centre after work.'

'And how well do you know her?'

'Not much at all, but she's a good laugh, she —'

'Well, she causes trouble for us in here, so I don't want you discussing me with her at all. Understand?'

Susan's eyes widened. She looked from Janet to Scott.

'I suppose Mum has her reasons,' Scott said carefully.

'Fine,' Susan said, crossing her arms and legs and rolling her eyes.

The next hour and a half dragged on for Janet. She felt as if she was tugging a heavy plough through sticky clay soil, with the progress stony and plodding. Susan hadn't really thought about whether she wanted a pattern or a plain, a glazed cotton, or a cotton satin, for her bedroom curtains, so heaps and humps of sample curtains, waterfall arrangements, and pattern books soon smothered the desk, and cluttered Janet's orderly mind.

Twice, Susan edged right over to Berkeley Fabrics, teetering on her stilettos, to look at the sample curtains, while Janet searched through the Crowson and Sanderson pattern books for a design she might like, sweating and flushed with frustration in the airless heat. Twice, Marian tried to reel Susan in, like a fish on a hook, directing triumphant smirks at Janet, when Susan *oohed* and *aahed* at Marian's suggested florals, while Marian draped and ruched the fabric over her arms like a dressmaker for full effect. Internally raging at Marian's bare-faced cheek, with her pulse rate thumping with indignation, Janet made her move. Before there could be a third opportunity to bag her catch, Janet stalked over to the desk where Scott was chatting to Daniel, and asked him to go and tell Susan she had to chose something from the main department. That it was only fair.

Scott frowned, but went over and had a word with Susan who returned to the desk.

'What's the problem? Why does it matter?' she asked Janet.

'Because it's a separate company, that's why.'

Susan open and shut her mouth like a landed fish. Wordlessly, she glared at Janet.

Janet noticed Scott put a restraining hand on Susan's arm and was very pleased to see it. It looked like her son had some control over his flighty mare after all.

'Come on, Susan, let's get this done.'

'Fine,' she responded in a clipped voice.

After much shilly-shallying which was typical of Susan, and after multiple quotes on different fabrics based on Scott's window measurements, with frequent cajolings, whinnyings and whinings from Susan, and frequent boasting about her pay rise at McReath's estate agency where she worked, Janet was finally able to write up their order.

Chosen fabric: Crowson, 'Wheatley floral multi' (a sumptuous overblown garden bouquet design, with pinks, greens, peaches, on a white ground) 54" wide, pattern repeat 25", to be ordered by the metre.

Order to be made up by Clothworks, as follows:

One pair of curtains, two widths each curtain (2WEC), by an overall drop of 92", pencil pleat heading, ivory lined, to be fitted to a track.

One valance, six widths, to fit width 102" plus two 6"returns, by overall drop of 13", pinch pleated, with contrast buttons and a contrast trim of 1.5" in stock fabric glazed cotton, colour 'plum', ivory lined. Valance to be Velcro fitted to a pelmet board.

One pair of tiebacks to fit 2WEC, crescent shaped, contrast piped in glazed cotton 'plum'.

Out of the spare fabric from the pattern repeat wastage, two 17" cushion covers to be made with contrast piping in 'plum'.

Scott had pulled Susan up on her penchant for frills, saying it would look frilly enough as it was, and he insisted he could do the fitting to save costs, with a bit of guidance from Janet, who agreed to help.

And the total order came to £490.50 – excluding track, pelmet board and sundries.

Susan gasped. 'That's a bit more than we were expecting! Marian said you could probably put it on your manager's store card for us. You get 50% off, don't you?'

Janet, who was just beginning to believe that this ordeal was coming to an end, felt her stiff spine give way, and she visibly collapsed back in her chair. No words came to her lips, she simply shook her head. For stretched out seconds, she felt disconnected, the wires connecting her to reality unplugged. But slowly, wire by wire, she plugged herself back in and began to feel adrenalin flow into her veins, a little trickle, a good current, then a gushing torrent. And her whole body tensed, ready to pounce. In her mind's eye, she saw herself shoving over the table, letting all the paperwork seesaw to the floor in fluttering floating arcs, she saw the pattern books thump down, in redundant finality…she saw herself thrusting her hands around silly, silly Susan's neck and squeezing and tightening, making Susan's eyes bulge out of their sockets, with the mounting pressure inside her head getting ready to explode through her skull and shatter it to pieces, spilling out her brains, but wait, she didn't have any brains, did she? Just blood would have to do, then. What was her lovely son doing married to this stupid, stupid woman? This woman, who she forced herself to tolerate because she was Daniel's mother. What had Scott seen in her? She'd become pregnant with Daniel so soon after their marriage. Had she manipulated Scott into marrying her by getting pregnant on purpose? She'd asked Scott when he told her the news of the pregnancy, but he'd denied it and she hadn't dared take it any further.

And it was Scott who came to her aid now.

'Susan, you can't ask that! If Mum agreed she could get into serious trouble!'

'Oh, come on. I bet staff do it all the time,' Susan said.

'That's enough, do you hear?' His tone was uncompromisingly authoritative.

Daniel began to sniffle, a tear or two fell down his chubby cheeks.

'Now look what you've done!' said Susan. She got up and took Daniel's hand. 'I'll take him outside for some fresh air, while you finish up the paperwork, Scott. I'll see you out there.'

'Bye, Grandma,' Daniel sniffed.

Janet's heart softened. 'Bye, Danny.'

Scott sighed as he watched them depart, then he turned to Janet.

'Sorry. She gets carried away sometimes.'

'Yes, I know.'

'I know you don't like her, but she is my wife.'

'I know. I do try.'

'I know you do, and believe it or not, so does she.'

'I suppose we just have to make the best of it.'

'Yes, but I get a bit sick of being stuck in the middle.'

Janet said nothing. There was nothing she could say.

'What have you got against this Marian?' He jerked his head towards Berkeley Fabrics.

Janet shrank back into herself. She'd never discussed her problem with Marian with anyone outside work, let alone her very own son. She'd always strived to keep work and her private life separate, but that had been when Frank was alive. Perhaps it just didn't matter anymore? Perhaps she owed Scott an explanation? So she gave him what she could.

'She makes life difficult here. She tries to steal our customers, and I'm pretty sure she gives unauthorised discounts as well. She's cheeky, she's rude, she dresses too provocatively. And she had the audacity to apply for the manager's job.'

Scott took a sharp intake of breath. 'Is that why you applied? In case she got it?'

Sharp, Janet thought. My son is a clever boy. 'Yes, I suppose so.'

'Whew, Mum! You're one tough cookie.'

They stared at each other. Then Scott smiled, and Janet smiled back.

They got back to business by Janet completing the

paperwork and giving Scott a copy. She explained no deposit was necessary and that it was a good price.

'I'm sure of that,' he said. Then he looked carefully at her. She was wearing her bottle green two-piece. 'You know, that suit looks really good on you, Mum. Is this you out of the black?'

Janet hesitated. 'I suppose so. If I carried on with the black in here, people wouldn't realise I was the manager.'

'Well you look very nice and you look the part. And you're enjoying the job – not too stressful?'

'No, it's fine.'

'Good. I'm pleased for you.'

And as she looked into the familiar warmth of his hazel eyes, she noted for the umpteenth time, how handsome her son was and how proud she was of him, and how proud she was of him putting his university education to good use by becoming an architect. But she had also recently noted that he hadn't mentioned Frank much since he died, not since the funeral in fact. She supposed she would have to talk to him about Frank at some point. But not today. She had something more pressing in mind.

And as she watched Scott leave and saw his fair head disappearing down the stairway by the lift at the far end of the department, her mind was pulled back to Marian – like an iron filing to a magnet. That little bitch had made taking the family order so much harder than it needed to have been. And now she'd really crossed the line by getting close to a family member, in a tight-crotched leotard, prancing about like Jane Fonda, in a 'feeling the burn' aerobics class. It was perfectly obvious now that there was no truce between them, so she'd have to up her game by crossing her own line and finding out more about her. After all, according to a far earlier sage than Dale Carnegie, knowledge is power. And little did she know that the opportunity for more knowledge would come this very evening after work.

Saturdays were frequently tricky for cashing up on time at

the end of the trading day. Usually this was done at around ten minutes to five, where the takings were bagged, with the credit card slips and cheques enclosed, and the float of £50 checked and bagged. Both of these were then taken to the cash office for processing after hours. If customers arrived late, say five minutes to five, or on the dot at five, Masons staff had to remain behind to serve them, which in the case of soft furnishing was often quite time consuming. *And* they had to cash up after that. There had been times in the past when Janet had been practically the last sales consultant left on the second floor, with the linen department beyond shrouded in a twilight zone of dimness with its bright dazzling day lights switched off. Not only was this staying behind a case of going above and beyond the call of duty, but there was no pay for this extra working. Still, this was Masons, a high-class store, which prided itself on delivering the very best in customer service, and if this was a measure of that quality, then Janet complied without a murmur. After all, she had her car, and the others had buses to catch.

Today, it was very different however. Closing the department down for its night's rest went smoothly, allowing Gemma plenty of opportunity to talk Kevin through the cashing up procedure. Ann had been owed an hour, so she'd already left, and Janet had told Claire to go because she'd looked a little pale after measuring out some lengthy metreages today, with table felt sales adding to the physical strain in the tropical heat. But what most interested Janet right now, was another marked difference today – Marian had a late customer for Berkeley Fabrics. And this was a rare occurrence.

So as 5pm ticked onto the hour, and after the store buzzer rang to nudge customers out of the grand emporium of Masons, Janet tidied the serving benches of scissors, pens, and pieces of scrap paper used for calculations, and she neatened up the ends of some of the rolls of fabric in the stands, all the while keeping her eye on Marian who was bent over her desk stabbing furiously at her calculator. And oh, how sweet the sight of seeing the shoe on the other foot. Marian always flew straight off as soon as the bell went, and now she was obviously stressed by not being able to. It was so nice to see her with her wings clipped.

And then it struck Janet, a light touch of a thought which turned into a resounding thump in her mind. Why Marian's customary urgency? What was her usual hurry all about? There must be something to it. Something worth finding out, perhaps? Well, maybe she'd be able to do just that. Maybe she could follow her. Follow her from the store to wherever she went that was so obviously urgent.

Janet smiled. It was a superb idea.

She strode up to the till to see how Gemma and Kevin were doing. Kevin was happy he was getting the hang of it, and they'd finished up, so she snatched the bags off them, told them they could go, and hurried past Marian to the cash office, dumping the bags into the serving slot. She was given the security disc for the till, for department number 15, and she quickly strutted back to chink it into the empty open till drawer. Then she hurried to her own office, once again passing Marian who looked up and scowled at her. The middle-aged woman she was serving finally got the message that the store was actually closed now and began apologising. Janet saw that time was of the essence. She charged into the office, grabbed her bag from the filing cabinet's lowest drawer, stomped out and rounded the corner. Customer lift or stairs, she couldn't decide. She stood stock-still rapidly considering her options, her feet itching to move. She had no shopping to collect, so if she took the lift she might be able to go straight out into Pilgrim Street via the food hall entrance if they hadn't locked the doors yet, and so avoid going through the labyrinth and exiting through the staff entrance. But if she chose this route she wouldn't be able to change from her heel-tapping court shoes into her more comfortable and more strategically quiet flats. And this latter thought decided it. Flats it had to be for effective surveillance.

She darted down the stairs with hot throbbing feet, one flight, then through the shadows of ladieswear to a 'staff only' door in the back corner of Jaeger, bashing through it into the dim coolness of a concrete corridor, and on she went, her patent leather shoes flashing and twisting as she ran down steps and turned corners, finally arriving at the room housing her locker – number 149. After she swapped her shoes and felt the sweet relief of the cushioned Rohde sandals, she had a thought. She'll easily recognise me in this suit if she catches a glimpse of me. What can I do? I can't change it! Her eyes shifted about her and happened upon Ann's locker, two doors down, number 147. She darted to it and grabbed the door. Most lockers had busted locks, so she yanked it open. And right there was a most marvellous solution hanging from a coat hanger. Ann's beige trench raincoat. She kept it here for emergencies. Well, this *was* an emergency. Janet shrugged into it, tightened the belt, grabbed her bag, and flew up the old fire escape, past the portly cheeky chappy in security who liked to chat up the middle-aged ladies and give them something to snicker over, but who never wasted his efforts on Janet, and out…into the cool balmy air of a midsummer's day, with the cooing sounds of pigeons roosting up above. It was 5.45pm.

There was no sign of Marian, and Pilgrim Street was deserted, so Janet ran across the road and positioned herself behind a red post box. She was ready to track Marian as soon as she emerged. Minutes tick-tocked past, while Janet waited. And just as her heart sank, with her deciding Marian must have flaunted the rules and exited via the front store entrance, out she came from the murkiness of the staff entrance doorway, into the light. Clutching hold of her handbag, she strutted fast down Pilgrim Street in her spandex skirt, her heels clacking on the heat-struck pavement, with Janet following silently behind.

The surveillance began. Janet followed Marian around the corner of Lloyds bank, then they turned right and south-east down the High Street. Janet found this easy work as Marian was so focused on rushing, like a missile locked onto a target. In fact, Janet was periodically forced into trotting. She earned a few puzzled frowns from passing pedestrians, which she presumed were due to her wearing a raincoat beneath a plate blue sky, but needs must.

On past Clarks, past Harvey Furnishings (Janet and Marian's main local competitors), past WHSmith, past Dorothy Perkins, and on past Marks and Spencer and Timpson's key cutters…and then Marian slowed down outside Sainsbury's on a junction corner.

Janet nipped inside the locked entrance doorway to Timpson's to shadow herself and watched as Marian cocked her head to one side and checked her watch. Then to Janet's surprise, Marian stalked into Sainsbury's. And Janet hadn't been expecting this. Her mind teemed with thoughts like busy ants in their nest. What was she to do now? Should she follow? Could she do this unobserved? She had Ann's mac on, that would help. What was the likes of Marian doing in Sainsbury's, anyway? What would she buy? Should she try to follow her into the store to find out? But there again, did it really matter what Marian bought? Was it even worth the risk trying to find out?

She came to her senses. No, it was not worth the risk. And any information she might glean from what Marian stuck in her basket would be meagre pickings. She would turn the corner and find somewhere to secrete herself in Winchcombe Street until Marian came out of Sainsbury's.

When Marian emerged about ten minutes later, Janet spotted her in the Cute Cutz hairdresser's window which she was using as stakeout mirror, ostensibly checking the hair salon's price list. Marian was weighed down by two sagging carrier bags in each hand. She raised one wrist to check her watch, frowned, then began to walk stiffly on down the High Street. Janet felt a surge of adrenalin pump through her veins, this was so exciting. This was so easy. Why hadn't she done it before?

On down the High Street Marian hurried, now and again breaking into a jog, despite her heavy shopping bags, with Janet close on her heels about ten yards behind. And finally, after another ten minutes, just past the entrance to Sandford Park, on the right side of the road, Marian slowed up at a row of flat-roofed, white, four-storey houses, with balconies and railings, so typical of Cheltenham's older regency residences. At first Janet was stunned. How could the likes of Marian be living in one of these? Then as she looked more closely, she could see there was no window dressing coordination from one level to the next, so they had probably been converted into flats. Her heart thudding in her chest, she ducked into an open telephone booth just outside one of the park's entrance pillars. Around twelve yards away now, she watched as Marian dashed up to the steps of number 14, High Street, on which a man was sitting with a little girl.

Eyes wide, Janet was able to play close attention to what followed, ears pricked for the raised voice altercation which now commenced.

The man got to his feet and shouted at Marian. 'What fucking time do you call this?'

He was dressed in a white t-shirt and tight faded jeans, sporting tattoos on the forearms he was now flexing. Well built, tall, and tanned, he towered over Marian's slight figure, while the little girl stepped down and stood close next to her. They clasped each other's hands.

'I'm sorry, Rick! I had a late customer, then I stopped off to get us something for tea and I got you some cans.'

'I don't want your bleedin cans. I told you. I changed my mind. I'm supposed to be already round at my mates. But instead I've been looking after your girl for you!'

'Look, I'm sorry, Rick. I do appreciate it.'

'Not again.' Rick pointed at Marian. 'You hear me! This is the only time. If you want us to work, I can't be your babysitter. In fact, I'm having doubts about us, anyway. It's too fucking complicated!'

'Look, I'm sorry! I didn't think you'd mind just this once!'

Rick pushed his face right up close to Marian's. 'Well, you thought wrong, didn't you!' he shouted.

'But Sharon usually does it when my parents can't. You won't ever have to do it again.'

Rick shoved past Marian, who was still holding onto the carrier bags, and he strode off towards Janet. Janet gasped and turned to the phone. She grabbed the receiver and frantically punched some numbers to make it look as if she was making a call. He glared at her as he rounded the telephone booth and the cold malice in his eyes made her breath hitch in her throat. This was something she recognised.

With Rick moving on down the street towards the town centre, her gaze turned slowly back to Marian, who was now down on her knees cuddling the little girl. The bags were lying collapsed on the pavement. The girl looked to be around the age of five or six. She had wavy light brown hair and was wearing a pretty floral smock dress, which looked like a Laura Ashley to Janet's well-trained eye.

Their voices were muffled by the distant traffic, but Janet strained to hear. She managed to pick up a little.

'I'm sorry, Jessie…wouldn't have left you with…' Marian said, stroking the girl's hair.

'It's okay, Mummy,' the little voice replied.

And this was enough. Enough to make Janet go rigid. Synapses fired off inside her, the nerves of her body flashed and fluttered and she was unable to drag her pinned gaze away from the two figures.

Marian had a daughter. The floozy, the little tart of Berkeley Fabrics who had been plaguing Janet's working life had a lovely little daughter.

Transfixed, with her feet turned into blocks of stone, Janet watched Marian and her daughter, Jessie, mount the steps with the carrier bags. Marian fiddled in her handbag for a second, then slid a key in the lock and pushed open the door. She ushered her daughter in first, then the door slammed shut behind them. Janet flinched at the sound, but continued to stare at the shut door which barred her until she finally managed to turn herself away.

As she trudged back down the High Street, past Sainsbury's, past Harveys, past Clarks, and turned right at Marks and Spencer into Pittville Street, she felt no pain in her hot and aching feet, no sweating inside Ann's raincoat. All she felt was a dull stupor, with her mind swaddled in thick fleece. Plodding up Portland Street, she crossed over to the all day car park she used in the summer months. And it was only when she banged shut her car door on the outside world, that she was able to breathe some of the stifling hot air locked inside the pressure cooker of her car.

Driving home with the window wound down blew some of the fleece away and she found herself feeling and thinking again. So Marian had a daughter. Was Marian married, divorced, separated? Was she bringing her daughter up by herself? Because it didn't sound like the thug of a boyfriend, Rick, was involved. Oh the poor little girl, having Marian for a mother. This was the problem, these days, anyone could bring a child into the world. And by the time she pulled into her drive at 9 Willow Lane, she was wondering what she could do with this new information to get Marian out of Masons.

Chapter 9

The sultry summer days inside Masons wore on into the solar cycle of September. Sales figures suffered in the heat, while the irresolute staff maintained their posts, upping their efforts with immaculate housekeeping. China and glass sparkled, the lighting department blazed in all its chandeliered glory, the counters in the beauty department gleamed, while the lipstick smiles of the concession staff grew even wider. Menswear and ladieswear garments on their hangers stood to attention in their rows, shoulder to shoulder, the latest fashions, the latest clearance racks, begging to be rifled through to give the bored staff standing around on sore legs some work to do in restoring order to the ranks. Women's accessories were flagrantly flamboyant, with their floating chiffon scarves and floppy brimmed sunhats with curlicued and feathered fascinators to rival those worn at the Cheltenham races. Childrenswear had the cutest new lines, to imprint children with identical mindsets to their parents.

But homewares struggled to tempt even a straggle of browsing customers, while the second floor, housing carpets, furniture, linens, and soft furnishing, was too high in the stratosphere of Masons to countenance custom with its tropical temperatures. Who wants to hack their way through a steamy jungle of duvets, pillows, Berber carpets and their loops, or hessian backed wool carpets with their twisted pile? Who wants to consider sinking into a over-stuffed wing chair, or take their ease on a pocket spring mattress, when they could get cool in the park with an ice cream? And who would want to set about making a pair of curtains for themselves, or even think about ordering some custom-mades when the hazy lazy days of summer were here?

And so this meant that the attentions within the soft furnishing department were able, oh so naturally of course, to shift from serving customers to focusing on the staff themselves, with more personal observations, reflections and determinations than possible at busier times.

From Gemma talking to Claire, and from Claire telling Ann, Janet found out that Gemma and Kevin had been out together a couple of times. Gemma had expressed concern that he was too 'straight' for her, and their circles of friends were never likely to overlap, but there again he was good looking and made her laugh. Making Gemma laugh at all was something Ann and Janet struggled to imagine, never having heard even a titter out of the gothic maiden. Kevin was most enamoured, but seemed to have learned from some wise owl to play it a bit cool, which was probably the best approach for Gemma, mused Claire. Claire's husband was spending a lot of time away at business conferences, and Claire was now suspecting him of having an affair, and if so, trying to work out if she cared. Ann was harping on about retirement again, now that Janet had settled into her managerial role, but Janet managed to persuade her to postpone it until the end of the year. Ann was a widow and lived alone, with a son and a daughter in the north who she didn't see very often. What was she going to do with herself instead? asked Janet. Just clean her Winchcombe bungalow, join the Women's Institute, and do coffee mornings? And Ann, who kept striving to be biddable, had characteristically capitulated for now.

Moving the focus to Berkeley Fabrics was also as natural as breathing at this quiet time, especially for Janet as she watched both Marian and Milly even more closely in light of her new knowledge. In fact her mind kept returning to Marian and her motherhood, like a tongue keeps probing a mouth ulcer. A few days after her Saturday surveillance, she tried to pump Milly-Molly-Mandy for more information, when Marian was on her day off.

Ostensibly going over to discuss what Berkeley Fabrics

charged customers for fitting, to make sure there was no yawning gap between themselves and Masons curtain fitters, she brought the subject up by first establishing that Marian had nothing to do with the measuring service and fitting that Berkeley Fabrics offered.

'No, not at all,' Milly said.

Today Milly's voluminous bosom was squashed into a white frilly blouse, and it gave her the look of a frigate in full sail, with her ruby ring flashing a suggestion of the spoils of war. Her Anais Anais perfume with its rich base notes of sandalwood and incense hinted at Eastern treasures. But the latitudes and longitudes plotted on her face with wiggly degrees of deviations told the truth of too many holidays on the Costa Brava.

'Yes, I thought so,' Janet replied. 'After all, where would she find the time after work? She must find it difficult enough holding down a full-time job with a little girl to look after.'

Milly looked up at Janet. Her eyes were pink-rimmed these days, rather than red, Janet mused, so she must have been making some progress through her grief-stricken days of widowhood. But Janet was surprised to spot some sharp splinters of shrewdness there now. Maybe Milly had learned a lesson or two?

'What do you know about her little girl?' asked Milly, fixing Janet with her gaze.

Janet felt wrong-footed by Milly and found irritation buzzing inside herself. 'Nothing. I just didn't realise she had one, then I saw them in the High Street.'

'So, what's it to you, anyway?'

'Nothing. I just didn't know she was married. Or maybe she's divorced?'

'Well it's none of your business actually, but –'

'Excuse me, I didn't say it was. It's just – '

'For your information, she's a single mother for all intents and purposes, and she could have done with your job!'

Janet stepped back. Her mouth dropped open. Milly's tone was insultingly aggressive, and as for the comment – well!

'That's…that's…ridiculous,' stammered Janet, overcome at the insolence in Milly's face. Where had the red-eyed, twitching rabbit gone?

After this encounter, she told Ann of her new intelligence. Ann was doing one of the department's jobs which was strictly reserved for when nothing more pressing presented itself. She was cutting out discontinued samples from a pile of pattern books, using the manufacturers' product brochures as a cross reference. These redundancies were recycled into the remnants during the sales, where patchwork fanatics pounced on them.

'There seem to be so many single mothers these days. How on earth do they manage?' commented Ann, as she sliced through the top of a particular luscious fruity floral dripping with bunches of grapes.

'I suppose they get child support from the fathers,' Janet said.

'Yes, but I've heard that it can be very difficult getting regular payments out of them.'

'Hmm.'

'And who looks after her daughter when she's at work?'

'Yes, it must be a problem.'

'It's irresponsible, getting pregnant and not getting married. I mean there's the pill, for goodness' sake. We never had that in our time! And a child needs a father.'

Janet bristled at this aphorism. 'Yes, but that depends on the father, doesn't it?'

In truth, she wasn't sure how she felt. She'd felt a strange confusion since she'd seen Marian with her daughter, despite being hell-bent on getting Marian out of Masons. And most notably, she hadn't been able to throw her Marian doll through the black hole in the wall every morning in the stairwell, because Marian was no longer quite the person Janet thought she was. And most disconcertingly for Janet, there was a tiny part of her which actually admired Marian for bringing up her daughter by herself. A tiny particle that was insoluble in the swish and swirl of her ruminations. And it bothered her. After all, she reflected, she should be applying to Marian the stereotype of a promiscuous young woman who sleeps around with a succession of boyfriends, then is irresponsible enough to get herself pregnant. Ann had no trouble applying the stereotype, so why did she?

'Well, it's a different world these days from when we were girls, isn't it?' observed Ann.

'Yes, it certainly is,' replied Janet.

And in this, the two matriarchs of the soft furnishing department were in agreement. The young had never had it so good. No having to do chores around the house, or suffer limited educations, no post-war deprivations, with the challenges of rationing, no housing shortages, no outdoor privies with newspaper for toilet roll, no coal fires to set. Today they had everything. Birth control, more money, more houses, and young people could get on the property ladder, central heating, indoor toilets, bathrooms and showers, deep freezers, telephones, microwaves, colour TV. Nearly everyone had a car too, and there were more paid holidays, and going abroad was now an affordable option. And there were stores like Masons where you could buy anything you wanted with interest free credit for the more lavish spends. In this respect, it seemed Louis Armstrong was indeed right – it was a 'wonderful world.'

And the two women nodded in agreement, with Janet feeling very much on course on the unchartered ocean of her new life. But unbeknown to her, there was a cloud burst hanging on the horizon and a rough sea ahead, because into this wonderful world of Masons serenely sailed a new addition by the name of Samantha Dixon-Wright.

It was Patrick King, the store manager, who introduced Janet to this new phenomenon, one week later, on the morning of the 17th September. He came into her office followed by a middle-aged woman Janet had never seen before.

'Good Morning, Janet,' he said, beaming like a Pillsbury Doughboy. 'I want you to meet our new interior designer, Ms Samantha Dixon-Wright. Samantha, this is Mrs Janet Brewer, manager of the soft furnishing department.'

Janet gaped at the store manager and his broadly smiling stockade of teeth, then her gaze switched to the woman in beige with blonde hair, who was proffering her hand to Janet, then it swivelled back to Patrick King still baring his teeth, then back to the woman in beige, as if her eyes were swinging like a pendulum under their own momentum, finally coming to rest upon the woman. The woman smiling sweetly at her with her pastel pink lipstick, looking cool and serene in a white blouse and cream suit, and smelling of roses. Her hair like Janet's, tied back at the nape of the neck, but with a soft fringe above her pale blue eyes – eyes which were now fixed on Janet, as round and innocent as a new born babe's.

Shaking the woman's hand Janet found to be a distinctly limp affair. 'Good to meet you,' she muttered.

Then, as her numbness ebbed away, a wave of burning heat flooded though her, which threatened to turn into a full-blown hot flush, of which she'd had a few lately. She rounded upon Patrick King. 'I was never told about this.'

'Oh dear, weren't you? I'm sure I passed it by you.' His massive brow overhung his flinty eyes in an exaggerated frown. 'Oh dear, I'm so sorry. Let me explain…'

Janet was now subjected to a lengthy explanation for the new appointment, while the woman was sitting right there opposite her in her office. Legs folded neatly to one side, like a lady celebrity giving an interview, her hands in her lap, all the time wearing a saccharine expression of concern on her well-powdered face. There was no opportunity for private consultation, as Janet listened to what Patrick King had to say. And as she listened, suppressing her triggered needs to interrupt which were firing off in all directions like shrapnel, she became convinced that Patrick King had deliberately kept her in the dark so it could be presented to her as a fait accompli – a battle won without even having been fought.

Samantha was to have a section of the furniture department's floor space, just around the corner from carpets, to provide an interior design consultancy for customers with more expensive tastes wanting a personalised service, and who were naturally willing to pay for it. She was to have her own budget for her own pattern books, and she would visit clients' homes to consult and take her own measurements, but she would have to liaise with the soft furnishing staff over the placing of orders, in particular with Masons own makers, Clothworks, in Cirencester. She would also be on the 1% commission rate. Patrick King knew, *of course*, that Janet and her staff would be more than willing to help Samantha settle in and find her feet for the sake of Masons.

'In general though, you just carry on as normal, Janet,' he added. 'Samantha being here shouldn't have to affect the soft furnishing department at all!'

Janet was seething with objections, knee-jerk reactions, hurts and resentments, and she wondered what on earth her staff were going to make of it. Having to teach a jumped-up, snotty interior designer the ways and working practice of Clothworks? Having a powder puff of a woman flouncing around purporting to know more in matters of aesthetic taste than themselves, who, by the way, had been doing very well for years, thank you. And of course Patrick King didn't know how important taking correct measurements was and giving precise making-up instructions, so that the all-important fitting went according to plan with Masons fitting service – no unwanted puddling, no unwanted shortfall, with curtains having to go back to the makers for alterations, or having to be made up again from scratch, with the costs of errors escalating and cutting deep into the profit margins. But oh, no. These boringly practical aspects didn't fit with the glamorous image of interior design, did they? It wasn't all about pretty swatches, frilly fancies, swags, tassels and tails.

Just how much bother and extra work were they going to get?

But Janet remained quiet and just bobbed her head in agreement, and remembering Dale's advice, she forced herself to crack a smile. She was acutely conscious of the fact that she had only just completed her six month probationary period and hadn't yet received her permanent contract. Nothing must jeopardise that.

So, as the 'discussion' came to a close, she adopted a practical compliancy and offered to introduce Samantha to the staff, thinking it would be best to get it over with. Patrick King grinned his victorious approval, swept his majestic proportions out of the office, and left them to it.

Janet introduced Samantha to Ann, Gemma, and Claire, explaining the situation. Kevin was on his day off, but Gemma promised to fill him in.

An open-mouthed Ann tried to appear gracious. 'Oh, really? An interior designer! How…how nice.'

Gemma looked hard at Janet, as she often did at times when Janet knew she was trying to guess her true feelings. Then she shrugged and turned to Samantha. 'Oh well, I guess we'll get used to it.'

Claire, who perhaps amongst the four of them, relished the design consultation aspects of the job the most, stood stiffly with her arms folded. 'Nice to meet you,' she said in a tight voice.

And with a few more stilted efforts of conversation with the angelically smiling Samantha Dixon-Wright, they found she lived in the charming village of Lower Slaughter, east of Cheltenham, and she'd be commuting into town every day. Having done some freelance work, most recently for the seventeenth century Oakbury Manor Hotel in Lower Slaughter, involving huge damask interlined drapes and goblet stuffed pelmets, she was *so* looking forward to working at Masons.

Private reactions, once the power puff smelling of roses had gone, were of a very different nature.

'Are we going to have to *teach* her everything? Asked Gemma. 'I don't see why we should! I'm sick of teaching new people and we don't get any credit for it or any extra pay. We're just expected to do it.'

'Like Ann and I taught you,' Janet observed.

'Yes, I know. But she's different. I bet she'll get paid more too. Why should we be expected to teach her? It's not fair!'

'No, it's not,' Ann said.

'Well, I'm not going to do it,' vowed Claire.

'I'm sorry,' Janet said, 'I don't like it either, but we're going to have to cooperate. She may know more than we think. She must do from what she was saying.' She sighed. 'But in any case, we have no choice. We'll have to put up with her. And of course, there's a chance she might not like it here.'

'Let's hope not!' Claire said.

Telling Marian and Milly was strikingly similar. But Janet found she actually enjoyed enlightening them on the new development that afternoon.

'Does my area manager know about this?' demanded Marian.

'I shouldn't think so,' Janet replied. 'Mr King didn't mention it.'

'Well, she'll have to be told! It affects our position here, our potential custom could be seriously affected. Not to mention our jobs being on the line.' She slumped into her chair behind her desk. Milly stood by her side, fidgeting with her hands. She looked down at Marian with puckers and pouches of concern crumpling up her face.

Marian sighed. 'I'll pass it on to Gillian. She'll be the one that'll have to fight our corner.'

Janet looked at her, surprised. She hadn't been expecting this grudging acceptance. She'd expected Marian to strut through the linen department, with her bottom wiggling, making a beeline for Patrick King's office, to go in there, even if he was in the middle of a meeting, and demand to know what was going on – why hadn't Berkeley Fabrics been consulted? That's what she would have done with Ron. But of course, Janet reflected, Ron had been tolerant, and now he was gone, and Marian had a little girl to support. Risky strategies were harder to act upon if you couldn't tell management to get stuffed and walk away from the job.

She scrutinised Marian for a few moments as Marian stared down at a order pad, lost in thought. She noticed she'd lost some weight. Her usually tight-fitting blouse and skirt seemed to sit on her slackly now and she was already of a petite size. And then there was her makeup. Janet could swear it looked thicker than usual. Her foundation was claggy, and her mascara and eyeliner had become practically Egyptian-esque. Plus she'd been strangely quiet lately too – almost withdrawn. Ann had commented the other day, that she wasn't being half as flirty with the customers. Her time keeping had also been erratic on a few mornings. And then there was Milly fussing around her when they were on shift together. It's so odd, reflected Janet. Something has changed. What's up with you? She directed this thought at Marian. Then she smiled, thinking, if you start being late regularly, I'll have you. I'll report you and get you out of here.

Marian snapped her head up. 'What are *you* looking at?'

Janet stepped back, a little shocked at the ferocity flashing in Marian's frowning face.

'Nothing,' she said. Then she grabbed at something else to say. 'We'll just have to weather Samantha Dixon-Wright, I suppose. All of us are in the same boat.'

'Yes, well that certainly makes a change!'

Chapter 10

And change is what happened in the following few weeks as Samantha found her feet. By the beginning of October she was in residence in her own consulting area in the furniture department, just around the corner from carpets. Out of sight of the soft furnishing department, but not out of mind.

A regal procession of new pattern books, with their freshly minted aroma, followed her in, while the staff of soft furnishing and Berkeley Fabrics watched helplessly from the wings. The elite crowd of manufacturers had arrived, with which the main department rarely dealt with. There was GP & J Baker, in production since 1884, and holder of the Queen's royal warrant since 1982 – most revered for their flamboyant florals, full of exotic birds and meandering stems. There was Wemyss, valued for their natural fibre weaves and chenilles for all upholstery needs, founded by two enterprising merchant brothers. There was the more recent company of Zoffany, and its prints and wallpapers inspired by Eastern decorative art and Italian architecture, offering a splendiferous wealth of botanicals, stripes, classic damasks, Chinoiserie, Toiles de Jouy, and Elizabethan and Rococo designs. And tripping over their heels, a few select worthies made up the entourage, allowed to rub shoulders with this royal vanguard, such as Jane Churchill, Designers Guild, Osborne & Little. You get the picture. Fabrics for customers who wanted to live in their very own palaces or English country homes, and most importantly for Masons, were willing to pay for it. And this is where Samantha came in, she of the double-barrelled name who was so truly fit for purpose.

At first, it had been a case of Janet explaining how Clothworks orders operated, how to calculate their fabric requirements, such as their hem allowances, and how to write out the making-up instructions for them. She'd decided that Samantha getting this right would save the actual department a lot of potential trouble. Mistakes were costly in this business and she didn't want the department's excellent service and good working relationship with Clothworks to be tainted by Samantha.

Samantha seemed most agreeable and she was grateful for the help.

'Thank you so much for making me welcome, Janet,' she murmured. 'I'm sure we'll all get on marvellously.'

And when she didn't know something, she asked for help in a deferential way.

'So sorry to disturb. I know you're busy, but could you just…'

'That's so good of you. I'm so grateful…'

But inevitably, because she was doing the measuring for her clients, and because this is a bit of fine art in itself, mistakes stealthily crept in, and the couple who did Masons fitting had to bring some of Samantha's customers drapes back in to the main department to be returned to Clothworks for alterations. And sometimes such alterations were unfeasible due to not enough fabric allowance available on the width or the drop to do the design task in hand. And this is where things got tricky, and this is where Samantha showed a stubborn unwillingness, bordering upon stupidity, to accept the facts.

'But can't you just order some more fabric?' she asked Janet one day in early November, with respect to a particular curtain order for which she'd taken faulty measurements. 'Just enough for the extra width to make up the fullness?'

'No, I've told you. We can't get the same batch number it came from, and this sample of what they *do* have available is much lighter in colour. Look, you can see the difference for yourself,' Janet said, holding the swatch of damask against the faulty made-up curtains lying folded on the serving bench.

'What does that mean?'

'It means you'll have to do the whole order again.'

'What? Surely not. The customer is getting impatient now. Can't we remake the heading, so it doesn't need so much fullness.' Her tone of voice became simpering.

'Well, if you can get the customers to go for a different style…but then the goblets will have to be unpicked, and that's costly. I don't think Clothworks would ever agree to do it.'

'But why not?'

'Because it's very time consuming, let alone expensive.'

'But can't they just make an exception?'

'Well, I'm not asking them.'

'But why not?'

'Because we have a good relationship with them. I can't ask them that.'

'But can't you just…'

And so it went on – *But can't you just? But why not?* – until Janet was mentally firing arrows into Samantha Dixon-Wright's majestic backside as she minced off after an encounter and disappeared through the linen department. But she always reappeared, and always too soon.

Ann, Gemma, Claire, and even Kevin, took their turns in trying to handle her problems, frequently having to rewrite her orders for the makers. But by mid November, the wheedlings of the English rose of Lower Slaughter had become thorny and tempers were fraying.

Another bugbear was the fact that she often took pattern books from the soft furnishing department to her consultancy area and never returned them, which meant when Janet and her staff went to find them in their usual places to serve *their* customers, they found the books missing. Gemma was the self-appointed retriever, stamping back through the linen department with four or five big books straining the muscles of her slender forearms, and thumping them onto the benches.

One Saturday near the end of November, Janet went

over to the Sanderson stand on their department to show some William Morris designs to a customer of hers, only to find that particular pattern book was missing. Her patience was all tattered and torn by now, and as she'd passed her probationary period with flying colours and had her new contract she felt she had little to lose in addressing the issue with Ms Dixon-Wright. She handed her customer over to Claire and marched through linens with her body tensing in readiness for an all-encompassing tackle with the English rose. An accumulation of objections and resentments popped and fizzed in her mind as she rounded the corner through carpets and stepped into Samantha's holy citadel. But what she found there stopped her in her tracks.

Marian, who'd been pretty quiet for weeks and had, disappointingly for Janet, given her no reason to be reported to Gillian Makepeace, was having words with Samantha. Marian had her back to Janet, which meant Janet was hidden from Samantha's line of sight. So she tucked herself by a display stand, making a show of fingering some swatches, while she strained to hear the conversation.

She didn't have to strain too hard.

'But I *can't* order the fabric by the metre,' Marian said angrily, clutching a sample curtain of Berkeley Fabrics 'Harvest Fruits', which was bursting with cornucopias of ripe lemons and limes, peaches and plums, grapes and vines. 'They've said they're discontinuing this colour 2 very soon, so they won't be printing any more. And even if it was available, it can't go through Masons makers. Any fabric of ours has to be ordered as custom-mades with *us*. Can't you get your customer to choose one of *your* manufacturers. You should have plenty of fruity ones to choose from.'

'I've tried! She's adamant she wants this one for her living and dining rooms. She saw it in your section before coming over to me and insists upon this design in this colour. Colour 1 won't do. I've tried her with that option. And she wants them interlined, and you don't do interlined. If this order goes well, she's going to be ordering a whole house worth of other soft furnishings, for goodness' sake. This is the Royal Crescent we're talking about. We can't botch up an order for a Royal Crescent client. We just have to oblige her with this. She's a very important person!'

'It doesn't matter if she's the Queen of Sheba and lives in Buckingham Palace. We can't supply the material – it's as simple as that.'

'But why not? Why can't they just print off a last roll?'

'I've told you. This comes from the top. They can't do it! They won't do it!'

'What if Mr King spoke to them?'

'The answer would be the same!'

'But we could try.'

'Well, I'm washing my hands of it. You can try!' Marian flung the curtain down on Samantha's desk and strutted off in the direction of the ladies powder room, adjacent to the carpets and furniture office.

Janet found this a highly amusing exchange, which functioned to flatten the fizz of her irritation. Now seizing her moment, she stepped out into full view of Samantha to find her staring dismally down at the sample of Forest Fruits, which had taken on the rarefied value of a much sought after commodity like a vintage wine.

'Can I have a word?' Janet asked.

Samantha looked up at her. Her blue eyes were over-bright, almost feverish, her powdered calm betrayed by a sheen of perspiration. 'What is it?'

'It's the pattern book situation. You must return ones that are taken from our department.'

'Oh. But sometimes it's the clients that bring them over. I can't possible keep track of them all, Janet. And after all, we are all a team.'

'No, we're not, actually. Just because we've helped you settle in doesn't mean we're a team. You have your own budget. Buy your own books. Don't take ours.'

Samantha's mouth dropped open. Her face creased into crinkles of distress. 'But Janet...there's no need for all this aggression! I thought we were getting on so well.'

'That's what you would think when we've been bending over backwards to give you what you need. Well, you're on your own now. You'll have to sort your own messes.'

Samantha gazed down at Harvest Fruits again. She opened and closed her mouth, then began to work it into contortions like a little girl determined not to cry.

Janet decided Samantha had got the message and it was time to leave. Needing the toilet she strode to the ladies powder room by the second floor office.

It looked empty as she bolted her cubicle door. But after flushing she heard a sniffling sound coming from the adjacent cubicle, then a hard blowing of a nose. Someone was in there, crying.

Opening her door she walked quietly to the basins and began to wash her hands. The snuffling continued. Janet became curious, so she tiptoed over to the locked door, bent right down, and looked through the gap at the bottom. She saw a pair of black suede stilettos which she instantly recognised. They were Marian's. Well, well. Marian was sitting on the toilet bubbling, something she had never imagined could happen. How thrilling. How perfect. What with Samantha, a certain favourite phrase concerning two birds and one stone came to mind for this afternoon.

The door flew open and Marian stood there. 'What the hell are you doing?' she shouted. 'I saw your shoes beneath the door. You're spying on me!'

'Don't be ridiculous. I was talking to Samantha and came in here afterwards. And keep your voice down, there's an office right next door.'

Marian flounced over to the basin and started washing her hands. 'Don't mention that stuck-up bitch to me. She's been nothing but trouble for me and Milly since she came. Our takings have gone down too. And do you know what she just asked me?'

'Yes,' Janet said. 'I heard the argument about Forest Fruits.'

'Oh, did you now? Lurking in a corner, spying were you?'

Janet felt rising indignation burn in her gut. 'No! I was not spying. I don't go around spying on people!'

Marian began wiping her tear-streaked face and mopping up sooty runnels of mascara in the mirror with a dampened hand towel.

Janet watched her. 'Look, as a matter of fact, she's been a serious pain for us too.'

'So can't we get rid of her?'

Oh, the irony, thought Janet, smirking now.

Marian turned around before she could hide the smirk. Her eyes flashed venom. 'What's so fucking funny?'

Janet flinched at the swearing and Marian's anger directed straight at her as sharp as a rapier. She was just about to spit out a tasty retort, when she noticed a dark patch, a shadow blooming over the edge of Marian's right eye.

She froze.

She knew what this was.

A tidal wave of emotions flooded her, the currents shifting their course, as she stared at Marian. There was something she liked about seeing an obvious bruise in the face of this trumped-up little tart, who had probably asked for a thump, seeing as she was so full of flirt, fluff and fancy, so disobedient too…it was an absolute delight to see she had got what she had coming to her, and Janet felt a fluttering of excitement.

But then she remembered Marian had a daughter. Marian was a mother. Had the little girl seen this happen? Was it that loutish Rick who had done this?

And now, not being able to drag her eyes away from Marian's bruise, time shifted within her as she remembered the first time Frank had punched her in the face, just like Marian. The shock and the pain of it. How she'd staggered away and collapsed on the floor, while he carried on yelling down at her, while any second she'd expected him to kick her in the stomach with his standard-issue police boots. Feeling the threat of the pending impact. But how she didn't dare get up. And she remembered why he had done it. And how humiliating it felt, how so ashamed she'd been when striving to cover the bruising with foundation for days and days until it finally faded from view, but never from memory. As if being hit, even if seemingly unjustified, conferred a lowering of status upon you, turning you into someone who deserved to be put in their place and who had brought it upon themselves – it's just you never knew you deserved it before, you never knew you needed correction, and now you'd been enlightened. Just like Marian.

The she caught hold of herself and stiffened.

Just like Marian?

Her cheeks flushed with heat and she trembled. She remembered how Frank had gone on to devise more imaginative ways of hurting her, ways that didn't show – with his hands and with his words.

'What are you staring at?' Marian shouted, jerking Janet back into the present.

Janet's throat felt swollen and thick, as if there wasn't enough room to squeeze any words out. She coughed instead.

'Well?' Marian yelled.

She swallowed, still staring at Marian. 'You can't let that happen,' she croaked, finding her voice at last and pointing to Marian's bruised eye.

Marian stepped back. 'What? What are you talking about?' She gaped at Janet.

'You can't let it begin. Once they start, that's it.'

'What are you talking about?' Marian shouted.

'Will you keep your voice down, there's an office next door!'

'I want to know what you're fucking talking about!'

'Your bruise! What do you think I'm talking about?' Janet said, her voice rising. She pointed again at Marian's eye. 'You've let that lout thump you. Did your little girl see him do it? Was she there?'

'What do you know about my life? What lout? And what

do you know of my little girl? Has Milly been talking?' Marian was yelling now, slipping into her West Country accent, which Janet hadn't heard from her in a while, her tendons bulging in her neck while a silver pendant strained to break off its chain.

Janet shut her mouth, realising what she'd revealed.

'Well? What do you know about my private life?'

'Nothing...I just caught sight of the three of you in the street. That's all.'

'That's all?' Marian screamed at her.

'For God's sake, calm down! You'll get us into trouble,' Janet hissed. 'They'll come running in here to see what's going on! There are probably some customers that have nearly come in and then turned around.'

'Fuck the customers! What have you been doing? Spying on me?' Her English accent was restored much to Janet's relief, as she was finding the West Country burr disorientating.

'I just saw you the once,' Janet sighed. 'What does it matter? The point is what are you going to do about *that*?' Janet gestured to the bruise again.

'I bashed into the side of the kitchen door, for your information. Not that it's any of your business.'

'No you didn't. You were punched.'

'No, I bloody well wasn't!'

Janet stepped up close to Marian, making direct eye contact. She saw Marian's eyes darting in confusion, tears puddling in the corners.

'Yes, you were. There's no point denying it. Just admit it!' She was feeling irritated now by Marian's stubbornness and was worried they were causing a scene that was being listened to through the wall.

Marian's shoulders sagged. Her face dropped. 'What would the likes of you know about it, anyway? You're a stuck-up cow, who nobody would dare mess with. You're as hard as nails.' The West Country burr had returned.

Janet gasped and her blood stirred in her veins. She heard

her own mother's West Country voice, back in Bristol in the forties – *You're as hard as nails, Janet.* Her own mother accusing her of the same thing, all those years ago, when in her own mind she'd simply been sticking up for herself, not wanting to bend to her mother's will, while her father silently dipped his head to his paper.

'What would I know about it?' she replied. 'You might be surprised what I know about it.'

'Well, what?' Marian shouted.

Marian placed herself squarely in front of Janet, hands on her hips, all puffed up with eyes as narrow as arrow slits in a fortress wall. A wrestling fury of defence and attack.

'So what would you know, Janet?' She sneered through her tears in the same accent.

Janet felt the old sores inside her opening up. Her mind buzzed with a kind of white noise building into frenzied static she couldn't penetrate, while her vision clouded. All she felt was a quivering rage. A rage from the dark place inside her, in the very black she had always worn, a rage that had never been allowed out into the light. She let it out now.

'I know what it's like to be punched or slapped across the face, when you say a wrong word, look the wrong way, to dare to answer back. I know what it's like to have a cigarette put out on your very own skin. To lie to the hospital or your GP about the bruises and cuts. I know what it's like to live in fear, on a knife edge, day in day out, while they keep on saying you're asking for it. What it's like to be ridiculed, spat at with vicious words, to have things you love smashed up, to have the wellbeing of your child threatened, to try and make sure your child doesn't see or hear anything, when their father is hitting their mother. To be terrified that they will see or hear. And I know what it's like not to be able to tell anyone because you feel so stupid and ashamed for putting up with it.' She hesitated. 'So what part of that haven't I got right, Marian?'

Marian eyes bulged in their sockets. She tottered backwards against a hand basin.

'Jesus, Janet!'

'Well? Come on! You've been thumped, haven't you?'

Marian paled. 'No, it's not like that. It's not the same as all *that!*'

'No. But it's probably the start. You need to get rid of him. For your own sake and for the sake of your daughter. I saw him. He's a thug. I saw the look in his eyes. I know that look.'

'What? When? But he said he was sorry…'

'No buts, no sorries. You need to get rid of him!'

'But you put up with it! You put up with your husband. You didn't do anything by the sounds of things! You didn't leave him. Why didn't *you* do something?'

'I did in the end.'

'What? What did you do?

Janet was silent.

'Come on, Mrs Know-it-all! What did you do?'

'I killed him,' Janet said quietly. 'That's what I did. In the end it was him or me.'

PART THREE

Chapter 11

The silence in the powder room swelled with the shock that had befallen it, as Marian gaped at Janet, her eyes as round as paperweights.

Janet stared back at her, registering the shock only externally at first. Look, there's Marian looking all horrified. How strange. Then slowly she came to realise that she'd actually said what she'd said out loud, not just in her own head, but right out loud.

'Oh, my God,' she whispered.

She felt her legs turn to water and she collapsed to the tiled floor.

Marian, still standing, found her voice. 'But Ann told me your husband died of a heart attack.'

Janet looked up at her. Now she saw confusion in Marian's face, and that was easier to bear. Still in a state of trauma, she groped for some guile to extricate herself from this horror, the horror of confessing her sin to the likes of Marian, the one person who she'd never have wanted to put her trust in. But she found herself drawn only in one relentless direction and that was to tell *someone* what had really happened that evening. And that someone was Marian. Ten minutes ago her life had been practically perfect, now it was all over.

The words of explanation came easily enough. 'I wound him up,' she said, glancing up at Marian. 'He had angina. He used to take pills for angina attacks. I wound him up. I knew what I was doing. He was going on about my working here *again,* insisting that I quit. He'd never approved, you see. This time it was a golfing friend's wife who'd recognised me working here in Masons, and she'd made some comments about my obviously needing to work which had got around their stupid club. He said it kept looking to his friends like we needed the money and he didn't want *his* wife working. He also said that these days it was giving me ideas above my station. I saw him getting really angry and instead of backing down, saying that I'd think about it, as I would have done in the past, I told him I'd work here as long as I liked and there was nothing he could do about it. Well, he wasn't used to that. He got red in the face, began yelling at me, spitting at me, and then it happened. He was on the floor by the sofa. He managed to grab for his pills that he kept down the side of his chair. I'd forgotten about those, but I knocked them out of his grasp, and then I kicked them under the sofa. He saw me do it.'

Janet covered her face with her hands and kneaded her forehead as if to get her thoughts in the right order. 'He knew I was killing him, you see, he knew. That's why he called me a bitch, right at the end. And I couldn't do anything after that. I just froze until it was all over.'

She felt Marian's hands on her own, tugging them from her face. Marian was sitting on her knees in front of her now. Janet stared into her eyes, and found an absence of hardness she'd never seen before.

Marian shook her head. 'But Janet, that's not murder or anything like it.'

'Isn't it? He'd be alive if I hadn't wound him up. I knew what I was doing.'

'But you'd had a lifetime of his behaviour. You were a victim fighting back.'

Janet clutched hold of Marian's hand. 'And you'll be a victim if you let yourself be punched. Don't you see?' she said, her voice rising. 'Don't you see?'

'Shush, shush, Janet. Yes, I see.'

Being told to shush brought a jolt of reality crashing in on Janet and she leapt to her feet. Here she was in the ladies powder room of Masons, her beloved store, confessing her sin to Marian, while anyone, just anyone, might be listening in from next door.

Her hand fluttered to her mouth. 'Oh no…no…NO! she wailed. She felt a wave of cold sweat wash through her, leaving her shivering with panic with goose bumps prickling her skin.

'What? What is it?'

Janet's eyes darted to where the office was behind the power room wall.

Marian caught hold of her hand. 'It's alright, there's no one there, I checked before I came in. I knew I was probably going to get upset, so I checked. I didn't want anyone to hear me.'

'No…no…'

'Do you hear me, Janet, I checked.' Marian looked hard at her, still clasping her hand.

'But…but that was ages ago,' Janet stammered. 'What about now?'

'Stay here. I'll go and see.'

Marian was gone for a few seconds which ballooned with dread for Janet as she paced the powder room trying to control the pounding inside her chest. What had she done? Now, everyone would know. She'd gone and ripped a hole in the fabric of her new life which was only to be torn open wider and wider, as more and more people found out, until her new life lay in shreds.

When Marian returned, she was smiling. 'It's fine. There's only Niall in there. He said he's only been in there a couple of minutes and only heard vague mumblings.'

'But what if he's lying? What if he heard everything? What if-'

He didn't, Janet. I got him to swear. He fancies me and to be honest he's a bit of a pushover. But he wasn't lying. I'd know.'

'You'd know?'

'Yes, I'd know.'

Janet let out a deep breath and her shoulders slumped. She looked at Marian. 'What do I do now?'

Marian chewed on her thumbnail, frowning. 'Well, you

need a friend to talk to, I reckon. Talk it all through with. You've got to see you're not to blame. He could have died anyway, regardless of what you think you did. And the fact that you were a victim all those years, well no one could take it seriously, Janet.'

'But I am to blame! I know I am!'

'No. That's the problem. You need to see you're not, but how to do it, I don't know...' Then her eyes brightened. 'What about Ann? She's a friend, isn't she?'

Janet hesitated. 'At work, yes, I suppose. But we don't see each other on the outside.'

'Well, is there anyone else?'

Janet shook her head. She felt miserable. She had no friends. Frank had seen to that. And by the time she was sticking up for herself, it felt far too late to put her trust in anyone.

'It'll have to be Ann, then. Come on. I'll walk you back to your office and I'll fetch Ann.'

'I can't go out there.'

'Yes, you can.'

'I can't!'

'Of course you can. Just be your buttoned-up usual self, Janet. You fucking show them.'

Janet responded to the challenge with a grimace of understanding and she stiffened herself to the task.

She and Marian both emerged through the doorway of the ladies toilet into the spotlights of the second floor, shoulder by shoulder. A poker-faced Samantha Dixon-Wright followed them with her narrowed eyes as they walked steadily past her, without even a glance in her direction. It felt like a long public parade of humiliation to her office, through carpets, through linens, past the customer lift, around the corner, past the cash office, and finally the sanctuary of her very own office, where she collapsed into her chair. Marian went to fetch Ann.

For the next few minutes Janet felt as if she was groping her way through a swirling mist. She was aware that there was still an hour to go until closing time and all she could do was sit there, trying to concentrate, trying to see her way through this disaster that was sure to mark the end of her new life. Her mind felt so confused and tied up with knots of fleece, but she was conscious of things outside herself moving on. The inane chatter from the cash office was a cruel torture, while she listened with a muted and dumb helplessness she'd never experienced before, as her emotional circuits shut down, one by one.

When Marian returned with Ann, in the confines of the office, she briefly explained to Ann what Janet had revealed in the powder room, and just before she left she assured Janet she would tell no one. This jump-started Janet into life again.

'You mustn't let it happen to you! Do you hear?' she said in a shrill voice.

'Yes, I hear, Janet,' Marian said, closing the door.

Janet turned to look at Ann. She looked close to tears and her ivory complexion had given way to a waxy whiteness. What good could she possibly do?

Janet found she could say nothing, emptied out of all emotion and will. But much to her surprise, Ann took care of her will.

Rising to her feet, she said, 'Come on, Janet. You've got a department to put to bed for the night. Then you're coming home with me. You can drive us.'

Janet's mouth dropped. 'I can't go out there, Ann. I just can't!'

Ann stood close in front of her. She took hold of Janet's shoulders and gave them a little shake. Her watery pale blue eyes looked into Janet's green ones, and right into the soul of her. 'The Janet I know can do anything!'

That very evening, after a quick ham salad which Ann insisted upon preparing, but which neither of them had much appetite for, Ann and Janet talked in the living room of Ann's Winchcombe retirement bungalow. A November rain sputtered on the picture window, while the flames of the fire in the grate licked the coals for nourishment.

Janet had succumbed to this sudden change of routine, meekly going through the motions and doing as she was bidden in a kind of suspended animation born of shock. The only real alarm she'd actually felt through the numbness which was keeping her safe for the moment, had been triggered by remembering Thomas, so they had first called at Janet's house in Charlton Kings, to check on him and leave him some food. Janet caught a typical look of haughty disinterest from him just before he slid through the cat flap. So, as Thomas was unperturbed and Janet was resigned to spending the night with Ann, she gathered together a pair of trousers, a jumper, and some night things into a small suitcase, while Ann prompted her to remember the essentials whenever Janet's panic threatened to break through her daze. Since it was a Saturday evening, they both had a day off tomorrow, and they agreed that it was fortuitous. That much logical thinking Janet could manage.

Ann surprised Janet by doing most of the talking to start with as they sat together on Ann's green draylon Parker Knoll sofa, a previous sale purchase from Masons, while they sipped a sherry each. And the sherry helped because by now, being in a somewhat alien environment, Janet was full of whirling thoughts and feelings she just couldn't handle, as if a gigantic black scribble was trying to wrap her up and carry her off to a place of no return and beyond all hope. But her senses had somewhat restored themselves and Ann was a voice in the midst of this chaos and she clung to it, while the sherry bestowed some living warmth to her body and some darkly undeserved sweetness to her taste buds.

'I thought you were handling his death too well. And the things you let slip in the past about his temper and his not having given you much freedom. I didn't think it could have been a happy marriage.'

Janet grimaced, staring into the fireside flames.

'And he never came to pick you up from work, like some

husbands do, like my Bob used to do.'

'He hated me working at Masons,' Janet muttered.

'He sounds like he was very controlling…and as for hitting you. Well, it's inexcusable! I can't imagine what you've been through, Janet! And you say it went on for years?'

'Yes. Pretty much all through our marriage – 34 years of it.' Her breath hitched in her throat, but she found she was ready to talk. 'Of course, it was worse after he retired, with him being around the house more, and with time on his hands. Picking on every little thing. And Scott was married by then, so there were just the two of us. At least when he was at work or at the pub with his colleagues, I saw a lot less of him. But after he retired, I knew that I had do something, so I got a job. He tried to stop me, because he'd never wanted me working, but by then there wasn't really anything he could do about it, and I stuck to my guns. He wouldn't let me use his car, so I got the bus.'

Ann turned and looked at her, wide-eyed. 'Why didn't you tell anyone, Janet? Why?'

Janet sighed and gazed at the fire, after catching a glimpse of Ann's face drawn into a dramatic mask of innocent disbelief. She desperately needed to distance herself in order to talk about what she'd so neatly packaged up and shoved into the back of the pitch-black cupboard of her memories of the past – but of course the cupboard had been opened now, and for some reason, which she still couldn't fathom, she'd opened it herself.

'There were lots of reasons,' she said wearily. 'I felt ashamed. I felt dirty. I wasn't sure anyone would believe me because he was very careful later on, and he usually slapped me so nothing would show. And of course he was a policeman; they're supposed to be beyond reproach. And he was always quite personable in public. He could be quite charming when he wanted to be. People would never have believed it.' She paused. 'He did have this best friend from school, Cliff was his name. He was a policeman in the same division. He once asked me whether Frank treated me right. But this was much earlier on and I just couldn't tell him.'

'Why not?'

'Because I didn't know if I could trust him, did I? They'd been friends for years. How was I supposed to know if I could trust him? It might have been some kind of sick test!' Janet heard herself wailing now and she flinched at the pathetic keening sound. What's happening to me? she wondered. Why is this happening? She shook her head and clamped her hand over her mouth, but Ann gently drew it back down.

'No, you must carry on now, Janet. I'm sorry, I can see why you wouldn't trust Frank's friend.'

'That's right, I just couldn't risk it. It's funny, because shortly before that Frank took up with a different crowd. They'd pick him up from the house and go on somewhere, a men's club of some kind, I think he said, but I didn't want to know. I never saw Cliff again and Frank never mentioned him again. I think he may have been promoted and Frank would have resented that. I suppose I missed a chance with Cliff, but how was I to know?' She turned and stared at Ann. 'You see, he was always threatening me. That was the main reason I didn't say anything to anyone. Whenever I stood up to him, he threatened me and…well, I believed him.' Janet felt tears burning their way out, but she rubbed them away with her fists. There were to be no more tears shed over Frank.

'Threatened you with what?'

Janet spoke now in a dull monotonous voice she barely recognised belonging to her. 'In the early years it was about Scott. He'd use his contacts at work to make sure that if I ever left him, I'd never get custody. He reckoned he could make it stick that I was an unfit mother.'

Ann drew a sharp intake of breath.

'So I put up with it for Scott. I don't know how much he remembers; I tried to shield him from it. But we've never talked about it. He never brought it up, so neither did I.'

Ann looked hard at her. 'You know it wasn't your fault though, don't you? And as for what you think you did to him, well he had it coming. And you can't very well be responsible for his lack of control over his own temper!'

'I don't know. I'm not sure it works like that. I kicked his pills away, and before the doctor arrived I threw them in the bin. I knew what I was doing.'

'Yes, but you'd had years of misery and he provoked you!'

'Yes…' Janet said, shaking her head slowly. 'But I was glad he was dead. I was relieved.'

'Well, any other woman in your position would have felt the same after all those years! The bastard had it coming. I never liked him anyway. Whenever I bumped into you and him in Sainsbury's he was always impatient to be off. He was rude, never saying hello to me, and he had an arrogance about him. I used to wonder what you saw in him.'

Janet glanced at Ann. She'd never heard her sound like this, so venomous. Her mouth was set into a hard line. Was this the same compliant woman she thought she knew? The one she could rely upon to be so biddable?

They both sat brooding in silence, sipping the dregs of their glasses, with just the snap and crackle of the fire and a golden light haloing from Ann's pleated corn silk lampshade. The television had remained switched off since they got home, a grey eye in the room picking up their dull reflections. But now Janet yearned for a soap or two, to force her mind into the banal repeating dramas of other people's lives, because she knew there was yet more for her to tell, to drag out of the back of the cupboard, and she was dreading it.

When Ann finally asked the question she was expecting, her skin crawled into goose bumps. It was the question the answer to which was sure to rend the frayed tear in her life wide open. If what she had already admitted to wasn't enough to do that, this surely would be.

'Was there any reason,' Ann asked, 'why he started it in

the first place? I mean, I know sometimes there's no reason, but …' she tailed off, picking at the piping on her seat cushion.

'Yes, there was a reason.'

Ann stopped picking and turned to look at her.

Eyes cast into the fire, her mouth now dry and tasting sour, Janet told Ann what she'd never told anyone except Frank all those years ago. She was surprised at how the words came out so easily after all this time.

'You see, I had a baby, before I married him. And I had to give her away. I got sent to a mother and baby home and I *had* to give her up.' She shook her head, her hands kneading each other in her lap. 'I thought it was the decent thing to do to tell Frank after we'd had Scott. My mother had made me promise not to tell him anything. She made me marry him really. She said she and Dad couldn't support me at home anymore and that's what girls my age did, got married, and she insisted he came from a good family. He did seem okay at first, attentive and so on, so I decided to tell him. It felt like the right thing to do for our marriage. But when I told him, everything changed. He hated it and he hated me.'

Janet searched Ann's face for her reaction. What she found there astonished her. Tears brimmed in Ann's eyes and ran down her cheeks. She made no effort to mop them up and she grasped hold of Janet's hand and squeezed it.

'I can't believe what you've been through, Janet. How very strong, you've been.'

As Janet lost herself in Ann's gaze, as she registered the simpering sympathy she so disdained, she found herself craving this sick comfort nonetheless, like a cactus in the desert still needs occasional rain to survive on – despite all appearances to the contrary. So she soaked up the sympathy and felt it touch that dark black place she'd kept inside her – that black hole, just like the one in the stairwell at Masons, the place of the defeated and the dammed. That was where she belonged. But as she stared into Ann's face, Ann's tears reached her there, and her own rising sobs pushed and clawed their way up and out to be heard. And before she could grope for purchase on any last bastions of her usual defences, out tumbled keening convulsions of hurt. Hurt long held onto. With Ann's arm around her shoulder, she gave in. She cried. Long juddering intakes of breath and harsh exhales to sob harder and harder, remembering Frank, remembering her mother, remembering the one man she'd loved. But most of all remembering the baby girl she had given away at six weeks old.

Chapter 12

The night pressed in on the Winchcombe bungalow and Ann had already drawn the curtains against the late November rain as it turned to a slurry of sleet. Now she shovelled a few more coals on the fire and topped up their sherry glasses. The carriage clock on the mantelpiece read ten minutes to ten. Janet glanced at it and then at Ann. Her emotions had run dry, but she knew she had to carry on. Better now, than in the cold night of day. She knew a bare-faced chilling reality was waiting for her the next morning, where the full enormity of what had happened today would hit her like an overturned piano crashing to a marble floor, and she was dreading it. But for now, Ann wanted to know the full story and Janet wanted to tell it, and at least Frank wasn't around to stop her.

'My mother always told me, *You make your bed, you lie in it*,' Janet said, sipping at her sherry.

'Yes, that was around in my day too,' Ann observed. 'They were pretty hard back then in the post-war years, weren't they?'

'Yes.'

Janet glanced at Ann. She'd changed into a blue velour tracksuit with matching slippers, just for comfort, she'd said, an outfit that looked like one you might see advertised in the *Radio Times*. It was odd seeing Ann out of her staff uniform and in trousers, it was strange them sitting side by side like this, and it was even more remarkable that she was in Ann's home revealing her innermost secrets. And all because that silly Marian wouldn't listen to her, and she'd lost control. But it was too late now; the milk had been spilt.

She swallowed hard. 'He was called Joe,' she said. 'Joe Fairlie. He was a local farmer's son and worked at the Coop in Castle Street in Bristol. I was seventeen at the time, he was twenty. We met when we were working there in 1952, him driving one of the mobile grocery vans, me in ladieswear. We actually met at one of the staff do's in the autumn at The Palace and we hit it off straightaway. We did a lot of dancing that night, ballroom, a lot of jive, and by the time the band was playing Nat King Cole's 'Unforgettable' – well, the spark had been lit. I'd never felt anything like it before.' She hesitated and looked at Ann. 'And I never have since.'

Ann's eyes widened. 'What was he like?'

Janet gazed down into her glass of amber elixir. 'Handsome, of course. He had the most lovely deep blue eyes and dark blonde hair. His fringe kept flopping down onto his forehead. But it wasn't just his looks. He was kind, and funny – that was important, I didn't get many laughs at home. My friend at the time, Babs, said he was a catch, that he looked like a blonde Gary Cooper.' She smiled and looked at Ann. 'He did, too.'

And as Janet took her walk down memory lane, accompanied by Ann, she went straight to the pretty scenic spots first, to smell the full-bodied roses there.

That first meeting she'd been wearing her brand new, ready-to-wear dress, made of silky Sea Island cotton. Her friend, Babs, had persuaded her to buy it from a local dress shop called Peacocks, in Bishopsworth, Bristol, where they both lived, after they'd seen it in the window there. Janet felt it was a bit too flamboyant, but the red dress with the white spots, its buttoned bodice and shirt collar, had fitted her to perfection after Babs bossed her into trying it on. And after Babs had insisted it wasn't flamboyant, but rather, it was *très chic*, Janet paid ten pounds for it, which was two weeks wages then. She kept the cost to herself and the dress well away from her mother's prying eyes. She'd also recently adopted a new hairstyle for her glossy dark brown hair which was being popularised through film stars, Gina Lollobrigida and Sophie Loren. It was short, strategically shaggy, and was known as the Italian cut.

That night at the dance, Babs told her she looked amazing and in truth, she felt amazing. She felt even more amazing when this tall, good-looking man in a smart double-breasted suit approached her and asked her if she fancied a dance. Fancy it, she did, and found herself quickly fancying him. And as they danced, one dance after another, and as he moved her around the floor with assured ease, and as they finally succumbed to moving their bodies closer together, arms encircling, as they shifted to the slow and sultry strains of 'Unforgettable', neck to neck, *then* Janet knew she wanted to see this young man again, and again. Joe Fairlie was now Janet's first serious contender to fit the role of being her beau.

And she couldn't quite believe it had happened. She'd always thought she must be too steely and resistant a person to fall in love, because her mother was always telling her *You're as hard as nails*. Why this character judgment, her mother had never explained, but it may have been because she tried to stand up for herself in response to Mildred's carping and criticizing. However, after that first meeting with Joe, she knew her mother's view of her wasn't true. Indeed she'd felt quite the opposite of hard in his arms, more of a melting feeling deep inside. And she felt all fluttery and excited when he asked her to the Ritz to see *The Bad and the Beautiful*, on the following Saturday night.

Their first date went well. He picked her up at her home, 14 Marguerite Road in Bishopsworth, where he briefly met her mother and father. Her father was friendly, her mother stiff and questioning. They caught the bus into town to the picture house. Lana Turner and Kirk Douglas were on good form, smoldering and scowling respectively, and Janet and Joe eagerly watched the drama unfold with an ice cream each. Then Joe escorted her home, said goodnight on the doorstep, just giving her a kiss on the cheek. He'd been the perfect gentleman, and her mother could find no fault, which in those days was quite an achievement.

After that, things developed quickly. Christmas came and went, but then they met each other most weekends, going to dances, or to the pictures, or just to chat in a coffee house, and sometimes they went on outings with mutual friends from the Coop. But when spring came, Joe used to collect her in his truck and they'd go over to his father's farm a few miles out of town. Ash Farm, it was called, and Janet was pleased to find some ash trees lining the driveway. His mum and dad were a little cool with her, but Joe explained it was because they had their hearts set on him marrying the neighbouring farmer's daughter, which he had no intention of doing, so until they accepted this, he told her not to take any notice of their cold shoulder routine. They'd be sure to come around.

Although parental approval was considered a must for respectable young people at the time, Janet put this inconvenience out of her mind and they carried on seeing one another. Babs told her to be careful, asking her if she knew how not to fall pregnant, but when Janet stared back at her in shocked silence at her insinuations, Babs left the subject well alone. The days in the countryside brought back happy memories of when Janet was evacuated as a little girl to the village of Camelford in Cornwall, to stay with her grandparents and her mother's youngest sister, Auntie Florrie. Family picnics were her favourite times, out in the meadows with a rug to sit on and a hamper, lying on her tummy and listening to her grandfather's stories about his days as a policeman with the Devon and Cornwall Constabulary, while her grandmother tutted at his tall tales. So with this in mind, Janet would prepare a picnic basket for herself and Joe, with meat and potato pie, devilled eggs, cheese and crackers, plus a homemade chocolate cake, all washed down with a flask of sweet tea. And then they'd lie back on their picnic rug and stare at the sky, talking about all sorts of nonsense, while periodically leaning in to kiss each other - gently, or passionately, but always blissfully. And by the time July came around, on such a picnic like this, looking at the sky, Joe told Janet he loved her.

'But there's a problem,' he said, sitting up and gazing down at her, as her wide smile turned to a frown. 'I should have told you about it already, but I just couldn't bring myself…and anyway, I don't want it to be a problem. I love you.'

'I think I love you too,' she replied. 'But what is it?' She propped herself up on her elbow to examine him, to closely study every shifting expression in this face which she now loved, whilst her heart thudded in her chest. From his cracked brow, to his long lashes shielding an uncertain confused look in his eyes which she'd never seen before. This look scared her. 'What is it?'

'I'm going to have to go to America,' he said, looking at the horizon. 'To help run my uncle's farm in Connecticut. He died recently in a tractor accident. And now my aunt and my two young cousins are really struggling to run the farm. I'm supposed to go over there after harvest time.'

He turned to look deeply into her eyes. 'We can write,' he said. 'It won't be forever, just a couple of years probably.'

'A couple of years…' Janet repeated mechanically, trying the words out on her tongue.

'Yes. And of course it's a great opportunity too. There have been so many advances over there with machinery and that.'

Now Janet felt goose bumps pimple her skin and she shivered. He sounded excited. He wanted to do this. He really wanted to go.

'But you will come back?' she asked in a small voice.

He clasped hold of her hand. 'Of course I will. I love you!'

Janet took a deep breath. 'So when do you go?'

'Around the middle of September.'

Janet fell silent for a little while, then they ended the conversation by vowing to make the most of the time they had left, around eight weeks. They would make this time blissful, and when he came back they would marry. And then

Joe did what so many lovers did back in those days, using his pen knife he carved his and Janet's initials, JT and JF, inside a heart, in the trunk of a tree, a huge ash tree on the fringe of their favourite field. This marked the end of that day when their futures looked blessed.

As the days of summer passed, they spent all their spare time together, rain or shine, and they grew closer, driven by a new sense of urgency. Their kisses and caresses became more heated, more passionate…more vitally necessary somehow, as they explored the dizzy heights and mysterious depths of where this relationship was taking them. And on a warm sunny afternoon in early September, their mutual need finally overtook their senses and they found themselves making love for the very first time, on a picnic rug underneath their ash tree. And although at first, it hurt a little for Janet, soon their bodies adjusted to what they were doing, both of them, for the very first time. And it was romantic, it was beautiful, it was like they'd seen in the movies. They truly felt as one. But there was no protection on Joe's part, other than to attempt the withdrawal method which some of his mates had told him about, and no protection on Janet's part, as mothers back in the fifties didn't discuss such things with their daughters, and she hadn't pursued the subject with Babs. And as they said their goodbyes the night before Joe left for America, on the 15th September, taking a passage on a ship bound for New York from Bristol Docks, Janet watched him stride out of her life into the darkness beyond. And not once did she think she'd never see him again.

It was Babs who first worked out Janet might be pregnant, after Janet mentioned at work one day in late November that she'd missed her monthlies twice. Joe and Janet's innocent bliss had led to a social catastrophe.

At this point in Janet's story, Ann gently suggested a break while she made them some hot chocolate, then she soon settled herself back on the sofa.

She sighed. 'It was a different world back then, wasn't it?' she said. 'They've got it so good these days.'

Janet nodded mutely, taking a sip from her mug, then she grimaced. Now came the part of memory lane which was rocky, the roses withered with blight and thorned with heartache.

While Janet desperately waited for a letter from Joe, it was her mother who'd noticed something was wrong. She was in the habit of buying sanitary towels for them both and when she realised Janet hadn't used any for two months, she suspected the truth.

'I sincerely hope this isn't what I think it is?' she ranted, pacing around in the kitchen with her hands thrust into the pockets of her pinny. Her hair was just out of its curlers, which gave her the austere look of a high court barrister for the prosecution.

'It might be,' replied Janet in a small voice.

Then quickly her mother rounded on her and whipping out her right hand, she slapped Janet hard on the face.

'You slut!' she hissed at her. 'I knew you and that Joe Fairlie were up to no good. You cheap slut! How could you do this to us? Opening your legs to the first man that sniffs around you and bringing shame to our door! We're a respectable family! I'm a Catholic, for goodness' sake! He'll have to do the right thing by you. He'll have to marry you!'

With her cheek smarting from her mother's rage, Janet quailed. 'But I don't want it to be like that, Mam! I don't want to trap him like that.'

'Oh, you don't want it to be like that, do you?' her mother said in a mincing tone, with her hands on her hips. 'Well, what do you think the alternative is? Because we can't have the brat here!'

At this point her father appeared. He'd been sitting in the lounge, reading his paper and smoking his pipe. With rounded shoulders and thin greying hair, he was wearing a worn woollen pullover, many times darned by Janet, but originally knitted by Mildred before the war years had hardened her into peanut brittle. His face was settled into its customary resigned folds, sculpted by so many full-of-strife occasions during his married life with Mildred.

'Now, Millie, we don't know for certain…' he said to his granite-faced wife standing by the sink.

He took Janet's hand. 'We'll work something out, Janie, love. Don't fret.'

'Don't fret! Don't fret!' shouted his wife, picking up a plate and flinging it across the kitchen where it crashed against the tiled wall and shattered into an avalanche of shards down onto the linoleum. 'It's no use taking the soft approach, Albert Turner! That's you all over! She'll have to reap what she's –'

'And she *will*.' Her father's voice cut in firmly over her mother's. She'd never heard him do this before and her mother's mouth dropped open. He looked hard at his wife. 'But first things first, Millie, you take her to the doctors to make sure, or I will.'

'Well, he won't be able to tell! It's far too early for that!'

'He can put things in motion.'

So a few days later a tight-lipped Mildred marched Janet to an appointment at their family doctor's office. There was no reliably accurate urine test back then to help a doctor to confirm pregnancy, other than to send a sample off to be injected into a rabbit. If the rabbit died, the woman was pregnant. But it was more usually a case of waiting until the heartbeat could be heard, which could be as late as twenty weeks. In the meantime, Janet was given the name of a welfare worker who the doctor said would *sort her out* when the time came. This meant a referral to a mother and baby home, where the child would be born in secret in a different location, and from where the baby could be put up for adoption, unless Janet's circumstances were to change. If Joe didn't get in touch, she would be an unmarried mother, of socially unacceptable status, and unable to support her child.

And so the waiting began in earnest for Janet. And it was

a time of shame, despair, and discord. Shame due to her condition, despair in her not hearing from Joe, and discord between Janet and her mother, with increased discord between her father and her mother, while her younger brother, Norman, who knew nothing of Janet's pregnancy, and who was hell-bent on being a Teddy Boy much to his mother's mortification, was now wanting to join the merchant navy and see the world. 'Over my dead body,' yelled Mildred.

And when Mildred found out that Joe had forgotten to give his forwarding address to Janet, and that she'd forgotten to ask for it, it seemed to be the final straw for her.

'How could you be so stupid?' she screamed. 'Now he's got the perfect excuse never to do the right thing because he's never going to know! The child will have to be adopted for certain now!'

'But he's bound to write to me, Mam,' insisted Janet, blinking at her mother through her swollen red eyelids.

But this apparent hopelessness in the situation tipped her mother's stress over the brink and she retreated to the tiny box room upstairs, now designated as her sewing room, to work on her hat designs. As a young woman she'd dreamed of being a professional milliner, before married life had dashed her hopes. So it seemed she'd washed her hands of motherhood and wifedom for the time being.

Soon after this, Janet's father suggested he and Janet go and visit the Fairlies at the farm, to tell them what had happened and ask for Joe's address as he had a right to know. This was usually something that was more appropriate for a mother to do with her daughter, but Mildred felt far too aggrieved to 'go begging to them' as she put it. Janet perked up, allowing herself to believe that Joe's parents would be sure to help.

But as Janet and her father sat in the Fairlie's farmhouse kitchen, decorated for the festive season with berried holly, they weren't even offered so much as a cup of tea. And Janet was shocked at their hardness, especially coming from Joe's mother. While her husband grunted noises of agreement with his wife from the fireplace where he sat throughout, chewing on some tobacco and periodically spitting into the fire, she was doing all the talking. She vowed that Joe's life was not going to be ruined by a loose town girl, who'd obviously been around a bit. Janet tried to explain it wasn't like that at all. *She* wasn't like that. It was love. It was *first* love. But Mrs Fairlie wasn't interested in Janet's interpretation of what she called her son's 'silly infatuation', and refused point-blank to give Joe's address to Janet and she refused to let him know of Janet's condition. Mrs Fairlie looked Janet square in the eye as she stated that when Joe returned from America, he was to marry the neighbouring farmer's daughter, sweet Elspeth, who was used to farming life and would make an excellent farmer's wife. That, she said, curtly, was all there was to it, as she briskly smoothed her hands down the front of her apron.

Despite Janet's sobbing, and despite the reasonings and counter-arguments that her father offered, such as pointing out that this would be their grandchild, their very own flesh and blood, that if Joe ever found out they hadn't told him, he might never forgive them, that love was precious and this baby was an outcome of that - the door of the farmhouse was still shut behind them with a resounding shudder.

They walked all the way home in a cold drizzle, her father sighing and shaking his head, while Janet's tears finally dried up in despair. The heady days of her and Joe's romance seemed so unreal to her now. And if it wasn't for the initials Joe had carved in that old ash tree, which she visited now and again to feel close to him, it could easily have felt like it had never happened – *if* it wasn't for the new life now inside her.

Chapter 13

Christmas, in that year of 1953, was horrendous. Mildred thumped bowls around the kitchen making the usual fare but with the added ingredient of bitter acrimony, and since she cared so much about appearances, all the paper chains went up in the downstairs rooms for visitors, while the Christmas tree was positioned centre stage in the middle of the front window, so that passing neighbours were sure to see that Christmas was being celebrated in the Turner household, just as usual. In fact, Mildred smothered the tree with so many baubles and draped it with so much tinsel, it looked as if the Turner household was positively choking on Christmas.

Albert tried to rescue a grim Christmas Day by gathering them around the radio after dinner to listen to some classic Christmas songs. But his daughter, son, and wife, soon skulked off to lick wounds aggravated by the confinement of the festive season. Norman didn't know what was up with Janet, though much to her surprise he did ask her. But her mother had sworn her to secrecy with respect to Norman, who was the apple of his mother's eye. She didn't want him exposed to his sister's shame, she said, and besides, he'd be sure to tell his friends and then 'all and sundry' would find out. And young boys mustn't be told of such things by their sisters, she said with her characteristic scowl. So Janet told Norman that she was just missing Joe.

She worked numbly on into January at the Coop in ladieswear, running to the toilet now and again when she needed to be sick, explaining she had a tummy upset. Auntie Vi, who she'd been happy to confide in, advised she carry on working until she began to 'show'. Janet fretted over how on earth she was to judge this, with chicken and egg coming to mind, until she noticed the floor manager staring at her tummy despite the girdle she was wearing. By this time she was about four months into her pregnancy, so she promptly resigned saying she needed a change.

'Good idea,' observed Mrs Dart, the thin-as-a-pin floor manager, as she frowned at Janet over her horn-rimmed spectacles. 'I should think so too, young lady.'

During this time, her loyal friend, Babs, had suggested various methods she'd heard of for getting rid of the baby. It turned out that Babs had some experience in these matters, and she was also feeling guilty that she hadn't warned Janet enough about the risks of getting pregnant.

'I just never thought you two would actually *do* it,' she said anxiously, then drawing hard on her cigarette, as they sat in their favourite coffee house.

So, to make up for this error, she tried to help Janet now. She shared a small flat with her sister, so Janet could go over and try drinking gin in a hot bath and use a douche. That was supposed to do the trick. Or she could try falling down stairs a few times. Or maybe if these approaches didn't work, she could find someone to 'sort her out' for a fee. So it was made very clear to Janet that this pregnancy needed sorting out one way or the other. But she still believed that Joe would write, so how could she do something like this? How could she try to kill his baby? *Their* baby. And once she began to feel it moving in her womb, the very idea of trying to kill it filled her with horror.

As she began to show more, she had to stay in her room when they had visitors. When she did go out, she wore a jacket and skirt, trying to avoid the nipped in waist look that was so prevalent, and she took to wearing a baggy duffle coat that her Auntie Vi gave her, so she could leave the house looking like a respectable girl going to the shops or to meet her friends. In truth, the only friend she was keeping in touch with was Babs, who was diligently guarding her secret. She carefully avoided the others, because, although she felt strongly she'd done nothing wrong other than to fall in love, she still felt ashamed because, well, because she was meant to feel ashamed, wasn't she?

The tension at home was unbearable as they all waited through the months of spring for the day she was to go to the mother and baby home she'd been booked into by her social worker. Her mother barely spoke to her. Her father tried to be kind, but kept being snapped at for his pains by his wife. And Norman kept out of the way by staying out for longer with his Teddy Boy mates who were forming a skiffle and jazz band, much to Mildred's disapproval.

When the time did come for Janet to leave home in the last week of April, six weeks before the baby was due, and having still received no letter from Joe, her heart felt so heavy and dragged down, she didn't know what was keeping her upright. But upright she stayed, in more ways than one, as she packed the weathered wartime suitcase her father gave her. Into it went her night things, toiletries, and some smock tops and wrap-around skirts she'd made herself from a pattern Auntie Vi had bought for her from the local haberdashers, to save Janet's own embarrassment.

Saying her goodbyes, before she left by train for Hope Lodge in Swindon, and embarking upon her first time ever away from home, was the beginning of the worst time of her whole life.

First, Babs came to see her at home the day before she left, and she cried in the privacy of Janet's bedroom. Then she rubbed her eyes and looked hard at Janet.

'Don't let then grind you down, do you hear?'

Janet stared back at Bab's red face in confusion. 'What do you mean?' she said, whilst a flush of fear chilled her heart.

'Just that they can be strict. A cousin of mine went to one of those Catholic places. A bloody nightmare, it was, they had her doing all this washing and praying all the time.'

'But this one isn't Catholic,' Janet replied, cold fear now snaking up her spine. 'It's Church of England.'

'Well, just take care of yourself. You're my best friend, you know?'

Janet had been touched and they hugged each other

goodbye, before Babs hurried down the stairs and into Marguerite Road. As Janet watched from the window, Babs made a smart figure, tripping down the street in her new flared mustard coat, with her neat French pleat of a hairdo, then disappearing around the corner, while Janet couldn't help wondering for no logical reason whether she would ever see her again. An ache twisted in Janet's heart like a rag being wrung out of feeling. All she had left of Babs were the musky undertones of her favourite Arpege perfume lingering in Janet's bedroom like a precious memory of good times gone by, surely never to be had again.

Norman had been easier to say goodbye to. He was off to band practice shortly after Babs left, so he said goodbye then. He knew by now what the situation was, because despite Mildred's attempts to keep him tied to her apron strings, he wasn't a child anymore and Janet's bump was now beyond obvious. At the age of seventeen, he'd just got himself an apprenticeship at a printworks, which pleased Mildred because this meant he wouldn't have to do national service. He was on his way to becoming a man, but he was still understandably tongue-tied with Janet.

'See you soon, Sis...good luck with the...err...the baby thing,' he said, frowning and looking at her bump. 'But, hey,' he said, brightening, 'it won't be long before you're back again.'

No, she thought, but then what? Her mother had been dropping hints like bricks that she'd have to set about finding a husband as soon as she got back. When Janet protested that she wanted a good job instead, her mother retorted, 'Just who do you think you are? Single women can't be self-supporting. Marriage was good enough for me, it can be good enough for you!' Janet kept her opinion that her mother's marriage had hardly been a match made in heaven to herself.

Her mother's farewell, in the hallway inside the front door, to save making an exhibition of themselves in front of the neighbours, had been typically curt. 'Just get it done and over with, then our lives can get back to normal.' Then she'd turned and gone into the kitchen.

Her father had been so different. He gave her a hug, looking watery-eyed and said, 'I'm sorry, Janie. It will be hard...but you can do it. It's the best thing for the baby, it can go to a good home. Just you take care of yourself and come back to us.'

'She'll be fine,' her mother called from the kitchen. 'She's as hard as nails.'

Her father shook his head and turned away, mumbling, 'I'm so sorry, Janet.'

And Janet knew he meant sorry about her own mother.

By the time Auntie Vi and Uncle Ted arrived to drive her to the station in the firm's grocery van, she actually wanted to go, to get away from the claustrophobia of family life which she'd had to endure for the last few months of her confinement, confinement being a very apt expression, she decided.

The three of them were very quiet on the way to the station, then Ted gave Janet a hug farewell on the platform, leaving her with her Auntie Vi. Auntie Vi, her mother's younger sister, who'd been nothing but supportive to Janet, whilst having been accused of *always being too soft* by Mildred. Auntie Vi had retaliated by declaring Mildred to be far *too hard*, and that she ought to be ashamed of herself taking her own frustrations out on her daughter. Janet found this hard and soft business very confusing, but she knew where her affiliations ultimately lay. And now she was to be parted from her aunt, and the train was due in ten minutes so they had little time left for talking.

Auntie Vi placed her hand on Janet's arm. 'I'm so sorry you're going to have to go through this, Janet.'

Janet looked surprised at her. 'But I've got no choice.'

'Oh, Janet...I wish Ted and I could adopt your baby. We talked about it, but Ted says he really wants us to keep trying for our own.'

A hook caught in Janet's throat and she couldn't reply.

Tears stung her eyes. Wouldn't that have been just perfect? If her aunt and uncle had raised her child, she'd have been able to visit, and who knew what could have transpired in the future, maybe when Joe returned?

Now her aunt was crying too, as she held Janet's gaze. She reached into her handbag and placed something soft into Janet's grasp. Janet looked down. It was a small knitted rabbit with upright ears, satin stitch blue eyes, and a pink nose, and it was wearing a blue, red, and yellow striped jumper and trousers. It was beautiful, and Janet knew her auntie had knitted it especially for her baby. And this made her baby so much more real now. Even though she could often feel it moving around inside her, this little toy would soon be clasped in its tiny hands.

The train was now puffing into the station with a wheezing of steam and a blaring of whistles, and all too soon the doors began to open and the smell of cigarette smoke snaked out with the passengers. Her aunt grabbed her, gave a her tight squeeze, then nudged her forward, and Janet stepped onto the train with her suitcase.

In a hazy daze she lurched into the first empty compartment she came to, facing east in the direction of travel. And as the train slowly rolled out of the station, she and her aunt waved to each other, and she craned her neck for as long as possible out of the window, to see the trim figure of her aunt in her sage green tailored suit, becoming fainter, veiled by the steam, then disappearing altogether. And she wished, not for the first time, that her Auntie Vi had been her mother instead of Mildred, who thought her own daughter was as hard as nails, when really it was very much the other way around.

What ensued next, the older Janet of today had done her utmost to forget, but as she was in the mode of telling the full story to Ann, she was surprised at how fast the memories began to flash in her mind – visuals and sounds and feelings, like a slideshow running faster and faster. It became overwhelming, as if the past was trying to reach out and drag her back there. So in order to handle it, she tried to keep the telling brief and just to capture the pictures which best told the story, sticking to the facts as best she could.

The first thing that hit her senses when she entered through the doors of the massive victorian block of red brick with its windows frowning down at her, rather despairingly known as Hope Lodge, was the smell of disinfectant. It hung in the air of the passageways as if to press home the point that this was a clean, sterile environment as befitted its purpose, which would cleanse and purify the sins of the flesh.

Then there was a polite, but curt, checking-in procedure at reception. The matron told her she was to be there for six weeks prior to the birth, where she would be transferred to the local hospital. She and 'baby' would then return to the home for a further six weeks, during which time 'baby' would be put up for adoption. Her mother and father had not been able to afford the full fee of her stay, so her Auntie Vi and Uncle Ted had made up the difference, so she didn't have to apply for benefits or work in the home to help pay for her time there. This was considered a real boon.

'You're a very fortunate young lady,' observed the matron, as she snapped a glance up at Janet from the ledger on her polished mahogany desk. 'Most of the girls here have to work.'

The matron also reiterated to Janet, that since she was under 21, and her parents weren't in a position to offer the baby a home, and seeing as the father was out of the picture – and even if was in the picture and wanted to marry her, he'd still need parental consent – then the baby would have to be adopted.

'It's best for baby and best for you,' she said.

Janet nodded mutely, having already been told by her mother that there was no way Janet could expect her to give the baby a home. It was, she said, 'Quite unthinkable! How dare you even ask! How many times do we have to go through this, you have no choice, no choice at all!'

Then after a briefing on the rules of the home, she remembered following the robust bottom of a member of staff as she squeaked her rubber souls on the polished floorboards, with Janet in her wake, carrying her battered suitcase. She was shown the recreation room first, with a few very pregnant women present, and some noticeably 'no longer pregnant' women smoking and playing cards at wooden trestle tables. Then she was shown the nursery, where she stared blankly at a few babies in their cribs, then came the laundry and kitchen, and then her assigned room, which she was to share with three other girls, also waiting to give birth. Finally, she was able to unpack her belongings.

Until the birth, it was pretty much the same routine every day, and the time felt as flat and stretched out as the sheets being pressed in the laundry, which she felt obliged to help with to avoid looking 'stuck up' to the other mothers.

There were chores in the morning, then in the afternoons they could go into town or knit, have tea and chat. Some of the women made close friendships, and Janet did get along with her roommates, but all the while she felt either a brain-fogged disconnection to her surroundings, unable to comprehend that this was actually happening to her, or a razor-edged worrying about what the future would hold for her. The baby's life was soon to begin, and when that moment came, she felt hers would be over. Without Joe, *nothing* made sense.

There was also the crying that would resound fitfully down the sanitised corridors, when another mother had to give her baby up, revealing the naked truth of the function of this building, and warning the mothers-to-be that their time too would come. And in town there was no escape, with the intrusive stares from locals looking at the girls 'from the home'. On Sundays they were obliged to attend a religious service, where they were alligator-marched to the local church in which they had to occupy the back row pews. It seemed to Janet they were seated there so they wouldn't upset the sensibilities of the ever so righteous.

Another compulsory requirement was the preparing of a baby box. And Janet hated this. They had to buy a plain box with a lid on it from a local shop, which ever so conveniently kept a stock of them, then decorate it to make it look 'pretty'. Janet kept this decoration to a minimum, and interpreted the whole process as humiliatingly trite rather than purely practicable. So she didn't knit a stitch for anything to go inside it. Nevertheless, she was forced to buy blankets, nappies, booties, hats, and matinee jackets for her baby, and her roommates urged some of their knitted items onto her, for use after the baby was born, and to hand over with the baby to its new parents. 'It's the last thing you can do for baby,' declared the matron, as she inspected the contents of Janet's box.

By this time Janet was feeling the weight of her unborn child, and the kicking inside her, light flutterings giving way to distinct jabs. Her lower back ached a little and to offset the weight she found herself leaning backwards and waddling around like a penguin, something she found highly distasteful. She couldn't sleep, and her ankles swelled. Mentally and emotionally, she crawled through the days, until finally her waters broke at midday, on Friday, the 2nd of June, where it was like having one huge uncontrollable pee.

What followed next was like a blur of shifting images down the tube of a kaleidoscope of horror: being ambulanced to Swindon General Hospital; lying on starched-to-a-crisp white sheets; being called 'Mrs Turner', to which she had an inbuilt revulsion; horrendous cramps in her belly like really bad period pains; being left alone with her fears for hours at a time, where they ballooned inside her mind to bursting point, while slowly and relentlessly her contractions increased. Finally, a nurse was there, telling her to push, while a wave of pressure built up inside her and there was no going back. The pain was the kind of pain she couldn't believe it was actually possible to survive, like it was tearing her in half. And then, just as she thought she was actually dying, and when she couldn't hold back the screams any longer, it was over. Her baby was born at ten minutes to five on the 2nd June, 1954. A swift clean up followed, and suddenly, her baby was there in front of her eyes – Janet's new baby girl. Fair hair, blue eyes.

'Such lovely blue eyes,' she said.

'All new babies have blue eyes,' the nurse replied. 'And of course, you'll not get to see what they become if you're giving her up for adoption.'

Janet flinched at the words 'giving her up.' It was so real now, and she looked from the impassive plank-faced nurse to the other beds on the ward, to see if any of the other 'legitimate' mothers had heard those words too.

She and her baby were soon transferred back to Hope Lodge where six weeks of tension ensued. The protocol of care was carefully prescribed and monitored. Like the other new mothers, Janet washed her baby, changed its nappies, bottle fed her baby to keep any potential bonding at bay, whilst taking tablets to stop her own breast milk flowing. And she took her baby in a pram for a walk into town, while the rest of the time her baby was with the others in the nursery. She named her baby girl, Vivien, after Vivien Leigh, and so she could always be called Vi, after her own beloved aunt. And Vivien just happened to take a liking to Auntie Vi's rabbit. She kept it clutched in her perfect tiny fingers, and squealed when matron moved to take it off her, declaring it far too personal a toy. But Vivien won her battle with matron, much to Janet's satisfaction and pride. In the meantime, Janet was getting accustomed to Vivien. She felt a twist in her heart every time she had to say goodnight to her. She worried when she cried more than usual. She increasingly sought to comfort her, give her cuddles, all under the hawk-eyed scrutiny of the matron, who dissuaded such actions for attachment reasons.

It was an emotional day when her father and Auntie Vi

came to visit and take her and Vivien to the South West Adoption Agency office in town, where Vivien would be handed over to her new parents, along with the baby box. Janet could only presume these new parents had visited the nursery and picked Vivien out of the line-up of cots. Her father took pictures with his Brownie. Some of Vivien, and one of Janet holding her, standing by the nursery window in a warm bar of golden light. Her father's lip kept twitching and his hands trembled, and Auntie Vi kept turning away with her hand pressed hard to her mouth, to hold back her sobs that otherwise escaped now and again to make more explicit the tragedy of the situation.

By the time they got to the agency and were seated in the office, all their eyes were misty, all except for Vivien's. Hers were wide with wonder as she looked around at all the faces, which caused Janet to break down into a stream of tears for the very first time. Auntie Vi took Vivien gently from Janet and bounced her a little on her own knee.

Her father put his arm around Janet and squeezed. 'I know, I know. I'm so sorry, Janie, love.'

Paperwork was signed, Janet's signature blurring in and out of focus as if demonstrate to her own mind her profound indecision right up until the very last moment. But she had no way of obtaining legal consent, as far as she was aware of, by which to keep her lovely baby girl. And so she had no choice but to give her up. This had been repeatedly made so clear – *best for baby, best for you.*

Then, as she held on tight to Vivien, with Vivien in turn holding tightly onto her rabbit, the welfare worker said the words Janet would remember for the rest of her life, like a day of judgment pronouncement chanted after her down the corridors of the years. 'I'm going to have to take her now.'

One swift pair of arms extracted Vivien from her own. The welfare worker tried to take the rabbit off Vivien, but Vivien screamed. Auntie Vi turned her back to the scene, shoulders hitching, while her father looked on with a twisted expression on his face.

'This isn't right. Oh, this just isn't right,' he said, shifting around in his chair.

'Try and stay calm, Sir, for your daughter's sake,' said the welfare worker.

Then the door swung slowly shut as the welfare worker swished her skirts from the room, carrying Vivien away.

Janet could hear Vivien crying in the next room, then some muffled shushing trying to appease her. All these sounds ripped through her like knives, as she doubled over, her whole world shrinking in on her, squeezing her in a vice-like grip. Then while they all sat there, trying desperately to turn to stone, things went quiet in the next room. And after half an hour, they heard the new family leave, when the heavy oak door of the front of the building boomed its closure. This was now their cue to leave too.

Overcome by one frantic thought, Janet rushed into the next room. The welfare worker shot to her feet from her desk.

'Did they let her keep the rabbit?' Janet rasped.

The welfare worker frowned. 'Yes. But it really was an exception to the rule.' Then her face softened. 'Your baby will be taken good care of. You can get on with your own life now, look forward.'

'Look forward,' Janet mumbled as she stumbled backwards into the arms of her father and Auntie Vi.

Chapter 14

When she got home to 14 Marguerite Road in Bristol with her father, to the smell of frying onions in the kitchen, her mother's greeting was a tight-lipped hello. And she delivered another one of those slamming-the-door-on-the-past platitudes Janet had heard trotted out so many times in the last few days, by staff at the home, and by other mothers trying so hard to persuade themselves using head over heart.

'You can get on with your life now, and we can all get back to normal,' Mildred said, with a smile plucking at the corners of her mouth. 'I'm sure the neighbours are none the wiser, they just think you were visiting your Auntie Florrie down in Cornwall, helping her while she wasn't very well.' Janet gaped at her mother's inventiveness. Her Auntie Florrie was a spinster school teacher who played the church organ. What a perfect foil for Janet's own sins!

And then it came. All too soon. Before Janet had any time to get her head together or begin to try and recover from her loss.

'We can concentrate on finding you a decent husband now,' her mother said as she mashed some potatoes, thumping the masher into the pan like she wanted to smash them into pulp.

'For crying out loud, Millie! Let the girl get her bag unpacked before you start on that one! She's just given up a sweet little baby girl, and you've nothing to say about it!'

'What's to say, Albert Turner? It's no good getting all sentimental about it! What in God's name can I say, except you make your bed, you lie in it!'

She turned to Janet, frowning. 'I know it must have been hard. Really, I do. But you've got the rest of your life ahead of you and the best thing is to take the bull by the horns and get on with it. Make a good marriage and *then* have a family.'

Janet went into a benumbed state of limbo after this, suspended in a state of uncertainty over an abyss of oblivion. Feeling little, thinking little, as the weeks became months, trying to forget about Joe, and repeatedly trying to sand down thoughts of her baby which chiselled grooves into her stony heart and mind. She didn't want to connect with her usual crowd of friends, she felt different from them now. She might have relented for Babs, but Babs had got married to the boy she'd been crazy about while Janet had been in the mother and baby home, and she'd moved to London with him. It was a bit of a rush job apparently, but Janet knew to take this 'information' with a pinch of salt. Still, she was surprised she hadn't got a letter from Babs and had only managed to find out what had become of her through Smith's, the local newsagent, who delivered local gossip for free.

Shortly after this in September, she saw an ad for trainee typists in the Bristol Telegraph, and since she'd decided she wanted a fresh start, and encouraged by her father (rather than her mother who thought it was a waste of time), she enrolled in the year long course. She found the work suited her. Touch typing was an enjoyable challenge, while the necessary qualities of fastidiousness, attention to detail, and professional attire, were custom-made for her. Her aim was to become a secretary rather than a run-of-the-mill typist, swimming in a pool of the very same fish.

Just before Christmas 54, her mother told her about Frank Brewer, an eligible young man, who might make a good match. He was the son of a new friend of Mildred's, namely Betty Brewer, who had just joined the local WI. Frank was ex-army and now a policeman, as yet unmarried, and a very good catch, her mother insisted. She would be secure for life with a policeman's pension and they would get a police house. After all, her own father, Janet's grandfather, had been a policeman in Cornwall and they'd had a good life growing up.

But Janet was far from keen and didn't want to discuss it. She was enjoying her training and for the first time in months was able to envisage a future for herself, perhaps *by* herself, if she could manage it. She was, after all, only nineteen, and should have her whole life ahead of her. But her mother hammered home the point that a husband was a necessity. And she kept her hammering going all through the spring and she delivered more and more thrusting blows in response to any objection Janet could raise, until Janet felt battered and bruised with their impact. It was all very well, her mother said, for her father to tell her life is what you make it, but it simply wasn't respectable for a girl to live alone. She'd get a reputation. *No one* lived alone. And she simply wouldn't be able to support herself, she needed a husband for that. It was a girl's duty to get married and have children, look after her husband, and keep a good home.

'Look what's happened to your Auntie Florrie,' her mother continued, skinning potatoes at the kitchen table. 'She's a spinster because she was too picky and her pupils have to be her substitute children.'

'Yes, but she supports herself and has a profession,' argued Janet, shelling some peas into a pan. She quickly checked her mother's face for signs of irritation.

'Only because she got a schoolhouse with the job and got some money from my Mam and Dad when they passed,' her mother said, sneering.

'But maybe she's happy the way she is?'

Her mother's face shrank sharply into the lines of vitriol she'd etched into it over the years and she slammed the peeler down on the table and glared at Janet. 'Happy!' she shrieked. 'Of course she's not happy! She's not married!'

'So all married women are happy, then? If so, what about you?'

A siren fired off within Janet and her nerve endings kindled – the words had popped out before she could stop them. She flinched backwards in her chair, expecting her mother to lash out with a slap.

Her mother flicked a hand out, saw Janet wasn't within reach, so bashed her fist down on the table instead. Then after a few bloated moments of silence, to Janet's astonishment, she saw tears brimming in her mother's eyes.

'You don't know what it was like, Janet. The war years. They were hard, and they've taken their toll on your dad and me. It's not your father's fault I don't seem happy, he's a bit soft, but he's a good provider and a good father. But you, you can have a better life, get nice things, make a nice home of your own. Times are changing for the better now. Get yourself a husband and make a fresh start. Married life is the *only* way. You can't have a career like a man and be self supporting. You can't get a loan from a bank to start your own business. I tried to be a milliner before I met your dad, but neighbours who became customers didn't expect to pay what the hats were really worth. It was impossible, because they didn't rate it any higher than a domestic skill. The only kind of freedom you *can* have is to be a married to a man with a good job. So forget all about Joe Fairlie, forget all about the baby, and never tell your future husband about them. Do you hear me? Never!'

Janet stared back at her mother. She was trying to imagine keeping the most significant thing that had ever happened to her, a secret. But she couldn't imagine it. What about trust? 'But…' she began to argue. 'But wouldn't he – '

'But, nothing. You act like you've never even done it before and go on from there. Men categorise women into two types, pure respectable girls or slappers. There's no middle ground. You hear me?'

Janet shook her head in desperation.

'Do You Hear Me?' Her mother intoned each word with menacing weight to drive home their force.

Janet bowed her head. 'Yes.'

Then a thought, long seeded in her mind, budded and burst open. Something she wanted to know. And maybe this rare heart-to-heart with her mother, as scarce as water in a desert in the Turner household, was the best chance she was ever going to get.

'Why do you call me hard?' she asked in a small voice.

Her mother looked up and a blush of red burned hot on her cheeks.

'Because...because you stick up for yourself, Janet. You were always so stubborn because of it. You never let me put your hair in ringlets because you hated them, you used to go and wet your hair to get them out, despite knowing you'd get a right telling off. And as for big ribbons, which were the fashion back then, you hated them too, and I caught you once about to cut off your pigtails to get rid of them. You know your own mind. You won't be pushed around. Not like your Auntie Vi who is too soft for her own good. Why, she lets the less well-off customers have more credit which affects the takings. Ted's always on at her about it. And she bends over backwards for people, and gets no thanks whatsoever! She's too sensitive and gets upset too easily. You've got to shift for yourself in this life, especially if you're a woman. You need to be tough, and if I've been too hard on you at times, it was only for your own good.'

Janet pondered this for a few moments and then a penny dropped. It tinkled to the floor and shimmied and shone. Her mother thought being hard was an asset, a strength of character in order to compete in the rigorous playing field of life as she saw it, rather than to be kind and caring about the local community, and sensitive of people's feelings the way her aunt was. And maybe her mother had a point. Look where her trust in Joe and her love for him had got her? What about the pain it had led to? Maybe it was better to shift for yourself after all.

And soon after this conversation, and unbeknown to Janet, her mother invited Frank Brewer over for afternoon tea one Sunday in early June. And in the parlour, with her mother, father and brother Norman present, and whilst her mother poured tea into her best Aynsley bluebell wood bone china set, a wedding present from her own parents, Janet first met

Frank.

He was thirty, eleven years her senior. Men his age were usually married by now, but when Mildred asked him why he wasn't, he told her he'd been concentrating on his career. Albert changed the subject while Janet studied Frank. He had a long face with even features, a strong Roman nose, pale blue eyes, and brown hair styled in a standard issue short back and sides, though his chin was a little weak. His voice was quite deep, lending it a commanding quality which she imagined came in handy for his police work and which she quite liked. He was lean, if a little lanky, but tall – he'd had to stoop when he entered the parlour. He was polite, asking Norman about his work at the printers and her father's work at the office, and he complimented Mildred on her Victoria sponge, to which she responded with a triumphantly beaming smile directed right at Janet.

When he suggested a walk around the park, seeing as it was a sunny afternoon, Janet complied, eager to get away from the scrutiny of her mother, though she was perturbed to see her father wearing his worried frown as he shook out his newspaper to read. Wearing her new burnt orange swing coat, Frank escorted her with a relaxed ease, and apologised for the contrived nature of the afternoon. She found him pleasant and attentive to her needs, as they selected a bench to sit on and chat. He liked going to dances, so he said, he enjoyed films, so he said, and as they got to know each other over the next few months, he did seem to enjoy these activities, and sometimes they'd make a foursome with his old school friend, Cliff Ward, who'd also joined the force, and his wife, Angie. He'd buy her orange roses, he'd tell her she was beautiful, he'd always paid for their dinners out, and they would only kiss, nothing else. He seemed the proverbial perfect gentleman and slowly won the approval of Albert too. What was there not to like? Meanwhile Janet continued with her secretarial course, and carefully considered what married life to Frank could be like, realising that they were now officially courting.

A few months later in October, when Janet was now twenty, Frank declared he loved her and popped the question on the same bench they'd sat on that first time in the park. Autumn leaves showered down like confetti on their bare heads, as they leaned into each other, and Janet had her answer ready. Her mother approved, but more importantly, her Auntie Vi seemed to like him and her father offered no concerns. She'd given up believing in true love, or so she told herself, and providing she could work part-time using her new secretarial skills after they were married, the answer was yes. Frank was delighted. That was no problem, he said, he wanted her to be happy. He'd apply for a posting to the Gloucestershire Constabulary and by being married they'd get a police house or housing allowance to buy their very own home. Was she happy to leave Bristol?

'It'll be exciting,' she replied, looking into his cool blue eyes which held her resolute gaze.

Then he kissed her with a passion she'd not felt from him before. And he smelled of the aftershave she was to become so familiar with in future years, Aqua Valva, with its faint minty top notes and floral base.

With Mildred, and Frank's mother, Betty, at the helm, Frank and Janet (as they were now so speedily referred to) set a wedding date for the following month. It would be a winter wedding and be held at St Peter's church, Bishopsworth, Janet's mother still clinging on to the fraying threads of her Catholic upbringing.

With a boulder rolling over the entrance to her past, like an impenetrable seal to an ancient crypt, she said 'I do' to Frank Brewer at the stone altar, on the 12th November 1955. There was to be no going back now, only forward into a brighter future.

When she looked at their wedding photographs a few years later, trying to understand the man she'd married, and *why* she'd married him, she was always first struck by what a good couple they made. And that's what everyone had told them too. She, in her tea-length, beautifully fitted bridal dress of white tulle, with lace sleeves and bodice, sculpted to a figure that revealed no signs of childbirth, holding her cascading bouquet of red roses and ferns. Frank, tall and distinguished in his double-breasted blue serge suit and matching cravat. Both smiling, surrounded by their suitably togged-out family, with Mildred's smile stretching the widest of all, which Janet felt to be a little frightening for its rarity. So there they were. The perfect couple, who moved into their perfect new home of 9 Willow Lane, Charlton Kings, Cheltenham, just in the nick of time for their first Christmas together.

But there were a few flaws beneath the surface of this shining perfection right from the start. Janet was surprised to find Frank's lovemaking a little rough and perfunctory, as if he was carrying out his duty at home exactly like he did his police work. She found his alternating eight hour shifts a little hard to adjust to as a housewife. Was he going to be home for his tea or not? And when he was home, and she asked him how his day had been, like any loving wife would do, he very soon became disinclined to talk about it. So their conversation could quickly dry up like a rain puddle on a hot day. And of course, when he was on day shifts, he naturally expected his dinner to be in the oven when he got home, proving irritable if it wasn't, quite perturbed in fact, wearing a twisted frown she came to recognize the meaning of without him having to say a single word. And this was a form of communication she didn't relish. He'd go to the King's Arms down the road at least twice a week where he would meet up with colleagues like Cliff Ward, who had also transferred to the area, but he didn't take her out very often. And much to her frustration, despite his earlier agreement, he kept putting her off the idea of working as a secretary, despite her qualification now going to waste.

'You don't need to work, love. You've got everything you need. What would they think at the station, anyway? Isn't looking after me good enough for you?'

But he kept telling her he loved her. He bought her little

presents. And he allowed her to furnish the house just the way she liked it, using her ideas from *Good Housekeeping* magazine. She even had a twin tub washing machine, the envy of her older women friends at the local WI, and even more to be jealous of, an actual telephone. The couple also made regular Sunday visits to family in Bristol, in their new green Ford Anglia, which Frank kept clean and polished for the occasion. So she spent her days doing housework, cooking, washing and sewing, while listening to radio programs like Housewives' Choice, Mrs Dale's Diary or Music While You Work, so she could keep up with the latest hits.

But this lacklustre 'perfect marriage' began to disintegrate with the arrival of their son, Scott. When Janet gave birth for the second time at Cheltenham General in the March of 1957, memories of Vivien bulldozed their way back into her consciousness out from the tomb where she had laid them to rest. And the pictures her father had taken, that she'd hidden in the old wartime suitcase she used for her Hope Lodge stay and had secreted in the attic of this new home, began to twitch in the dark, urging her to come, look, and remember. The pain of the contractions brought the pain of her loss. And when she used Johnsons Baby Powder on Scott after diaper changing and at bath time, the sweet smell brought back the feel of Vivien in her arms, and tears welled up inside her bursting to get out. She kept trying to slam shut the door of her memory, but it pressed hard from the other side until she couldn't hold it back any longer.

And one evening, when Scott was sleeping in his cot upstairs in the nursery, and when Frank was settled in his armchair with his favourite tipple of a whisky and soda, and she was sipping her Martini, she found herself telling him about Vivien. Her mother's warning was countered by her desire to have an honest marriage and by the hope that he would support her. Perhaps they could try to find Vivien together?

But when she saw his face change into a stiff mask as she

told him the full story, and saw his free hand on the arm of his chair curl into a fist, an icy finger of fear stroked down her spine. His mask soon slid away to dramatically reveal his changing states of mind by the contortions of his features, just like a slow motion close-up series of film frames. First wide-eyed astonishment, then a snarling of the lips and flaring nostrils, then finally blood-hot fury erupted, as he smashed down his glass on the coffee table, got to his feet, squared up to her and glared at her. His fists clenched and unclenched and his icy blue eyes hooked into hers like claws.

'You slut,' he said. 'You fucking slut.'

She teetered backwards away from him, ripples of fear charging through her like electric shocks. She'd never heard him sound like this before. He'd never sworn at her before. She'd made a mistake. Oh God, she'd made such a mistake! What was he going to do? How could she explain…

His face was inches away from hers now, bearing down on her with his bulk, where he'd backed her up against the living room wall.

'How do I know *this* baby is mine?' He stabbed his thumb upwards.

Janet felt some fighting spirit spark in her veins. How dare he? she thought. How bloody dare he? 'Of course he's yours!' she insisted. 'The other time was just the once. For goodness' sake, Frank, there's been no one else. How could there be? We made wedding vows.'

He poked his index finger right at her. 'Don't you take that tone with me! And don't talk to me about wedding vows, while all the while you were damaged goods.'

Janet squeezed away from him and backed into the centre of the room, the phrase *damaged goods* ringing in her ears.

'But Frank, I thought you'd understand. It was a silly mistake! I was very young!'

When she saw his eyes glinting at her in the lamplight, as mean and menacing as a mad wolf's, her mouth went dry. Who was this man she'd married?

Then he came at her. She saw the raised fist as he lunged

forward, and she managed to snap her head to the left. His fist smashed into the right side of her face. The shooting pain crashed through her head like a thunderbolt and her legs caught the edge of the coffee table and she collapsed to the floor like a bag of bones, whilst wave after wave of stinging heat flared in her cheek. She curled up into herself, grateful that at least he hadn't broken her nose, while he stood over her, shouting, raining down expletives and recriminations upon her like stones to batter her. Any second she expected him to kick her around the room with his shiny police boots. Muffling a hysterical giggle, that caught her unawares, she wished she'd reminded him to change into his slippers.

As she lay there waiting, for what she didn't know, he snatched his jacket off the peg by the door and stamped out of the house. When he slammed the door behind him and the shuddering through the house settled, she breathed out long and slow, not realising she'd been holding onto her breath the whole time. Gingerly getting to her feet, she went upstairs to the bathroom to examine her face. The whole right side was swelling up already and rosy pink. In the days to come the bruising was to give quite a show – from purple to green, to yellow, to brown, taking two whole weeks to fade altogether. Two whole weeks to take away the stain of her sin and the stain of her marriage.

When he got back two hours later, she was sitting on the sofa with a cup of coffee, her face throbbing, but resolved to show some strength of will, to draw on some of that hardness her mother so admired. Maybe she was her mother's daughter after all? she wondered, with a grimace.
He sank into his armchair and sighed. Then he lit up one of his Camels, inhaled deeply and blew the smoke up towards the ceiling where it hung there like a foul-smelling shroud covering their marriage, while he proceeded to tell her how it was going to be.

They'd been getting along pretty well. He hadn't really

wanted to get married, that's why he'd left it quite late, but she was a good wife, with a bit of spirit about her, not like his mother, and it suited the force that he was married. Divorce was certainly out of the question, far too much of a stigma there, so he'd forgive her past as best he could.

Very big of you, thought Janet, as she forced herself to meet his gaze.

But under no circumstances, he continued, was she ever to try finding her daughter. She didn't stand a cat in hell's chance anyway, because such records just couldn't be accessed. Her daughter was better off where she was, and there was no point in raking up the past. He did concede he was the father of Scott, the likeness was there. But if she ever tried to leave the marriage, wanted a divorce, or thought of searching for her daughter in the years to come, he'd make sure she didn't get to keep Scott. He had contacts, lots of them, and he'd make sure she was declared an unfit mother and never get custody. Such were his terms.

Then he tried to smile at her. And the twisted sneer he produced was the birth of that rictus smile of his. The one she was to see just before he slapped her over the face to make his point in the subsequent years of their marriage – knowing all too well that slapping wouldn't show. Naturally, he'd get a bit too carried away now and again, and he'd have to take her to the hospital with a lie, while he waited in the car outside.

But in the following months, Janet decided she had no choice but to accept his terms – the terms of a man she no longer recognised, and who had obviously married her as a matter of convenience. Because after feeling beaten, mentally and physically, she came to love Scott as much as she'd loved Vivien for that very short time. And despite being trapped in a loveless marriage without the job she'd been promised, her son became the centre of her life and she wasn't going to lose him. If that meant staying with Frank, then so be it. Frank controlled the finances, giving her a weekly allowance for housekeeping, but she got to receive the family allowance and that gave her a tiny bit of freedom. And she got more free time than some wives did because of Frank's variable shifts. So with Scott tucked in his pram, she'd walk into town and treat herself to a milkshake or a coffee. Sometimes it was with friends she'd made at the local mother and toddler group, or other times it was by herself, where she'd watch the straggles and streams of pedestrians at a table by a window, a window that reflected her back to herself, which she found comforting, and which at the same time was a portal into other peoples lives.

But the strange thing was that contact with her family began to trickle to a bare minimum. She did phone up her Auntie Vi for a chat, and was delighted to hear that her aunt was with child, but dismayed to hear that she and Ted were moving to Bournemouth in a few months to set up shop there, and then retire, while Ted's younger brother was taking over the Bristol premises.

'But naturally, I'll write, Janet. I'll let you know what's happening,' said Auntie Vi.

But she only received a couple of letters, with no useful forwarding address or telephone number, as they were renting for a while, and then the letters ceased altogether. At first she was just puzzled, and asked Frank whether he'd seen any letters from her aunt. He said he hadn't, so she soon felt abandoned to her fate by the aunt who had loved her most dearly, but who now most likely had her hands full with a baby of her own. She'd wanted to confide in her, but how could she have talked about it over the phone anyway?

By the time she managed to speak to her mother and father on the phone, she had no such quivering qualms. She was desperate for someone to know what she was going through. It seemed important in case anything happened to her. Her parents didn't have a phone so she had to arrange to speak to them through their next door neighbour's line, whose number she had for emergencies. She told them both in turn what had happened.

'What did I tell you?' her mother screeched. 'I told you,

didn't I? I warned you! And just trust *him* not to be the forgiving type, it's all about appearances with *him*.'

Janet cringed at the irony here.

Then she talked to her father.

'Oh, Janie, love,' her father said, when she repeated it all to him, 'I never did quite take to him, but I couldn't put my finger on what it was. I'm so sorry, I feel I've let you down...so bad.' She could hear his choking sobs as Mildred grabbed the phone back off him.

'You'll be fine,' she said. 'You hear me? You'll make it work if you're any daughter of mine.'

Janet was silent.

'Do you hear me?'

Yes, Mum. I'll be fine,' she replied and bowed her head. She bit her lip hard and tasted blood on her tongue. If only she'd listened the first time.

It was when she was trying to be fine that she found herself gathering all the pearls of wisdom she remembered people saying at some point or other in response to life's adversities. She strung them together into a sermonic necklace of solace and protection to wear right next to her skin like a rosary: life's a bitch and then you die, no use asking why, life is tough, just one dammed thing after another, the truth will out, you reap what you sow, what goes around comes around, God helps those who help themselves...and so on...

It also soon became apparent that Frank was no longer inclined to make family visits to Bristol. He was sick of the relationship between his mother and father, he told her, his father was a bully, who'd liked giving his sons a licking once too often as well as attacking his mother, but she was weak and silly and just took it. He and Janet were best off out of it. They had their own family now. And as for visiting *her* family, so Scott could get to know his grandparents, well he had opinions here too.

'You father's too soft. He lets your mother we ar the

trousers. What sort of example is that to set the boy?'

Janet quailed at his language and the paradoxical nature of his opinions didn't escape her. Not liking his father because he was a bully? And now he'd turned into one himself? And just how was he planning to bring up Scott? In the same way? Well that would be over her dead body!

But after some consideration, she didn't relish the idea of visits either. She couldn't stand Frank's father, Bill, who certainly was a thick brute of a man, always hitching up his leather belt because his beer belly kept pushing it back down. And Betty Brewer fluttered and flapped around her kitchen like a frightened starling trapped in an attic, unable to settle for one minute in case she was pounced upon by Bill for some little misdemeanour. And as for her own parents, she knew they'd watch every move Frank made from now on. And he was sharp. He'd get wind of her having told them about him – him and his fists, him and his chillingly cold 'conditions', and it would only be the worse for her, and by proxy, worse for Scott.

Her last sight of her family was at her father's funeral in 1968, which Frank conceded they must attend. They left Scott with Cliff Ward's wife, Angie, and Frank drove Janet to Bristol in stony silence. Janet was numb with shock that her beloved father had passed away. He'd only been 51 years of age and she could barely get her head around it. An embolism they said, must have been a family history of it. She stood with her mother during the service, who let Janet hold her limp hand. Mildred seemed so wilted and broken, with a confused look in her eyes, and Janet was unable to get much of a word out of her, not even later at the tea at home in Marguerite Road. Her brother, Norman, wasn't able to attend, because he'd just recently emigrated with his wife to New England in America to work in the textile industry there, and he didn't really want to take any time off so soon. Naturally, Mildred understood.

Auntie Vi and Uncle Ted were the only truly friendly faces there for Janet, having driven from their new home in

Bournemouth. Their daughter, Sarah, was now around ten years of age, but they'd left her with Auntie Florrie in Camelford en route. On their return journey, Mildred was going to accompany them to stay with Florrie in the family home, and maybe do her millinery, because she said there was nothing to keep her in Bristol any longer. Much to Janet's frustration, it had been impossible to have a private conversation with her aunt, who'd so obviously been wanting one, because Frank stuck to Janet's side like a prison officer with his ward out on parole for the day. Her aunt managed to hand her a piece of paper with her new Bournemouth address on, with Frank interrogating Violet about what it was she was passing to Janet, but it had gone missing later on. So, all Janet could feel in the end was a gnawing ache in her heart for her father and a cognisance of the fact that everyone had new lives to get on with. The wheels always kept turning. And finally, all she wanted was to get back to Cheltenham, to her son.

Her lovely son, Scott, who she'd tried to protect from Frank's bitterness and prevent him being a witness to his father's temper and violence, which became worse over the years the longer he stayed in the force, gathering resentments and frustrations like a snowball rolling down hill, getting heavier and heavier, harder and harder. No wonder he got angina with all that stress inside him.

Until finally, after Frank had retired, he'd simply become unbearable, and he made the mistake of trying to control Janet just one time too many, saying she'd been seen by one of his golf crony's wives in Masons, who was *so surprised* Frank Brewer's wife needed to work. His point being, yet again, that she showed him up by her working. As if she'd give up the job she had fought so hard for, and that he should have let her have years ago. So, with Scott all grown up and safely out of the way, she decided, in that moment of his temper, to stand her ground. She'd fantasized of several ways over the years to avenge herself upon him, from the bloodily intimate to the more classically detached, yet here was a real opportunity that she just couldn't miss. And she had wanted him to die, so she had done what she could to help it along in a situation which she ironically had never fantasized about.

And now…it was out in the open. She'd told Marian and Ann. And Scott – he'd have to be told. And that frightened her more than anything. Blistering tears swelled up in her again and slid down her mascara-sooted cheeks.

Ann put an arm around her and Janet welcomed it. They sat slumped on the sofa together, staring into the grey ashes of the fireplace in the early hours of the morning, with the dawn of a Sunday in late November 1990 seeming so far away.

Chapter 15

A burst of morning sunlight thrust through the gap in the lined curtains of Ann's spare room, waking Janet with a red glare behind her shut eyelids. The light filtered through the fine network of capillary vessels there and for a moment she was able to enjoy the sensation. Like she had as a child when she had Saturday to stretch out in bed and have that one weekly lie in.

But when she opened her eyes wider and slowly groped her way to the surface of consciousness, she recognised the distinct country house features of Ann's spare room in her tiny Winchcombe bungalow. It was the epitome of a designer's mood board come to life, incorporating a heavenly coordination of Dorma's Harewood bedding design, with its delicate floral sprays and scrolls in cool pastel tints with lace trim on the pillows and cushions, with coordinating fringed lampshades, and a pale pink carpet and stencilled white furniture. Almost all of it had been bought by Ann from Masons during sale periods over the years, with strategic use of her store card and some determined sewing and painting skills to bring the boudoir into being.

But there was nothing heavenly about it for Janet. Sweet chintzes and Pollyanna paint effects could do nothing for her when she realised where she was. And when she remembered the day and night before, that piano she had been expecting crashed right down on her, and she doubled up under the weight of it, folding her body into a tight ball, with her arms clutched around her, while burying her face into pink roses that had no smell. And as the remembering pinned her to the bed, her nerve endings jangled like unleashed piano wires, vibrating such flashes of feeling in hellish randomness with no control – aversion, disgust, fear, guilt, and shame, with old feelings of hate, anger, regret and confusion marching in. All she could do was lie there and feel and wait and hope, hope for them to settle themselves into some order so she could take control, like she always did. But this time, all was chaos. She moaned and squeezed herself tighter into her ball. She lay like this, wanting to be swallowed up by the bed and disposed of in a cocoon of Dorma Harewood, never to see the light of day again.

But after a spell, and she had no idea how long because she was purposefully not looking at the ticking clock on the bedside table, which would drag her further into the harsh brightness of reality, she heard sounds from the next room. A delicate cough, the thud of a wardrobe door closing, the shuffle of slippered feet into the bathroom. Ann was getting up and Ann now knew everything. And then it hit Janet, the big question, the biggest of her whole life. What was she going to do now?

Dragging herself out of her cocoon, she shivered and groped for Ann's spare dressing gown on the back of the door. Belting it around her, she padded to the bathroom. When she looked into the cabinet mirror she saw a Janet she didn't recognise. A pale drawn face, tightened into knots and lines of worry, with puffy eyes full of fear. Where was her usual self? That composed, sure, and determined Janet she'd lived with and cultivated for so long, to beat the world at its whimsical games of destruction and sorrow, to survive and succeed instead? She didn't know who or what she was looking at now and it scared her. But she sighed, pressed her lips together, and headed into the kitchen.

Ann sat at a pine table by the window overlooking her back garden, which was soaking up some rare November sunshine like a special treat, with a glittering gauze of dewdrops catching colours of the rainbow stretched across the lawn. She was still in her pyjamas and dressing gown, for which Janet was thankful because getting dressed felt like far too much of a responsibility-shouldering and reality-facing act right now and she didn't want to be alone in her shabby dilapidation. But the kitchen clock read half ten, and snatching a glance at it dragged Janet into her present predicament like a criminal being taken into custody – despite the dressing gown. And there was *the* question stamping around in her head, making her shudder but demanding her attention. *What am I going to do now?*

A pot of tea and toast were waiting for her, so she poured herself a cup. That, she could at least manage to do.

'How are you feeling?' Ann asked her tenderly.

She reached for Janet's hand.

Janet looked at her. Ann's silver hair was standing on end, probably the result of a hasty backcombing to bring it back to waking life from being flattened in sleep. But the effect looked comical, like someone in a horror film having finally seen the ghost they were searching for, but regretted the meeting for its sheer terror. It would normally have looked comical to Janet, but she was registering instead, the kindness in Ann's eyes. Real caring concern. And in that moment she realised for the very first time that Ann was a good friend. Perhaps her only friend. Someone she had taken for granted. Someone she had used for her own ends.

Janet pulled her hand away from Ann's. 'Why do you care about me? I can be hard and ruthless, only after what I want. I can be downright bitchy. I don't deserve your caring.'

Ann took hold of her hand again and clutched it tightly. 'Yes, you're hard. But you're also determined, assertive, capable, and very reliable. And you're ambitious. I admire you for it. I always have, since you first started working at Masons. I was your typical housewife with dreams I let go of and what have I got to show for it? Children who are too busy getting on with their own lives to visit very often. I wish I'd been more like you.'

Janet's eyebrows shot up and her mouth dropped open.

'Yes, I mean it. And now I know what you've been through, it all makes a lot of sense.'

'Does it?'

Ann nodded. 'And now we have to figure out what to do

– figure it out together.'

'You mean, you're going to help me?'

'Try stopping me.'

Janet squeezed Ann's hand in return and managed a smile. Tears welled up in her again and gratitude and relief warmed up the cold dread wrapped around her heart. She wasn't going to have to do it alone.

After two hours of discussion, debate and decision-making between the two women over the kitchen table, and after draining the dregs of numerous cups of coffee, Janet found herself driving to 9 Willow Lane in Charlton Kings with Ann alongside her. The sunshine had done its short shift for the day and rain now spattered on the windscreen, with Janet's car wipers beating back and forth trying to clear her vision. She was trying to get a clear vision of herself too – of what she was going to do. But Ann had told her to take one small step at a time. They had made a plan, they would stick to the plan, all that mattered was working with the present, in the present moment. And this was enough for Janet. It was all her husked-out self could manage.

Above them the sky was iron grey with twisted rags of cloud hanging on the horizon. Ann was going to stay with Janet for a couple of weeks, no arguments, Ann said, and there was a packed suitcase in the boot to prove her intention. Janet had phoned Scott for him to come over later on that afternoon. She was going to tell him everything. That, at least, was crystal clear unlike the rest of her life, which seemed to have succumbed to a deadly poison spreading through it like clouds of ink in water.

As Janet trudged up the drive with Ann, carrying her suitcase, she spotted Winnie Parsons, her neighbour from the adjoining house at number 7, sneaking a peak through the gap in her nets, her nose sharpened like a pencil for reporting.

Tutting as she turned her key in the clock, she swung open the door to a warm house. But the warmth was all she could find welcoming about it. Somehow it all looked different, almost tawdry, yet she knew it was really a 'little palace' because Scott was always telling her. The smell was the same; the vanilla room freshener she'd used over the years had breathed its scent into the fabric of the building and all its furnishings. But it was mostly the living room she didn't like, the floral three piece suite, the marble fireplace, the Chinese rug, the coffee table, and she realised that after having confessed about Frank's death, it now looked like the scene of a crime – *her* crime.

While Ann unpacked her case in the spare room overlooking the garden and fields at the back, Janet put the kettle on, then examined Thomas's feeding bowls. One was all licked clean, the other had just a few nibbles remaining. She went to the bottom of the stairs and called for him, but there was no answering patter of paws. Ann called down to say he wasn't upstairs.

Janet frowned. She snatched an anorak off the peg on the back of the kitchen door and hurried outside, yanking on the coat.

'Thomas!' she called out, in her usual high shrilled tone.

No response. No slinking feline form emerging from shelter under a bedraggled shrub. No sudden twitching of autumn leaves as Thomas headed down the garden path for home.

She made her way to the end of the garden by the rose bed, scanning the edge of the field just beyond the wire fence, where the long grass hid voles and shrews and other prey for cats' passions and pastimes. 'Thomas! Where are you?'

From behind her came a response, but not one she welcomed.

'He came into mine for a little while last night.'

Janet spun around to see *just a quick chat* Winnie, huddled in a bright yellow Mackintosh with the hood up, as hard and shiny as a fisherman dressed for stormy weather at sea. She stood close by the fence which divided her garden from

Janet's, her eyes drawn into slits to stop the rain getting in. She was a short woman, well under five feet, with bowed legs. And instead of her usual clumpy high heels, she was wearing black wellington boots which were sinking into the boggy lawn. And right now she reminded Janet of the meat cleaver-wielding dwarf in the film *Don't Look Now*. All that stricken grief and throat slitting, then a funeral boat cortège sliding through a sludgy winter canal in Venice. But she gave herself a mental shake to bring herself back into the present.

'Hello, Winnie. How was he?' she asked, thinking what a traitor Thomas was, decamping to next door when she'd only been gone for one night.

'Fine, he seemed fine. Where were you? It's not like *you* to spend the night away.'

Janet stepped back, puzzled for a moment. Winnie Parsons had lived next door for all of Janet's married life with Frank. Winnie and her husband, Charles, had welcomed them when they first moved into Willow Lane in December 1955. An older more experienced couple, the Parsons had known the Cheltenham area well, which had been a godsend for Janet, and she'd particularly been fond of Charles for his gentle manners and his willingness to do occasional jobs for her around the house, which Frank disdained to do because he didn't like getting his hands dirty. She'd never known what to make of Winnie, but she'd brought cakes and scones and the occasional casserole around for the Brewer household, which had been received by Janet with heavy-hearted acceptance over the years, because she just couldn't get her to stop.

Winnie had been a widow for ten years now, Charles having died from lung cancer. After his death, Winnie's compulsion to avail herself by whatever means, of neighbourly knowledge and the minutiae of other people's private lives, had appeared to be her very own solution to the eternal question of how to live a meaningful life. Well, Winnie had it sorted. Who needed existential philosophers to help work it out? And here she was honing in, with her nose on the scent, tracking the fact that something out of the ordinary must have happened in Janet's life to explain her staying away from home for one single night. And of course she was right. Just play it straight, Janet told herself, but be careful.

'I stayed the night at a friend's. Now she's visiting me for a while.'

'Oh, so who's that, then?'

'A friend of mine from work,' Janet snapped, turning her gaze back to the misted murk of the field, and shielding her eyes from the spitting rain.

'But you are alright, aren't you?' Winnie shuffled even closer to the fence, peering at Janet from inside her hood, with wrinkled lines of enquiry drawn in her wizened face and with eyes that glittered like nailheads.

Janet turned to face her, feeling the hackles rising on the nape of her neck. Something was very wrong here.

'Of course, I'm alright. Why wouldn't I be?'

'Just if you need to talk, I'm only next door.'

Then Janet lost her cool. She didn't have time for this. Didn't she have enough on her plate? She had to get rid of Winnie and her strange insinuations.

'What is it, Winnie? What are you getting at?'

Winnie lowered her voice and leaned towards Janet over the fence, her eyes taking on a twinkle. 'I saw what you did, you know.'

Janet's breath caught in her throat. Her hand fluttered to her mouth. She tried to swallow, to say something, but all she could do was stare back at Winnie, while she stood there taking root, fears flashing through her body in hot and cold flushes and down into the ground. She couldn't move.

'It's okay, I'm not going to tell anyone, dear. You needn't worry about that. That husband of yours was a right bastard. He had it coming. Pity, never mind.'

All Janet could do was open her mouth to try to say something, but that gave Winnie her cue to deliver more shocking facts. And she'd only just begun.

'That Frank of yours. All he cared about were his roses. Didn't take care when he was parking that blasted car of his, running over my marigolds planted out front. He was always rude too, what a mouth on him, he had. And after he retired. Well! Do you know he once told me I was a nosy cow and to mind my own bloody business. Those were his words! And he came home drunk a few times from the pub, didn't he? I couldn't stand the man. So no wonder you did what you did. You put up with him for years. Why shouldn't you have a life of your own now?'

Janet found her voice. She tried to keep it steady. 'Frank died of a heart attack, Winnie. You know that. You were there when the ambulance came. What is it you think I did exactly?'

'I saw you just standing there. Doing nothing. I was on my way around that day with some lamb stew I thought you might like. But then I heard the shouting and because the lights were on in the living room and the curtains were open, I could see through the nets. I saw you kick the pills away from him. And that was all you had to do, wasn't it? So no need to worry, you didn't have to lay a finger on him.'

Janet gasped and gaped at Winnie, while Winnie smiled broadly back at her.

'I'm telling you, it's okay! To tell you the truth I tried a few times to get rid of Charles without having to lay a finger on him. I had him going on the roof on a windy day to fix some loose tiles. But he didn't fall off the roof or the ladder, which I fiddled with by putting the foot of it at more of an angle while he was up there. I tried to poison him with some weed killer in his tomato soup, but he just got the runs. I even tried to smother him with a pillow when he was snoring, but he soon woke up, and I had to pretend I was having a nightmare. And there were a few other things I tried, but that man was indestructible. Oh well, in the end nature took him.'

'Why?' Janet croaked.

'Cancer, you know that.'

'No why…why did you want to – '

'Why did I want him gone?'

Janet nodded mutely, now dumb with disbelief at what was unfolding. Like she was watching a tabloid newspaper in her mind's eye, turning its own pages to publically shock with scandal after scandal, horror after horror, taking place over the years in 7 Willow Lane, to feed the voyeurs with salacious headlines and scurrilous details.

Just then Ann called down the garden to Janet from the back door. 'Are you coming in soon? The kettle's on.'

Janet managed to wave at her. 'In a minute,' she shouted back.

'Nice lady, looks like,' Winnie said. 'Now, as for why Charles had to go, well it was the garden gnomes. When I married him, he wasn't fussed about them. Disgusting evil little things, they are. But when his father died he brought his dad's collection home. A bequest, apparently. All of them hand-painted in lurid colours. And I couldn't stop him after that. He built a rockery for them and got more when they came back into fashion in the seventies – remember? The whole of the back garden was littered with the nasty little buggers.'

Janet remembered. Charles had allowed Scott to play with them when he was little, and she and the teenage Scott had frequently surveyed the growing population from the back bedroom. Frank had said that Charles was 'off his tiny rocker.' But whenever Janet went to the garden shed at night in winter with her torch, to fetch some sticks for the coal fire, the beam would flash on a maniacal grin on the other side of the fence, or eyebrows hitched high over eyes wide open in mock surprise, and fleshy faces with bulbous red noses and cheeks, as if their owners had partaken of a few too many 'wee drams' during their regular flits to fairyland. She could almost hear the raucous laughter. They had been positively spooky.

She looked at Winnie. 'So that's why you got rid of them all after he died? You hated them that much?'

'God, yes. I swear he thought more of them than me!' Then she hesitated. 'I have just one left though. Charles's favourite. A gardener gnome with his shovel.' She pointed to the back door where Janet could just make out the figure of a white-bearded cheeky chappie wearing a pointed hat. 'That's my Charles,' she said.

Janet gasped. 'What do you mean?'

'I put Charles's ashes in there – it seems fitting somehow, don't you think?'

Janet stared hard at Winnie. She was totally serious and Janet shuddered.

'So no worries about your Frank. Us widows have to stick together.'

Janet decided she had to tackle Winnie further right now and get it over with. 'Why are you telling me what you think you saw now? Why not tell me earlier?'

'Because I can tell something's happened. You've lived next door to me for over thirty years! Something's upset your routine, so something's upset you. What else could it be? You've been getting on grand this year, haven't you?'

'Yes…yes, I have…' Janet stammered.

'So don't you think of doing anything stupid like confessing, you hear me? I was the only witness and I'm staying stumm.'

Winnie drew her finger over her closed lips which made Janet recoil. Then she lifted her wellies one by one, sucking them out of the lawn and waddled to her back door. And watching her, Janet was struck by the realisation that gnomes were always male. Was there even such a thing as a lady garden gnome? Well, she reflected, if there wasn't, then Winnie would make a fine model.

After her conversation with Winnie, with Thomas hurled to the back of her mind for the present, she warmed herself in the living room with Ann and a cup of tea. Ann's eyes grew as round as paperweights while Janet told her everything Winnie had said.

'I feel as if I'm in some sick nightmare,' moaned Janet, sitting on the edge of the sofa with Ann, and brushing snaggles of wet hair away from her face.

Ann shook her head. 'It's so unbelievable! I don't know what to say or think, except now there's technically a witness, I suppose. We could do without that!'

'I know!' Janet wailed. Then she cast her eyes around the room, focusing first on Frank's chair, then the coffee table and the fireplace. She dropped her gaze to the floor, to the edge of the rug by her feet.

She jumped up. 'I've got to change this room around.'

'What?'

'Right now. I can't stand this arrangement any longer.'

'Why?' Ann stared at Janet pacing around the room.

'It reminds me too much of that day. I can't stand it like this anymore!'

'No, Janet. Leave it for now. Talk to Scott first! He won't be long. Talk to him first and you can show him what happened if you leave the room alone.'

Janet stopped pacing. Her knees felt weak and she sank back into the sofa and clutched her head in her hands, rocking herself backwards and forwards. 'I don't know if I can go through with this!'

Ann sat beside her and took Janet's hands in her own. 'You can. You have to. It'll be alright.'

Janet looked at Ann, feeling like a little girl seeking reassurance from her mother for something awful she'd done or was about to do. Something so shameful, her throat felt swollen and thick with it. And tears came once more, whilst Winnie's shrunken face peered right into her mind's eye, and a garden gnome with his spade grinned at her with grotesque empathy.

Chapter 16

When Scott arrived at around three o'clock that Sunday afternoon, coming alone as instructed, he gaped when he saw Janet's red and puffy face greeting him at the front door. 'What's happened?' he asked, taking hold of her arm and scrutinizing her.

'I'm so sorry,' she said in a small voice, barely able to meet the gaze of her beloved son.

Retrieving a soggy tissue from the inside of her pullover sleeve, she blew her nose, then wiped her eyes with the back of her hands. Turning to Ann, she introduced her to Scott, who said he'd seen Ann a few times on the shop floor of Masons, but he greeted her warmly and shook her hand. Then Janet asked Scott to please sit down, she had something to tell him. Many things to tell him, actually, and she hoped he would bear with her.

He lowered himself uneasily into his mother's fireside chair and looked hard at both Janet and Ann perched on the edge of the sofa, their legs crossed tightly at the ankles, as if primed for a formal interview.

But despite her extreme apprehensions only moments before, Janet found the words came easily. They wanted to come out of her like a suppurating infection held in her body for too long, pus, seeping its way out, drop by drop, to alleviate the pain she'd had to hold within herself for far too long. And the infection of Frank had felt like a lifetime's affliction.

As she talked, Ann gave prompts here and there to help Scott understand.

Janet began with Frank's death, Scott's very own father's death. This was the worst aspect of all for Scott, and it had to come first. Scott's eyes grew wide as he listened and they settled into a hard stare, which Janet recognised for what it was – acute disbelief and shock. He watched her demonstrate by the fireplace and coffee table what had happened that day, moment by moment, while he sat there in his mother's chair, with this arms and legs loosely arranged like a beached and restless starfish, uncertain of which direction to take next.

When she came to describing Frank's actual heart attack and her making sure he couldn't take one of his glyceryl trinitrate pills, Scott burst through his silence.

'Jesus, Mum, that's serious! What were you thinking?'

'Wait for the rest, Scott…there are things you don't know yet,' Ann said.

Scott crumpled his brow and slumped back in his chair, drumming his fingers on one of the arms while Janet continued the telling, and when she got to the why of it, Scott interjected again.

'He was still doing that bullying stuff? I thought he'd eased off after retiring.'

'It was more verbal than physical by then.'

Janet suddenly realised the implications in what she'd just said. It was a little too soon…she'd got things in the wrong order.

Scott stared fixedly at her. 'You mean he used to *hit* you?' His voice rose higher. 'That he physically…he physically abused you?' His face was blanched and bloodless in the glare of the table lamp by his side.

She sighed. There was no going back now.

'Yes, ever since we were married. You never noticed anything? I tried hard to protect you from knowing. But you did used to have trouble sleeping when you were at primary school. I wondered if you'd picked up on it.'

Scott scratched his cheek and drummed his fingers faster on the arm of the chair. He shook his head. 'I don't think I remember anything like that. You two never seemed happy. A lot of tense atmospheres, I got that much. And I used to hear you arguing. So when you seemed very quiet, I thought it was to do with the arguing, that's all…and I thought you could handle him, Mum. And you always said things were fine. He certainly had a temper. I remember the time he smashed up the kitchen. I must have been around ten then.'

Janet flinched. She remembered too. Accusations of her being 'useless' over the burnt crust of a pie, with too many Johnnie Walkers fermenting in his gut and stirring up his temper.

'And after he retired, Thomas seemed to irritate him more. I saw him kick him once.'

More than once, Janet thought. But Thomas had toughed it out too.

Janet had brought Thomas home twelve years ago after seeing his picture in the local post office, a tabby kitten needing a good home. She'd wanted some company in the house after Scott had left home, and she'd always related to cats for being able to take care of themselves. As a girl, one of her favourite Just So stories had been about the cat who walked by himself and she'd memorized the lines, 'I am not a friend, and I am not a servant. I am the Cat who walks by himself'. She'd loved that. So she'd brought her very own cat home as a cute and cuddly fait accompli to serve as an independent companion. This was a risky strategy where Frank was concerned, but he was going through a more mellow phase at the time and enjoying his new weekend golfing with his cronies. He'd only muttered 'Make sure he doesn't get under my feet.' And Thomas had quickly learned not to.

Right now, there was a heavy silence in the room, made more oppressively cloistered by the darkening sky outside pushing against the window, and the low glow of Janet's table lamps striving to penetrate the gloom. The only sound was the tick-tocking of the mantelpiece carriage clock, persuading, with its inexorable rhythm that nothing could hold back time.

Ann cleared her throat. 'So your mother had provocation going on for years, and if she snapped in the end, you can hardly blame her.' She looked at Scott beseechingly.

Scott shook his head. 'I can see that. Of course I can. But surely there must have been someone who could help? Why didn't you tell anyone, Mum? What about your family?'

Janet explained this was the sixties they were talking about. There was nothing back then. No refuges, no help for victims, no divorces. Married women had to put up with it, learn to live with it. Marriage was for life. Looking back now, she could hardly believe this was how it was, but it was true.

And she told Scott about Frank's threats to use his policeman's clout to make sure that if she left him, she wouldn't be able to take Scott with her. Her family knew, at least her mother and father did, and probably her aunt too. They were sorry of course, but they were of the same mind – there was nothing she could do, and there was nothing *they* could do. And she'd seen less and less of them after that. It seemed easier all round. There were very few letters that she knew of, just some birthday and Christmas cards, but Frank had always made a point of getting the post in the morning with that air he had of being master of the house, so she wouldn't have put it past him to vet or destroy any family letters sent to her. And before she knew it her father had passed on with his embolism and her mother had gone to live in Camelford with her aunt Florrie, while she concentrated on bringing up Scott. She did find out from Florrie that her mother had a major stroke when she was just 64 and had to go into a care home when Florrie felt she couldn't cope any longer. Janet had written to them a few times over the years, with progress reports and pictures of Scott, Susan, and baby Daniel, but she'd had no replies that she knew about. Mildred had died in 1988 at the age of 71. *That* letter did get through. But Janet had been unable to attend the funeral because she'd had a really bad dose of flu at the time. So, family had become estranged over many years which seemed to keep Frank happy, but for which she felt partially responsible.

Time ticked on in the present as Janet explained to Scott

what married life had been like with Frank. She wanted him to know everything now that she'd opened her padlocked strong box, rusting and creaking at the hinges, to pull out the tattered and torn memories she'd sealed up like old clothes over the years, one after the other after the other, out for an airing at last.

He got up to examine the scar on her left cheek, after she'd told him what had really caused it – not falling over and cutting her cheek on gravel as she'd always maintained when he'd asked as a boy – but Frank's cygnet ring. The one she'd ended up pawning. The scar was to be seen in a new light, that was important to her now, because she needed Scott to see the only physical evidence that remained. She needed him to believe her. Scott kept shaking his head, Ann kept darting glances at them both, and Janet kept twisting her hands in her lap.

And right now, there was something itching inside her that she just had to know about, now that all the rest was coming out of the shadows and into the light.

'Did you love your father, Scott? I need to know.' Her voice broke as she said the words that sounded like some sick oxymoron – love and Frank just didn't go together.

Scott ran his hand through his hair, leaving it sticking up in spikes. 'Well, he wasn't much of a father, no. He didn't exactly show affection, and he wasn't around much with the shifts that he did. I remember him taking me fishing sometimes when I was little, and we had some walks around Pittville Park or up Cleeve Hill a few times. That was okay, but when I got older it was obvious I wasn't the kind of son he wanted. He used to think I was soft, as he put it. And when I stuck up for you when you weren't around, after he'd been over-bearing, he'd call me a 'mummy's boy.'

'Yes, that sounds about right,' Janet said wearily.

'One day,' Scott continued, 'I remember I was taking your part when you were at the shops. I can't remember what it was about, except I said he should stop treating you like a dogsbody, and he tried to throw a punch at me…but I caught hold of his arm and stopped him. By then I was just as strong as he was, so he backed down after that. You should have seen the twisted look on his face.'

Janet smiled for a second, a feeling of relief breaking through at Frank not having got his way for once.

'And when I told him I was going to study architecture at Uni, he called it a namby pamby job and said I was no son of his.' Scott paused and looked at Janet. 'To be honest Mum, I couldn't stand him. I used to wonder why in God's name you'd ever married him. And when he died…well, I was glad you were free.'

Janet stared hard at him. 'Really?' Could it be true, she wondered. And if so, how was it she hadn't known?

Scott got out of his chair, moved the coffee table aside, and kneeled down on the Chinese rug before his mother, taking hold of her hands in his. 'Yes, really, Mum. So, no, I didn't love him. He didn't earn it like you did. You were the one who brought me up, and considering the circumstances, you did a good job.'

Ann got to her feet. 'Time for a cup of tea, I think.'

Janet barely heard her, as she examined Scott's earnest face.

'But why didn't you say anything?'

'Like what? That I couldn't stand my own father?'

'Yes, that.'

'What good would it have done you or me? I just wish you'd been able to leave him.'

Janet shook her head.

'I know,' he said.

'I'm so sorry.'

'I know. It doesn't matter now.'

Then he took Janet in his arms and gave her a hug, the kind of hug she only allowed from him when he instinctively knew she needed one. These hugs were scattered over the years behind them like precious jewels, all the more valuable for their rarity. But they both knew their worth and she squeezed him back in return.

Then something else occurred to Janet. Something she really wanted an answer to.

She broke out of the hug. 'I'm so sorry, Scott, but I need to know. Did you really marry Susan for love?'

Scott frowned as he straightened up and returned to his chair.

He sighed. 'I thought I did at the time when we met at University. When she got pregnant we'd already been living together for a few years, and she'd been working by then to see me through my studying. We were taking precautions, but I just can't believe she got pregnant on purpose. I couldn't really have done anything else but marry her under those circumstances, could I? No, I don't suppose she's the love of my life, but she's great with Daniel, very bubbly and lots of fun as a mother. I needed some fun in my life at the time, and I wanted my son to grow up with that too.'

Janet nodded. 'Of course you did.' After growing up with herself and Frank for parents, he'd have fully deserved some fun times. And this was where the ripple effects of her and Frank's stifling marriage would have naturally led him. Fun at all costs. 'Thanks for telling me,' she added.

She was struck by the irony that her son was married to a woman he didn't fully love for the sake of a child, and in a way, she'd been in the same position with Frank. And of course there was losing the love of her life and *his* child. But that was just too big to think about right now, other matters needed airing first, and when Ann set down the tea tray Janet was ready to go on. But Scott got in first, while leaning forward to pour the tea.

'How come you're telling me all this now, Mum? Has anything happened?'

Yes, she thought. Marian happened. And if she hadn't let that thug of a boyfriend of hers hit her, and if she hadn't followed Marian into the ladies, none of this would have had to come out. But she checked herself. She had confessed to Marian, and Marian hadn't made her do it. She'd lost control because somewhere deep inside her, she'd needed to.

Ann nudged Janet with her elbow. 'Tell him about Marian and what happened yesterday.'

So Janet described her breakdown in the ladies toilet when she saw Marian's bruise and blurted out the truth to her.

'Will she tell anyone?' Scott asked, looking concerned.

Janet's body tensed, as if held in a vice, as she thought about this. The teacup she was holding froze in mid air, half way to her mouth. Why hadn't she considered this already? Why hadn't she and Ann discussed this? She imagined the little floozy Marian telling her own abominable secret first to her flighty perfumery pals, then the rumour being fed and spreading outwards and then upwards from the ground floor, like a rank fungus, up the escalators and stairs, right up to the second floor, with its fruiting bodies popping up everywhere for all to see, then finally stretching its invasive roots right into the heart of the management offices. I'll lose my job, she thought, her heart beating wildly, I'll lose everything.

She stared back at Scott and her hand trembled, making some tea slop into her lap.

'Janet!' Ann said. 'Marian promised not to say anything. Remember? She thought it was nothing, anyway. That it was just your interpretation! Which it honestly really is!'

Janet turned to Ann, a sweat breaking out and flushing from her feet to her chest. 'Yes, but...how do we know she'll keep her word,' she stuttered.

'Mum, look at me!'

She forced her head to swivel on its stiff stalk and turned to Scott.

'It doesn't matter what she says. Let's hope she says nothing. But if she does, it's just her word against yours, isn't it?'

Janet swallowed hard. 'Well, she checked the office and promised no one was in there who could have overheard.'

'Right, well there's no need to worry about that then. And as for the general circumstances, it's not as if there was a witness, so it's really –'

'But there was!' Janet exclaimed. She began to squeeze herself with her arms, thinking of Winnie.

Scott looked wildly from Ann to Janet. 'What do you mean?'

Ann replied. 'The next door neighbour says she saw everything. She just told Janet in the garden before you came.'

Janet explained to Scott what Winnie had told her. What she said she'd seen the day of Frank's death. And how the secret was safe with her because she'd tried to do the same to her own husband. 'To be honest,' she added, 'I don't think she's worth worrying about because she's obviously a bit touched in the head.'

Soon Scott was pacing around the living room brushing his hair into spikes again. 'It's all so unbelievable! I need to think about this.'

Meanwhile Janet sagged back into the safety of the sofa, surprising herself by thinking more clearly again. And she picked up the threads of the resolution she'd been trying to make since her chat with Winnie, a resolution that she'd been trying out for size to settle within her, just like the absent Thomas padding around on a seat cushion, trying out different positions to see which one suited him best under these present circumstances. And this resolution was based on refusing to be afraid of what seemed inevitable, and the repugnance of having to be beholden to anyone's goodwill. If she had to lose everything, so be it.

'I think I'll have to confess,' she said. 'Under the circumstances, it seems the best thing.'

Ann gasped and the teacup she was holding rattled in its saucer. She slammed it down on the coffee table. 'No! You can't! It was an accident. You know it was. It's ridiculous even to consider it, Janet! And we've talked about this. He had it coming.'

Scott stood still and stared at Janet. 'You can't be serious, Mum! Why would you do that? It will affect the family too.'

Then he kneeled by her again and held her gaze so directly that his words struck right to her core, along with the alarmed look in his eyes. 'You were a victim of domestic abuse, Mum. Years later you finally fought back. That's all that happened, do you hear me? And you didn't actually touch him, you just stopped him taking a pill that might not even have worked. If he got himself in a rage, that's his responsibility. That's the way I see it.'

Janet opened her mouth to protest, but he cut in on her.

'I'm going to get some legal advice before we do anything else. Do we know anyone we can talk to with some discretion?'

Janet shook her head without thinking. She simply wasn't used to having any advantages or useful contacts in her life. Frank had seen to that.

'Anyone from the past?'

'Hang on!' Ann exclaimed. 'What about Cliff Ward, Janet? Frank's old policeman friend? He asked you if you were alright once, then later fell out with Frank. He became an inspector, didn't he?'

As Janet sat in a fog of exhausted numbness with a headache beginning to throb, Ann and Scott discussed going to Cliff Ward for advice, but first, Scott said, he'd find out if he was still alive and where to find him. Going to ask for help from someone who knew the legal system and Frank at the same time was ideal, he said, just what they needed. And his eyes shone bright with enthusiasm.

Still one more thing to do, thought Janet, steeling herself for the final telling. And it must be now. Mumbling she had to go to the toilet, she left Scott and Ann chatting as she dragged her aching calves upstairs. Using the pole on the landing, she reached up and hooked it under the loft hatch handle and pulled. The hatch swung away from its frame and the step ladder creaked and juddered down through long lack of use. Wearing the same slacks and jumper she'd had on since yesterday at Ann's, she climbed up and eased herself through the black mouth of the hatch. Snapping on the bare light bulb, she began crawling along the flimsy support boards, which warped under her weight, towards the dimmest reach of the loft.

Frank had never ventured into this loft very often because his height meant that he had to bend over considerably, and he certainly wouldn't have tolerated *crawling* to access the recesses in the eaves, so Janet had been able to hide something up here all their married life. It was the only part of herself she'd been able to keep from him, and so hadn't been within his reach to violate, as he had so many of her other treasured items over the years.

Such violations had included the bottle green chiffon and lace cocktail dress he'd ripped up after she'd worn it at a policemen's Christmas party they attended, because he maintained the dress had been attracting the stares of too many of his colleagues. He said it made her look like a common tart, and her claim that it was perfectly respectable, having come from a designer section of John Lewis, fell on his deaf ears. And what about Angie in her pink mini dress, she'd argued? Was she a common tart as well?

Then there was the Royal Doulton dinner service her mother and father had given the couple as a wedding present, a beautiful leafy design in autumnal colours called Larchmont. When they gave a rare dinner party once, inviting only Cliff and his wife, Angie, something had set Frank off afterwards when she was doing the washing up. He'd carefully put down his tumbler of Johnnie Walker, then plucked piece after piece of the china covered in washing up liquid suds out of the drainer and smashed them onto the floor, accusing her of too many airs and graces. She knew he liked to impress his peers, but somehow she always seemed to get it wrong. Steak and kidney pie would have been more apt, he declared, than her poncy Chicken à la King. She could still remember the splintering cracks of plates and bowls shattering and skidding across the kitchen floor, and the final defeated tinkling sounds as she brushed the broken shards into the bin along with some of her tears. She'd loved that dinner set, as she had the cross stitch embroidery of spring flowers she'd almost finished, before he dragged his pen knife through it to make another of his points.

And of course that was what it was all about. He knew exactly how to cut her deeply, and so keep her in line. She could always sense his rumbling frustration bubbling away under the surface. But her attempts to get to the bottom of his anger, or even perhaps to help him with it, simply led to nothing but a cold front of hostility which was his standard fallback position, and he'd forestall further scrutiny by escaping to the pub. So all she felt she could do was to tow that line of his as much as she could, to protect herself and her son, and the few things that remained still precious to her were kept well out of Frank's sight.

Brushing the archival weavings of dead spiders from her shoulders, and picking up a layer of fluff on her hands and knees, she crawled past cardboard boxes of her life with Frank. Past a fifties Bakelite radio, some bare teak picture frames, long since out of fashion, and some piles of old books, including a set of gilt embossed Encyclopedia Britannica that she'd saved up for from her housekeeping money for Scott.

Finally, she squeezed her shoulders into the east facing eave and plunged her right arm into the darkness. Her fingers groped around, then grasped hold of a stiff leather handle that shook a little on its metal hinges, and she dragged out the old wartime suitcase her father had given her to go to the mother and baby home all those years ago. She'd come up here sometimes when Frank was sure to be out all day to refamiliarise herself with its contents in the light of a torch, and always it had felt as if she was dragging out her past to light up her shame. But today was different. Her past had festered in here long enough like an unhealed wound, and it was time to carry it into the present for some tending to. It was time to tell Scott about Vivien.

'Where have you been, Mum?' Scott exclaimed. He had

resumed his pacing around the living room, with Ann looking on. 'We've been waiting -'

But when he noticed the scuffed and scarred brown leather suitcase in her arms, he went silent and dropped back into his chair, leant forward and propped his forearms on his knees. He looked up at her sharply with a deep frown nicking his brow. 'What now?'

'Shall I make another pot of tea?' asked Ann, rising to her feet.

'No! No more tea!' he said. 'Is this the last thing? Because if it isn't, I don't know what – '

'Yes,' Janet replied. 'It's the very last thing, I promise. But it's a good thing, I hope. It's the reason your father set against me in the first place.'

'Oh,' Ann squeaked. Then she clamped her mouth shut and sat back down.

Janet settled herself next to Ann with the suitcase on her lap and using her thumbs she flicked open the catches and slowly opened the case. The faint aroma of the Miss Dior perfume she used to wear escaped from its confinement to conjure back her youth, and she shook out the red and white spotted Sea Island dress she had worn the night she met Joe, which had been preserved in the perfume's tones.

Scott gasped. 'Is that yours?'

Janet nodded, remembering that night of the dance at The Palace and how full of promise her future had seemed under its starry ceiling.

'But I didn't think you ever wore bright colours.'

'Well, she obviously used to,' exclaimed Ann.

Janet felt as if she was performing some kind of inexorable and long-deferred ritual as she folded the dress and placed it on the coffee table, and then proceeded to pull out all the contents of the suitcase, one by one, and position them carefully side by side, like revered relics for new eyes to bear witness to.

Scott and Ann watched in silence.

There were the two novels she had read at the mother

and baby home, namely, *Bridal Path* by Nigel Tranter, about a man in search of a suitable wife, and *Martha Quest* by Doris Lessing, which she remembered with a little more personal affinity, for its theme of a young woman wanting to break away from the narrow confines of her life and make her own way in the world. The irony of this at the time of reading had upset her, and the plot of the former struck a chord of recognition within her now, but she let the *Martha Quest* book fall open in her hands to reveal a pressed four leaf clover, as thin as a tissue sample, and which she dared not touch lest it crumble into fragments. Joe had found it for her in their favourite field that summer of 53 and she'd carefully pressed it between the paper leaves.

There was a green velour box which she opened to reveal an opulent ivory satin lining cosseting a multiple stranded and woven necklace of creamy pearlised beads – her one Christmas present from Joe and as precious to her as the crown jewels.

And still remaining inside the suitcase were two brown envelopes, one large and one small.

She drew out the larger one and pulled out her secretarial course certificates with their embossed stamps of approval, which she'd fingered many times in the past as tactile symbols of a future she might have had if she'd never met and married Frank. As she reached forward to place them on the table, Scott took them from her and began reading them.

Then her hand shook as she grasped hold of the small finger-smudged envelope. Pausing for a moment to mark her father's writing on the front, with its familiar copperplate looping hand, and simply reading 'Janie', she prised out the black and white photographs cradled within. There were three. One of these she'd inserted herself. A young man with a crew cut, grinning broadly and wearing a woollen tank-top over a cotton shirt rolled up at the sleeves. She'd borrowed her father's Box Brownie one afternoon and had taken a picture of Joe at the farm. And despite the passing years, and the danger of Frank finding it, she'd been unable to let it go.

The other two pictures were poses, moments apart, and trapped beneath the creased and crackled glaze of time. Herself as a young woman in June 1954, with a Liz Taylor hairstyle, standing by a window and baptised in a beam of light. She was holding her new-born baby girl wrapped in a blanket with Auntie Vi's knitted rabbit tucked inside, while she herself smiled at the camera. Then herself again, but caught unawares this time, with her smile turned downwards as she gazed into the eyes of her baby who in the next few hours she'd be giving away to strangers.

Her heart twisting once again at the memory, she handed all three pictures to Scott.

'This is the reason your father took against me. Before I met him, I had a baby by this man.' She pointed at Joe. 'He left for America and I never saw him again, but he was the father of our baby, Vivien. And he was the love of my life.'

The tightness in her chest eased and tears slid down her cheeks. A sense of relief which she hadn't been expecting made her feel swimmy and she sank back into the cushions of the sofa as she watched Scott scrutinise the photographs.

Seconds ticked by, building a wall of silence, as Ann looked nervously from Janet to Scott to Janet. But after a while Scott cleared his throat and broke through the wall.

'You mean I have a sister?'

Janet looked straight into his eyes of hazed confusion. 'Yes, you have a sister. Well, somewhere anyway. I had to give her up. There was no other way, Scott. Not back then. I do hope wherever she is she's had a good life. I hope she's happy.' The use of the present tense stuck in her throat and swelled with recognition, making her feel like choking. Yes, Vivien was out there somewhere, had been all this time. But there again, she might be dead, for all she knew and she'd never ever know, would she? She had no right to know. Her laced-together fingers tightened in her lap turning her knuckles white.

As Scott continued to gape at both herself and then down at

the photographic evidence of these fleeting moments tossed into the future for his viewing, Janet explained what had happened, leaving nothing out, just as she'd told Ann less than 24 hours ago. Sometimes Ann chipped in with prompts which helped Janet as she went through the whole painful story once again, until finally reaching the night she'd told Frank. She explained she'd genuinely believed she was fond of Frank and trusted he would make a good husband, so in order to have a honest relationship with him, she had told him about Vivien. But it had been a big mistake, as her mother had warned it would be. He just couldn't handle it and it had triggered his abuse, despite all her reassurances and her efforts to be a good wife and make him happy.

'Everything changed that night,' she said. 'He began to hate me and there was nothing I could do. I just made sure we never had another child after you, Scott. There were more options later on in that regard. It would have been just too much for him and probably for me too.'

Scott stared hard at the picture of Janet and Vivien clutched tightly in his hand. Then he looked sharply up at Janet. 'Did you ever try to find her?'

Janet groped for a reply to try to soften the bluntness of his words which hit her like hammer blows. But there was nothing. What could there possibly be to soften this?

'No,' she rasped, 'Frank would never have allowed it, not with all those threats and those contacts he went on about. I had to think of you. I did make some enquiries a couple of years later with the Citizens Advice Bureau and the Social Services office in town, to see if there was any way I could find her, but they said I didn't stand a chance accessing those kind of records, which were well and truly closed to protect the adoptees and their adoptive families. So it was best to leave it alone for everyone's sake.' She looked at him searchingly, trying to read his expression. 'I tried to forget all about it then. I felt I had no choice, Scott. I pushed it to the back of my mind and got on with the present, and as the years went by, it seemed even more out of reach.'

Scott slowly got to his feet. 'I need a walk around the block, Mum.'

Ann's eyes widened. 'Surely not in this weather!' She began to get up.

'I need to have a think.'

'Of course you do,' Janet said in a monotone voice, recognising the irony in Frank having done the same thing. She grabbed Ann's arm to make her sit back down.

'I'll be back in an hour or so.'

After he shouldered himself into his anorak and shut the front door behind him, as her son walked off into the dank spitting of the night with his back bent to the rain and to the task of processing all she had told him, with his mind and with his heart, Janet's heart now went out to him. Such a burden she'd given him to carry. How had it come to all this? Then she remembered, it had come to this by her blurting out the first big secret to Marian at work. Then it had been a swift and sure unravelling until all the threads were laid bare with all her hard work undone.

She sighed.

Ann squeezed her knee.

There wasn't anything to say, so they both gazed into the artificial flames of Janet's electric fire, with the same instinctive need to find, in any living fireside, a modicum of comfort or enlightenment there – just like man through the ages has done, for good or ill.

Scott was true to his word. One hour later he knocked on the door. Janet rose to let him in. Without even taking off his coat, he stood dripping on the carpet. Janet saw determination in the set of his jaw, just like she'd seen him when Frank was ribbing him about being a stuck-up varsity student. But she also saw something else – was it a glimmer of excitement in his eyes?

'This is the plan, you two,' he said. 'I was talking to Ann while you were in the loft, Mum. First, we find out if Cliff Ward is still around. If so, we talk to him about the circumstances of Dad's death, looking at where you stand, Mum, and taking into consideration the nosy next door neighbour as a witness. Sounds like he'd be sympathetic and very useful as he knew what Dad was like. We need professional legal advice, and he might be able to give it or at least help us get some. In the meantime it's business as usual, for you, Mum, with no more confessions.'

'What…what do you mean?' Janet asked, her mind whirling in confusion. He surely didn't mean she went back to work?

'Give yourself tomorrow off with a tummy bug or something to get your head together, then get back into your routine.'

'But I can't go back there!' she cried, shaking her head at Scott and then at Ann.

Scott and Ann spoke in unison. 'Yes, you can.'

She gaped at them both.

Then Scott said more gently, 'You can do it, Mum. I know you can. It will keep your mind occupied, while Ann and I do some investigating.'

Ann nodded at Janet. 'That's right.'

'Ann is going in tomorrow to hand in her resignation. She was telling me earlier she's been wanting to retire for ages now, so it's a good time. She's only contractually obliged to give them a weeks notice and she has some holiday owing so she's happy to leave forthwith and can help me out with some investigations. I'll give her a lift home tonight, then she'll come back here to stay as arranged.'

Janet turned and stared at Ann, who looked straight back at her. Her light blue eyes glimmered like steel in the dim light of the room.

'It's the perfect time to retire, Janet,' she said. 'And as far as the short notice in concerned, I can't say I care. I just hung on for you.'

Janet nodded mutely, now wondering how on earth she was going to do without her at work, especially now, when she felt so ripped open and exposed. But Ann would be helping her in a far more important way, and she realised that had to come first.

She grasped hold of Ann's hand. 'Thank you, Ann. And thank you for everything you've done already.'

She turned to Scott. 'But what about *your* work?'

'Well I get to keep my own hours since I went freelance, don't I? So there's no problem with that. And before you ask, I won't be telling Susan anything for now, not until we get somewhere with it.'

Janet gasped. She just couldn't quite believe the sheer directedness of his taking control of the situation. Yet relief began to seep into her like a warming balm, just a little though, because she'd never been in the habit of trusting feelings like this. They'd always proved far too premature.

'And shortly after trying to find Cliff,' he continued, 'depending on what crops up, we'll find out if that Aunt Vi of yours is still alive, and maybe your brother. We need to reconnect with our family. Family is important. And that's why, with your permission, I'd like to see if we can find Vivien.'

Janet's mouth fell open. Her heart quickened and thumped hard against her rib cage. 'You really want to?'

'Of course.' Then he frowned at her. 'You do want to, don't you?'

She nodded. Could this be really happening? What she'd not dared let herself imagine for so long?

Scott read her expression and cracked a smile at her. 'If I can get a sister out of this mess, then that's really something!'

That night, while Janet lay upstairs in an exhausted dreamless slumber, Thomas the missing cat, crawled stealthily through the cat flap, but not for the first time tonight. He'd come in earlier from his nest in the hedgerow when he spotted the lady who he shared the house with had returned and the lights were shining out like flares for him. He'd disdainfully ignored her calls. Just who did she think he was? A dog? Perish the thought. So he'd come in when it suited him, but when he heard all the conversations going on, he'd slunk out again in disgust. Wasn't she missing him yet? Did he have to spend another night outside? That kind of out all night behaviour was for the local ruffian moggies, who he was forced to put in their place whenever they ventured onto his patch, but not for himself who was of finer calibre. And he didn't fancy going around to that funny lady next door. He didn't like the clucking sounds she made at him, or that staring little man with the shovel just outside her door. But now, he was finally home. The man and the other woman had driven off in a car so his life was back to normal. And as he chewed at some tuna the lady had left him, her knowing it was his favourite delicacy apart from the juicy little bodies of house sparrows, he felt in the mood to push his luck with a distinct change in his routine.

The temperatures had been dropping outside and despite having fluffed out his coat and tail, he was still feeling chilly. So to test his theory that the lady was sure to have missed him, he ventured past the chair that the big nasty man used to sit in, but which was now for his own personal use, and slowly padded upstairs and into the front bedroom where the lady was. He lightly jumped onto the bed and curled up by her side, relishing the softness of the duvet and the warmth of her body. This was the life! Things had been on the up since the nasty man had gone, and now he was to sleep on the lady's bed, something she'd never let him do.

As he began to doze, he felt a hand reach out and begin to stroke him. Yes, he decided, she's learned her lesson, and he purred in appreciation to verify the new contractual living arrangements.

Chapter 17

On Tuesday morning after taking Monday off sick, when her feet were approaching the staff entrance to Masons, and she saw hunched figures bent under the freezing rain trudging to work like people in a Lowry painting, she came to a halt by a post box. This post box served as a rare brushstroke of bright colour in what was otherwise a bleak late November townscape with December waiting just around the corner, getting ready to flash its tinsel. The post box also acted as a form of cover for Janet to huddle by, giving her some time to briefly remind herself of her immediate options, because the thought of joining the struggle of workers entering the mothership of mass employment was now repellent for many reasons. And these reasons pulsed like amber warnings in her mind.

First and foremost was Marian. Would Marian tell anyone about her confession? Scott had been quite insistent that Janet tell no one else for now, but Marian already knew, and that was a danger to Janet, because knowledge was power. And it stuck in her heart like a thorn that Marian of all people should have this kind of power over her. She'd have to tread so very carefully, but was she up to it?

Secondly, and it was a critically close second, her nerves had been pinging in all directions since she'd got up this morning and contemplated the day ahead. And then they'd been twisting themselves into knots making her feel nauseous as she drove in and parked her Polo. And she hadn't been able to park it in her usual spot in Grosvenor Place because all the spaces were taken, so she'd had to resort instead to the paying car park she used on Saturdays in Portland Street. This had caused new and tender nerves to shoot from her and flail around in a fluster of agitation. So she didn't even know if she could control herself and be able to work, because she had no experience in getting the measure of this level of tension and turmoil. She'd phoned Ann before leaving home, bewildered at how she was feeling. But Ann had assured her that her nerves would calm down, that everything in the department was running smoothly, there was nothing urgent to do, and that she'd see Janet later on at the house. To finish, Ann reported feeling a great sense of freedom at her forthcoming retirement now she'd actually handed in her resignation, and she obviously couldn't help but sound as chirpy as a chipmunk despite the dark drama going on in Janet's life. And although Janet could appreciate Ann's sentiments, she couldn't vocalise this for Ann's sake due to her own current state of feeling trapped by her past, her present, and potentially, her future.

And thirdly, going back to work in Masons seemed to have lost its gloss. Why this was, she couldn't understand. The staff entrance looked even more grubby and dilapidated than usual beneath the prevailing funereal sky, as if deemed suitable only for the 'lowly' workers to use to gain access to serve the shining citadel until death us do part. And she feared that descending the internal fire escape to the staff lockers, and hearing her own footsteps reverberating from the iron fretwork, would feel like taking a stairway to some kind of purgatory rather than her usual Masons heaven.

But yesterday she'd finally resolved within herself to follow Scott's advice and return to work. This came at the end of a day of mixed emotions and strange contemplations. She'd awoken at around nine in the morning to a thrumming sound ticking over like an idling engine, and despite her dread of the solitary day ahead, she'd been pleased to find Thomas on the duvet. Instead of throbbing panic, as anticipated, she found her feelings soothed by stroking her missing cat. Smoothing down his fur, she delivered a soft admonishment for him being on the bed, but they both knew she didn't really mean it because she was so relieved to have him back. She even left him there on the unmade bed, while she got dressed and went downstairs for breakfast.

She'd always been a good eater despite sorrows and adversities, never having been one of those women who professes, during some minor or overblown crisis of her own making, *Oh no, I just couldn't eat a thing!* So she managed a couple of boiled eggs, sitting at the kitchen table. It was here that she finally registered the weather outside beyond the kitchen window. And her breath caught in her throat.

Last night's dripping rain had frozen in the chilling temperatures of the crystal clear night under a swarm of shimmering stars, to form an ice-frosted wonderland worthy of Narnia, blanketing the fields and hedgerows beyond the confines of her white veiled garden. She gasped out loud. It had been so long since she'd seen a hoar frost like this, and she knew from her childhood romps in them that she simply must get out into this one. She marvelled at how she could find anything stimulating when the lens through which she'd observed the world, and through which she had found meaning, had cracked apart after confronting her role in the death of Frank, and after facing up to the past where all her troubles and losses had begun.

And yet despite her deep despair over all this, she still wanted to take a walk in the wonderland. So as she washed up and stared at the enticing mantle of white beyond the window frame, and feeling infused with a long forgotten sense of excited anticipation, she decided to go on a particular field walk she'd done by herself occasionally when Scott was at school and Frank was at work. She'd go east from the back of her house into the farmland beyond, where she could extend the distance into the thick expanse of woodland higher up. She could relish the frost so much better there than in one of Cheltenham's busy parks made for doggy toileting and children's play.

Just half an hour later she was trudging along, crunching crispy blades of grass beneath her boots and inhaling the clean freshness of the biting cold air. She quickly felt transported into a now that she wanted to last forever. Hedgerows were silent and thick with a multitude of frosted forms, all feathered with interlocking particles of ice. Dead stems of hogweed stood erect in the stillness, their fanned umbels of seeds powder-sprinkled with flakes of ice, with lacy festoons of spiders webs draped between. The trees which lined the hedgerows stretched out branches encrusted with needles and spines drawn and distilled from the moist cold air. And as the sun raised its head to the day, as Janet trekked on, shafts of golden light began to split the trees and everywhere, and on everything, the white frost particles were transformed into a dusting of glittering diamonds. And everything looked tranquil and beautiful to Janet. And she wondered that if these muddy farmers' fields, usually pock-marked by cowpats, could be so magically transformed by nature into something as fresh and pure as this, then maybe she could be changed a little too, and maybe there was even a tiny chance, as thin as a splinter of ice, that she would find her daughter.

When she reached the upper woodlands and found herself wandering along a track with tall oaks and sycamores fringing the path and forming an arching canopy high above, it seemed as if she was walking down the aisle of an enchanted winter cathedral, the trees forming colonnades on either side of her, with a stately vaulted ceiling above. She wanted to meander on, but she noticed the light had begun to dim and the cold was nipping harder at her cheeks, so recognising that all pleasures come to an end, and they certainly always seemed to in her case, she turned on her heels and back-tracked the way she'd come, descending the slopes and hurrying through the fields as the sun began to doze, all the way back to the rear gardens of Willow Lane.

When she was climbing over the fence of her garden she spotted Winnie's sucked-in face squinting across at her from a low elevation in the frame of her kitchen window. Janet was used to seeing this neighbourly 'interest' from Winnie, but she knew the vertically-challenged Winnie usually dragged a fit-for-function footstool to her window to stand on, in order to achieve a more efficient vantage point for her very own specialised form of Neighbourhood Watch. Pretending she hadn't seen her, Janet hurried indoors, eyes pinned to the garden path, but the sight of this meddlesome woman acted as a slap in the face to bring her back to the jagged edges of her worries.

By then it was around three thirty in the afternoon, so she made herself a ham sandwich and a coffee, and after putting on a load of washing she settled in her living room by the glowing bars of the fire. But her mood turned dark again. She began worrying whether or not she could really face the next day, and even constructive visualisations didn't help, like they recommended in her books.

So to distract herself from her thoughts, she sought a tried and tested personal palliative by perusing in detail a Comfy Life catalogue which came free with her *Radio Times*. The range of inventions for the middle-aged and elderly was truly staggering: foam cushioning for sensitive toes, clip on magnifying lenses to wear on your regular spectacles, folding trays for when you're sick in bed and lap trays for hobbies, elasticated trousers for expanding waistlines with intractable front ironed creases, stretch at the side belts for men (now Frank could have used one of those, mused Janet), adjustable wide-fit slippers in navy or wine velour for when bunions bulge, clever little bra extenders for when your breasts swell and sag but you want to pretend you're still the same size, quilted armchair protectors, facial hair removers, protective knee braces, companion tables with multiples of compartments on castors for easy manoeuvrability, doughnut cushions with washable stretch covers for use when suffering spinal or lower back pain, and finally thinking of Thomas, veterinary pet beds with luxury foam. As if he'd ever use one, reflected Janet.

But what was it about these items which usually gave her solace? Because Janet knew full well many were plain ridiculous, with a touch of having been invented for the sheer conceptual sake of it rather than true practical application. Perhaps it was something to do with all the aches, pains, and disabilities, which were assumed to plague the elderly, being so thoroughly catered for with these aids for the home. *Everything* could be taken care of. It was a feeling of security, funded by a lifelong pension scheme with a good return, of somehow living a cosy life in one's twilight years, with a both literal and metaphorical protective blanket over your knees. There'd be a sense of a full life having been lived, with time for reflection and no regrets, snuggled beneath the 100% wool tartan rug bought on a former coach tour of the Highlands. But alternatively, there might be the realisation that you'd misjudged life, that you'd got it wrong in some ways, but it's okay, no one could possibly expect you to make any life changes *now*.

And there it was. Janet had, understandably perhaps, been visualising this very direction of security after a hard life with Frank. She hadn't wanted any more challenges. Becoming manager of her department, and being thought well of by upper management, formed the very pinnacle of her 'life after Frank' ambitions. But now all this felt shadowed by doubts. And these doubts crept over her in the night, as she contemplated going to work the next day. And in the morning, with the frosted wonderland having vanished like a mirage in a desert, while getting dressed for Masons, her hand had reached out for a black suit from the wardrobe, and she'd slipped on the black skirt before remembering that she wore colour now she was a manager. And as she fingered the purple suit, then the bottle green, not being able to decide, it struck her like a punch in the gut that all this Masons stuff didn't really matter one iota now, because confessing her crimes over Frank and over Vivien had blasted the post-Christmas Janet apart, and people in Masons had better watch out for the flying shrapnel.

So standing here now by the post box behind Masons in the chilling dankness of Pilgrim Street, in a fatalistic frame of mind having gone through her options, and despite being surreptitiously glanced at by some Lowry figures plodding along the path, she relinquished her cover and assertively stalked up to the staff entrance vowing not to give a damm.

Her heels clattered down the iron steps. She tossed her coat in her locker, changed her shoes, and slapped on her Masons badge. Eyes averted from the black hole in the wall, she ascended the staircase and marched through the first floor. Then emerging from the escalator onto the second floor, she finally found herself in familiar terrain, but with a somewhat dislocated mindset. Take it moment by moment she told herself, minute by minute, hour by hour, just like the books say. *Bend like a reed in wind. This too shall pass. Nothing is good or bad but thinking makes it so.* And there was always the back-handed compliment her mother used to pay her: *You're as hard as nails, you are*. I've only been absent for one day, she told herself. Just *one* day. Nobody has reason to be suspicious. No one has any reason to suspect anything is wrong. It's just business as usual as far as they are concerned.

As she made her way through carpets, she nodded a greeting at the lofty Hugh Boatman, manager of furniture, who was consulting with Niall Walsh, the question mark of a manager of carpets, who was looking just as uncertain and shifty as usual. The work station on the left, belonging to Samantha Dixon-Wright, the powder puff interior designer, was vacant. This was par for the course because the English rose obviously didn't think she was bound by the same rules as a plebeian workforce, and that she was therefore entitled to a leisurely and scenic drive into town from her beautifully draped cottage in Lower Slaughter. Next up was Shirley Appleton, the boiled sweet manager of linens, who offered a sugary greeting.

'Good morning, Janet. How *are* you? I *do* hope you're feeling better.'

Janet groped to remember what she'd said she'd been ill with. Damm, she should have had this ready on the tip of her tongue. Then it came to her, just as Shirley's sustained expression of feigned concern, with her pencilled-in eyebrows reaching their maximum elevation and her blue eyes rounded to the size of marbles, would have become farcical to the point of self-parody.

'Thank you, Shirley, it was a tummy upset. I'm a lot better now.'

'So glad to hear it,' she murmured. 'Oh well, so much to do in preparation for the Christmas sales. I'll probably be in my office all day.' She glided away in her pastel suit as if she was balancing an invisible book on her head from her days at Lucie Clayton's finishing school which she'd once boasted to Janet she'd attended.

Janet sailed past her in turn onto her department to find Gemma and Claire stuffing their handbags into the till cupboard and locking it. This wasn't officially allowed, but all the female staff did it so they could get swiftly to the canteen at break time or straight out to do some shopping in town, without having to go down to security to retrieve their handbags first. It was a rule of Masons that was made to be broken. And Janet was to be witnessing and being asked to take part in more rule breaking before long, the surprise being from which front this would be coming.

Since the approach to Christmas was generally a quiet time for the whole store, compounded by the fact that the soft furnishing department in particular wouldn't be first port of call for eager shoppers cruising for bargains during a Masons January sale, Janet realised it was as good a time as any to try and take it easy, putting little pressure upon herself, while Scott and Ann went about their delicate business on her behalf. She was having to continually remind herself that they had offered to do this for her because she couldn't get over the fact that they were actually sympathetic and that they were helping her.

Her gratitude was an uncomfortable feeling, because it was a feeling which had rusted and corroded within her through lack of use, like an old garden hoe, no longer fit for tending a garden and bringing forth any blooms. She hadn't trusted feeling grateful since her youth when her troubles had begun through meeting Joe, and ever since Auntie Vi, her beloved aunt, for whatever reason hadn't been able to stay in touch. Her father had died many years ago, and her mother only two years ago. The Sunrise care home near Camelford, where Mildred had gone when her sister, Florrie, couldn't take care of her anymore after Mildred had a bad stroke, had notified Janet along with Florrie, of her death. And this loss, and remembering her mother's vitriolic bitterness about life and her regrets, had made Janet determined to get some measure of happiness out of her own life. No matter what it took. And there was the rub. Just look what it had taken and where it had got her now! Having to find out if she'd committed a crime. And what if it was decided she had? What was she going to do?

Giving herself a mental shake to return to the present, she answered Claire's and Gemma's enquiries about her health. Yes she was fine, thank you, just a tummy bug, she said as she emptied the float that Gemma had collected from the cash office into the coin wells in the till with a jangle of silver and coppers.

'Never known you to be ill before, Mrs B,' Gemma observed, her forehead drawn into a knot of curiosity.

'Well, let's get on, shall we?' Janet said, unable to look Gemma in the eye, as she slammed the till drawer shut with a ping. Gemma was a highly perceptive girl.

Janet marched over to the right-hand serving bench, which functioned as the main helm for the department, with Claire and Gemma in tow. Gathered together here, she began to leaf through the girls' order books. All looked well. There were a few stock fabric orders to go to Clothworks, which would be entered on the new forms she had designed herself, and a few Crowson and Sanderson custom-made orders with some nice commission to be earned. She also noticed that a few entries were in Ann's handwriting. She'd obviously been sharing out her last orders between Claire and Gemma in light of her imminent retirement. Always considerate, that that was Ann for you. And she felt a hot pang of guilt as the realisation hit home that she'd never truly appreciated these qualities in Ann before. She'd judged her as being 'too soft', just like her mother judged Auntie Vi for the same qualities.

But this slipping into the past wouldn't do and she coughed to clear her throat. 'Very good work, you two.'

She remembered Kevin, who was on his day off. 'How's Kevin getting along?'

Gemma handed her Kevin's order book and she scrutinised it. He was a messy writer, all wild loops with jauntily angled figures and numbers, but it looked more or less comprehensible.

'Would you say he's up to par yet?' Janet asked Gemma.

'He's not doing too badly for a boy.'

Janet felt a grin tugging at the corners of her mouth. She covered her mouth with her hand but Gemma had seen and she smiled as widely and as cheekily as was permitted for a pale-faced, 'life is so dire', committed Goth. Janet noticed she'd painted her fingernails black now too, but she simply wasn't in any mood to take her to task about it.

Instead, she took them through what the sale offers would be in soft furnishing just after Christmas: free making with Clothworks for all unlined curtains and half price for lined; 25% off company custom-mades; discounted stock fabrics by the metre; discounted ready-mades; sale cushions and of course, remnants. She told them to prepare their orders, but since no stock had come in yet, they could then measure up remnants and price them. This was a job Janet used to love, because staff were allowed to have first pickings for their own crafts projects at home and could reserve the fabric lengths in the stockroom for themselves to pay for later on. She'd been thrilled two years ago to have been able to make a whole patchwork quilt this way.

She moved to go to her office, but Claire, who'd been very quiet, caught hold of her arm.

'I think you should know that something might have

kicked off yesterday,' she said.

She looked at Claire sharply. 'What do you mean? Ann didn't say anything.'

'It was when Ann was at lunch. I thought I'd wait to tell you myself. Mr King and Samantha were having heated words with Marian over by her desk. And Milly was all over the place, scuttling around them looking all frightened like she does.'

Janet glanced in the direction of Berkeley Fabrics. Milly-Molly-Mandy was there with her shaggy head of bleached blonde hair bent over some paperwork, at present keeping a low profile.

'Could you work out what it was about?' Janet asked.

'Well, Mr King was shaking that sample curtain at Marian. You know, the Harvest Fruits colour 2, the discontinued one. The one she's been repeatedly asked about. Samantha just won't let it drop! And she's obviously dragged the store manager into it now. I know you're not fond of Marian, but I really felt for her.'

'How did it end?'

'I'm not sure, but I think *you* were mentioned.'

Janet groaned. Then she looked at Claire. Claire, of diminutive stature and good figure in her navy suit and frilly white blouse, but whose husband she'd admitted didn't really appreciate her and didn't show her much love. She was around fifteen years younger than Janet, so much more time to make a fresh start if she could break away from her marriage. Just how common was being trapped like this? she wondered.

Janet smiled at Claire. 'Thank you for the warning, Claire. I expect I'll find out soon enough.'

And she did. That very afternoon.

Janet had been so nervous about seeing Marian again. But all morning there was no sign of her and she didn't want to get into any discussion with Milly-Molly-Mandy as to when Marian would next be making an appearance, so she busied herself in her office by listing the sale signage needed and making sure they had plenty of stock fabrics on order. Her palms kept oozing stickiness, and she repeatedly wiped them on her purple woollen skirt, wishing she'd worn the more subdued green suit as purple felt far too showy for her mood today.

At lunchtime she escaped into town, where the bare trees on the Promenade looked like black charcoal scribbles smudged into the grey winter sky. It was nose-pinchingly cold but her body was nicely insulated in her thick black woollen coat, for which she was grateful. She periodically checked herself in the Christmas windows as if to make sure, from moment to moment, of her physical reality, despite her weekend confessions. She could scarcely believe the visual evidence. She *did* still exist *and* she looked exactly the same.

With her stomach growling a reminder, she grabbed a sandwich and a bottle of water from Marks and Spencer's food hall, then later found herself roaming restlessly through ladieswear in C&A at the top of the High Street, wondering why she'd come in here of all places, where she'd never be caught dead shopping since her Masons promotion.

Pausing by a rack of raincoats, which she was currently feigning interest in purely for her own self image's sake of keeping up an appearance of normality, she felt a tugging on her arm.

'Janet! I need to talk to you!'

Janet twitched her head around to see Marian standing by her, wearing a double-breasted teal raincoat, short in length and belted at the waist, which could very well have come right off a C&A clothes rail itself. Her red hair was fluffed out around her upturned collar and shoulder pads. Janet's eyes locked onto the bruise by Marian's right eye which was smothered with cover-up. Despite the camouflage she was surprised to see it had hardly faded, and yet it was a stark reminder that only two days had passed since their last encounter in the ladies powder room.

'I need to talk to you!' Marian repeated, her brow puckered and her eyes steely. 'You are on your lunch break, aren't you? You are back at work today?'

Staring at Marian, who was standing very close in front of her now, all Janet could think was, *You know what I did, You know what I did...* She tried to open her mouth to speak, but her lips were glued together.

As if reading Janet's mind, Marian pulled at her arm again. 'Snap out of it, Janet! I told you that stuff doesn't matter as far as I'm concerned. That husband of yours got what was coming to him. To hell with all that! We've got a problem in the here and now with our snotty Samantha over that Harvest Fruits problem. She's only gone and taken it to Mr King! And he's siding with her!'

Janet's lockjaw slackened with shock. And up close like this, she noticed the glittering determination in Marian's eyes, rendered by pinprick pupils sharply focused by the slight to herself and her professionalism, while revealing a pale amber glow in her brown irises. She'd seen this contracted pupil look in her own eyes when vowing to herself in a mirror, after yet another of Frank's slaps or goads, that she would not be brought low by the likes of him. It was a visual reminder to herself and she knew the look well.

'Janet! Snap out of it! Do you hear me? He's siding with her!'

Janet held Marian's gaze, her point now sinking in like a lance into quicksand. 'But what has it got to do with *him*?'

'He's taking her side because of Mrs Harrison, the customer, being very well off and very well connected. She's the wife of an local MP apparently, and they live on the Royal Crescent. Mr King says we can't afford to disappoint them. He says it's our duty to satisfy the customer. It's one rule for the rich and one rule for the poor, if you ask me!'

Janet now caught on. 'But what's he expecting you or Berkeley Fabrics to do if the colour she wants is discontinued?'

'Well, I've been on the phone to them at home this morning, after he was insisting we meet the order yesterday. Turns out he's been onto *them*. Asking them to print a roll of the colour especially for the customer as a gesture of goodwill. They've told *me* they haven't decided yet and have to hold a meeting at head office.'

'But that's just ridiculous. Going to all that trouble for one customer?'

'Exactly!'

'But what has any of this got to do with me?'

'Because the order will have to go through your curtain makers, Clothworks. Because Berkeley Fabrics don't do interlining, or stuffed goblet headings – and that's what she wants the Harvest Fruits for, for her living and dining rooms. And if those are okay, she's intending to order a whole load of other designs for upstairs. She's been pouring over pattern books from all of us and Miss Fancy Pants has been doing all the measuring too.'

'Oh, no! Not the measuring! She's useless at it!'

'Exactly. And who's going to tell Mr King that? You? Me? Your fitters should be doing it. It's a fucking nightmare.' Marian paused and relaxed her shoulders. 'Anyway, I'm just letting you know because I think the big man will be having a word with you and me about the whole thing very soon.'

Janet groaned. Why did this have to be kicking off now? Just when she needed to stay under Masons radar and fly low through the day. Her last meeting with Mr King had been about having to be supportive to the powder puff and work as a team. But how on earth could they do that under these conditions?

'So you'll have to think about the position you're going to take,' observed Marian, turning to leave, with a flick of her hair. Her diminutive figure strutted away, disappearing into a patchy milieu of fashion displays, customers grappling with coat hangers surely designed to let clothes slide off them rather than hold them, and mannequins strutting their stuff in freeze-frame with attitudes of chilly indifference to the shoppers' plight.

Perhaps nothing will happen today? Janet thought. Then I can talk to Ann about it tonight and sort out a strategy.

But, unfortunately, this proved to be wishful thinking.

That afternoon, just after 2.30pm, when she was cloistered safely in her office, there was a sharp rap of three knuckle strikes on the door. Janet jumped at the harsh sound and turned to see the door swing open. Three people entered.

First was Samantha in an apricot woollen suit, looking flushed just as an English rose should, followed by the portly Patrick King, brandishing the Harvest Fruits colour 2 in his sausage-fingered hand. His smiling stockade of teeth were concealed by his drawbridge of a mouth, now tightly shut. To Janet's mind, this meant he was going to be unwilling to brook any negotiations in aiming for his usual fallback win-win argument. The look on his cast-in-concrete face, the set of his gravity-fed jowls, communicated a taking no quarter mindset, with total surrender being the only outcome he was interested in. Janet had never seen him look like this before and her nerves began to flutter. She dragged her eyes away from his nail-headed eyes to see the third figure was Marian in one of her tightly fitted navy suits, with the skirt a little longer than her usual style. She was standing behind the others, arms folded across her chest. She raised her eyebrows at Janet.

Janet stood up.

'Let's all sit down shall we?' Patrick King said.

He began to scrape a few chairs together around Janet's desk, pinning her back into her own chair and blocking off her means of escape.

When they were all seated, Janet felt she had to say something. But her nerves were now snapping in all directions. She didn't need this today. Why did she have to deal with this today? Her nerves began twisting and they tightened in her throat like a noose on a condemned man every time she tried to speak.

'You are aware of this problem, Janet?' Mr King cast the sample curtain onto her desk. All their eyes locked onto the target. The fabric bulged with its abundance of swelling lemons, limes, peaches and plums, now taking on the appearance of a brash and flagrant flouting of decorum and fair play.

She managed to free herself of the noose. 'Yes, I'm aware. A very difficult situation.'

'Yes, well it's what we're going to do to fix it that counts, isn't it?' Patrick King said, leaning back and thrusting forward his paunch. 'Working as a team, all pulling together, that's what matters here. And of course the customer always comes first.'

Janet flinched at the old retail slogan, with which she had been forced to disagree at times, and she disagreed even more so with the battering ram maxim of *the customer is always right*. And there were many logical reasons why she'd had to contest this, but of course she'd always managed to keep them to herself. There was always a way of solving such difficulties with graciously given apologies, or financial concessions, or a reassessment of the order and measurements, a gentle steering in another direction.

But this! How could the customer come first this time? And why *should* they come first this time? She remembered having to tell a lovely couple from Gloucester that they couldn't have Crowson Papillion colour 4, the lilac colourway, which they had set their hearts on for their bedroom, because when the department had ordered the fabric from Crowson, they were told there was none of it left and there wouldn't be any more. Sorry, they said, it should have been listed as discontinued. Would the pink or the peach do instead? Janet had asked if they could print a roll of the lilac, but she'd got nowhere, so why should this situation with the Harrisons be any different? How come a customer with clout, that the store manager feels he has to pander to, get their own way, when that lovely couple from Gloucester didn't?

While she was thinking all this, Patrick King was summing up the situation and then stating what was now going to happen. She tuned in properly when he said he'd been on the phone this very morning with the director of Berkeley Fabrics, going to the top, as he put it.

'And I'm happy to tell you,' he continued, 'that the director has agreed to order a roll of colour 2 to be especially printed for the customer. There is to be no meeting to decide, no pussy-footing about.'

Marian gasped.

Janet frowned.

Samantha smiled.

'They're setting up the printing of it as we speak and have promised to get it to us in the next seven days at the latest. Samantha here has done the measuring already, so it will be full steam ahead. And once they're fitted I expect Mrs Harrison to be fully satisfied, enough to go ahead with more orders and more business for Masons.

'But they told *me* it would be too difficult an operation to print the fabric now,' Marian said, 'and they absolutely had to discuss –'

'Never mind all that!' Mr King rasped, pointing a finger at Marian. 'It's sorted. And you'd better change your attitude if you value your job. I told them we didn't have to have a Berkeley Fabrics concession here at all.'

Marian shrank back into her chair, her face flashing fear.

Janet felt shocked at Mr. King's aggressive treatment of Marian, something she would usually have relished, but not under these unfair circumstances. Her mouth also dropped when the penny did. He'd threatened the manufacturers to get what he wanted. Unbelievable! She glanced again at Marian. Her face was now as blanched of colour as a whiteout in winter.

Then she checked out Samantha. Her eyes were as wide as a newborn babe's. All innocence, while she clasped her hands neatly in her lap with fingers smoothly interlaced. She'd no doubt been to Lucie Clayton's too, along with

Shirley from bed linens. Such a picture of demure contrition. But it didn't wash with Janet, and she felt like grabbing hold of Samantha and shaking her so she could see what trouble she'd caused by simply not being firm enough with the customer, and by going to the big man to stir it up further. What a mess!

But Janet was always a realist. And despite the hairs on the back of her neck bristling and her stomach hardening with the injustice of it all, she tried to calm herself and consider what could still go wrong with the order. A whole newsreel of disasters flickered across her mind. Inaccurate measurements, because the powder puff had done them, would lead to curtains being made from a one-off, especially-printed, roll of fabric that simply wouldn't fit. There'd be shock horror when the poor Steadmans, such conscientious fitters, and not too good with the gift of the gab when it came to the posh folk, discovered curtain drops either puddling on the floor like the cast off bloomers of a generously hospitable tavern wench, or curtains hoisted high from the floor like the indecorous petticoats of a Moll Flanders.

She tried to reason and forced herself to look at Patrick King. 'I don't want to cause offence to Samantha here, but I think it would be best to let the Steadmans do all the measuring for the whole house.'

With a look as direct as a power drill, Patrick King snapped, 'And why would that be necessary?'

Holding his gaze, while trying not to let her buzzing nerves make her neck twitch, she tried to explain as kindly as possible, to demonstrate to Mr King that they did indeed work as a team for the benefit of the customer and for Masons, why the Steadmans should do the measuring. 'You see…' She hesitated, her heart rapping against her ribcage, in anticipation of the ire to come. 'Samantha's measurements have already been problematical, less than ideal.'

'What do you mean, less than ideal? Samantha here is a professional interior designer! She's had some notable clients who've been well-satisfied customers. Hotels and the like. Despite any personal feelings of certain noses out of joint, I've asked that you all work as a team, but there doesn't seem to be much evidence of that, does there?' He turned to Samantha. 'Do you see there being any problems?'

Janet groaned inwardly. Teamwork was exactly what she was supporting.

Samantha's mouth wobbled and Janet was surprised to see this discomposure. 'No,' she said quietly. 'I don't see there being any problems at all.'

Marian looked hard at Janet.

Janet looked hard at Samantha. But there was to be nothing further from her. No truths. No owning up to her weak areas.

So Janet went for it – because someone had to, even though her mouth was as dry as blotting paper.

'But what will happen when Samantha's measurements are wrong, the curtains are made and go to be fitted by the Steadmans, where the errors are discovered and they have to be remade? It's happened a few times already. And is there going to be another roll of fabric especially printed? And what about all the other windows? We could lose a lot of business, not to mention damaging our reputation. I really would advise getting the Steadmans to measure the whole house.'

She took a deep breath after getting to the end and Marian gave her a surreptitious thumbs up.

Samantha looked into her lap. Her fingers were now squeezing her hands so hard that her knuckles were paling.

Patrick King thrust his body upright and shoved his chair back. 'I really am disappointed in you, Janet, and I certainly don't have time for all this pettiness,' he said in clipped tones. 'Samantha has done all the measuring already. She's the professional around here, not you. You will help her with the order, make sure the curtain makers have everything they need. I don't want to hear any more about it.'

A fast flash of heat surged through Janet and she gasped.

He halted by the doorway and turned around. He forced a smile, with teeth as white as a glacier and a chilling look to match. 'You work as a team, do you hear me? And if you can't do that, you shouldn't be working for Masons.'

They all murmured, 'Yes, Mr King.'

Just like a group of naughty children in the headmaster's office, thought Janet, being threatened with expulsion. And she hated it. The sheer injustice of it. She was too old and had been through too much for this kind of treatment.

After he left, Janet stared at Samantha. 'You know full well you get the measuring wrong. What are you thinking of?'

Marian was harsher and she grabbed the sample curtain from Janet's desk. 'This whole situation is your fault,' she said to Samantha. 'You should have accepted that *no* meant *no* in this case,' and she flung the sample into Samantha's lap.

Samantha gathered it to her like a security blanket, folded it neatly, then stood up to take her leave. 'I don't know why you two are so worried, I really don't. Everything will be just fine,' she said, with her serene mask back in place. Her tone sounded smooth and sincere, exactly like her usual pouring of verbal syrup onto anything she found distasteful. Janet had come to recognise this tone and she detested it.

Samantha exited the office leaving the door wide open just as Mr King had left it.

Janet was left looking at her nemesis, Marian. But she realised that for the first time they were on the same side. Perhaps just as well, as she couldn't fight a war on two fronts.

'Have you got any suggestions?' she asked Marian.

She shrugged her shoulders. 'No. You said it all. I suppose we'll have to let her hang herself, won't we? If she insists on using her measurements and they are wrong, then the blame will all be hers.'

While Janet traipsed down to the staff entrance to leave another day of hell behind, she found herself feeling at odds with the store for the very first time. She'd always believed that the management played fair by their employees and so in turn she'd always observed their rules and respected the management. But today she'd been hurt. There an twisting ache in her heart as she remembered Patrick King, who now fitted Marian's description of the big man, saying he was disappointed in her and implying she wasn't a professional when she knew she could do a better job than Samantha. He'd reminded her of Frank and his aggressive put-downs. And then, he'd effectively threatened them with the loss of their jobs if they didn't go along with something they knew was going to turn out to be a disaster for the customer and for the store. Would he have treated them like this if they'd been men? Another consideration. She'd tried her very best to warn him, she'd stuck her neck on the block to do it, but he hadn't recognised it came from a caring place, a place of loyalty to Masons.

Just as the damp evening air blew into her face at the exit, a shoulder brushed past her, then stopped on the pavement outside. It was Marian in her teal mac. She caught hold of Janet's arm and tugged her out of the way of the other bodies all scurrying to get home.

Standing beneath the sodium haze of the street lamp opposite the staff entrance, Janet could see that Marian's eyes were swollen, brimming with wetness, and sooty from smudged mascara – once again. Slowly, Janet's thoughts veered off course from her own upset to register Marian's.

'I've had a verbal warning on the phone from Gillian Makepeace,' Marian said, with her eyebrows pinched together. 'She admitted to me that she didn't want to give it and didn't agree with it, but she'd been told she had to, for my supposedly being obstructive to Samantha. She says I'd better tow the line or else they might sack me.' She stared down at the greasy pavement. 'I really need this job to look after my daughter. I can't afford to lose it,' she said, her voice rising.

Janet was surprised to find herself sympathising. Perhaps

it was because of her newly-born antipathy towards her own duplicitous employers, where it would only take a little more of her staying true to herself to be in a very similar position. Perhaps it was because Marian knew her secret and she was protecting herself by being agreeable towards her. Or perhaps it was because they were both incensed at the turn of events all caused by the English rose, their common enemy.

'Well I might not be far behind you,' she commented. 'It's disgusting.'

Marian nodded and shivered in the cold and damp November air.

'But you're right,' Janet said. 'We'll have to stand by and watch the developments. It's on Samantha's head.'

'Wait for the shit to hit the fan.'

Disliking the expression, but seeing little point in criticising, Janet simply agreed. 'Yes, exactly.'

'Goodnight, then.'

'Goodnight.'

As Janet walked behind Marian, watching her smartly marching figure fade into a street fog blurry with the murky cheer of Christmas lights, her thoughts once more turned to Frank's death, her daughter, and the mess she was in, which Scott and Ann were going to help her with. At least in the meantime work would function to keep her distracted, if nothing else, just as Scott had suggested it might, and she'd be able to discuss the Samantha situation with Ann tonight.

As she got into her Polo, fired the engine, and pointed her car towards home, she was so very relieved that she wouldn't be going home to an empty house full of memories of another big man – her very own dear Frank, to whom she had also told the truth, and only received punishment for her honesty.

Chapter 18

Two days passed while the winter drizzle continued unabated, the sun so rarely parting the clotted rainclouds to lighten spirits. Ann was in full agreement with Janet that the double standard hypocrisies being imposed by Mr King and the directors of Berkeley Fabrics just wasn't acceptable behaviour. They should stand by their staff if their staff were upholding the very regulations that they themselves laid down. She concurred that management only had themselves and Samantha Dixon-Wright to blame when the order went pear-shaped, as it surely would. Janet phoned Ron Richardson on his home number, which he had given her for emergencies. After relaying the situation to him, his reply shocked her.

'Why do you think I wanted out, Janet? Crap like this used to happen to me regularly. I had to get out for my health, but I thought if anyone could take it, you could.'

Janet appreciated the validation but was still disturbed. 'But I had no idea Masons management wouldn't stand by their staff.'

'They act according to what suits them. What looks good on the books. And staff can easily be replaced if they don't do what's expected of them.'

'But what can I do?'

'Nothing. In this case there is nothing you can do but wait. Wait for the shit to hit the fan.'

There it was again, Marian's expression that had been buzzing around in her mind over the last few days at work, as well as her own internal urgings such as *Bend like a reed in the wind*, and *This too shall pass.* Meanwhile the department was unnaturally calm, with so few customers, just like a sailing ship drifting on a tranquil sea, waiting for the winds to pick up, only to get more than it bargains for and to be blown straight into the heart of a raging storm. And Janet felt that storm was just around the corner. But it was, at least, something to focus on, rather than her own inner turmoil and an alien sense of being out of control over what Scott and Ann were looking into on her behalf. With respect to *that*, she felt as if she was standing on the edge of a precipice, trying to keep her balance with blustery breezes buffeting her.

But Ann managed to keep her steady. And they even had a couple of cosy evenings watching the telly, while chatting and working on some cross stitch patterns Janet had bought for them from Masons haberdashery, while Thomas stretched out in Frank's chair. There was some shared concern between them over the aftermath of Prime Minister, Margaret Thatcher, having resigned her leadership of the conservative party, and they watched some political discussions on that topic, worried that the grey and hesitant John Major, simply wouldn't be up to the job that their bright and shining Maggie had executed with such cutting precision. But soon they reverted to soaps, catching up with *Brookside*, where bad boy, Jimmy Corkhill, had some business plans, no doubt once again of a dubious nature. Yet despite these diversions, the pressure from Janet's confessions was rising each day Scott hadn't been in touch. And she could feel this pressure slowly building and squeezing around her heart, making her gasp out loud in unguarded moments. The waiting was proving barely tolerable, and it had only been two days.

On the third evening of Ann's stay she showed Janet a leaflet she'd picked up in town. It was for Victim Support, a confidential counselling service for anyone who'd been a victim of a crime.

'But what good will that be?' Janet exclaimed. 'I'm the one who did the crime.'

'No you didn't, Janet! This attitude is why I think you

should go. You were only responding to Frank the way you did because you'd been his victim for all your married life. And you need to see that. They deal with victims of domestic abuse, I checked when I popped in for the leaflet. I think you should see them for a few sessions. You can go in your lunch hour, and I can go with you if you like.'

Janet took some convincing. Her mother's voice rapped into her mind again – *You don't go airing your dirty linen in public* had been in Mildred's very own top twenty life-surviving maxims.

'But I've never talked about it in that way before,' Janet argued. 'I don't know if I can, I don't know if – '

'You told me. You told Scott. You even told Marian. And even that woman next door seems to have an inkling. You can tell someone else,' insisted Ann and she thrust the leaflet on top of Janet's embroidery in her lap.

Janet dragged her eyes from the blue silk threaded through the needle she was using to stitch a blue iris into the bouquet on her canvas, to the leaflet. She picked it up by its folded edge with the tips of her fingers in the manner of someone fearful of being contaminated. As she read it, her defences came stamping in to protest when certain words and phrases assaulted her sensibilities: Independent charity (*I'm not a charity case!*) Emotional support (*hand holding slush!*) No matter how long ago the crime took place (*how long is a piece of string?*) Confidential (*but how can I really trust that?*) Counselling (*having to go over it all again, and to what end, anyway?*)

Nevertheless, Ann, who argued the case for the defence and hammered down Janet's vocalised objections, got her way. It was a new service and she should take advantage, she said, and the time was right to prepare Janet for what was to come. The drilling look in Ann's ice-blue eyes bored deep into Janet's core. She found herself astonished at Ann's display of sheer determination and was once again struck by how she'd underestimated this woman. This woman from work whom she'd always judged to be as pliable as her grandson Daniel's Play-Doh. How could she have got her so wrong? Had she been wearing blinkers?

In any event, Janet found herself agreeing to try, and as the Victim Support office was open in the evening as well as during the day, she picked up the phone, got a voice at the other end and stuttered her needs into the receiver while Ann hovered by her side. She was extremely fortunate to get an appointment for the very next day at 2pm, which would fit in with her regular lunch break period. Janet liked this late slot because it gave her a short afternoon and she was on the department for the regular lunchtime trade. She promised Ann she wouldn't cut the visit short by saying she had to get back to work, she'd take the time necessary. Ann insisted that for once she should put her own needs first before Masons, and remembering the way she'd been spoken to by big man, Mr King, Janet found herself nodding. Ann would be there with her for the first visit and would meet her at the office in Crescent Place, only a five minute walk from the store.

The blond wood chairs with their waterproof vinyl coverings made Janet squirm as she tried to settle herself into one of them. Ann was by her side and they both sat opposite the counsellor who was sporting a neat blonde bob as if to coordinate with the furniture. The sanitised feel of the chairs reminded Janet of the sterile functionalism of hospitals, and then in turn of Hope Lodge, the mother and baby home, making her want to retreat further into her skin, rather than reveal any naked truths. If only the mess she seemed to have made of her life could so easily be wiped clean.

Mrs Liz Waring, who insisted on the use of her first name, seemed friendly and efficient, but Janet kneaded her clammy hands together in her lap when Liz began making some notes of Janet's personal contact details 'for the file' as she put it.

'What do you have to keep a file for?' Janet asked, her tone rising, annoyed at the secretarial demeanour of this all too neat and petite middle-aged madam, who looked just how she would imagine one of Samantha Dixon-Wright's friends might – another powder puff with her string of pearls and cashmere jumper. What could she possibly understand about the pains of giving a child away and a loveless bullying marriage?

A frown nicked Liz's brow, as if she was reading Janet's mind. 'Everyone has to have a file, Mrs Brewer, may I call you Janet? It's just in case you enlist our services later on down the line.' Then she smiled sweetly. 'Don't worry. Whatever you say here, whatever is written down, it's all totally confidential.'

'It's fine, Janet,' urged Ann.

'Okay,' said Janet tensing her stomach muscles and deciding to keep it brief so she could get out of here as soon as possible.

'Lovely,' Liz said, closing the file and sliding the cap back on her pen. 'Why don't you start at the beginning and tell me how you come to be here?'

Jane began the telling, tentatively at first, as hesitant as a newborn calf trying to walk on wobbly legs. But after half an hour, her 'brief' telling had protracted itself into almost the whole story, with promptings from Ann and clarifying questions, paraphrasing, and summarising from Liz. When Janet got to the climax of the story, now feeling like a runaway steam train building up speed through more frantic engine stoking, Liz leaned further over the desk on her sharp pointy elbows, and when Janet described the circumstances of Frank's death, that frown cut into Liz's forehead again. But there was no shock in her expression, just concern.

'I see,' she said, her eyes softening as she leaned even closer. 'What a lot you've had to bear. You must have had to be very strong.'

Janet held her gaze, searching it for the judgment which was sure to come, but she found nothing but sympathy. She tried to trust this but didn't know how to handle it. Besides, she didn't deserve any after killing her husband.

'But I caused his death,' she exclaimed.

'That remains to be seen,' Liz said. 'Of course you must feel a massive amount of conflict over it, but setting any legal issues aside, why don't we just consider how you may have got to the stage where you felt unable to help Frank at that crucial moment.'

'But what's the point? I did what I did,' she insisted.

'But you're here at Victim Support, Janet. And let me assure you, you're in the right place. No matter what you've done or didn't do, you've been a victim of domestic abuse – that much is clear. And times have changed. The law has changed and women are no longer expected to just put up with it. They no longer have to be a victim of this.'

Janet flinched at the words 'domestic abuse' and 'victim' which she had read in the leaflet and which Ann had previously used, but which she herself had never said out loud. These terms being applied to herself sounded so utterly pathetic and pitiful, riddled with weakness and wretchedness, terms that only applied to women who couldn't stand up for themselves. Women who let themselves be treated like doormats. Who didn't fight back. Who said they'd walked into doors. But then she caught hold of herself. She wouldn't describe herself like that…and then there was Marian too. Far too tough to be a victim…and yet she was becoming one through her bruiser of a boyfriend.

'We don't have much time left this session, Janet,' said Liz. 'But I'll over run a little because I feel its very important for you to consider some of the typical behaviour of domestic abuse that many women report, and see how they fit with your husband, so that you can begin to accept how he could have affected you over the long term.'

'Yes, exactly,' interrupted Ann. 'That's what I was hoping for.'

Liz didn't look at Ann. She kept her eyes fixed on Janet. 'Is that alright with you?'

Janet nodded mutely.

And as Liz talked on, Janet began nodding more. Her

eyes began to widen, and her bottom lip slowly dropped as she began to hear other women's truths for the very first time, truths that so easily matched her own. How much Frank had changed once they were married. That he'd become a bully just like his father. How he'd become jealous and possessive, criticising her clothes for being too revealing. There had also been the public put-downs, the not wanting her to have any friends, the not wanting her to do the secretarial job she'd trained for, the cutting her off from her family – all familiar territory to all these other women. As was his being socially engaging in public, but morose and easily triggered to slapping her in private. If she *would* wind him up, what did she expect? The constant criticizing, telling her she was useless, *Just who do you think you are, Janet?* That she'd never amount to anything, then conversely, that she was all airs and graces and needed taking down a peg or two. The smashed dinner set after the dinner party with Cliff and Angie, and more of her favourite china over the years, the ripped embroideries of her own handiwork, the turned-up nose at her new culinary dishes, sometimes being flung at the kitchen wall, the deliberate cigarette burns on her favourite soft furnishings. The rough sex, which she felt she had to put up with, but which sometimes became more violent crossing the line into rape – yes, she remembered saying 'no', but he said it was his right. The assurances that he wouldn't do it again, but doing it again anyway. The threats over using his police work connections to declare her an unfit mother and prevent her from getting custody of Scott if she tried to leave him or tried searching for Vivien.

And finally, there was the paralysing shame that held her back, the fear of not being believed – just like all the others. And the slowly acquired lack of trust in other people she'd laid down year after year, like the secreted protective layers of a marine animal. A building up of a tough exoskeleton, to safeguard her vulnerable inner self. And through having done this, feeling cut off from other people and even her own feelings. It all fitted and Janet's head was spinning with it all.

'There is one thing I'm wondering though,' Liz asked her. 'When your son grew up, you could have tried to leave your husband then. Did this possibility occur to you?'

Janet flinched, feeling a hot stab of pain in her chest. 'Yes. But by then I'd become hardened to him. I used to argue back. And I didn't see why I should be the one to leave the home I'd made with nothing to show for all those years. When he retired and was at home more and increased the verbal stuff again, I stood up to him by getting a job and my own car. And that helped so much.' She faltered. 'But at the same time I began to realise it was never going to end, and so I felt it had to be him or me…'

'Yes, I can see that,' Liz said softly. 'And then you finally snapped, didn't you? You see the thing you have to bear in mind, Janet, is that the repetition of the abuse over the years of your marriage may have rendered you powerless to radically change the situation. And although you are obviously a resourceful and assertive woman, there is a name for this kind of learned passivity known as battered person syndrome, which sometimes leads to the wife causing the death of her husband abuser, because they feel there is no other way out. And in your case, your husband being a policeman made it much harder for you over the long term to extricate yourself. So if you *do* decide to confess, to clear your conscience – because that's all it would achieve – you should use this syndrome in your defence.'

'You think she should confess?' Ann sounded incredulous, staring at Liz with eyes as round as saucers.

'No, I'm not saying that at all. I don't think the case would stand, and really speaking, he got what he deserved.'

'Are you allowed say that? I thought you weren't allowed to judge,' asked Janet, feeling confused. 'After all, what would someone like you know about any of this?' she said, her tone becoming desperate.

Liz bent forward again and clasped her hands together on the desk. 'I know, Janet, because it happened to me too.'

Janet and Ann gasped.

'You?' Janet felt she must have heard wrong. Surely not this well-to-do woman with the cashmere and pearls.

'Yes. That's why I trained in counselling and work for Victim Support. It's the kind of field where personal experience naturally helps. Of course, it wouldn't be professional of me to share my story, but believe me when I say I know, and I hope I've helped you see that you are a victim, Janet, and whatever you decide to do you should take that into account.'

When Janet returned to Masons, her thoughts were dashing around at tangents to one another like schoolchildren in a playground, bashing into each other, shouting and screaming. She'd made an appointment with Liz for the following week on her day off, and Ann had gone to Sainsbury's to get 'something nice' for tea. She had her own key to Janet's house now so could come and go more easily. Unable to contemplate food however, and not even having had a sandwich for lunch on the hoof, all Janet wanted right now was some peace. To call time on the chaos in the schoolyard by ringing her teacher's bell, and withdraw into her office sanctum.

But it was not to be.

Marian burst through the sanctum's door, like an impatient zealot, eyes bright with what looked like a strange sheen of fervour and fright. 'There's been a new development with the Harrison order!'

From Marian's expression Janet found it impossible to grope for an appropriate reaction – good news or bad news, celebration or commiseration, success is failure turned inside out and vice versa, was it to be or not to be…

'Well, ask me what,' Marian said. 'Go on!'

'Alright. What?'

'I was just coming back from the powder room, and Mr King was talking to Samantha at her desk, so I paused in the carpet department, pretending to look at some swatches. Well, Mrs Harrison has only gone and asked that the curtain order be fitted in time for Christmas.'

'What? But that's impossible! Clothworks have a cut off date of the 18th December, that's the day they'll deliver the last of the orders promised for Christmas. And it takes them at least four weeks to process an order. And even if that *was* possible there'll be no time to correct measuring mistakes. The whole idea is just – '

'I know! But Samantha *told* him it would be possible.'

Janet jumped to her feet. 'But he shouldn't have asked her. He should have asked me!'

'I know.'

'There's just no way this is going to work.'

'I know. But who will get the blame?'

'You're safe enough, because the fabric is coming any day now.'

'It's in! It came while you were at lunch. And we already have the contrast fabric needed.'

'Well, that's something! That would give them two weeks if Samantha doesn't dither about getting the order ready to send off. But it's still not enough time. I've never known them to do a curtain order in two weeks, especially a complex one like this with handmade goblet headings.' Janet sighed. 'Let's sit down for a minute and think about this.'

They sat. Janet with her chin propped in her hands, elbows on the desk, and Marian with her legs plaited tightly and nibbling at her nails.

Janet groaned. 'I'm going to have to ring Clothworks and ask them if it's at all feasible. And that's ignoring altogether the question of whether the measurements are right, which is Samantha's responsibility. I'm going to have to ask them if they will agree under any circumstances to do the order in time for a pre-Christmas fitting. Then if they can't accommodate, which I doubt they can, I'm going to have to tell Mr King.'

Marian stopped biting her nails. 'Right, okay, that sounds

good. I took the fabric around to Fancy Pants as soon as I checked it in. But she was leaving to have lunch with a 'potential client' as she put it. She said she'd do it later. It was still on its end propped against her desk when she was talking to Mr King.'

'Right,' said Janet. 'So it's no hurry, no rush, what's all the fuss about? That's her. You can just see her paddling her own canoe serenely over Niagara Falls.'

Marian giggled.

'I'll get onto Clothworks right now,' Janet said.

'Yes, but if you have to go to Mr King, he'll wonder how you know about the promised deadline before she's passed the fabric and the instructions over to your department to send off. And what if he thinks he'll get a different answer from Clothworks if he insists? Like the job he pulled on me.'

'Good point.'

Janet was finding it hard to think straight. Her personal life troubles and work troubles were jockeying for top dog position in her mind and she'd developed a late afternoon headache which was threatening to intensify like distant thunder clouds gathering on the horizon.

'You'd better go back to the department,' she said to Marian. 'I'll have a think.'

After a few angry moments of realising that what had happened to Marian could easily happen to her, she decided to make the call anyway. She had to do something. She wasn't ready to let the whole thing hit the fan just yet. It simply wasn't in her Masons programming.

Marian left her to it, but brought her what Samantha had given her in writing when she was first trying to order the Harvest Fruits. It was a big help to Janet. In Samantha's lightly-pressured and loopy handwriting, which a graphologist could easily match to Samantha's ethereal and slippery personality, Janet decided, the order described two pairs of floor length curtains, 2.5 widths each curtain by 92" drop, goblet headings, to hang on brass poles of which there was no mention of their respective widths. And God help the hook drops, thought Janet, which in this case would be a vital component of the order. But in any event, there was no way the powder puff would have got hook drops right. Her eyes had drawn down their gauzy blinds to the term when Janet had mentioned it to her one day. There was also to be contrast trimming on the leading edges of the drapes, along the top of the goblets, and as piping on the additional two pairs of crescented tiebacks. All so time consuming and expensive to make. Now she had something more concrete to ask Clothworks. Perfect!

A young efficient lady called Tracy answered the phone. Janet had spoken to her many times before and had fostered a good relationship with her. When she described the order, Tracy made a whistling noise, and then fell silent.

'Tracy? Are you still there?'

'Janet, it's just impossible. The 18th is our deadline for getting orders back to you. We haven't even got your fabric and instructions yet and with all the work involved? It's an absolute no.'

'Not even if we pay you extra?'

'Not even then. The staff get one decent break a year, and that's at Christmas. There is no way they will do overtime.'

'Not even if our store manager puts pressure on your directors.'

'One of those directors is my dad, so I know it will be a no, not even then. Not even if your manager is Father Christmas himself.'

Janet breathed out heavily. 'Okay, that's what I wanted to know. Sorry, Tracy, I know it's ridiculous, but I needed to know exactly where we stood.'

'Happy to help, Janet. Have a happy Christmas, won't you?'

'Yes, you too. Thanks very much, Tracy.'

When she went back onto the department, she found Samantha was bringing the order over. She gently lowered the roll of Harvest Fruits down on the bench as if it was a holy relic, with her making up instructions taped to it. Claire snapped a thank you at her and she and Janet watched the rear view of the interior designer, somehow with the essence of her character summed up in the fleshiness of her backside, saunter away, with Louis Armstrong somewhere in the ether singing, 'We Have All The Time In The World'. This was as far from Masons programming as Mercury is from Neptune and Samantha was all set to crash and burn.

As soon as Janet spotted the written instruction *'to be finished by the 18th, so fitting can be done before Christmas'* she knew the moment had come. Fired up and fully charged by the sight of Samantha's airy-fairy instructions, she went and retrieved a spare Clothworks leaflet from her office and together with the written instructions, she stalked along the vinyl walkway, rapping her heels on its polished hardness, to Mr King's office in the far corner of the linen department. His secretary was there, all pursed lips and horn-rimmed spectacles on a chain. She looked up in surprise when Janet entered by thrusting open the door and causing it to bang against the adjacent wall.

'I need to see Mr King. It's urgent,' she said, adopting her habitual first position in ballet with her feet, which she reserved for formal occasions to help her gain her poise.

'He's on the phone.'

'Then I'll wait.'

Janet dropped into one of the easy chairs, usually reserved for visiting management dignitaries, industry buyers, or sales representatives, and neatly crossed her legs. Her own personal problems and past history, as reflected upon in the counselling session, were right now functioning to harden her resolve.

Mrs Grant, the secretary, phoned through to Mr King to inform him Janet was waiting, and after five minutes he appeared. Grey silk suit, as usual, but with a blue tie today. Deep furrows ploughed across his brow.

'What's so important, Janet?'

'Sorry to disturb you, Mr King, but I thought I'd better

warn you, if you're under the impression that the Harrison order can be ready and fitted before Christmas, well, it will be impossible, I'm afraid.'

Mr King locked his gaze upon her and a silence fell between them with an almost audible thump. Mrs Grant, behind her desk, coughed as if fill it.

Patrick King thrust his considerable belly forward and drew himself and his shaggy eyebrows up to full elevation. 'What did you say?'

Janet held tight onto her resolve. 'The Harrison order can't be ready for Christmas. I checked with the curtain makers.'

He paused, drawing his face into a scowl. 'So how is it that Ms Dixon-Wright assures me it will be?'

'It isn't up to Samantha to give such assurances. She doesn't have the jurisdiction.'

'That's quite a word, isn't it? Jurisdiction. And I suppose you do have it? The jurisdiction, that is.'

The sarcasm in his voice began to press an old button she still had inside her, a button worn thin by Frank. But she still held tight.

'No, not me. Clothworks. They won't be able to process the order in time for Christmas.'

And then it struck Janet, how simply ridiculous it all was. Curtains for Christmas, ever so vital, weren't they? Just so a family living on the Royal Crescent could have *the* perfect Christmas, around their perfect fire, with its garlanded mantle, with their perfect Christmas tree, the expensive kind that doesn't shed its needles, dripping with tinsel, with a literally stuck-up fairy at the top to bring their Christmas wishes true. A perfect turkey, especially ordered from a free range organic supplier, and it might even have had a living name, like Bertha. Gobble up Bertha everyone. She's so nicely glazed. Sitting around a massive drop-leaf mahogany table buffed to a mirror finish. And don't forget the poinsettia as the centrepiece will you? The one that was especially ordered from a London florist and came to the door in a pretty green van, rather than being bought in a queue in the local Safeway. And what about the Baileys? And the after dinner mints. Bendicks anyone? And there she was, back to realising that she couldn't stand Christmas and all its rituals, and here she was facing another one. "Christmas won't be Christmas without any presents", grumbled Jo, lying on the rug, in the opening line of *Little Women*. Only Louisa May had got it wrong, Janet decided. It was more a case of "Christmas won't be Christmas without our new curtains" insisted Mrs Harrison, working through her 'to do' list and sipping sherry from an Edinburgh Crystal glass.

'So this is what the makers have told you. That it can't be done.' Mr King's gravelly voice disturbed her musings like an Greek oracle with the prophetic power of foresight.

'Yes,' she said, with a cutting edge of defiance.

'Well, we'll see about that. I'll phone them. Give me their number.' He flicked his right hand towards himself to hurry her up, and she handed him the Clothworks leaflet and the making instructions she'd come prepared with. So far, so good.

'Leave it with me. I'll sort it out.'

She turned to leave. The oracle had spoken. Now it was in the hands of fate.

After Janet returned to her department, she glanced at her watch. It was just after 4pm. Only an hour to go until closing time and surely not enough time for any further developments this afternoon.

But she was in for a surprise. At 4.30, Mr. King's raised voice could be heard from the direction of the carpet department, with simpering sounding replies which served to turn up the store manager's volume control even higher. Luckily there were only a couple of customers in discussion with an assistant in the bedding department discussing duvet tog ratings. But members of staff's noses began to twitch in the direction of carpets, and they scuttled nearer to tidy up stands of merchandise which were already immaculately displayed. Shirley Appleton told one assistant to cash up and thrust a duster into another assistant's grasp. Claire on soft furnishing began cashing up, periodically raising her eyebrows at Janet.

'Gemma will be sorry to be missing this,' she muttered.

On Berkeley Fabrics Milly bustled around the hanging display curtains, tweaking the pinch pleats even straighter while snapping worried glances at Marian.

Janet and Marian stood like sentinels with their arms folded staring at each other.

After five minutes or so the argument stopped and everyone paused in their diversions and strained to hear what was coming next. Then Niall Walsh from carpets slalomed and slunk around the fixtures and fittings noiselessly making his way over to soft furnishing with his hands tucked deep into his pockets.

'He wants to see you, Janet,' he said, not making any eye contact with her and his shoulders more gravity slumped than ever. 'He wants both you and Marian to go around to the interior designer's desk.'

Marian heard and made her way over to Janet. 'What does he want us for?' she asked Janet.

Janet shook her head.

'You went and warned him, didn't you?'

Janet nodded.

'Best not keep him waiting,' muttered Niall.

So Janet and Marian hit the vinyl and rapped their heels over to Samantha's section, giving each other mutual glances of misgiving, while Niall slithered silently behind them like a shadow.

When they rounded the corner they saw the store manager pacing around Samantha like a wounded beast. Red in the face, mouth set like concrete above his tucked-in chin, with a protruding vein popping in his right temple. Samantha was standing behind her desk with her lip wobbling, looking down at her feet.

When Patrick King saw Janet and Marian he rounded on

them. He pointed at Samantha and declared to them, 'I'm very disappointed in Samantha here. I've given her a verbal warning. The makers will not be able to have those curtains ready for Christmas. They refuse point blank.' He flung the leaflet and the instructions onto Samantha's desk. 'Frankly, they don't deserve to be on our payroll if they can't accommodate emergencies, and I fully intend to look into finding an alternative company at some point. But that aside, I've personally been made a fool of! Masons has been made a fool of! I was misled by Ms Dixon-Wright here, who assured me a Christmas delivery was possible. I promised the customer based on that assurance and now look at us! I've had to smooth things over with Mrs Harrison for now, but let's just hope things go all right from now on, because I'll be watching you. All of you!' He hooked his gaze into all three of them as if marking his prey.

'I expect you to work as a team. Do you hear me? Whatever it takes. I have better things to do with my time than supervise a cock-up like this.' Then he looked at Janet. 'I can't quite figure you out. I don't know if I can trust you. You're good at finding problems, but not necessarily at solving them. Remember, you haven't done a full year yet as manager, and you're still on probation as far as I'm concerned. I'm beginning to question my judgment in giving you the position.'

Janet gasped. 'But with all due respect, there -'

'No! I don't want to hear it.' He thrust his hand at her, palm out and upright, at her like a policeman stopping traffic. 'I've had more than enough for one day.'

And with that, he swivelled on his heels and marched away, leaving Janet, Marian and Samantha staring at one another. The main department lights had been turned off, the whole of the second floor seemed deserted, and there was an atmosphere of repose that falls like dusk when both customers and staff have left a busy space alone for the night. No doubt Claire and Milly were probably waiting to hear what had happened, but otherwise the floor seemed to sigh, stretch itself out and recline with some relief that another day of carrying the heavy weight of consumerism was over.

Marian shook her head at Samantha.

Janet saw that Samantha's eyes were red and filmy, and in her peach linen suit with its wrinkles of wear from the trials of the day all too evident, she looked like a crushed bloom.

'Samantha! Why did you promise it would be okay? Why didn't you ask me?' Janet said, feeling a caustic cocktail mix of fury at Patrick King for treating her so unjustly and fear at the idea of losing the position she had fought for and already proved herself worthy of many times over.

With her eyes narrowed into slits in a way Janet hadn't observed before, for once Samantha made her feelings plain. 'Because I'm sick and tired of having to pass things by you both, that's why. I know you don't like me. You've made that pretty obvious.'

'But it's because of your airs and graces,' Marian exclaimed. 'This is a department store, not a high class interior designers.'

'But that's what I was brought in for. Just *that*. That is my role!'

'But you've never learned the systems,' Janet said. 'And we've tried so hard to teach you. That's what's caused all this! And you've got us into trouble along with you!'

Then Samantha's demeanour changed. Her azure eyes regained their soft, slightly out of focus appearance. She retrieved her leather briefcase from beneath her desk, shouldered it and smiled sweetly at them both.

'I'm sure it will all turn out for the best,' she said, with the wobbly worry on show only minutes earlier swept from her face like dirt brushed under a rug.

As she left, Marian and Janet wordlessly followed in her wake, pausing to tell Claire and Milly what had happened. Then they all descended the staircase, their aching feet now suffering after a long day in court shoes and begging for relief at home, to wend their way down through the labyrinth to the staff exit, and out into the pinching chill of a late November evening. It was going to be the 1st December the very next day, and the first shopping weekend of December would begin. What was usually a quiet Yuletide time for soft furnishing, was now threatened by ill omen, because although one Harrison order crisis had been managed, another was looming after Christmas in the New Year when those curtains *would* be ready for fitting.

When Janet got home she found Ann waiting with a broad smile and sparkling eyes, and there was the delicious aroma of roast chicken floating from the kitchen to remind Janet that she'd barely eaten anything all day. Despite this welcome, and without taking off her coat, Janet slumped into the sofa.

'A terrible afternoon,' she muttered. She shook off her shoes and propped her elbow on the arm of the sofa, with her fingers splayed on the side of her temple. 'The Harrison order just got a whole lot worse.'

'Never mind about that,' Ann said excitedly. 'You can tell me about that later. You need to ring Scott, he's got some news about Cliff Ward! He said for you to ring him straightaway.'

At the mention of this name, this former friend and colleague of her husband's, Janet felt a sick kind of fear creep into her bones. The past had just yanked her back into its depths again, like being tugged through a thick hedge backwards.

'Oh God,' she said, slowly getting to her feet. 'I can't believe this is happening.'

Ann pulled her coat from her and Janet edged to the phone in the hall. She looked back at Ann, her face drawn into a grimace.

'Go on! It's good news, nothing bad.'

Scott answered on the second ring and he got straight to the point. Like mother, like son, she thought. 'Cliff Ward will see us on Sunday at his place in Toddington, Mum, at two o' clock. You, me, and Ann.'

'How…how did you find him? I can't believe you've found him.'

'Through the police headquarters. It took some doing. He's retired now and they refused to give me his contact details, even though I explained I was the son of a former friend of his. I named Dad of course, in case that helped, but it didn't seem to. But I kept asking, so in the end they got in touch with Cliff to see if he would ring me. And he did! And he said he'd be more than happy to see us all.'

Janet swallowed hard. 'What have you told him?'

'Just that you want his advice and it's about Frank's death. I said it would be better if we told him everything face to face.'

'Oh God.'

'He sounded fine, Mum. Really. He became a detective chief inspector. Said he'd often thought about you over the years. And when he found out Dad had died, he wondered about getting in touch with you, but he didn't want to drag up the past in case it upset you.'

'Well…that was considerate.' Janet tried to remember what she'd liked about Cliff. He was always cheerful in contrast to Frank, always courteous. But mostly, it had to be his sensitivity with his wife, Angie, something Janet had never had from Frank, and she remembered feeling jealous of Angie. Dear harmless Angie, who loved her dancing, her Babychams, and short skirts and dresses, who just wanted to have some fun, and who Frank called a floozy for her pains in later years.

'Did he say how his wife, Angie, is?'

'Yes, kind of. She died two years ago. Heart disease apparently. They never had any children, so he's on his own now.'

'He'd take that hard. He adored her.'

'Right. That would be tough…well, I'll pick you and Ann up at half one on Sunday.'

'Alright. Thank you, Scott. Bye –'

'Just a minute. Ann said you'd been putting up with some bullshit at work.'

'Yes, I'd say it qualifies as that.'

'Well, you can give as good as you get, remember that, won't you?'

Janet smiled weakly. 'I think I've already begun.'

Scott said goodbye and she held the receiver for a while with a shaking hand, listening to the sonorous dialling tone resounding in her head with a sense of confirmed finality that there was to be no going back now. She got the message, and slowly lowered the receiver into its cradle with a barely audible click. Things were changing so fast, racing out of her grasp, with none of the familiar control she'd relied on over the years. This was a whole new unfamiliar territory which she was finding vaguely terrifying.

But after explaining the details of the Sunday visit to Ann over their chicken dinner and bringing her up to date with the latest blow-up at work, the tensions of the day began to seep out through Janet's pores. She listened to Ann's soothing tones of support and glanced periodically at a curled up Thomas sleeping in Frank's old chair. And as the evening drew further in, it slowly dawned upon her that she had a true friend in Ann, that she'd done little to deserve her, and that if Ann wasn't keeping her company right now, she'd probably be a black heap in her woollen coat huddled on her bed.

'Thank you for being here,' she said.

'You don't have to thank me.'

'I'm scared.'

'I know.'

Chapter 19

Cliff Ward's home in Toddington was a bit of a surprise to Janet. It was of rustic style in a quiet leafy lane in the new town area, and was presently glazed in the honey glow of some rare December sunshine, bestowing upon it the feel of a house straight out of *Grimm's Fairy Tales*. As Scott parked his white Toyota Corolla at the kerbside, and he, Ann, and Janet began walking up the front flagstone path, she examined the house further to distract herself from her quivering nerves and the hard knot in her stomach. It was semi-detached, with a red brick ground floor and a slate-tiled first floor, with the upstairs windows featuring black and white tudor-style gables reminiscent of Tewkesbury High Street. A white picket fence edged the path to the front door and its quaint overhanging tiled roof. As they approached, she noticed a tall shadow inside the front room rise to full height.

Just as Scott's hand reached for the brass bumble bee door knocker, the red door opened and a man she hadn't seen for over 25 years stood in front of them with a half smile on his face, as if in readiness to assess the situation and decide on the appropriate expression in due course.

Introductions were made. Cliff shook hands with Scott and Ann, but he held himself back when greeting Janet and they both examined each other carefully.

Cliff had always been on the slim side, but he'd lost weight over the years, becoming reed-like with his flesh more loosely shrink-wrapping his bones, and he'd developed a faint stoop which seemed a little advanced for his 66 years of age. He and Frank had been exactly the same age, but where Frank had laid down fleshy mass into late middle age, Cliff had pared himself to the core. But when she looked up at his face and into his eyes, the Cliff she used to know was still there. Despite the shaggy eyebrows, the receding stiff grey hair, the square set of his jaw with the grooves around his mouth deep enough to plant seeds in, and his long chiselled nose, his sharp blue eyes had lost none of their vigour. And as she stared into them, he grinned.

'Long time, no see, eh, Jan?'

She smiled at the use of his old nickname for her, which no one else had ever used.

'You're looking as good as ever, holding back the years well,' he smiled.

Then he came forward and she found herself enveloped in a pair of surprisingly strong arms and being tightly squeezed. And this was something, she reflected, that he'd never have done if Frank had been around. And come to think of it, just a week ago she wouldn't have been able to tolerate it.

'I'm very glad to see you,' he said quietly in her ear. 'I miss Angie so much. I've been thinking about the old days lately.'

As he ushered them into the living room and offered them a seat, he asked them what they wanted to drink – tea, coffee, or something stronger – and orders duly noted, he went off into the kitchen, giving Janet time to assess the interior design. This was a compulsion in her blood now, as much a matter of procedure as Cliff's police work had been to him.

The ceiling was beamed and the fireplace was made of buttery Cotswold stone, with a single gilded photograph of Cliff and Angie in their younger halcyon days in pride of place on the mantle. Angie looked radiant, as she always had; with her loose blonde curls framing her bright open face and made up in quintessential sixties fashion with sweeping eyeliner, powder-blue eye shadow, and pale pink lipstick. She was wearing a printed frilly blouse right out of the seventies and Cliff was by her side, with a full head of shaggy hair and an untidy moustache, while he looked at Angie with a sloppy grin on his face. This was a picture of a couple truly in love. A couple sharing the kind of love she'd only known so fleetingly with Joe. Frank had killed off whatever love may have come in time for himself and Janet, as purposefully as he'd killed the greenfly on his roses, but with such devastatingly different results. She felt her eyes itching with tears so she continued assessing the interior. Pinks, terracottas and greens were the main coordinating colours, as represented in their togetherness in the cotton-satin loose covers of the three piece suite, which Janet recognised as Crowson 'Amadour' colour 40 from the Country Gardens collection. And as she cast her eyes around further she could see the distinctly light and feminine qualities with an edge of the frivolous that had been Angie's very own taste. A cottage garden out the back was in harmony with this, though it presently appeared overgrown and neglected.

When Cliff brought in the tea and coffee and set the cups on the coffee table, Janet felt she had to say something about Angie first.

'I'm so sorry to hear about Angie, Cliff. She was always so full of life, so kind too.' In fact she remembered Angie telling her in later years of their acquaintance that she should leave that husband of hers. *That bastard*, that's what she'd called him. Probably not long after the Chicken A la King party where Frank had smashed up their wedding present after Cliff and Angie had left. The tensions had obviously already been sensed despite Janet's best efforts to hide them.

Cliff sighed as he lowered himself stiffly into his easy chair. 'Thank you, Jan. Yes we had some amazing times. It's so different without her. I don't know what to do with myself to be honest…and everywhere I look in this house, she's here.' He cast his arms wide. 'This was her choice of house, her décor. It was her thing, not so much mine. All that mattered to me was that she was happy. After I became a detective inspector with the CID I spent more time away from home, but she was always here for me, at home.'

His voice was cracking now, and Janet felt she had to

help him. Even though she considered herself useless at giving empathy, it was right that it should come from her.

'As far as I could see she was a happy free spirit, despite you being in the police force. Maybe that's what worked so well?'

Cliff's frown lines smoothed out. 'Yes, actually, Jan, I think that's exactly how it was.'

He hesitated for a moment. 'Well, what brings you here today? Scott, here, said it was to do with Frank's death? Sorry I couldn't make it to the funeral by the way.'

'It doesn't matter,' Janet replied. 'There was hardly anyone there.' Then she paused, head bowed over the coffee cup she was holding.

'Do you want me to fill Cliff in, Mum?' Scott asked.

No,' she said quickly. 'It should be me.'

The telling of the story *again* was something she'd been dreading, and the knot in her stomach had drawn even tighter since she'd sat down. But as she began telling once more what amounted to her life story – all that was before Frank and after Frank – she was surprised to find it was becoming easier each time she told it. And it felt as if she was unpacking a loaded bag of mossy rocks that she'd barely been aware of shouldering all these years, unpacking it now in front of others who actually wanted to help her examine them. She was turning over these memories, these rotting mossy stones, and watching the hidden insects scuttle away. And she knew these memories would never be quite the same again now she was truly sharing them.

Ann interjected periodically, or Scott broke in to clarify or prompt her, and Cliff asked questions, calmly, with his head nodding understanding or encouragement, as she tried to describe events as chronologically as possible. But there was one moment when he jumped in fast just as Janet was explaining about the domestic abuse.

'Do you remember me asking you if he treated you right?' Cliff asked, frowning. 'You said things were fine.'

'Yes, I know,' Janet replied. 'In a way that's why we're here now. But at the time I just didn't dare tell you the truth in case it got back to him. You were a close friend of his, not really mine.'

Cliff shook his head slowly. 'Yes, but we were all reasonably close once. I feel I let you down, Jan. I suspected he might have been taking his frustrations out on you, but you said you were alright. I should have known better. I feel so badly that I let you down.'

'No, Cliff. I never blamed you in any – '

'There are things you need to know about him, what he was like at work. It might help. But carry on and get to the end first.'

So she carried on and when she got to describing Frank's death and all the particulars, Cliff shifted onto the edge of his seat, hands clasped between his knees. And now came the first pertinent questions. They were of a rapid kind, inviting only yes or no answers.

'So, you're worried you contributed to his death?'

Her tongue felt stuck to the roof of her mouth. The question hovered and flapped in the room like a trapped bird.

'Is that it, Jan?'

She breathed out and took a sip of coffee. 'Yes.'

'Because you kicked away the pills he might have benefited from?'

'Yes.'

'Because right in that very moment when he was having his angina attack, you saw an opportunity?'

'Well, kind of, yes – if I'm totally honest with myself. All I knew was I just couldn't take any more. No more of him telling me what to do, no more of him having a go at me, belittling me, no more of him trying to stop me working at Masons. And right in that moment I just couldn't let myself help him, and when he tried to get his pills, something in me just snapped and I felt he mustn't have that chance. So I stopped him.' She hesitated. 'And then I froze, I couldn't move. But afterwards, when I got rid of the pills in the kitchen waste bin before the ambulance came, I felt guilty…I began to realise that by doing this I was covering up. And if I was covering up I must have committed a crime.'

'Hmm. So the emergency services arrived, found he was dead, and then called the doctor?'

'Yes.'

'Was it Frank's GP?'

'Yes, Dr Blake.'

'And did he ask about Frank's medication?'

'No. He just told me it was due to his condition. And as far as he was concerned not unexpected.'

'Hmm. Did you think that was a bit odd?'

'No, not at the time. I was just relieved.'

'Hmm, well never mind that for now. So what made you bring all this out into the open recently with Ann and your son?'

'I blurted it out to someone at work. Someone I know is probably being hit by her boyfriend. Marian's her name. I don't know what happened. She wouldn't listen and it got very heated, she pushed me I suppose, and I ended up blurting it out…and that was the beginning of this, well, unravelling, I suppose you could call it.'

'I see. Do you think she will tell anyone?'

'She says not.'

'Do you trust her?'

'Not really, no.'

Ann interrupted. 'But I've got a feeling she won't tell anyone. She didn't think Janet had done anything wrong.'

'Well not to worry, it would just be her word against yours, Jan, unless you were overheard?'

'No. She checked. Apparently we weren't overheard.'

'But there might have been a witness,' observed Scott. 'The next door neighbour claims she was peeping through the curtains at the time. She's told Mum she saw the whole thing.'

Janet explained what Winnie was like. What Winnie had

told her. And why she swore she wouldn't say anything, because of having tried to get rid of her own husband and repeatedly failing until fate had finally intervened.

Cliff's eyebrows shot up. 'What are we in here? A farce? A Noel Coward play? Or maybe we need Poirot and his little grey cells? I think I need something stronger.' He hoisted himself to his feet and sidled over to a dark wood mock-Tudor drinks cabinet in the corner of the room. Pouring himself a one finger measure of scotch, he stood at the window and stared out at the road.

'So the only people really in the know are Ann, the close friend, Scott, the son, this Marian at work with the lousy boyfriend, and Winnie the weird neighbour.'

'Yes,' Janet said, inwardly wincing at these part-playing descriptions. 'But now also a Victim Support woman called Liz.'

Cliff turned around smiling. 'Oh, I know Liz from work. Smart woman. Knows her stuff.'

'Yes, very helpful.'

'And that's it?'

'That's it.'

'Okay, so you want to know where you may stand legally?'

'Yes,' Janet, Scott and Ann said in unison.

'Right,' said Cliff. He swirled his whisky around in his glass, took a sip, then returned to his armchair.

Well, technically,' he said, crossing his legs, 'it's a kind of manslaughter, specifically gross negligence manslaughter.'

Janet shivered and felt herself beginning to shake.

Scott drew a sharp intake of breath and Ann gasped.

'Bear with me,' Cliff smiled. 'I'll lay it out as factually as possible. Then we'll look at the mitigating circumstances, okay?'

They nodded.

'So gross negligence involuntary manslaughter. A form of homicide where one person causes the death of another in circumstances where there is an extreme lack of care within a position of liability. In your case they might call it a crime of omission, where the death can be seen to occur due to a failure to take action to help prevent the death. Was there a duty of care that should have been in operation that was breached? In this case, between a husband and wife? It would be a yes, I'm afraid. You see, it's really the kicking away of the pills that makes this a tougher one to defend – because technically that would be called an endangering act.'

Janet nodded.

Ann and Scott stared at each other.

'But the mitigating circumstances are that you were repeatedly bullied and abused throughout a long-term marriage, and after he retired the situation became more tense. There's this syndrome, a kind of learned behaviour, that can affect victims of domestic abuse called battered person syndrome –'

'Liz mentioned that,' interrupted Ann.

'It's sometimes used as a defence in cases where a wife is accused of killing her husband abuser because there seems to be no alternative. That it's a matter of survival.'

'But it wasn't like *that!*' Janet exclaimed.

'No, I'm sure it wasn't,' Cliff said. 'Or certainly that you didn't *feel* as helpless as that. You're too tough for that. And I wouldn't say you killed him at all, Jan, believe me, but I'm just saying this syndrome can argue a case for diminished responsibility, due to the long-term abuse, and could be taken into account for your defence if it hypothetically went to court. I'm just giving you the facts.'

'Yes…I know.'

Scott jumped to his feet. 'But this is mad! She didn't do anything really.'

'Yes, but there's that word, 'really', isn't there? Jan here failed to help her abusive husband of many years because she'd had enough. After all those years she didn't back down. Many people would find it totally acceptable, they'd say that it was Frank's due, that it was his responsibility not to get into an anger tantrum in the first place, that he could have got angry anywhere at anytime without access to his pills, and I'm one of those people who would say these things, but legally it's not that simple, and what makes it more significant is the deliberate withdrawal of the pills, because in that very moment the intent was there for Frank to die, and in law, that counts. Do you see? And it's the action, not the state of mind that counts.'

'Oh shit,' Scott said.

'Exactly,' Cliff replied.

'I just don't know what to do,' Janet said. 'But I do know that each day that passes I feel like I need to wipe the slate clean. I've lived under enough clouds. I want a clean slate and I want to find my daughter if at all possible.'

'Yes,' Cliff said gently, 'and I want to help you. I'm *going* to help you. This retired detective chief inspector is going to tone up his detecting muscles to turn private investigator for you, so – '

'But you don't owe me anything, Cliff, really! I don't expect anything!'

'But I feel I owe you, Jan. That's what counts.'

'That would be amazing,' Scott said.

Ann beamed approval.

Janet opened and shut her mouth, not knowing what to think or feel anymore. This whole business of people helping, people actually caring about her enough to help, was something she had never experienced since she'd been a girl through her father and Auntie Vi. She'd long given up even bothering to imagine it. And yet it was happening right now. Her head felt swimmy and she couldn't speak.

'So lets look at your options, Jan. So that you can go away and have a think, bearing in mind that clean slate you're after,' Cliff said.

'First up, you could do nothing and learn to live with it, as you've been doing this year. But now that means trusting that this Marian and, most importantly, the weird neighbour, will keep their mouths shut. Liz certainly will.

'Or you could walk into the police station and confess,

taking Liz with you as support. Now if you do that, they really need evidence. A confession from you alone isn't enough. So they'd at least need a witness statement. But would the weird Winnie comply? She doesn't sound inclined to. They could also request access to Frank's medical records which may or may not help. They might want to talk to the GP. And they'd want to know about your history of domestic abuse too. So, even if you confess, by the time they assess the case and begin investigating, they may decide that despite your confession, if they don't have a witness then they won't have enough evidence to get a warrant to arrest you. And they won't have enough evidence to submit to the Criminal Prosecution Service. It's the CPS which decides on which cases can legitimately go to trial or not. But on the other hand, there is a chance it might go the other way, if Winnie plays ball with the police or if something else turns up. If that happens, you might be looking at a manslaughter charge and a suspended sentence.'

Janet took a deep breath, then slowly exhaled. 'Right.'

'Now there's no real rush, Jan. You need to go away and think about it. I have a solicitor contact who might be able to help if necessary. But I want you to know that what happened is a very grey area indeed. And I'm sure many similar incidents go unreported. But it strikes me that this is all about your conscience, so that is what we need to work with for your peace of mind so you can move on. Have I got that right?'

'Yes. Oh yes.'

'And you have some excellent defence material on your side. And the knowledge that a policeman got away with this abusive behaviour will be a bitter taste indeed.'

'Yes, I can see that,' replied Janet. But it was now sounding so frightening. Could she see this through? Because right at this moment just the idea of walking into the police station made her shudder. The pure shame of it.

Cliff turned to Scott and Ann. 'Do you both see where Jan is coming from with this? Because we all need to work together with whatever she decides.'

Scott and Ann looked at Janet – two worried faces seeking some kind of sanction. She cracked an encouraging smile, then they both turned to Cliff and nodded.

'Okay, that's good. Now how about we all stretch our legs, amble over to the pub down the road, and I can tell you about Frank, the stuff that really broke up our friendship. And you need to know it, Jan, especially now.'

Sitting in rays of low winter sunshine glancing through leaded windows, and ensconced around a table in the Traveller's Rest, the four of them sipped at their beverages. White wine for Janet and Ann, a pint of local bitter for Cliff and Scott, and they had some packets of crisps to dip into. It was a typical Ye Olde English Inn. Dust motes rolled lazily in the golden glow of the sun, black beams propped up the ceiling stained by tobacco fumes puffed out over the centuries, and the smell of hops infused the air with a warm familiarity of time out of mind. Fading scenes of red-jacketed huntsmen and their hounds racing across country estates after their quarry, decorated the knobbly whitewashed walls, and the oak tables and chairs had been burnished and hollowed by a ceaseless flow of human contact. How many yarns and jokes had been told inside these walls? How many had propped up the bar while they vented their spleen? It felt to Janet like a place where stories were told. And what she was about to hear now sounded exactly like one.

'Now let me tell you about Frank,' Cliff said, looking at Janet and Scott. 'You need to understand what I think went wrong with him, to do with the job.'

Janet and Scott looked sharply at one another, then at Cliff.

'Okay?' he asked.

They nodded.

'Go ahead,' said Scott. 'He never did talk much about work.'

'No,' Janet murmured. 'Certainly not after the first couple

of years moving to Cheltenham. I used to ask him about his day, but he just said, 'same old, same old, you don't need to know."

'Right,' Cliff said, 'that sounds like him. The job certainly altered him. Back in the days when we were at school together we were mostly pals because our mothers were friends, so we'd be around at each other's houses a lot. I never saw much of Frank's father, he was always either at work at the factory, or at the pub, but I got the idea he was what you might call a hard man, pretty strict, and his wife seemed scared to death of him. No doubt he was a bully. Anyway, I have to say Frank was a good friend. He was loyal, thoughtful, a bit on the priggish side at times, but okay. We used to get up to what all teenage boys got up to back then in the forties, building shelters, going on bike rides, mucking around on bomb sites. Later on we went walking and camping in the Mendips together. And after we did our national service we decided to apply to the police force. Looked like a good secure job for life with a police house and a decent pension.'

'Do you think that's all it was to him – security and good prospects?' Janet asked.

'No, I think it was more than that at first. He seemed to be genuinely interested in helping people. I *do* think he wanted to impress his dad though and I think he came to enjoy the power. He was good at the job for the first couple of years, enjoyed being on his beat, though he didn't approve of the women police officers who were coming into the job. He was a bit sexist actually, got warned a few times. Wouldn't listen to me by then. He was also pretty squeamish where road accident work was concerned…to be honest after those first two years we just drifted apart. I was working towards promotion, so I was doing everything by the book. Frank didn't seem bothered about advancing. He got to the rank of sergeant, but I think he lacked the diplomacy and sensitivity to get any higher – and then of course, later on, like quite a few officers in the sixties, there was a bit of a kicking against standard procedure.'

'How do you mean?' Scott asked.

Cliff took an extra large swallow of his pint. 'Too much cutting of corners and bending the law to get results, I suppose you could call it. To be honest, it was a bit like you see in The Sweeney. He used to be easily provoked and use his fists too readily when he was arresting someone who gave him some verbal, or when he got frustrated with a suspect. Any excuse, and he was in there, at least that's what I heard. On one occasion I heard he only narrowly escaped being dismissed. It was just around that time when I asked you if he was treating you right, Jan, because this violence seemed to have been triggered off in him by the job and was sort of turning him.'

'Or it might have been me telling him about Vivien?' Janet said, frowning.

'No.' Cliff shook his head. 'I think it was in him all the time. Remember his father? And the job created an outlet, and then it became a habit. He *did* like the power. I saw that in him. There were others just like him. His cronies. And I think he joined some kind of private police club, where they socialized and shared the same mindsets no doubt.'

'That gold signet ring of his,' Janet breathed. 'He caught me here with it once,' she said, touching the scar on her left cheek. 'Maybe it was an affiliation ring or something to do with the Freemasons? Not something he inherited from his father like he said.'

Cliff looked at her sharply. 'Can you describe it?'

'A spread eagle holding a sword.'

'That's not the Freemasons. Theirs is a square and compasses.' He paused, eyebrows drawn together. 'But…it kind of sounds familiar. I wonder if I've seen it before? Where is the ring now?'

'I never wanted to see it again. Scott didn't want it, so I pawned it at Money Spinners in the high street.'

'Hmm. It could well have been an affiliation or fraternity ring. It's the kind of thing a private club of bent police officers would do, dispensing their own kind of power and justice with the eagle and the sword symbolism.' Then he shook his head. 'But I was with CID by then, so I just didn't see much of Frank or his mates.' He paused. 'Anyway, what I'm saying is he seems to have changed for the worst in the service. And I'm sorry to say…' He glanced at Scott. 'I really don't want to upset you –'

'You won't,' Scott replied.

Cliff nodded. 'He was a sexist, bigoted, controlling bully boy in the end, who'd had plenty of chances to reform and who just managed to scrape by without getting dismissed. He smoked too many Camels and he drank too hard. And if you'll pardon the pun, quite *frankly*, he got what he deserved. And to put yourself through any further distress, Jan, would be doing him too much of a service. You had a child out of wedlock like so many other young women back in those tough judgmental days, and instead of showing any understanding whatsoever he made sure you were punished for it. Women were wives or whores in his world with nothing in-between. Just how long were you supposed to atone?'

They sat in silence for a few moments, munching their crisps. A low buzzing of conversation slowly drifted over from the far end of the bar like a drowsy bee seeking somewhere to rest. Janet felt tired herself. But it was a satisfying kind of weariness, like after a long trek, where every worked muscle sighs in relief after exertions made.

'Well, while you have a think about what you want to do about Frank's death, Jan, next up is getting going with trying to find your daughter,' Cliff said. He pressed his empty crisp packet flat, folded it repeatedly then made a knot in it. 'It won't be easy, but you know that, don't you, Jan?' His voice was gentle and his eyes were soft as he looked straight into her own.

She swallowed hard. 'Yes, I know.'

'It's not my field of course, but I know a little bit about it through liaising with social workers on certain cases over the years. I do know that if the adoption was in the fifties, it's far from straightforward trying to get any information.'

Janet, Scott and Ann all nodded.

'But there's the legal route and the not so legal route – by that I mean going down the road of private investigation, which is quite common for things like tracing family. That is where I can come in, so we can try a double-pronged approach.' He paused. 'What was the name of the mother and baby home?'

'Hope Lodge in Swindon, in the Pinehurst area,' replied Janet. 'That was in 1954. It was a Church of England place and all arranged through a social worker, though they called them moral welfare workers in those days.' Janet shivered at the memory of the antiseptic smelling corridors.

'What a judgmental job title,' observed Scott.

'Yes, those were the days, eh, Jan? Actually Swindon isn't too far away from the Bristol area, so that might help.' Cliff hesitated for a moment. 'I guess what we ideally need is access to the adoption certificate, naming Vivien's new name and her new parents.'

'I was told years ago it was impossible,' Janet said. 'It was a closed adoption with the South West Adoption Agency, and that was that,' they said.

'Right. Well, I know adult adopted children can now ask for their original birth certificate which would have *you* named on it...just you, was it?'

'Yes. I wanted to put Joe down as the father, but I wasn't allowed to if he wasn't present. So it had to be left blank. It looked awful – that empty space where I was desperate for his name to go.' And she remembered feeling flushed with indignation on Vivien's behalf.

'Right. That's what I thought.' He frowned. 'How old would Vivien be now?'

'36,' Janet replied.

She felt her cheeks redden and throb with guilt as she stated Vivien's current age out loud. All that time she'd missed or wasted. All that time. Oh, how she hoped Vivien had been well cared for and had led a happy life. These thoughts used to haunt her every night like faithful ghosts creeping in upon her just before she went to sleep, but now they were stalking her into her waking life too. And a sense of urgency and keenness to know what had happened to Vivien, that she'd held back all these years, was now flooding within her, like a dam that had suddenly burst. And instead of a trickle, now that they were discussing finding her daughter, it had become a deluge that she barely knew how to handle, such was the force of it. She dragged her attention back to what Cliff was saying.

'But what we need is to find out if we can get a copy of the adoption certificate or other amended birth certificate concerning Vivien held at the General Register Office. So we need to contact Swindon and Bristol offices, though I doubt we'll get anywhere by this route. That's why people sometimes end up hiring their own researchers. But it's worth checking the offices first.'

Janet forced her practical side to get the upper hand and they all talked on, making plans and assigning jobs, as the sunny afternoon made way for twilight, with an intense electric blue sky framed by the parted curtains of the pub window bestowing a witching hour feel to their discussion. This feeling intensified for Janet when the subject then shifted to her remaining family members. She realised she hadn't thought much about them since Frank died, so intent had she been on returning to her Masons life. More shame.

'Frank played a big part in cutting off contact,' Janet said. 'I'm sure of it.' So when he died, why didn't I think of them? she wondered. What's wrong with me?

'Control again,' commented Cliff, shaking his head at Frank's suspected behaviour. 'So where do you think we can start tracing your family from?'

'Camelford in Cornwall,' Scott replied. 'Where Mum's family originally came from.'

Janet nodded. 'Yes, it's the only place really. My Auntie Florrie should still be there, my mother lived with her for years before she went into a care home. Florrie must be in her late sixties now. She was the youngest sister and inherited the family home – Riverside Cottage, Camelford, that's the only address I have. And I'm sure there's no telephone there. She used to be a teacher and never married. There's also Auntie Vi and Uncle Ted and their daughter, Sarah, who'd be my cousin, that I'd really like to get back in touch with. I've never even met Sarah. And all I know is that they were living in Bournemouth, and I don't have the address. Auntie Vi wrote it down on a scrap of paper for me at Dad's funeral, but it went missing.' She sighed. 'As for my brother, Norman, all I know is that he got married and emigrated to New England in America for his work in the same year Dad died, in 1968.'

'So we start with Auntie Florrie in Camelford,' Scott said.

'Yes,' agreed Cliff. 'Maybe you could take a few days off, Jan, and drive down with Scott? Make sure Florrie is still there, of course. You could check with the local post office. It'll be a small place where everyone knows everyone else. And if she's there, you can begin with Camelford and then go on to Bournemouth to find the other aunt.'

'I can house-sit, take any phone messages, and look after Thomas,' Ann said. 'How does that sound?'

Janet swallowed hard, thinking about her Masons responsibilities. The Harrison order. Patrick King. But what about her responsibility to herself? December was a quiet month in soft furnishings and nothing was going to happen now with the Harrison order until after Christmas. It was the 2nd of December today, and she certainly had some time owing.

'That sounds fine,' she said slowly. Then a thought came to her, sounding in her mind like a heavily struck gong at the beginning of an old film. 'It will be the anniversary of Frank's death on Wednesday. The 5th of December.'

'So it will, Mum,' Scott said.

Another thought struck her, this time like a sledgehammer. Her mind whirled dizzily with the impact, but then it settled and her vision cleared. She felt her spine stiffen. Now she knew what she had to do. What had to come first, before trying to find Vivien, before tracing her family.

'I don't need time to consider whether to confess or not,' she said looking straight at Cliff. 'It's my day off on Wednesday, as it happens, and I have an appointment with Liz. I'm going to go to the police station to confess. Liz will probably be able to go with me. I want to do whatever it takes to get that man out of my mind, out of my life. He's still in it and I want him gone. I refuse to live under his influence any longer. I need to do it before I find my family. I'll take whatever comes.'

Ann's mouth sagged open. 'But Janet. It's not fair!'

Scott frowned. 'Are you sure, Mum?'

'Yes. And I'm going to name Winnie as a witness.'

'Oh, Christ, Mum. That's going to make it so much tougher,' Scott groaned.

'But it's exactly what I thought you'd decide to do,' Cliff said, nodding slowly. 'So I insist on getting you some advice from my solicitor friend. Just to cover any eventualities. I insist. Okay?'

'Alright. Thank you,' Janet said. 'And thank you so much for today.'

Cliff smiled. 'Come on, let's get home. It's been a long afternoon.'

As they left the inn and pulled their coats tight against the evening winter chill, Cliff walked Janet, Scott and Ann to their car, parked outside his house. There was little strength left in the day. They passed a few houses, lights on inside, but with no curtains drawn, displaying the cosy glow of other people's lives – where in the brightness and colour it's so hard to imagine any problems, any conflicts, any misery. Why had she never been able to live like this? Janet wondered. Well, she knew the answer to that. But perhaps one day she'd be on the inside of one of these windows.

Just as she was about to get into the passenger seat of

Scott's Toyota, Cliff caught hold of her arm, turned her around and gave her another hug. She was surprised to find herself returning the embrace.

'This time, I'll have your back, Jan,' he said.

'Thank you,' she said, looking into his craggy face. 'That means a lot.'

And as they drove off into the night back to Cheltenham, headlights scanning the grassy fringes of the dark country lanes, she saw his encouraging smile in her mind's eye. And she knew she was going to be doing exactly the right thing.

Chapter 20

By the time Wednesday, December the 5th arrived, three days later, Janet was straining to get the deed over with. Twitching nerves and a fluttery stomach had exhausted their efforts to prepare her for her visit to the police station, surrendering her into a kind of stupefied weariness. Liz was happy to accompany her using their appointment time, and said she'd rescheduled her next slot to be on the safe side. So they met up at Portland Street car park at ten thirty under cover of whipping cold rain and Liz drove them both to the police headquarters at Talbot House in Lansdown Road, which Cliff had recommended they go to rather than one of the local police stations. It was a stark rectilinear building with rows of windows spelling out functionalism and order and Liz parked her Maestro in the visitors area.

As they approached the main entrance, Liz squeezed Janet's hand, then she opened the door for Janet to go through first. Janet crossed the threshold, but when she spotted the desk sergeant at his post, she cringed and pulled back.

'What is it?' Liz asked, nearly bumping into her from behind.

'It's...it's the uniform,' Janet stuttered. The same uniform Frank had worn all those years. The uniform he had frequently worn with his rictus grin, or while slapping her, shouting at her and making his point. His policeman's uniform. That visual emblem of public protection and trust. Aren't children always told they can trust a policeman? Don't people always call them when they're in trouble? Or turn to them in despair and anguish? Well, she'd certainly never been able to since marrying one. She grew up thinking they were the good guys, like her own grandfather had been down in Cornwall, a pillar of the community and loved by all, who'd bounced her on his knee and always made sure his little Janie was happy on those family summer visits. So now, it all felt like a warped contradiction in terms for her. Nausea gripped her deep in her abdomen and tightened, sweat broke out on her forehead and in the palms of her hands, her breath came fast and ragged. She felt fixed to the spot, just like she'd been while Frank was dying. Where was the fireplace to hold onto?

'Janet, you don't have to do this,' Liz urged. 'God knows, most wouldn't.'

'No, no…I've decided.' She took some deep breaths and focused her mind on her feet and told them to move. One tiny step with her left, then another with her right. They obeyed. And before she was ready, she and Liz were standing in front of the desk sergeant. He looked up and smiled.

He was balding with a salt and pepper beard, a neatly trimmed moustache, and a firm paunch, making him an avuncular figure to report crimes too. His warm sparkly eyes full of merriment were not at all what Janet had envisaged as the first face she'd see in here and he caught her off guard.

'What can I help you with?' he asked.

She stared at him. She'd imagined someone with a hard bony face with a jaw set in concrete to maintain an aloof cynical disposition, eyes riveted upon her like a hawk's, not this round-faced genial character who'd make a perfect Santa. Then she realised she'd been imagining someone like Frank. This reality check helped her snap back into the present.

'I want to confess to a crime. One year ago today, my husband died, and I think I was responsible for his death. He was having a heart attack and I stopped him from taking one of his pills that might have helped.'

Santa's eyebrows shot up. 'Well, now…let me see…er…I'd better take some particulars in the first instance, then.' He opened a hard-backed notebook in front of him and picked up a biro.

'Your name?'

'Mrs Janet Brewer.'

Janet saw the tip of his pen stop it's trajectory of movement, poised in mid air. He didn't write her name.

'Your husband?'

'Frank Brewer. He was a local policeman, recently retired.'

The sergeant's brow puckered and his mouth twisted into a grimace. 'Yes, yes...I knew him – '

Then he looked hard at her. 'Are you sure about doing this? Really sure?'

'Yes, I'm sure. Liz here, Liz Waring, from Victim Support is here to help me. You see, Frank, well...he used to hit me, you see. I just couldn't carry on like – '

'Domestic abuse,' interrupted Liz. 'Verbal and physical. For years. That's why I'm here.'

Janet turned and looked at Liz. She stood regal and elegant with a Liberty paisley shawl swept around her shoulders like a robe of office. She oozed a sense of professionalism which Janet found truly comforting and she surprised herself by thanking God this woman was on her side.

'I see...' Santa knitted his brow and shook his head. 'I'm so sorry to hear about this...about the abuse I mean...' He hesitated, then straightened up and became more brisk. 'Well let's get some details down, shall we? I'm Sergeant Moffat, by the way. After I've taken your details, I'll find a detective inspector to take your statement in an interview room.'

Janet nodded, relieved to see the creaking wheels of this particular journey into the unknown beginning to turn.

After quickly taking her name and address and the nature of the confession, Sergeant Moffat further surprised Janet by offering them a cup of tea. Orders duly noted, he showed them into a small featureless magnolia room, just off the main entrance area, and snapped on the fluorescent overhead light which blinked frantically to charge itself. The room was small and cramped with a plain table and chairs, one chair on one side of the table, two on the other, and a small square window, too cell like for comfort, was shaded by a dusty venetian blind, slats currently allowing so little natural daylight in that the strip-light was left to do all the work and was making a harsh job of it. The two women were left alone, sitting together at one side of the table, the door slightly ajar.

'Now, remember Janet, just keep it simple,' Liz said, looking Janet straight in the eye.

'I intend to...but who knows what will happen?' Janet could feel her heart thumping inside her ribcage and a flash of heat surged through her. Surely only guilty people felt this nervous?

Five minutes later, Sergeant Moffat brought them each a cup of tea – milk and one sugar for Janet, milk and no sugar for Liz. Janet found the steam rising from her cup and condensing on her lips together with the hot sweet taste distinctly comforting. So that's why they always say 'have a cuppa, it'll make you feel better', she thought. Although, whoever *they* were, she'd never been able to figure out.

After another five minutes, Sergeant Moffat reappeared with a short, lean, plainclothes man behind him. Again, this man looked nothing like Frank. He was clean-shaven and narrow of face, looked to be in his late fifties, with wiry beetling brows overshadowing his soft grey eyes. His manner was brisk and courteous as he shook Janet's hand, then Liz's in turn, after Sergeant Moffat did the introductions. Then Detective Chief Inspector Bridges scraped the remaining chair up to the table and sat opposite them with some paperwork and a pen. The sergeant left them to it, but a uniformed constable appeared and stood just inside the closed door, hands behind his back wearing a suitably blank expression.

DCI Bridges leaned forward in his grey tweed sports jacket, white shirt and woollen tie, reminding Janet of Scott's former geography teacher who she'd met on a parent's evening once or twice. The jacket hung a little too loosely on him and could have done with a good ironing, but it rendered him unintimidating, which Janet appreciated. He examined them both in turn, then fixed upon Janet.

'Can I call you Janet, instead of Mrs Brewer?'

'Of course,' she replied.

'So I understand you want to confess to having contributed to your husband, Frank Brewer's death, exactly one year ago today?'

'Yes.'

'Because you stopped him taking some medication that might have helped him?'

'Yes. He got the bottle of pills from down the side of his chair, where he always kept them and…well…I somehow just couldn't let him…I knocked the bottle out of his grasp and when it fell on the floor I kicked it under the sofa. Then before the ambulance and the GP arrived I retrieved them and threw them into the kitchen bin.'

'I see. What is the name of this GP? Your own GP I take it?'

'Yes, Dr Blake, Charlton surgery. He was Frank's GP and is still mine.'

'Did he ask about the medication at all?'

'No.'

'And there were definitely pills in the bottle.'

'Oh, yes.'

'Hmm…' He paused for a moment. 'And did anyone see what you did?'

'Yes. My next door neighbour, Mrs Winnie Parsons, at number 7. She told me recently that she saw me through the window when she was bringing around some lamb stew. It was dark, but the main curtains were still open. She saw through the nets. She saw me kicking the pills away from Frank.'

'I see.' His face betrayed no surprise which puzzled Janet, but not for long.

'Okay, Janet. I should tell you that Cliff Ward, a former

colleague, did warn me that you'd be coming in and he did tell me a little of the background, so I thought I'd handle it today myself instead of you speaking to one of the detective inspectors here, to see if we can fast track this. I'll take your statement and we'll do some investigating – such as interviewing Mrs Parsons, accessing Frank's medical records, either through the coroner or, with your permission, speaking to Dr Blake – to see if there is a case to bring.' He hesitated. 'This is what you want, is it not?'

Janet nodded, sitting back in her chair and exhaling deeply.

'Obviously there is a bit of a nasty twist to this in Frank Brewer being a retired police sergeant from this constabulary. And on behalf of the force I so regret that you suffered at his hands for so long. I do wish you had felt you could report him, but I understand completely why you didn't. But in the here and now all lines of enquiry will be pursued objectively. Do you understand?'

Janet nodded. 'Yes, of course.'

'And I'm happy that Ms Waring is here to support you. Your having been a victim of domestic abuse will certainly have much to bear upon the case in your defence.'

'Yes.'

'She was a victim practically the whole of her married life,' added Liz.

DCI Bridges nodded sympathetically. 'And she's brave coming here today.'

Janet flushed. She didn't feel brave at all. She simply had no choice.

'Right,' he continued. 'Let's get the forms filled in, all the contact details, and then the statement sorted.'

They bent their heads to the task, and just one and a half hours later, Janet had signed a typed version of her statement, describing everything that had happened exactly one year ago on that fateful day, and had a folded-up copy of it in her handbag. She had also given formal permission, as the executor of Frank's estate, to the police for accessing

Frank's medical records.

Tucking the statement into his folder, DCI Bridges looked up and smiled warmly. 'Right, we're all done for now. I'll keep you informed of the progress we make. By phone, if that's okay with you?'

'Yes, fine,' Janet replied.

He reached inside his jacket pocket and handed her a card. 'My contact details. Just in case you need to get in touch about anything, or if you remember anything else – anything at all. And of course you have Ms Waring here for support in the meantime.'

She nodded and slipped the card into the deep pocket of her black woollen coat, selected not just to keep the rain out, but to blanket her too. It's cosy cocoon had indeed helped, but under the circumstances the black had made her feel like a hypocrite, not to mention inviting associations of the 'black widow', and she hoped DCI Bridges didn't think the same way.

'I'm not under arrest now, then?' she asked, feeling panicked that this was all going too smoothly.

DCI Bridges's scouring-pad brows shot up. 'Good heavens, no. We have to find out if there's enough evidence to apply for a charge warrant first. That's the procedure we go by,' he said to her more gently.

Liz's face crumpled in concern as she stared at Janet. 'I thought you knew you wouldn't be arrested straightaway?' Then she shook her head. 'And if I had my way, there's no way you could be arrested at all.'

Janet sighed. 'I wasn't thinking straight. It must be sitting here in this room, or all those television soaps. And I've already booked next week off from work to visit family in Camelford.'

'DCI Bridges grinned. 'Those soaps have a lot to answer for, we find. Just don't go flying out of the country.'

'Is Camelford, Cornwall and Bournemouth alright? I'll just be gone a few days on family business – all linked to Frank in a way.'

'Yes, that's fine. It will take a few days to get some cogs turning.'

So much to Janet's surprise at the process having been far easier than she'd envisaged, she and Liz walked out of the police station into the grey light of the December day, with a cheery goodbye from Sergeant Moffat. It was raining heavily now, so Liz flapped open her umbrella, only to find Janet declining its cover. The icy-cold drops pelting Janet's forehead and running down her cheeks felt strangely welcome. Like a baptismal wash cleansing her for a new beginning – at least for the time being.

Chapter 21

While having a late lunch with Liz at a table next to a steamy window in Betty's Tiffin in Montpellier, and looking out at the bleary figures of passing shoppers, hooded by their umbrellas, the two women discussed the situation. Liz thought it had gone very well and was trying to bolster Janet, because despite the dazzle from the regency-style chandeliers, Janet was very lacklustre. But Liz did have one very clear bit of advice.

'If you are determined to do this, you'd better warn your neighbour to expect a visit from the police.'

Janet looked at her with eyes as round as doorknobs.

'Why?'

'Because from what you've told me, she might not cooperate.'

Oh, yes,' Janet groaned. 'Cliff mentioned that. But what will I do if she doesn't back me up? I mean, she has to, hasn't she?'

'Legally yes, but what from what you've told me, it doesn't sound like she respects the law very much.'

Janet took a sip of her coffee, then planted the cup firmly on the saucer. 'I'll just explain to her how important it is to me.'

'Okay, well good luck it.'

When Janet returned home in the afternoon, her house was empty as Ann had gone with Scott today to visit Swindon's General Register Office as planned, to see if there was any chance of Janet gaining access to Vivien's adoption certificate. They felt a personal visit was in order, in case of any other help or information they might glean. A Bristol visit the previous day had been fruitless, but they wanted to eliminate this route of enquiry first. Even Thomas seemed to be otherwise occupied, so Janet decided to tackle Winnie straightaway, not even bothering to take off her coat.

Standing on the front doorstep of 7 Willow Lane, she pressed the doorbell and three harsh descending chimes struck her eardrums. The harsh vibrations made her shiver. She noticed the front window net flicker and saw Winnie's sparsely haired head peering at her. In the next moment the door opened and with a smell of roasting meat wafting into the chill of the day, Winnie stood in front of her – bow legged, high heels, and her face as wrinkled as tissue paper.

'What is it, dear?'

'Sorry to bother you, Winnie. But I need to tell you something important.'

Janet hesitated, grasping for the right words.

'Well, what is it?' Winnie sounded irritated.

'It's about Frank's death. Can I come in?'

Winnie stared hard at her. 'That's all done and dusted, isn't it?'

'Not quite. Can I explain?'

'Well, alright, come on in. I'm just in the middle of watching a Catherine Cookson film. *The Fifteen Streets*. Have you seen it yet? Lovely writer, I've got all her books. The full set.'

Winnie turned into her living room, snatched the remote off the back of the sofa and switched off the period drama with an exaggerated sigh. Janet followed her inside, keeping her attention solely on Winnie.

'I've just been to the police station and confessed about Frank's death, not allowing him to get to his pills. And since you saw what I did, I've named you as a witness, Winnie.'

Winnie stood so still Janet could have almost believed she had become a wax figure worthy of Madame Tussauds. Her eyes narrowed into the crevices of her face, but Janet could still see two tiny black beads glittering back at her.

Through tight lips, Winnie replied like Janet imagined a strict head teacher in a boarding school might, grasping a ruler to wield some punishing stings to a vulnerable palm.

'Now what did I tell you! I said don't go doing anything stupid like confessing! I said I would stay stumm. For God's sake woman, what planet are you on? That husband of yours was no good! He had it coming good and proper. What the hell are you playing at?'

'I want a clean slate, Winnie. I don't want this hanging over me the rest of my life. I'll take whatever comes.'

Winnie hopped from foot to foot. 'A clean slate! A clean slate! Since when did any of us get one of those? This is real life, girl! We all mucky up our slate, blot our copybook. The longer we live the more it happens. That's life! It's called survival! And to wipe your slate clean, you are dragging me into your guilty conscience!'

Janet felt a flash of anger. 'What about yours, over Charles? Don't you have a guilty conscience?'

'No, I bloody well don't.'

And as Winnie carried on ranting, vowing she wouldn't be telling the truth to the police, Janet now noticed the new additions to Winnie's living room.

On every available surface were ornaments of Winnie's she hadn't seen on previous visits over the years. These were new. On the windowsill, the mantelpiece, the side tables, the top of the television, on every available surface were clustered ceramic figurines of angels, cherubs, fairies and ladies. Ladies in all their frills and fancy, feathers and bows, carrying baskets of roses or posies, or willowy edwardian ladies, all bustle and sinuous line in their more refined elegance. Janet recognised the style and matt finish of a few of these from the popular Leonardo Collection. All this poise and pose on smart wooden bases with brass plaques, the total antithesis of the real woman stood right before her. She stared wide-eyed at Winnie who had fallen silent.

'When did you get all *these*?' Janet asked, waving her hands around the room.

Winnie shrugged her shoulders. 'I've had them for ages. I just had them upstairs before,' she replied, but her eyes were focused on the floor.

'Where did you get them all from?'

'Here and there. But it's none of your business, is it?' she snapped.

Janet picked up the nearest Leonardo figure next to her on a side table and turned it around in her hand. It was a 1920s dancing flapper girl in a gold lame dress with lots of bias-cut flounces at the hemline.

'But this is one from a very new range. I like to keep track of them in the china section of Masons.'

Then she had a creeping suspicion born of an instinct she'd developed for Winnie's defensive attitudes and reactions over the years, and she decided to air it as it might just suit her own purposes.

'You've just got your pension, haven't you? How can you afford all these?'

'I save up. That's how!'

'What's going on with you, Winnie?'

'Keep your nose out of my business.'

Janet was struck by the irony here. 'I'll do you a deal. I'll keep my nose out if you simply tell the truth to the police about what you saw that evening when Frank died.'

'But I don't want the police coming around! I can't stand the buggers! And here you are, dragging them to my door.'

'Just keep it short and simple and it will be over before you know it.'

Winnie slackened her shoulders and the fire faded from her eyes like a guttering candle.

'And I suggest you move some of these back upstairs as they're a bit of a distraction,' Janet observed.

'Oh, for goodness' sake, woman. Alright, I'll tell them the truth. It's such a shame though. I thought you were a savvy sort, like me, a kindred spirit. But have it your way, why don't you!'

And as she shooed Janet out, she shook her head and said with a distinct tone of regret, 'Pity, never mind.'

Reeling from the very idea of being considered a kindred spirit to the weird Winnie, as Cliff called her, Janet returned to her empty house with darkness falling fast, glad her encounter with Winnie was over with. After a quick cup of coffee by her electric fire to cosy herself, she decided to keep herself occupied by making a shepherd's pie for tea. Ann had done so much of the meal-making since she'd been staying, and after her visit to Swindon she'd be needing some decent nourishment. Scott could always have some too if Susan was alright about it.

Susan, she thought, while starting to peel some potatoes, Susan still didn't know what was going on. She'd be sure to be picking up vibes by now. She'd always had a nose for rooting things out. Scott had said he'd tell her when there was something important *to* tell. But not yet, Janet hoped. She didn't think she could bear Susan knowing anything just yet.

When she was rinsing the peeled and chopped potatoes the phone rang. It was Cliff calling to see how she'd got on at the station.

She described everything that had happened, what was said, and then her visit to Winnie afterwards. He found the Winnie situation distinctly amusing, saying he hoped to meet her one day, but emphasised that everything seemed to be going as well as expected. Janet thanked him for giving DCI Bridges some warning of her coming.

'It really helped,' she said.

'Just wanted to make sure you got someone I respect and trust, Jan. And I've got a solicitor for you. That contact of mine I told you about is happy to help. I've given him your contact details. He's a real professional, a bit brusque but a good sort, name of Michael Armstrong. He'll probably contact you in the next few days. And there'll be no charge either, not when I told him the circumstances, and he owes me a favour or two.'

Janet was once more taken aback by Cliff's generosity. 'I don't know how to thank you, Cliff, I really don't.'

'No need, Jan. No need at all. So hopefully next up can be your visit to Camelford with Scott. Have you confirmed your aunt is still there?'

'Yes, she's still at the cottage, no phone though. Scott found out through the local post office like you suggested. I'll post her a note about our visit.'

'Lovely. You've booked the time off?'

'Yes, next week from Monday 10th.'

'Excellent, I might follow you down, but do keep in touch. Feed back to me if you get any leads.'

Going back to chopping onions and carrots whilst sealing some mince in sunflower oil, her thoughts gently ambled to Masons. It had been so very quiet lately. Everything had been prepared for the Christmas sale now: signage, pricing, remnants, special buys, and old stock ready-mades marked down and all set to drag out again for the sale bins. What did sell well at this time of year was heat-resistant table felt, which they stocked in a wipeable vinyl cushioned form or a lighter-weight quilted version, both available in a choice of two widths off the roll by the metre. The only hitch was they were incredibly heavy for the predominantly female staff of the department to lift and carry from the fabric stands to the serving counters.

Gemma always thumped these rolls down onto the counter prior to unrolling, as if to make a non-verbal protest, essentially saying to the customer *Look at what we are expected to do!* And since Janet agreed, thinking of the all-male staff in carpets as somehow connected to this lack of appreciation by management of the versatility of the female soft furnishing staff, she did allow Gemma's behaviour to go unchecked. After all, before she'd been the manager, she used to do the same herself, so she wasn't going to be a hypocrite and criticize Gemma.

As for Claire, well her thumping was simply a necessity of having to let go of the weight as soon as possible, and guided by her athletic son, she was in the process of doing weight training exercises to strengthen her arms. If that wasn't devotion to duty, what was? Yes, Janet mused, despite Ann retiring, she had a good little team with Gemma, Claire and the new lad, Kevin, who was respectful and helpful. She hoped they'd be okay without her for a week.

Then her thoughts picked up pace and trotted towards her family, the object of the visit to Cornwall, to Riverside Cottage, and those summer picnics before she'd lost the innocence of childhood.

And finally her thoughts careered into a mad canter, then an uncontrollable gallop straight towards what she hadn't allowed herself to even venture to reflect upon for so many years – not since she was told by the authorities that there was no way of tracing Vivien. So often she had gazed at the baby picture of Vivien, trying to imagine what Vivien would look like in whatever present she'd viewed the picture in.

First of all, there was always the question of what colour her eyes had become? Then through to what she might look like at each birthday...to Vivien at three years old...to Vivien at ten....and from there through to a teenager? Wondering whether her adoptive parents were good and kind people? Whether they had loved her daughter with all their hearts and brought her up well? Whether she was happy? Whether she'd ever been told she was adopted? And if she had been told, had she ever wanted to know about her real mother? Then Janet would move on to where Vivien might be living, what she might love doing, what she wanted to do when she grew up, and whether her wishes came true? But one day it had stopped because she couldn't bear wondering anymore. This had been replaced by a simple daily feeling of reaching out to Vivien, a bit like saying a prayer.

But now Janet allowed herself to wonder once again where her Vivien was right now. She'd be a 36 year old woman now. More than old enough to have a family of her own, with her own experiences of having children, developing those special bonds, where she might well be horrified at the idea of being able to give a baby away, no matter what the circumstances, no matter how hard the times, the judgments, the shame, the intense guilt – the guilt coming from all directions so you feel pierced by a multitude of arrows like a painting she'd once seen in a church as a girl of Saint Sebastian, all rolling eyes and pain. The guilt coming from parents, neighbours, society, welfare workers, even nurses, and worst of all, from yourself. Dammed if you keep your baby, and dammed if you don't. Would Vivien be able to understand? To forgive?

Her hand froze in its action of stirring the mince with a wooden spoon. The mince began to bubble. Now her heart quickened and banged against her ribs. She bent over the pan slightly as her stomach clenched, and hot bitter tears pressed their way out of their prison. Her vision blurred, and she felt a long-buried sobbing, twisting and rising up inside her to burst out, and she was so frightened because she didn't know what would happen to her if she let it out – she'd go mad – she'd scream and hit out – she'd smash things – she'd sit all huddled up and rock in a corner – then she'd be given a shot – be put in a strait jacket – and hauled off to the nearest asylum – and they always had such horrible names like Winterburn, Dinglemoor, Huntlyhaven, and then there was always the name of the home she'd attended to give Vivien up – Hope Lodge. Hope for who exactly?

But just then there was a miaow behind her. She flinched and turned to see Thomas at her feet, his questing paw lightly batting at her ankle. It was his way of saying he was hungry. And looking into his wide open face, the face he put on to show he needed her, she wiped her eyes, turned down the heat on the cooker ring, and bent to the task of replenishing his feeding bowl, with whatever flavour of cat food he would no doubt disdain after he'd licked a bit of the jelly off.

By the time Ann and Scott arrived at around half six Janet had fastened herself together again. The shepherd's pie was in the oven with the cheese just about to crisp on the top, the vegetables were tender, and some gravy mix was ready in a Pyrex jug to pour boiling water into.

As Scott reported their findings, it was the same story as yesterday. There was no access to any records allowed for the birth mother, only for the adoptee. And no access to the Adopted Children Register either. It was the usual crushing intractability, but at least, Scott said, they now knew the score. It was all to the good. Janet wondered were he had inherited his optimism from, because it certainly hadn't been from herself or Frank.

Scott declined staying for tea because Susan had said theirs would be ready at seven and it was chicken curry, his favourite. But Ann was delighted with the shepherd's pie and she and Janet both managed to polish it off between them, allowing themselves a couple of glasses of red wine to wash it down with. Despite the intensity of her earlier feelings, Janet found herself relaxing, and she realised she felt so comfortable with Ann now, living together like this, sharing the domestic tasks and evening pursuits of sewing and television. She struggled to imagine ever being alone again in this house she'd shared with Frank for so long. Ann's presence kept him at bay. And this development she had never imagined, but she welcomed it nonetheless.

The remainder of the week at work was largely uneventful as she anticipated, with Gemma, Claire and Kevin having to find things to do, like tidying up the stockroom out the back, updating yet more pattern books, and dusting display cases and shelves. Dusting was the very last resort for a department that was usually far too busy to give this particular housekeeping job the time which Mason's demanded, and which quiet, easy to work in departments made a relentless show of doing. Who knew how stultifying it could be, to *appear* to be busy?

So since all was well on her own department, and her paperwork was bang up to date to allow for her week off, Janet found herself watching Milly-Molly-Mandy and Marian on their adjacent concession on the Saturday. As they sat at the desk, heads bent together over the Berkeley Fabrics order book, she noticed Milly's conscientious attitude in the way she listened hard to Marian, nodding and shaking her head, smiling or biting her lip. She had proved herself a loyal employee and an excellent part-timer for Marian. She'd also been coming out of her shell a bit recently, with less of the red-eyed look of a scared white rabbit in mourning for her ever-so-perfect husband. She'd been having a chat with Gemma and Claire since it was so quiet, even sharing a giggle or two. But whenever Janet had caught her eye, Milly had visibly twitched, snapped her permed head around, and returned to her section. This blatant aversion reminded Janet of how unpleasant she'd been to Milly when she'd first started, and how she'd tried to pump her for information about Marian – information that now seemed so utterly trivial in comparison to her current problems.

And then there was Marian. She felt she ought to tell Marian that she'd reported her involvement in Frank's death to the police. Somehow it was important that Marian be kept in the loop, perhaps because it was through her that she was now on this vital new path, necessary for her peace of mind, and as Liz emphasised, for her own healing. And she had something for Marian too.

So in light of these two issues, when Milly got up and began scurrying in the direction of the ladies powder room, Janet seized the opportunity and followed her.

When Milly emerged from her cubicle, she found Janet washing her hands at a basin. Milly halted and her gaze rapidly flickered around the empty rest room.

Janet saw her in the mirror and turned around, flicking water drops from her hands. 'Milly, can I have a word please?'

'What? What is it?' she rasped, still not moving towards the washing area.

'I want to apologise for being nasty to you when you first started, and for, well, for digging for information about

Marian. I'm sorry. I really am.'

'Are you indeed?' She stalked to a basin and squirted some soap into her palms, vigorously rubbing them together. 'And I'm supposed to believe you, am I?' She looked sharply at Janet in her basin mirror. 'Marian said to watch myself around you.'

'Yes, I don't blame her. I don't blame either of you. But you see, I've been under a strain of some kind which I didn't realise.' She shook her head, desperately wondering how she could explain without telling Milly all about her confession.

Milly arched her eyebrows, stuck out her ample bosom beneath the cardigan which had accrued more bobbles and planted her hands on her rolling hips. 'Really! Well, I can't imagine what strain that was. You got your promotion, after all.'

'Yes, I know. But you see I didn't have the kind of relationship with my husband that you did with your Archie. I never had what you had. I can't go into all the details, but Marian knows some of it. My husband used to hit me, call me names, for years it went on. All through the marriage.'

Milly's arms collapsed by her side, her eyes popping out on stalks. 'You! You were bullied by your husband? But…you're so strong, so…so tough.'

Janet gave her a small smile. 'I know that's how I seem.' And then she realised something and blurted it out before she knew what she saying. 'I don't really want to be like that anymore.'

Milly stared at her.

'So will you accept my apology? Please?'

Milly's shoulders sagged. She tried to smile at Janet, her mouth forming a crooked line. 'Alright,' she said. 'And Marian seems to have changed her mind about you a bit, if that helps.'

'It does,' replied Janet. 'And can you give her a message for me, in case I don't have a chance to speak to her privately?'

'What?'

'Just tell her I've confessed.'

'You've confessed.' Milly sounded like a hypnotist's subject repeating some instructions.

'Okay?'

'Okay.'

And Janet left Milly to the merciful routine blast of the hand blower which would hopefully restore her equilibrium.

It was around closing time when Marian sought Janet out. The cashing up was done and the soft furnishing staff had left. Janet was just in the process of leaving her office to switch off the department's lights when Marian pushed through the office door and slammed it shut behind her.

'What on earth have you gone and confessed for?' she asked.

Marian was standing close in front of her. Red hair, currently more Kim Wilde than Farrah Fawcett, fake tan, bangle earrings, thick mascara, and question marks in her amber eyes. But there was more. And at this proximity Janet spotted it straightaway. This time the tide-mark bruise plastered with foundation was on her *left* cheekbone, hard to detect to the untrained eye, but Janet was an expert.

She reached out and touched Marian's face. 'It's still going on, then.'

Marian slapped her hand away. 'I've told you before. It's not the same as it was for you, Janet. You're just going to have to mind your own bloody business.'

Then Janet noticed she was wearing a long-sleeved blouse. She'd been wearing her jacket earlier, but at present it was folded over her left arm. And what was it with long sleeves? Since when had she worn long sleeves? They were far too demure and non-revealing for Marian. So what were they hiding?

With a sudden instinct she grasped hold of Marian's left arm and pushed up the sleeve. The jacket slid to the floor in the process, but there was nothing to see. Then despite Marian trying to turn away, she got hold of her right arm and did the same. There was a batch of black bruises around her upper wrist which matched the finger holds of a nasty grip that hadn't let go.

'Ouch! What are you doing? That hurts!'

'I'm sorry, but – oh, Marian!'

Marian yanked her arm back down. She tried to hold Janet's gaze but her eyes flickered to the floor.

'Just leave it, Janet,' she said in a thick voice. 'I'll sort it.' She bent down and picked up her jacket.

'How? And what about your daughter?'

Marian looked hard at Janet, her eyes flashing. 'I'd never let him hurt Jessica! Never!'

'But if he's in your life, how can you protect her from him? Does he pick her up from school?'

'No! My parents do that. Then I collect her from them in Prestbury. Or I have a mate who helps out. But this is none of your – '

'What about the time I saw you and him. He'd been alone with her then!'

'That was a one-off time, when my parents were away and Sharon, my mate, was ill,' Marian shouted. 'I didn't have any other choice.' Then she sighed. 'Look, I don't like where you're going with this. I just wanted to say I think you're silly for going to the police.'

'Yes, well I'm doing what I have to do. The right thing. And so should you.'

She snatched hold of her own shoulder bag and dragged out a leaflet she'd been carrying around for days. A spare Victim Support leaflet from Liz's office, so she'd have the telephone number handy. She didn't need it now, but Marian did.

She pushed it at Marian. 'Please read this. I've been here for advice. It's really helped. Please take it.'

Marian looked at the red and white fronted leaflet, then glared at Janet.

'Take it!' Janet urged, pressing it against Marian's chest.

'Oh, for Christ's sake! Alright! Anything to shut you up!'

She snatched it off her and stuffed it into her quilted vinyl handbag.

'Now just leave it alone. Leave it to me!' Marian cried.

Because they both had some shopping to collect from the security hatch on the way out, they ended up being next to each other in the queue that snaked and laddered its way up the fire-escape stairway.

'You're nuts for confessing,' Marian hissed at Janet. 'You might end up losing your job here. Have you thought of that?'

Janet had thought of this only fleetingly. She didn't dare to imagine the repercussions if she was found guilty and sentenced. She was taking everything day by day as best she could. It was all she could manage. Her only recourse in this moment with Marian was to tough it out as usual.

'Yes, well, if that happens, you might stand a chance of getting it, mightn't you?' Her tone was distinctly sarcastic, but Marian didn't seem to mind.

'I don't think I'm Patrick King's favourite person right now.'

'None of us are,' Janet said.

Marian giggled.

As they hurried through the staff exit with their shopping, Marian eased ahead and Janet saw Rick, Marian's brutish boyfriend, waiting for her on the rain-slicked pavement. Hands thrust into the pockets of his jeans, shifting from foot to foot in his biker's jacket slashed with zips, good bone structure to his face, heavy-set jaw, and shoulder-length straggly blonde hair.

He and Marian immediately began chatting, and she heard Marian reminding him she had to collect Jessica from Sharon and take her over to Prestbury.

He scowled.

Janet had frozen in the doorway and was blocking the exit, so with a few people muttering 'excuse me' and shouldering her out of the way, she caught Rick's glance.

They stared hard at each other.

There was the same steely suspicion she'd seen before, when she'd been hiding in the telephone booth outside Marian's flat and he'd passed her by. When their eyes had locked onto each other's and they'd somehow sensed a mutually alien threat.

'What the fuck are you lookin' at?' he said, his eyes narrowing.

Marian got hold of his arm and tried to turn him away. 'Come on. She's just a colleague.'

He shook Marian's arm off and squared up to Janet, who'd now stepped aside from the exit.

'Feels like I've seen you somewhere before.'

Janet tilted up her chin. 'No, I don't think so. I'm sure I'd have remembered you.'

He eyed her carefully. 'Would you now?'

Her skin crawled into cold pimples. She knew this was a dangerous man. What the hell did Marian see in him? Was it the tough guy looks? The brawn? And then she shocked herself by wondering whether it was the sex. She snatched the thought back. None of her business.

Marian cut through the tension between them. 'For crying out loud, let's go, Rick! I'm going to be late, and then it'll spoil our evening.'

He looked at Marian and a smile plucked at the corners of his mouth. Then his face softened and he kissed her full on the lips, while Janet recoiled at the sight of it.

The couple both turned and headed towards the High Street. Marian did one quick flick of her head back in Janet's direction, then they disappeared into the night. Janet was going the same way, but she lingered to allow them to get ahead. She'd had enough of dwelling on *their* problems for now, she had enough of her own and didn't relish attracting more.

The street was lacquered black by the rain, and the sodium glow of the street lights bled orange into the shadows. She felt better when she got to her car, switched on her engine, and headed for home behind a pair of bright headlights. She was determined to put Masons aside and concentrate on the week ahead. She would focus on her long lost daughter, and reconnecting with her family while she was still free to do so. After all, who knew what the future held?

PART FOUR

Chapter 22

It was a frosty Monday morning. The previous day's rains had been alchemised into fine crystal on trees and hedges by plummeting temperatures, and there were mirrors of black ice on the roads. Janet sat in the front of Scott's Toyota, as he pointed the car towards the junction for the M5, heading for Cornwall, to Camelford, and to Riverside Cottage, where Janet's Auntie Florrie still lived.

Janet had written her a letter, brief and to the point, feeling an uncomfortable abstraction towards her aunt which prevented much in the way of pleasantries. She'd posted it first class on Thursday and hoped Florrie would have it by now and be expecting them that afternoon. They were planning to get directions to her cottage from the post office as Camelford's tourist information centre was closed for the season. And since an elderly single lady was used to her own space and company, she and Scott decided to find some accommodation for themselves when they arrived. If they felt they needed some assistance later on from Cliff, he was going to follow them down, whilst Ann was manning the fort at home and would take any messages that came through.

Everything was set, and as Scott joined the motorway he turned the radio on low, selecting Radio Gloucestershire. Janet welcomed its soothing strains and babbles, which meant she and Scott could go into their respective worlds without feeling the necessity to fill the silence with forced chatter – something neither of them had ever been in the habit of doing.

It was years since Janet had been outside Cheltenham, so she was happy to be a passenger for a change to register once again the local scenery, and it gave her a little time for reflection.

DCI Bridges had phoned her yesterday to let her know that Winnie had given her statement describing what she'd seen which exactly tallied with Janet's own. This meant they were now conducting a formal investigation, and he advised her to speak to a solicitor, which thanks to Cliff was already in hand. One of the police's next steps was accessing the coroner's report and Frank's medical records, and although not vital, they also wanted to talk to Dr Blake in person. Unfortunately, he was out of the country on holiday in the Canary Islands until the second week of January, so the case was on hold for now until after Christmas.

'Sounds about right,' Cliff had commented when Janet had phoned him, and he'd urged her to focus on her family instead. 'The police will be doing what they need to do for the investigation as fast as they can,' he assured her. 'And I'm going to see if I can pull in some favours and access any information about Vivien's adoption.'

That was promising news if he could pull it off, so now Janet shifted her attention back to the landscape.

Bypassing Gloucester town centre, she noticed a right signpost to Quedgeley, where Susan's family lived on one of the housing estates there, and where Scott and Susan had got married and held their small wedding reception in 1982. Then there was a right turning to Berkeley Castle, the medieval gothic residence where King Edward II was incarcerated and believed to be brutally murdered. She and Frank had gone for a very rare day trip there one Sunday with Scott, who'd revelled in the gruesome details of murder by insertion of hot poker, just like any little boy would. The picnic afterwards had been a swift affair when Frank had got bored and wanted to go home to watch a golf tournament.

On the left and eastern side was Stroud, and all its surrounding villages, with inviting names like Leonard Stanley, Dursley, Amberley, Sheepscombe – names to entice the visitors to this designated area of outstanding beauty in the beating heart of the Cotswolds. Villages Janet had never been to, because Frank was of the opinion that they were backward places full of thick country yokels with West Country accents to match. But why hadn't it occurred to her to visit some of these places after he'd died? she wondered. There had been nothing and no one to stop her. But her main focus had been her life at Masons, the promotion, the job. And she realised she had been as blinkered as a plodding workhorse, unable to see in any other direction but one, and she had fitted those blinkers to herself.

As the land flattened and industry and housing edged their bricks and mortar into the patchwork of fields on the suburbs of Bristol, and as Scott tuned into Radio Bristol, the next landmark was the sleek Clifton suspension bridge spanning the Avon Gorge. As the car trundled its way across the river Avon, Janet cast her mind east to the area of Bishopsworth and 14 Marguerite Road, her former family home. She wondered what it would look like now. Would the inside still be browns and creams and scratchy moquette bouclée furniture – an oppressive heaviness only lightened by floral curtains of ribbons and roses? Would the exterior paintwork still be burgundy? And would those leaded upper windows on the bays still be intact? Mildred had been proud of those. She wondered if there was any point in going to pay a visit to the street on the way back to satisfy her curiosity and because Scott had never seen it before. But there were more urgent matters pressing, and signposts directed her thoughts back into the present as she noted they were travelling past Western-super-Mare, then Bridgwater and Taunton. And at noon, just over two hours since leaving Cheltenham, they arrived in Exeter and decided to have lunch at the motorway services before heading west across country.

It was to a background din of cutlery clatter, when they were eating their sausage, beans and chips, that Scott told Janet he'd now told Susan what they were doing and why, and about Frank's death. He'd had no choice, seeing as they'd had to arrange extra childcare for Danny, to make up for Scott not being at home while Susan was at work. Scott scrutinised Janet's face for her reaction.

Her fork poised in her hand in mid air, Janet felt her spirits plummet like a rock rolling over a precipice at the idea of Susan now knowing everything. She expected Susan to be a harsh judge, seeing as they'd never seen eye to eye about anything.

'I had no choice, Mum,' Scott said.

Janet hesitated. 'I know. It's alright.'

The two of them were quiet for a while thinking it through. Someone else in the family knowing was a significant thing and right now it didn't feel alright to Janet at all.

'How did she react? What did she say?' Janet asked.

'Well I can't lie, Mum. She was shocked. It was a huge amount to take in. You and her don't get on that well, so she was saying what a dark horse you are.'

'Yes, I can hear her saying that, and a lot more besides.'

'Hmm…well she didn't seem bothered about the real circumstances of Dad's death. She never liked him, you know. She mostly didn't like his sexist behaviour. But she thinks you're doing the right thing in confessing. It was giving Vivien away that she felt the most about.'

'Yes, I can imagine.'

'But I explained the circumstances, the times back then, how hard it was. And when she'd had some time to think it over for a couple of days, she seemed to come around. Anyway, I explained what we were doing and she said I had to do what I could. She was actually quite supportive.'

Janet tried to imagine flighty Susan being supportive, without looking for some personal benefit attached, but she failed. It was simply asking too much.

One hour later they were travelling through Devon on roads crowded by thick hedgebanks on either side, like in a maze, making visibility over the countryside hard going even in a leafless winter. There was no veiling of frost here, with the dank wetness suggesting the lush and humid pasturelands of summertime to come. There was a sense of being channelled through roofless tunnels to their destination with the hedges becoming taller and thinner as they entered Cornwall. It seemed fitting the radio was switched off for their imminent arrival. And taking a right turn into the hamlet of Camelford at quarter past two, they crossed a road bridge over the river Camel, upon which Janet remarked, was the same spot where there used to be a humpback bridge. Then they headed for the main high street to find somewhere to park.

Camelford in winter, if given that prerequisite blanket of glittering snow so vital to all seasonal imaginings, would have made a perfect traditional Christmas card, where there's a coach and horses, carrying a family wearing cosy mittens, fur lined coats and top hats, trotting over a stone bridge, while the road winds on past quaint cottages to a distant church with a tower. Red scarves flying, the family makes its way to celebrate the yuletide season with Christmas cheer and much merriment while the bells peel out far and wide to gather the flock to the fold.

And some memories came back to Janet of when she was staying with her grandparents and her Auntie Florrie during the war years, when she'd been evacuated by train to Camelford for a spell at the age of eight. Her mother had kept Norman in Bristol, saying he was far too young to leave home, but it was more a case of wanting to keep him tied to her apron strings, her granny had observed. But the Davey family had made her so welcome. And as she looked out at the old town hall they were now passing, with its familiar golden weathervane shaped like a camel, she remembered shopping in the town with her granny where absolutely everyone knew everyone else's business – a state of living which her mother had told Janet she'd wanted to get away from as soon as she could. *It's full of busybodies,* she'd said.

Scott and Janet ended up parking outside an old coaching inn in the Market Place, called the Travellers Rest, where Scott suggested they could make enquiries about staying. The post office was directly opposite to get directions to the cottage from, so Scott went into the inn while Janet crossed the road to the tiny shop, with its low-set windows frowning over the pavements like a shop straight out of a Dickens novel. She felt relieved to be stretching her legs, but was also feeling a little jittery now with this jaunt into the past, where the blurry abstraction she'd felt about it before was now beginning to sharpen into reality. She pulled the scarf she was wearing closer around her neck and entered. The bell jangling on the door made her jump.

The lady inside the dim interior behind the counter was around Janet's age, and she beamed a greeting from behind her bottle-bottom spectacles. There was a smell of Sherbet Lemons from an open sweets jar she was topping up and the rattle of them stimulated memories of times gone by for Janet, spent in her own Uncle Ted and Auntie Vi's grocery shop in Bristol. She'd spent hours behind the counter there at weekends, listening to the local gossip while sucking on a Rhubarb and Custard.

When Janet explained to the post mistress who she was, her relationship to her aunt here in Camelford, and how her son had phoned to check that a Florence Davey was still living in the area, the lady got all excited and her eyes grew even more magnified, like well-fed goldfish behind curved glass.

'Oh, I remember that call! Oh, she'd love some visitors!' Her accent had a strong Cornish lilt which Janet found suddenly familiar from her childhood days.

'Is she well?' Janet asked.

'Oh, yes. Course she has knee trouble, walks with a stick. But apart from that...'

'And she really isn't on the phone?' Janet said, still finding it hard to believe how anyone could get by without one.

'No. But if I want to get hold of her I give her neighbour, Lowena, a ring, and she goes round and fetches her.'

'Oh, okay. Well, she should be expecting me and my son, Scott, this afternoon. But could you help me with some directions to the cottage?'

The post mistress obliged, marking the spot on an illustrated map of the town aimed at highlighting the local attractions more than providing town planning accuracy. After leaving the shop, with a promise to give the post mistress's best to Florence, Janet met Scott back at the car. He'd booked for one night in the first instance, two single rooms. But they could stay longer if they wished as it was low season.

'Now buckle up, and we'll get to Auntie Florrie's,' Scott said. 'I'm quite excited now.'

To get to Riverside Cottage, they turned onto the Market Place in the direction they had come from and drove back over the bridge heading east. Taking a left onto Trefrew Road, then the third left after that, they found themselves driving up a bumpy track with straggles of dead brambles nesting in the beech, and hawthorn hedges pressing from both sides. At the end of the road stood a detached house set amongst wintering trees and shrubs, the slate sign on its white front gate, confirming it to be Riverside Cottage. Scott parked at the end of the lane, and getting out of the car, they stood by the gate and surveyed the house in the grey of a December afternoon.

It was a traditional, whitewashed, stone Cornish cottage, with small square casement windows set into thick walls, and a slate roof, with a small slate overhang above the front door. If it had been summertime, it would have looked just like one of those cottages you see in a victorian pastoral painting, with maids wearing bonnets and carrying trugs in a garden bursting with hollyhocks and cabbages.

And visualizing this, Janet now managed to remember it for real. She could see her Granny Davey standing in the doorway, with her hair pinned in a bun and curls framing her face, wearing one of her numerous pocketed and frilled aprons, and waving Janet off to school – the very same school where Auntie Florrie would end up teaching, and later become headmistress of for the whole of her working life. Her grandfather, a tall and grave-mannered man, then retired from the police force, would probably have been stooped in his greenhouse seeing to his tomato plants.

And here she was again. At this very same cottage. She and Scott approached the blue front door together and a volley of barking reared up behind it. They stepped back and Janet heard a woman's voice saying, 'Hush, now, Blackie! 'It'll be our Janet.' The door opened wide and there stood a lady with a smiling face, holding onto a Border collie straining at its neck collar.

'Is it Janet and Scott? Why yes, I can see it is.'

Scott bent down to stroke Blackie and settle him, while Janet looked closely at her aunt. She looked remarkably youthful for someone who must be around the age of 68. Round faced, with large blue eyes, graceful eyebrows and a rosebud mouth, she seemed to have taken after her own mother's side of the family and had aged very well indeed, with only a sagging of her cheeks, marionette lines around her mouth and crow's feet at the corners of her eyes. Her hair was silver white, but Janet remembered from the few occasions she'd seen her, that it had been blonde. She'd had a wavy fringe and a long thick plait worn over her shoulder while playing the organ in church. Now her hair was cut into a bob which complimented her features. And Janet found herself wondering how on earth this woman had escaped the clutches of a husband.

'Auntie Florrie, you look so well!' Janet found herself exclaiming.

'Good country air, I expect,' she smiled. 'And you're not looking so bad yourself, though you could soften your hairstyle a little if you don't mind me saying so.'

Janet decided she didn't actually mind, since Florence was a member of the family. And how strange did that feel?

Florence ushered them through a flagstoned corridor covered with rag rugs, which looked of a thick homemade quality, into a living room dominated by a massive stone fireplace, deep within which a log fire crackled. The stone floor was covered by a large oriental rug, with deep sofa and chairs upon it. Heavy-set edwardian furniture lined the walls, while cushioned window seats looked out on Florrie's garden, which even in winter looked well-tended. Janet found the colour scheme a delightful blend of soft earthy colours, highlighted by strong reds and greens. And everywhere she looked she saw handicrafts. A tapestry fire screen, framed cross stitch embroideries, just like the ones she did herself at home, and silk cushions decorated with satin stitch flowers.

Janet gasped. 'What a beautiful room! Did you do all this craftwork?'

'Most of it, yes. Keeps me busy in the winter. Do you sew, Janet?'

'Yes, cross stitch mostly.'

'Like me, then. Maybe you take after me? Or Mildred of course. Violet was never that interested. But when your mother was staying with me, she began her millinery again and sold a few hats for weddings and the like, but there wasn't much call for posh hats by then.'

Janet nodded, feeling both perturbed at the idea of taking after Mildred for anything, and guilty that Florence had to look after her mother for so long. And she couldn't for the life of her imagine them getting along. But she also felt a warm affiliation with this aunt, a feeling she'd never had before with any of her family members apart from her own father and her Auntie Vi.

Scott was also impressed. 'Certainly looks like Mum takes after you, Aunt Florrie!' he said, inspecting a framed alphabet sampler in the same style as many of Janet's pieces.

The next hour was a dazzle of catching up on family facts, asking questions, and making observations, that only kin can be comfortable voicing after so many years of no contact. Janet had only ever met Florence a few times, because while Janet was staying with her grandparents, Florence had been at teacher training college in Truro. So, of all her mother's side of the family, Florence was the one she knew the least. But funnily enough, this made her all the more engaging. And as Florence answered their questions while they feasted on a traditional Cornish cream tea that she had prepared for them on her kitchen table, the life she'd led became more pinpointed in clarity and it was quite fascinating to Janet.

Just before she'd left for college, the young Florence had met a lovely local lad called Ruan, who she'd fallen for and became engaged to. But unfortunately, he'd died in the war, and heartbroken, she'd been unable to consider anyone else after him. She finished her training and then became a teacher at Camelford junior school which was when she got a little place of her own. She'd loved her work and that seemed enough for many years. Then Granny and Grandfather Davey had become more frail and asked if she'd move back into the cottage with them. As the spinster in the family who'd been living locally, this job naturally fell to her. She accepted the job with equanimity.

In terms of later romance, there *was* another man in her life. A history professor from London had come to the town in the mid sixties, when she was 42, to do research into the legend of King Arthur and Camelot. According to an old Cornish legend, Arthur's main fortress of Camelot lay buried beneath the town and the professor wanted to find out if there was any interesting evidence to uncover. Well, what he found there instead was Florence in the local library one day, and the two of them had an instant connection, as close to love at first sight as you can get, and duly became a proper couple for the few months he was living there. He wanted them to marry, but insisted they'd have to live in London for his work, and it was this that Florence just couldn't do. Family responsibilities, she'd said, and she preferred the rural life. They'd written to each other for years, but then he wrote to tell her he was getting married. Although she felt she'd missed out, she wished him well and they eventually lost contact.

'That's a real shame,' observed Janet.

'Sad,' added Scott.

'Ah well, you know what they say, Tennyson did anyway, *I hold it true, whate'er befall, I feel it, when I sorrow most, tis better to have loved and lost than never to have loved at all.* Now I'm very happy to see you both, but don't you think it's time to tell me why you're really here?'

Janet gulped and a mouthful of tea went down the wrong way. Florence thumped her on the back and Janet coughed.

'Thank you. Yes, yes of course,' she spluttered.

'Let's go into the living room, I'll put some more logs on the fire,' Florence said.

Scott got to his feet and began clearing the table to do the washing up. 'You go ahead and start, Mum, I'll follow you in later.'

And so Janet told her story again. And as another day shifted into the coal black darkness of a countryside night, unalleviated by street lamps, Janet did her telling by yet another fireplace. And as before, her feelings at first were muffled by the repetition. But Florence began to interject, which made it harder for Janet to stay focused, and not only that, Florence knew far more than Janet had ever imagined.

Janet began with the circumstances of Frank's death and how she'd prevented him from taking the pills.

Florence gasped. 'Oh my!'

Janet flinched from the cold shock in her tone. 'I know,' Janet said, hot with embarrassment. 'I know how it sounds. It sounds terrible. But I've owned up and we'll see what happens.' She explained about Victim Support, Cliff, and what the outcomes might be.

Florence was quiet for a few moments, then said, 'Probably for the best, love. You don't want the memory of that hanging over you. You've got the rest of your life to live now.'

Then when Janet explained the kind of relationship she'd had with Frank which had led to her stress and wanting a stop to it, Florence rose from her armchair and sat close to

Janet on the sofa.

She grasped Janet's hand and squeezed it. 'No man has a right to treat a woman like that. Like property, like a chattel. Like a punch bag. To oppress and belittle. Mildred did tell me of this, but I don't think she must have realised how bad it was.'

'She told you?' Janet stared at her aunt, astonished.

'Yes, she did. And you should know that she was sorry she'd been so hard on you, pressing you to marry him like that. Who you married could shape the rest of your life back then, and she knew it. In a way, that's why I wasn't so keen on the idea of marriage myself, though I'd have liked to have had children, of course.'

Janet nodded, then a realisation stamped into her mind and stood still tapping its foot, waiting for her to catch up. 'So if she told you about that, did she tell you about why Frank began doing it in the first place?'

Florence nodded gravely. 'Yes.'

'So you know about Vivien?' Janet felt a tightness building in her chest. It clenched harder into a painful spasm. She looked away from her aunt, suddenly desperate to be alone.

Her aunt patted her hand. 'Yes.'

Janet sat back, trying to regain some control.

'So, now you're going to try to find her?' asked Florence.

'Yes. Somehow.'

'Good.'

Scott poked his head around the door. 'I'll take Blackie for a walk, okay?'

Florence turned her head to him. 'That would be grand, Scott. There's a lead and a torch on a hook in the kitchen.'

Then after a scrabbling at the front door from Blackie and a 'See you later' from Scott, Florence turned back to Janet.

'You know, I was furious with your mother for making you give up the baby.'

'Why? I thought there was nothing else to be done. Even

my father thought so!' Janet said with a rising voice full of anguish.

'There, there, don't take on.' Florence put her arm around Janet. 'I'm not blaming here. I'm really not. It's just if people hadn't been so dammed concerned about reputations and appearances back then, there'd have been –'

'A lot of single mothers not able financially to look after their babies?'

'Yes, true, and they would have been vilified too. But look at what single women can do today? They work and have children at the same time. They can be single mothers if they want to be.'

'Yes, I know,' replied Janet, thinking of Marian.

'I tried to get the contraceptive pill when I was with the professor. Of course I was getting on then, in my early forties I was, but the doctor refused. It was only for married women as far as he was concerned. So we used the sheath instead, and I decided that if we had an accident, then I'd embrace it and make the best of it.'

Janet gaped at her. 'Why weren't you around when it was happening to me? I think you must have been the rebel in the family.'

Florence smiled briefly, then gazed into the fire, frowning.

Another thought occurred to Janet. 'How did you and Mam get on together? You seem so different.'

Florence shook her head. 'It wasn't easy at first. I was set in my ways here, and she had different ideas. Tried to organise me, she did, but I wasn't having any of that!'

Janet grinned. 'Yes, she liked her strict routines.'

'But we worked it out eventually over the years. She had the spare bedroom to do her millinery in and we shared the chores. We rubbed along like that for thirteen years, before she had her stroke. She missed your father, she missed you, not that she'd admit it, but it was Norman who upset her the most by emigrating.'

'Yes. He was always her favourite.'

'Yes, that's the way it goes sometimes. And the one who is fussed over the most is often the one who travels the furthest away, because they need to stretch their wings the most. You see?'

Janet nodded. 'I did write, you know. Lots of times. With pictures of Scott, and then Danny.'

'I know. She showed me. That's why I easily recognised you both. I've still got them around here somewhere.'

'If she replied –'

'Oh she replied, alright.'

'I never got them. I think Frank kept them from me. He always managed to get to the post first and he'd open any letters himself. He did right from the start. Or maybe he had some other way I didn't know about…'

'Control. He wanted to cut off your support.'

'Yes. I think so.'

Florence hesitated and fixed her gaze into the flames of the fire. 'Janet. There's something you don't know. And it's going to be hard to hear. I don't know how you'll take it. But it's the right time, I think.'

Janet's stomach clenched into a knot. She drew a deep breath to try to quell a sickly feeling from rising up. Surely there was nothing left to know now other than where Vivien was?

Florence turned to her and caught hold of her hand.

'What is it?' Janet whispered.

'It's about your lad, Joe.'

Janet reeled as if she'd been struck over the head. Hearing his name on someone else's lips after all these years was a shock. She tried to pull her hand away, but her aunt held it tight.

'Mildred did something I don't approve of. Violet caught her in the act one day and it stayed on your mother's conscience when Violet was so shocked at what she was doing. But I don't think your father ever knew.'

'What? What did she do?' Janet's felt panic bordering on terror beating like wings in her throat and she couldn't breathe.

'Joe did eventually write to you. We don't know why or how it took him so long. But by the time he did, you were married to Frank.'

'No,' Janet gasped.

'Your mother just opened the first letter to see who it was from. And I've made a point of remembering what she told Violet Joe said in it. He was wanting to know how you were, and telling you he was going to stay over there in America to run the family farm permanently. That he hoped you'd be happy and he wished you well, saying he'd always remember the time you spent together. Maybe he was testing the waters, I don't know. But Mildred never opened the others. She kept them for a while, then when you had Scott she decided it was best for everyone…best for your sake to leave the past alone. Vivien was adopted, you were married and expecting a baby when that first letter arrived. So she eventually did what she thought was best. Violet found her burning them on the fire at Marguerite Road.'

'I don't believe it. He actually wrote,' murmured Janet, looking dazed at Florence. 'Then he did care. He must have!'

'Yes, he obviously did. I think you can safely believe that, love.'

Janet felt her old hurt stirring. That feeling of being abandoned by Joe. It swelled from a trickle to a torrent and crashed through her, leaving her all tossed around and helpless. She found herself crying out old tears, tears that had never dried up. Struggling for breath, she wept, while Florence held her in her arms.

After she found there wasn't anything left to cry out, Florence began to wipe her tears with a hankie she'd drawn from her cardigan pocket.

'It's the way of life sometimes, you know,' she said dabbing at Janet's cheeks. 'Look what happened to my Ruan. These things are the stuff of Greek tragedies. That's why they were so popular, because so many people identified with them. Hearts break, that's a fact. But they can also mend. Now ask yourself, what would you have done if you'd known?'

Janet shook her head. 'I have no idea.'

'But your love was real.'

'Oh, yes. It was real. The only real love from a man I've ever known.'

'Well, that counts for a lot, Janet. That's your consolation. And Vivien was born out of love.'

Janet nodded. 'She was.'

They sat together in silence for a few minutes while the mantel clock ticked on.

Then Florence resumed talking about Mildred. 'I couldn't look after her following her stroke. I was still teaching and she hated the local help I got in. She'd get so frustrated, you see? All worked up, because communication was too difficult for her. So her financial estate went into the cost of a care home for her. She had more company that suited her at the Sunrise. It was a decent place. Vi used to visit her there from Bournemouth.'

'Thank you for everything you did her. I can't say I loved her. That would be going too far. She was too strict, too hard. And my priority was Scott. But I do appreciate you looking after her.'

'That's fine, Janet. I was probably the best person to do it, not too close to her. And Scott really does you credit.'

Janet smiled. 'Thank you.'

'Can I ask you, did Scott ever sense anything about you and Frank? Children don't miss much.'

Janet frowned. 'I know. I did try hard not to let him see or hear the violence. He said he felt the tense atmospheres and didn't like Frank's scolding me. To be honest I think Frank lost Scott as a teenager, when Scott started standing up to him, particularly physically on one occasion he's told me about. But yes, I think he saw more, and felt more, than he's let on.'

'He seems very well-adjusted nevertheless,' Florence smiled.

Janet looked hard at Florence. 'Oh, he is. I must have got something right. I just worry he married a woman that doesn't really suit him and who he doesn't really love. He married Susan when they discovered she was pregnant after they'd been living together. Danny's wonderful, but I simply can't take to Susan…she just comes across as too shallow, too thoughtless.'

'And how do you come across to her, do you think?'

'Oh, that's easy,' Janet said. 'A real bitch, who doesn't think she's good enough for her son. Mind you, I think I've given her *some* good cause over the years.'

'Living with Frank hardened you up, didn't it? Not surprising, mind.'

'Yes, I suppose it did. That's what my Victim Support advisor told me.'

'Time to soften up again, maybe?'

Janet stared at Florence. 'I don't know if I can.'

Florence laughed. 'I think you're already on your way.'

Just then the front door opened and slammed shut. Blackie came in, tail pumping, and nudged his nose into Florence's hand.

Scott popped his head around the living room door. 'Dog duly walked. I'll make a pot of tea now, shall I?'

'That would be grand, Scott,' Florence said. 'There's some biscuits in the tin near the kettle. And thank you for walking Blackie, he was hankering earlier for an outing. One or two local lads I used to teach come and do it for me most days, seeing as I've got this dodgy knee and I'm still on the waiting list for a knee replacement.'

This change of subject sparked an opportunity for Janet to finally ask Florence about Auntie Vi. She'd been floating invisibly in the background, waiting to materialise and be given some substance. Janet's mouth went dry and she squeezed her interlinked fingers in her lap. This was so important. She must see her Auntie Vi again.

Florence got up and tossed another log on the fire with a thud. Sparks snapped and popped.

'Auntie Florrie,' Janet said, turning to her aunt as she sat back down. 'About Auntie Vi. Have you got her address? I don't have any information at all. Just that she and Ted settled in Bournemouth. All I know is that she and Ted had a daughter called Sarah, who I've never met. She stayed with you during the time of Dad's funeral.'

Florence's face fell. 'Yes, that's right.'

'Well, do you have their address?'

'Yes. Ted's gone now, of course.'

'Oh, that's a shame. I'm sorry to hear that. Uncle Ted was great, always had time for me too. But is Auntie Vi still in Bournemouth?'

'Yes, she is. And I can give you an address and telephone number. Sarah went into nursing, you know, though she's married with two children now, Rowella and Cadan, but she visits me as often as she can.' She hesitated, frowning and the brightness in her eyes faded.

'What?' Janet felt a tingling crawl up her spine.

Florence turned to face her. 'Janet, Vi's got dementia. She's in a care home in Bournemouth close to where Sarah lives. She's only two years older than me, you know. I hate it, Janet. I can't visit with her anymore. It's too upsetting.'

Crystals of ice began forming in Janet's bones. Her hand slowly rose to her mouth.

'Sarah used to bring her here sometimes for the weekend, for a catch up, and it was wonderful. I always had a lot of time for Vi. We were pretty close. But I just can't do it now.'

'Oh, God, Auntie Florrie, that's awful. But how bad is her memory? Surely she can't be too bad, she's only, what –'

'71.' Florence pinched her lips together as if what she was going to say was too bitter a thing to form with her tongue. 'And she doesn't really know her family, Janet. She doesn't really know us at all.'

This was a crushing blow and it winded Janet's spirit, a spirit which had just been invigorated by knowing that Joe had finally written to her. But she'd so imagined meeting her

Auntie Vi again, and to tell her she was going to look for Vivien. That she'd never forgotten how kind her aunt had been all those years ago. But how could she do any of this if her aunt didn't know her?

But Janet rallied herself for Florence's sake. It was the least she could do after such a long time of no contact and for the information about Joe. So she and Scott stayed at the Travellers Rest in Camelford for two nights, time enough for Scott to convince Florence she should get new electrics put into the old cottage and take advantage of a phone line. And time enough to visit the Davey family plot within the grounds of the local church.

And it was here Janet stood, just before they left for Bournemouth on an early Wednesday morning stippled with frost. As she read the inscriptions on the headstones, lingering over her mother's, but feeling the same sense of alienation of old, despite the new revelations, she realised how fast the years had passed and how much time she'd missed with these family members, who now lay buried before her, the straggling weeds seemingly so bent upon covering their traces. Her father had insisted on cremation, perhaps due to what he's seen during the war Auntie Vi had suggested at the time. And Janet knew that Mildred had brought his ashes here to be with her when she passed. That at least seemed to prove she had loved him. And here it stood – a black granite memorial vase for her father, right next to Mildred's grave. 'Beloved husband and father,' it said in gold lettering after his name. And she heard him say again what he had said during special moments to fortify her, when Mildred was out of earshot, *Life is what you make it, Janie.*

'Yes, Dad, it is,' she replied now, 'and I'm going to change mine.'

Chapter 23

Travelling at speed along the A30 back to Exeter, then west through East Devon and into Dorset, was like rushing from Daphne du Maurier's Cornish coastal adventures to Thomas Hardy's rural tales of Wessex, with no time to take everything in. Even the town of Dorchester with its stately spires and towers had to serve only as a brief stop in the high street for a spot of lunch and a comfort break. The winter scenery was still compelling, with its rolling rhythms of ploughed fields of clotted earth, and trimmed hedgerows fringed with stately seed heads powder-sprinkled with frosting. The road was narrow and led them through the thatched villages of a county rich in archaeological interest and the mark of Iron Age man.

As they approached the outskirts of the seaside resort of Bournemouth, with the radio switched off, they were both quietly contemplating. They'd phoned Ann to see if everything was alright at home. Apart from Thomas having gone missing again for one night, and Winnie trying to winkle information out of Ann as to Janet's whereabouts over the garden hedge, everything was fine. They'd also contacted Cliff to see if he had any news. Unfortunately his efforts to gain information from the South West agency that had handled Vivien's adoption had proved fruitless and the actual office in Swindon was no longer there. But Janet was to have a meeting next week with Michael Armstrong, her new solicitor on the evening of Tuesday 18th at his office and Cliff would be with her for that.

In the meantime Janet's priority, on a shifting bed of hard and soft spots, was right now on connecting with her remaining family. And it had also become very important to Scott. As an only child he'd missed out on relatives and he seemed to have discovered a relish for making their acquaintance, being already smitten by Auntie Florrie. Indeed his enthusiasm was making the whole trip more of a natural venture for Janet, though she was feeling a queasy mixture of excitement at seeing her Auntie Vi again, but laced with a horrible dread that her aunt wouldn't even recognise her. There was also the question of how much to tell her cousin, Sarah, about Janet's past, the circumstances of Frank's death, and her current search for Vivien.

'I don't see what telling her about Dad's death will achieve,' remarked Scott, slowing down behind a lorry that was hogging the road. 'It will be more than enough telling her about Vivien.'

'Yes, but it was mainly through your father that the family contact was cut off.'

'Okay, well just describe what he was like in that respect, but there's no need for anything else. Sarah will have enough to take in.'

Janet nodded thoughtfully. 'You might have a point.'

They arrived at Sarah's house in Queensland Road in central Bournemouth at quarter to three under the glare of some winter sunshine. They were to stay for two nights with Sarah and then return to Cheltenham on the Friday. Sarah was expecting them, and due to Janet's anxiety about meeting her Auntie Vi, after a cup of tea, Sarah was going to drive them straight to Seaview Nursing Home where Violet was a resident. As she'd explained to them on the phone, their visit should easily coincide with afternoon visiting hours.

As Scott and Janet climbed out of the parked Toyota, a dark brunette woman with a trim figure strode briskly down the short drive of number 5 to greet them, as if they were right on cue. 5 Queensland Road was a detached house with a white painted façade and black window trims, surmounted by a decorative bargeboard gable above the bays. The adjacent houses were a snug, if not mean, fit alongside. But land was at a premium here in this tourist town, which attracted so many visitors for its seven miles of sandy beaches and night entertainments.

Sarah greeted Janet first. 'Wonderful to finally meet you,' she smiled, and she wrapped Janet in a hug. 'Do I call you Janet?'

Janet tried to relax her stiff posture, which it seemed she was having to train herself to do these days.

'Yes, that's fine,' she replied, now studying Sarah, who'd grasped her hand. She was the spitting image of how Auntie Vi had looked all those years ago. The same thick hair, as sleek and glossy as a raven's wing. Almost like her own dark brown had been before she'd gone grey and had decided to dye it black, thus needing to retouch her roots every few weeks. And the same brown eyes as Violet, with the shared nose of the Daveys, like her own, long and straight. Striking looks, they used to say in the family, rather than beautiful, though Florence had turned out to be an exception with her softer, more feminine features. But her cousin Sarah was a Davey through and through.

'You look just like I remember your mother!' Janet said, still holding Sarah's hand but stepping back to view her more clearly.

'Yes, everyone used to say that. You've got something of the look yourself. I've seen some teenage photos of you, so it's not so much of a surprise to me,' she said, laughing. She turned to Scott. 'And you're Scott. Totally not the Davey looks with that blonde hair. As I understand it we're first cousins once removed.'

'Yes, a bit of a mouthful, isn't it. But great to meet you,' Scott said, giving Sarah a kiss on the cheek.

'Right, let's have a cuppa, then we'll go over to Seaview.'

Sitting on Sarah's plush sofa in a room of peaches and creams, and trying hard not to rattle her cup in its saucer, Janet explained to Sarah the reasons why she'd lost contact with Violet, herself and Florence, and how much she regretted it. She told Sarah about giving away Vivien and how hard her life had subsequently been with Frank, about the domestic abuse, the bullying and how she was convinced that he'd destroyed any family letters sent to her. Sarah kept giving Scott worried glances, but he shrugged them off.

'I came out of it relatively unscathed,' he said. 'Mum saw to that.'

After listening hard for around half an hour, with a series of question marks flitting across her forehead, Sarah suddenly checked her watch. 'You can tell me the rest later, Janet. I think we'd better go to see Mum now. We can fit in a good visit before teatime.' She reached over and squeezed Janet's hand. 'Now, you mustn't expect too much. She may not know you.'

Janet put down her cup and saucer onto the coffee table with a clatter. 'But what about you, Sarah? Does she know you?'

'Sometimes.'

Janet felt a weight settle on her heart. 'Oh Sarah, how do you deal with it?'

Sarah sighed. 'It's not easy. But I think it helps that I'm a nurse. I try to use my training to be more objective, not to take it too personally. And I've got my husband, Doug, to talk to, he's a psychiatrist, so he comes in handy.'

'Right. That makes a lot of sense,' Scott said. 'But still...'

Seaview Nursing Home was a victorian pile of turrets, gables and balustraded balconies on East Overcliff Drive overlooking Poole Bay, and by the time they arrived at around four o'clock, dusk had crept over the shoreline. Lights in the home blazed from bay windows not yet sheathed by drawn curtains, giving it a welcoming aspect, but it wasn't warm enough to alleviate Janet's tension, and she felt as taut as a stretched bow.

Sarah parked her Ford Escort in the visitors area and they entered the home. At the reception desk Sarah signed them in, and a passing care assistant, who obviously knew Sarah well, said her mother was in her room and to just go on up.

The entrance hall they stood in was a rather grand affair

with two huge crystal chandeliers shedding drops of tears, as it seemed to Janet, and the carpet was a kinetic swirl of reds and mustard yellows which made her feel nauseous again. The air felt heavy, as if locked in place by a complex system of fire doors throughout the whole of the building, and it seemed to carry in it a saturation of odours of stale perfume, cleaning polish and fried breakfasts. But the lift they entered was mirrored and plushly upholstered. Only a liveried lift attendant was missing.

'It's a very grand place,' observed Scott.

'It used to be The Royal Hotel back in victorian times,' explained Sarah. 'Places like this convert very well into care homes.'

They exited on the first floor and Sarah led them down a blue-carpeted passage to a door with Violet's name on and a photograph of her which Janet scrutinised. Her aunt looked older of course, crinkled by time, her hair long since turned to ash-grey, but there was still the same open smile, the same brightness in her eyes that Janet remembered, so she relaxed a little. Maybe this was going to be alright?

Sarah knocked on the door and entered saying, 'Hi, Mum, you've got some visitors.'

Violet was seated in an armchair by the window, which during the day would provide a view of the sea. But all there was to see now were pinpricks of light from the piers.

Violet stirred herself and a *People's Friend* slid out of her lap onto the floor. Sarah picked it up, popped it onto a nearby pile of magazines, then dragged a couple of ladder-backed chairs close to Violet and settled herself on the adjacent bed. The room was spacious with an en-suite bathroom and seemed to have an eclectic mixture of furniture, featuring sideboards and tables with barley twist legs, Lloyd Loom chairs, and some china and ornaments, some of which Janet recognised from her aunt and uncle's rooms above the shop in Bristol.

'Look who's come to see you, Mum,' smiled Sarah. 'It's your niece, Janet, and her son, Scott. Do you remember

Janet?'

Janet and Scott sat in the chairs in front of Violet, and Janet allowed herself to look properly at her aunt.

Yes, she was Violet. The striking Davey features were still the same, but she didn't have the youthful vigour of Florence. Her skin appeared drier and her hair looked as if it had just come out of curlers and hadn't been brushed properly. But she was wearing a touch of make-up and was smartly dressed in a tweed skirt and red jumper, and her feet were swaddled in fleece-lined slippers. A large 1950s beige leather handbag with an alligator skin pattern was weighted on the floor beside her like a door stop. Janet felt a familiar connection with the bag, so she now locked eyes with her aunt. But immediately, she could see that Violet didn't recognise her. She had a faraway gaze, as if she was staring right through Janet into another reality. Those brown eyes were dimmed and she clutched for the magazine that was no longer in her lap. Janet's heart twisted with an ache she'd never felt before. An ache for family, and for the Janet she used to be, to be enfolded in the affectionate memory of this much-loved aunt, and to be given sanction to connect with her younger self. But Violet's eyes were clouded in confusion.

'Mum, it's your niece, Janet,' said Sarah again, now gently stroking a brush through her mother's hair. 'She married Frank, the policeman, and went to live in Cheltenham.'

Janet got down on her knees in front of Violet. She reached behind her own neck and yanked out the clasp pinning her hair back. Her hair fell to frame her face like she'd worn it as a girl. She grasped hold of her aunt's hands to stop them picking at her skirt in her lap.

'Auntie Vi, it's me, Janet.' She gave her aunt a piercing look. 'It's Janet, Auntie Vi!'

'Janet? I don't know any Janet. Leave me alone!'

Violet's tone was rushed and her breathing quickened. She snatched her hands away and turned to Sarah. 'Show them out now please. It'll be teatime soon.' Her voice wavered and she cast darting glances around the room.

Scott shook his head. 'It's no good, Mum. No use distressing her.'

'We could try again tomorrow,' offered Sarah. 'There are good days and bad days with dementia.'

Janet heaved herself to her feet. It was no use. 'We might as well go home tomorrow, Scott. I don't want to upset her with another visit.'

Sarah bent down and hugged her mother, an embrace which Violet accepted. 'Love you, Mum,' Sarah said, and she kissed her mother's cheek. 'See you soon.'

'Yes, come back soon,' said Violet. 'It's so nice to have visitors.'

They were just going through the door and saying goodbye when Violet called out something. 'Did she ever find her?'

'What, Mum?' Sarah asked, halting in the doorway.

Janet rushed back into the room and stared at Violet, who stared straight back at her.

'Did she ever find her? I hoped she would,' Violet said.

'Auntie Vi?' Janet asked. 'Do you mean Vivien?'

Violet looked blankly at Janet. 'I wrote to Janet telling her what I saw, you know.'

'You did? But I never got a letter, Auntie Vi. What was it? What did you see? What do you know?' Janet's tone was frantic.

'Steady, go steady, Mum,' Scott said, touching Janet's arm.

'It was sent back. I've still got it. I kept it safe,' Violet said.

'Where is it, Mum?' Sarah asked gently. She bent down in front of Violet and squeezed her hand. 'It could be very important. Where have you kept it?'

Violet reached down to her handbag and Sarah swiftly lifted it up and placed it in Violet's lap. Violet snapped open the clasp and stretched open the mouth of the bag to display the contents. Sarah brought into the light of day the objects held within this cavernous interior, placing them carefully on the floor: two metal spectacle cases, a powder compact, an old hearing aid, a hairbrush, a handkerchief, a worn purse bulging with bits of paper rather than money – but before she was finished, Violet pushed Sarah's hands away and she yanked open the zip of a side pocket. She reached inside and drew out a small brown envelope, ragged and fluffy around the edges.

She thrust it at Sarah.

Janet, Scott and Sarah scrutinised it as Sarah held it for them all to see.

'I've never seen this before,' she said, her eyes wide with wonder. 'Mum's always been so private about her handbag.'

The envelope was addressed to Mrs Janet Brewer, 9 Willow Lane, Charlton Kings, Cheltenham.

'That's Mum's handwriting,' Sarah said.

Janet pointed at the slash through the address and the words 'return to sender' scrawled in a fountain pen. 'And that's Frank's.'

There was a faded postmark on the envelope which showed it had been sent from Bournemouth on the November 21st 1958. Scott read the date out loud.

'That's shortly after I was born,' murmured Sarah. 'Here, Janet.' Sarah handed the envelope to Janet. 'It's for you to open.'

Janet took it from her with trembling fingers.

Violet sat transfixed, and with three pairs of eyes trained upon her, Janet slowly parted the torn opening and drew out two sheets of paper folded into quarters, yellowed with age and blotted with foxing, along with a deckle-edged, square black and white photograph.

The photograph showed a young woman and an older woman with a baby in a pram. The baby was visible because the pram hood was down and the baby was propped up on the pillow. The faces of the women were also clear. It looked like it had been taken at the seaside somewhere, as out of shot passers-by were caught frozen in the act of eating ice creams. It was also clear that the two women had no idea they were having their picture taken as they fussed over the baby. There was also a toy in the pram, but she couldn't make it out.

Janet stared at the picture, wondering what the significance could be. She turned the photo over. On the back was written in faded ink, '*Vivien (three months) in the pram at Western-super-Mare, with her adoptive mother, Mrs Ruth Matthews, and her grandmother, Jean Cookson – photo taken 10th September 1954.*'

Janet scrutinised the picture again, examining the baby's face. Could it really be her? Her hair was fair, like Joe's, and she thought the features were the same as those she'd gazed into when she held Vivien in her arms at the home. It was so very hard to tell, but what if it really was her? With the picture glued to her fingers and her legs giving way she collapsed onto one of the chairs. The letter fluttered to the floor. Her breaths began to shorten and become faster as she gulped in more and more air.

'Take some deep breaths!' Sarah said. 'Nice and slow, now, nice and slow.' She kneeled in front of Janet and drew in breaths with her to demonstrate the necessary pace. 'In...*and* out...'

'That's it Mum,' Scott said as Janet's breathing began returning to normal. He took the photograph from her hand and read the back. His eyebrows shot up.

Violet shuffled forward in her chair, bent over and snatched up the letter from the floor. This time she shoved it at Janet. 'Read!' she rasped.

Janet looked at her. 'I can't. I just can't, Auntie Vi.' Then she cast a look of despair at Scott. 'Will you read it?'

'Of course, Mum.'

Scott sat down in the chair next to Janet, while Sarah sat on the floor with her legs tucked to one side, and he read out loud the letter that had been posted in 1958, four years after the picture had been taken.

25 Wilson Road, Boscombe, Bournemouth

21st November 58

Dear Janet,

I'm writing to you about this because it's something I can only write and not say out loud over the phone in case anyone overhears. I don't know whether I'm doing the right thing, but after having Sarah, it got me thinking how very painful it must have been to give Vivien up, even though you did it for all the right reasons. Of course you've since built a life for yourself and have a son now, and that is indeed a wonderful blessing, but I know from Mildred that Frank is not making a good husband to you and I'm that upset for you. So sorry. This is partly why I'm writing. There are some things you should know if you ever decide to try to find Vivien. I've been sitting with this knowledge now for too long, Janet. I need to pass it on to you.

A couple of weeks after Vivien was adopted from Swindon, an older couple I knew as occasional customers came into the shop. I knew them as Mr and Mrs Cookson, a middle-aged couple from the Brislington area of Bristol. They had a baby in a pram, one of those posh silver cross ones. Well I peered into the pram and the first thing I saw was the rabbit I knitted for Vivien. It was in the pram, Janet! No mistake! The blue, yellow and red stripy jumper and trousers, the pink nose, blue eyes and the ears right up, not flopping. Then I saw the baby's face and could see instantly it was Vivien. I wanted to scoop her up, I did.

I tried hard to stay calm and I asked them who the baby belonged to, because they were too old to have adopted her. They told me their daughter, Ruth, and her husband had just adopted her and they'd named her Rosemary. I knew Ruth a little from the Women's Bright Hour. She's a nice girl, married to Leonard Matthews – so that makes our Vivien now Rosemary Matthews.

After talking it over with Ted, I decided I had to let it lie. You were making new plans for your future and what could we realistically do anyway? But when I saw them again on the Grand Pier at Western a couple of months later, that is, I saw Ruth and Jean Cookson with Vivien in her pram, I felt it was some sort of sign. So I got Ted to take a picture of them unawares, thinking I could put it in with a letter to you one day. After I've recently had Sarah, that day has come.

There is one more thing you need to know. Joe did write. In the end he did write. He was staying over there for good but wished you well. I found Mildred with some letters from him one day. But you'd just got married and were expecting, so she thought it best to get rid of them. I didn't approve, but again, what could any of us have done?

Well Janet, despite the past and your current difficulties, I so hope you find some happiness. I'm sending this letter now, but have to confess I just didn't know what to do for the best. But I am sure that the Matthews made good parents for Vivien. I think you can trust that much.

Much love,

Auntie Vi

(P.S I'll send this by registered post to be on the safe side)

During the reading of the letter, Violet had begun to chime in softly with Scott's reading, word for word in some places, as if she'd read the letter so many times she knew it by heart. Hers was the voice that ended the reading, following on from Scott's, with 'much love, Auntie Vi…to be on the safe side.'

Janet sat staring at her aunt, with her heart hammering.

Tears ran silently down Sarah's cheeks.

Scott stabbed his finger at the envelope. 'If she sent it by registered post, it would have to have had a signature. Dad would have received it, decided not to accept it, then he must have written return to sender on it and handed it back to the postman…then it made its way back to Auntie Vi and she read it over and over. Or Dad accepted it, opened it, read it, then posted it back.'

'Does it really matter now?' Sarah asked quietly, putting an arm around Janet's shoulders.

Scott frowned and put the letter back inside the envelope. 'No, I suppose it doesn't.' Then he brightened and looked at Janet. 'Cliff will be able to do something with this information for sure, Mum. It's a breakthrough!'

Janet nodded slowly, still trying to process what had just happened, while a sickening hot feeling of remorse built up inside her. All these years her aunt had known who Vivien's adopted parents were. All these years. And she'd never really tried to get in touch with Violet or her family. She'd made it easy for Frank to cut her off. Why? Why had she let it happen? There were buses and trains she could have got, weren't there? Tears swelled, edged down her face, then dripped off her chin, while she sat with her hands limply on her knees.

'Mum? This is a good thing! Don't get upset, please don't!'

He kneeled down in front of her and gripped her hands.

'I should have kept in touch…' Janet said. 'Somehow, I should have. There's no excuse.'

Violet reached to a side table by her armchair and tugged a tissue out of a box. She gingerly got to her feet and began to wipe Janet's tears away. 'There, lass. Don't take on so.'

Janet gazed into her aunt's face and began sobbing. Her shoulders heaved with her sobs as her shame overtook all her other emotions.

Scott held her in his arms. 'You mustn't punish yourself like this, Mum. You did your best. You always did your best. It's what we do from now on that counts. The past is done with.'

'Right,' Sarah said.

'Right, that's right,' said Violet.

All three of them stared at Violet. She smiled at them with such a look of serenity that they returned her smile.

'You know, I think it's done her some good getting that

letter off her chest,' observed Sarah.

And as they left Violet for the second time, Janet began to feel a little lighter in herself too. Scott was right. They'd had a breakthrough. A kind of miracle. And it was all thanks to her beloved aunt.

Chapter 24

Janet and Scott stayed with Sarah for the next two days, extending their planned visit by a day, and intending to travel back to Cheltenham on the Saturday. Only one week after that and it would be Christmas, and Scott had suggested that Janet, Ann, and Cliff, join himself, Susan, and Daniel for Christmas Day. This is something Janet would ordinarily have dreaded as Susan's company was so irksome, but if Ann didn't have any other plans, she thought she could manage it, as she certainly didn't feel like preparing for another Christmas herself. Not with everything going on.

On their stay in Bournemouth, Janet and Scott visited Violet twice a day, taking her out for wintry walks along the beach and watching the wind whip up the breakers as they scurried into shore. Janet found it didn't really matter that her aunt seemed unable to recognise her, because there was a trusting ease between them which Sarah said was a good sign of a sense of familiarity on Violet's part. Janet and Scott also got to know Sarah's children, Rowella and Cadan – so named, said Sarah, to keep the Cornish heritage on the Davey side going. *And* Janet told Sarah and her husband psychiatrist, Douglas, about her part in Frank's death, where their initial shock subsided into support.

The two days passed with Janet feeling a strange sense of freedom which she couldn't understand, while also trying to process her feelings about allowing herself to be cut off from her family all those years ago.

What she found most useful in so many respects was talking to Douglas, who Sarah was proud to announce only worked for the NHS, rather than privately, and whom she dubbed as the 'house shrink'. After hearing Janet's story and her recent concerns as to why she hadn't tried harder to stay in touch with her family, he was able to offer some insights.

He pointed out that she probably became repressed through Frank's treatment of her over so many years. His controlling and punishing behaviour could easily have cut her off from her inner self – the self that her family knew, the self that *she* knew. In a sense *that* Janet had gone to ground. It was common for victims of domestic abuse to develop a lack of trust in others and become emotionally detached with a damaged self-esteem. It didn't surprise him in the least that she'd allowed contact to dwindle under those circumstances. But when she'd gone to work after Frank retired, the dynamics had shifted a little. She had taken some of the power back. The job would have slowly boosted her confidence, so that later on, when Frank demanded again that she should give her job up, the job that had effectively helped her to be herself again, a need to take back full control from him had kicked in. And it was this dynamic which explained why she felt she had to let him die by doing what she did.

Scott and Sarah listened in, as the four of them sat in the lounge after dinner having a glass of wine, with Rowena and Cadan tucked in bed upstairs.

'I always knew you were a smart arse,' Sarah said to Douglas, giving him a kiss on the cheek, 'but I think you've just surpassed yourself.'

'Thank you, sweet pea,' Douglas grinned.

'It's fascinating,' Scott said.

'Yes, that's why I went into psychiatry.'

As Janet listened carefully to Douglas, she felt as if something inside her, a block as hard as polished granite, was developing more cracks. The cracks had been forming ever since she had shared her guilt about Vivien and about Frank's death. In the past she would have been terrified by this feeling of impending shattering, of falling apart. She'd have tried to plug the gaps with anything. She'd have bled to plug those gaps. But it had gone too far now.

'Are you alright, Janet?' Douglas asked.

Janet looked at him. 'I just feel so strange, like I don't know what's happening to me. It's…I don't know…'

'Scary?'

'Yes.'

'Try to just go with it. Change is frightening, but it's vital to recovery. To heal yourself and move forward. To be a happier you.'

Janet nodded.

'And if you ever fancy a chat, you know where I am. After all, we're family now.'

Driving back to Cheltenham the next day, Janet pondered on what Douglas had said, and instead of driving straight home, Janet asked Scott if he minded detouring west to Bishopsworth in Bristol for a quick visit. She wanted to see if the parents of her old friend, Babs, still lived at 23 Greylands Road, and if so, to ask them for Bab's current address. She had suppressed a long-term need to know how her best friend from her youth was doing, and at the same time Scott could take a gander at her old family home in Marguerite Road. So after heading north to Swindon, they joined the M4 to Bristol.

Two and a half hours later, they were standing by the car in front of 14 Marguerite Road – a semi-detached house with a tarmac drive scarred by patching. The burgundy windows were now white and double-glazed, but they were still leaded, if not the original pattern. And above the top and bottom bays was the barge-boarded gable. The lower floor was still brick, the upper pebble-dashed, but there was now an extension on the left side of the house providing an extra room upstairs and a garage below. What Janet felt most familiar with was the front door, set in a brick arch with that same concrete step which Mildred always made sure was scrubbed clean, and the bedroom window above, from which she'd viewed Babs disappearing out of her life. Scott, who'd been taking pictures on this whole trip took a few snaps, and asked her if she wanted to knock on the door and see if she could look around inside.

Janet shuddered. 'God, no!' But she described to him how it used to look.

'A classic 1940s council house,' he observed. 'With a vegetable garden out the back.'

When they got to 23 Greylands Road, they found Babs's parents had moved to 46 Highridge Green just a few blocks away. They had to wait for half an hour before anyone showed up, but at half one an elderly bowed lady, walking slowly with a limp and loaded with carrier bags, turned into the drive. Janet and Scott dashed over to her, and the lady, who Janet just about recognised through her camouflage of wrinkles, as Babs's mother, Ivy, peered at her with suspicion.

Janet introduced herself and Scott, and searched for some signs of recognition on Ivy's part while explaining the situation. When Ivy finally realised who Janet was, her eyes brightened.

'Of course, it's you! I can it see now. Such shiny dark hair. Come on in, love,' she said. 'Fred's away at his bowls, but come in for a brew.'

And just one hour later they resumed their journey with Babs's London address tucked safely in Janet's handbag along with Auntie Vi's letter and photograph.

Darkness was creeping in as they arrived back in Charlton Kings at half three. Janet felt a bit giddy with the mental and emotional impact of all the visiting she and Scott had done in the last few days. And the long preceding years now seemed like some strange state of suspended animation with all her vital signs cut off. She was now desperate to tell her news to Ann, then relax and reflect, and was thankful the next day was a Sunday which meant no Masons.

But as soon as they stepped over the threshold of number 9 Willow Lane, after greeting Ann, Scott wanted to collect together all the documents they had so far – the photographs which had been in Janet's suitcase, Violet's photograph and letter, with relevant dates and addresses – to take home and photocopy for Cliff. He was going to ring him as soon as he got home with the news. His energetic enthusiasm further stirred Janet's disequilibrium.

'I'm sure Cliff can do something with Violet's information, Mum. We just might get somewhere!' he said, sliding everything into a brown manila envelope that Ann found for him in Janet's desk under the stairs. 'But I'd better be off now.'

'Thanks for everything, Scott. I just couldn't be doing all this without you,' Janet said. 'And do give my best to Susan, and give Danny a kiss from me.'

'Of course, Mum,' Scott said, giving her a brief hug, then making for the front door. 'Now just have a nice day off and don't forget you've got the meeting with the solicitor on Tuesday night.'

The door slammed behind him and the house shook with Scott's departure.

Janet and Ann stared at each other in the silence.

Ann slowly grinned. 'Worn out?'

Janet nodded. Ann always seemed to perceive what she was feeling. It was uncanny. It had unnerved her in the past. But where was the threat now that Ann knew everything about her?

Tuesday evening came more quickly than Janet was prepared for, and at six o'clock she found herself seated across a vast mahogany desk buffed to a mirror finish so smooth you could have skated on it. Brown leather tomes dutifully lined the bookshelves in their regimented rows like an army of knowledge, and Janet and Cliff sat in regency-style chairs opposite the man himself, Michael Armstrong, at his office in Clarence Square.

He was an intimidating figure. Thick curly black hair, closely shaven, yet still with a shadow of relentless new growth, dark eyes under bristling brows, and a mouth that worked his words like a Shakespearean stage actor. His massive hands with their bony knuckles looked as if he could easily restrain thugs, let alone crack walnuts with them for his delectation, and some strange knobbles on his forehead imparted a sense of him having worked his frontal lobes so hard his brain was striving to advertise its labour by modifying his external form.

After the introductions were done, and he'd shaken Janet's hand surprisingly gently, he cast some swift glances at the brand new case file in front of him and thought it best to outline what the possible procedures and outcomes might be, before looking at the issues surrounding her defence.

Janet and Cliff agreed it was a good place to begin.

So gesticulating now and again for dramatic emphasis, Michael Armstrong, began to explain.

'So far, DCI Bridges is conducting an investigation to see if they can accrue enough evidence to take to the Crown Prosecution Service and request an order for your arrest, Janet, with a view to taking your case to trial. This is a distinct possibility as they have a witness in Winifred Parsons. They've checked the coroner's report and found nothing amiss, but they also want to interview your GP, Dr Blake, who was at the scene. It seems a little excessive to me, but it's by no means unusual, and since he's out of the country it means they are not likely to proceed further until they've spoken to him after the second week in January, after he returns.'

Janet and Cliff nodded firmly. But Janet was shrinking from the legal language which she couldn't believe had anything to do with her. She found herself pushing her back into the bones of the chair. Here was this legal expert talking about her *case*. She was a *case*? And yet she had to acknowledge that she was. And the sooner she got it into her head the better she could handle it. So she let the abrasive terms have their way with her.

'Now, if they do get an order for an arrest,' Armstrong continued, 'then they'll obviously be thinking they might have a strong case to take it to trial. So, Janet, you'd be arrested and charged...however,' he said, waving away

Janet's look of fright, 'you'd most likely be released on bail. And next up would be a plea hearing date at the magistrate's court, to assess the case as to whether it should go to a trial. And if you are pleading guilty, which you are by virtue of having confessed, then the hearing judge will take into account any presented extenuating circumstances, and issue what they feel to be a suitable sentence. If you're pleading guilty there will be no trial by jury, you understand? And the sentencing takes place there and then at the hearing.'

'So what do you think the sentence might be if it goes that far?' Cliff asked.

'With the mitigating circumstances, you're probably talking about being found guilty of involuntary manslaughter, rather than voluntary. But that could still go either way between gross negligence, through breaching a duty of care, or an unlawful and dangerous act, because of the conscious intent in that moment you made the medication unavailable, Janet. If it's gross negligence, you're most likely looking at a suspended sentence of one to two years, with the minimum being one year, maybe with some community service.'

'That's what I thought,' commented Cliff.

'But if it's classed as unlawful, with Janet being judged to have *intended* to kill Frank by removing his possible aid to life, then it could be a prison sentence.'

Janet gasped, and she found herself shaking. Her bladder loosened and she urgently needed the toilet, but she didn't dare move from her chair. 'But…but how will I find Vivien then? What will happen if – '

'Janet, listen to me. That's the unpleasant stuff, which I have to make you aware of, but now let me tell you what I am going to do to help you.'

'I think you'd better,' Cliff said, grabbing hold of Janet's hand to squeeze it and frowning at Michael Armstrong.

'We'll use the long-term domestic abuse as a defence, which rendered you fearful for your survival every time there was an argument. And the fact that Frank was a policeman made your position even more desperate for trying to get help. And finally, due to this long pattern of oppression, there was a fear-driven provocational instinct to protect yourself in that moment in which you saw Frank's anger escalating yet again. It was the last straw in this sense. We can also draw upon battered person syndrome if necessary.'

Janet wrinkled her nose. Not that awful term, again, she thought.

'Yes, I know, not a nice phrase, but to the point,' the solicitor smiled, reading her mind. 'But maybe your GP can corroborate a history of unexplained bruising and so forth. Do you think that's possible?'

Janet nodded. 'Yes, I'm sure Dr Blake suspected, though I never admitted it to him.'

'Good. So for now, we'll wait and see what the police do next. And if they do charge you, I need to be present at the station. Understand?'

Janet nodded. 'Yes.'

'And please try not to worry. I'm on your side, and I'm going to do everything I can on your behalf.'

'Yes, thank you. Can I use your bathroom?'

'On the landing, first door on the left.'

'Can I have a word with you?' Cliff asked Michael.

Cliff turned to Janet and said, 'I'll see you in the waiting room, okay?'

'Okay, fine.'

Janet was keen to get away from the close atmosphere of the room and the distinct feeling that all the books on the shelves were frowning down upon her. In the bathroom she noticed how she did look somewhat strained with her hair tied back again. Ann had told her the other day, after seeing her arrive home with it loose, to give it a try at work because it really suited her. Well, she wasn't ready for that yet, but wearing it down outside of work was a start. Little changes, little bites at a time were in order, towards a new Janet, or a rediscovered young Janet, but certainly not the one in-between. And as she eyed herself in the mirror, she vowed she would fight this legal fight no matter what the outcome. She had to go forward. She wanted to find Vivien, to connect with her family, and she wanted to find some peace.

Finding any peace on Christmas day was a bit of a bumpy ride, though they had all fastened their seatbelts and were on their best behaviour, before coming in for a relatively smooth landing.

Janet resolved to set aside worrying about her potential arrest, together with the vivid imagery it conjured up, and tried to enter into the spirit of the festive season this year, by doing some Christmas shopping in her lunch breaks from Masons. This motivation was kindled by the store's bright decorations and banners, by the fairy-dust sprinkling of lights in the Promenade's rows of elm and plane trees, and the central arcade being strung with festive garlands and glittering reindeer leaping to catch stars.

She'd asked Scott what to get for Daniel, and he'd suggested a Nintendo Game Boy which she could get from Toys 'R' Us. It was the latest hot toy and Danny had been trying out his friend's and was now asking for one.

'It's either that, Mum, or the Teenage Mutant Ninja Turtles,' Scott said. 'So take your pick.' She picked the Game Boy and Scott laughed. 'Thought so!'

She got some perfume for Susan, as she knew she loved Christian Dior's Poison. It was a rather heady and spicy scent which Janet felt to be stifling, but this was Susan's taste and that was what mattered. Since she'd noticed Scott's briefcase was getting worn when he was collecting her documents for photocopying, she double-checked with Susan first, then found him a lovely red brown leather one with an optional shoulder strap from House of Fraser. For Ann, she chose a set of fine crystal sherry glasses from Masons, and for Cliff, a Filofax, as he'd mentioned he'd better be getting an organiser if he was going to become a private investigator – it was a joke on his part, but Janet decided it might just have a grain of truth to it. So armed with these beautifully wrapped presents she and Ann turned out of the drive in Willow Lane in Janet's Polo and headed for Scott's house over in Andoversford, four miles to the east.

As she passed the Reynolds house opposite, she wondered, not for the first time in the last few days, why there wasn't the usual exuberant display of outdoor illuminations as there had been last year, though Winnie had forced some gossip on Ann over the garden fence, suggesting that the couple were almost at breaking point and they'd be splitting up for sure – 'Just mark my words,' Winnie had said. Ann was now trying to steer clear of Winnie and Winnie was steering clear of Janet. So it was nice to get away for the day and steer in another direction altogether.

Around the dining table centrepiece of a blood-red poinsettia, which made Janet wince every time it caught her eye, Susan put on a fine spread of a traditional roast turkey dinner. But she'd been moved to mess around with tried and tested fare by experimenting with some new ideas, specifically to be a cut above, Janet felt. For example the chestnut stuffing was a bit of a risk when sage and onion would have done perfectly well. And the fresh cranberry sauce was unnecessary when you could buy good sauce in a jar from Sainsbury's. But she caught hold of herself, noticing her critical thinking, so she forced a smile, pretended to enjoy a mouthful of stuffing, and said how delicious it was.

Ann was chatty and said how much she was enjoying the change from going to her son's or daughter's up north. 'Gives them a break from doing their duty,' she said.

Cliff was enjoying the food and the company. He hadn't had a family Christmas like this, he said, for so long. Even with Angie, it had usually been just the two of them.

Scott and Daniel were their usual amiable selves, but Susan was notably quiet, and she struggled at first to cope with not knowing Ann or Cliff. There was a visible strain around her eyes and a tightness to her mouth as she tried to be a good hostess and say nothing about what had brought this group of people together – namely, Janet's past 'misdemeanours', which she'd been forced to reckon with at such short notice.

After dinner the present giving commenced by the real-deal Christmas tree, decked out with this year's fashionable duo of silver and purple tones. While they had coffee and mints, everyone was polite and friendly and all seemed thrilled with their gifts.

Janet got a bottle of *her* favourite Obsession perfume from Susan, as safe an exchange of gifts as you could possibly get, which the two of them managed to do at Christmas time when they strived to feign mutual acceptance. From Ann, Janet received a Paisley shawl similar in style to the one she'd described to her as Liz from Victim Support wearing. The reds, burnt oranges, and touches of jade were a little bright, but Ann told her, 'This is the new you.' Janet's thanks were strangled short by thinking, yes, but, I can't wear this if I go to jail. From Cliff she got a swanky photograph album with red silk ties. 'For the future,' he said. And again, she groped to escape the grip of a stomach clench, thinking, yes, but what if I don't find Vivien and what if there is no future? Scott played safer with a couple of tapestry embroidery kits, two large coordinating floral panels which she decided she could probably still work on in prison.

The mood lightened with some fizzy wine, while they watched Daniel play with his new Mutant Ninjas – Michelangelo, Donatello, Raphael and Leonardo – as they battled in their bandanas, wielded their weapons, and performed some masterly martial arts moves in Danny's expert hands.

After this interlude, Scott and Cliff helped Daniel figure out how to use his Game Boy using the manual which they began to bicker over, and then declare was no use whatsoever, while Susan went into the kitchen to wash up. Ann moved to join her, but Janet shook her head at Ann and followed Susan into the kitchen herself.

'Oh, it's you,' Susan said, looking startled, and much to Janet's horror, with a touch of fear crossing her face.

Janet put a hand on Susan's shoulder and looked sideways at her. 'Listen, Susan. It was so good of you to have all of us over today. This must so strange and worrying for you. And a shock of course. But with all that's being going on, you've made sure today is a good day.'

Susan looked hard at her. 'I didn't really have any choice, Janet. I didn't want to say no to Scott, because I could see how important it was to him.'

Janet's hand fell from Susan's shoulder. 'Well, if it means anything to you, I do appreciate it, and all the trouble you've gone to.'

She was finding Susan to be her usual intractable self, but in a different way than before. And in that moment, she noticed the fear in Susan's eyes had shifted to a steely glint, and she realised she'd probably lost the upper hand in their tenuous relationship. Her two great sins, which Susan was now in full knowledge of, had seen to that. And Susan knew it too.

'I suppose you think I'm a hypocrite,' Janet said.

A silence fell between them and Janet stared beyond the kitchen window into the back garden of Scott and Susan's honey-coloured stone detached house. It was in a prime location close to the A40 for Scott's commuting to Oxford and London for work. Susan had used her connections where she worked at McReath's estate agents to get a good deal for 6 Station Road, Andoversford, when she and Scott were looking to buy just after Daniel was born over seven years ago. And it had served them well, but Scott was now looking for a plot of land on which to design and manage the building of a home to their own specifications. 'Our dream home' he called it, but Janet was unsure whether Susan and he shared the same dream, as he loved minimalism and she loved flounces and frills.

Susan sighed as she tipped more Fairy Liquid into the

washing up bowl. Her shoulders sagged. 'You know, what you've just said is typical. You assume I'm judging you, because you judge me.' She flashed a look at Janet. 'And don't deny it, I know you do. I'm not *stupid*, you know.' She agitated the water with her fingers and dumped some dinner plates into it. 'But I really love Scott and Danny. They need me. I know Scott and I are quite different, but we complement each other and I'm not going anywhere, despite what you think of me.' She turned and stared at Janet full in the face. 'As for what you did. Giving away your baby is something I can't understand, but then I've never been in the terrible position you were in. And you aren't the only one who was made to suffer for those times when women barely had any rights. As for Frank, he was unpleasant to me. Snide, if fact. He didn't want to get to know me at all, and he gave me the creeps when I was alone in his company. At least you made an effort with me at first. If you ask me, if you can be guilty of something like manslaughter for not backing down in an argument and not wanting him to recover from a heart attack because of the ramifications to come, then I'd probably have done the same thing in your place.'

Janet gaped at Susan. She didn't think she'd ever heard Susan say so much in one go that didn't sound like trivial babble. But maybe her usual babble was nervousness? Then Janet was overcome with a warm feeling, which she realised was gratitude. And there she'd been, assuming Susan would think the very worst just because she could get her own back for the way she'd treated her sometimes.

She shook her head. 'Susan, I've misjudged you. I'm sorry. What you've just said means a great deal to me. Some people may not see it your way, that's what I've been told. So I'll take my punishment. But can we start again, do you think?'

Susan nodded and smiled briefly at her. She flicked a tea towel from a side drawer and thrust it at Janet. 'Sure we can.'

And just like that, much to her astonishment, another tide in Janet's life turned.

Chapter 25

After the Christmas holidays, whether it's a generous two weeks grace from an office, or a paltry few days off in the retail world, the new year can be a difficult business. As people trudge back to work under the heavy burden of new resolutions made and a scarily low bank balance, they are expected to snap back into shape and stand to attention like weary soldiers on parade, sick of the old routine but bound to serve. And in this respect, Masons was no exception. But within the soft furnishing department and the concession of Berkeley Fabrics there was an added tension, spiced with a fearful anticipation of trouble to come. And that trouble came in the form of the fitting of the Harrison curtains.

But Janet had further fearful anticipations of her own. She was waiting for Dr Blake to be interviewed by the police when he returned from the Canary Islands any day now in the second week of January. Shortly after that, she expected to be arrested and brought to justice for Frank's death. Her recent dreams had been so troubling, she'd shared them with Ann, who urged they were only symbolic. She'd dreamt of being trapped in her car with the engine unable to fire, of being in a city teeming with people she didn't know and who wouldn't help her as she tried to clutch hold of their grey slippery shadows. She'd been confined in a room with wormy pap to eat and rats for company. She'd sunk into quicksand, only managing to wake up just before she choked on sludge.

After these dreams, wiping sweat from her brow, she'd drag herself from her bed to make a cup of tea, accidentally disturbing Ann, and then they'd huddle together by the glowing bars of the electric fire, talking into the early morning. Thomas would cast his eyes upon them from

Frank's chair, then go back to his own world of imaginings, soon to quiver with the thrill of a fresh catch. But Janet felt if she hadn't had Ann to talk to, she might very well have gone insane by now. She could feel her anxiety slowly creeping and building inside her, rising inside like another kind of quicksand riddled with crawling bugs, rendering her twitchy. She had to keep reminding herself to relax, to let be and float through, as her books said, to remember the serenity prayer. But these tactics would only go so far.

What she desperately needed were outcomes, and the biggest one of all was whether or not Cliff could find Vivien's parents. He was her only hope now, and he was waiting for someone he knew to come back to work, someone in CID, he said, who could help him access the Police National Computer system, where he might find something useful. He was also going to visit Bristol to make enquiries about Vivien's adoptive grandparents, the Cooksons, to see if they were still living in the Brislington area as Violet had said in her letter. This could lead him to Ruth and Leonard Matthews. If no luck there, he was going to have to trawl through microfiches and telephone books at the library to try to trace the Matthews, or apply for access to the Electoral Register at Bristol City Council. If successful in finding them, he was planning to act as a mediator for Janet, as she'd have to go through the adoptive parents to stand any chance of connecting with her daughter.

But in the meantime, for all of this, it was a matter of waiting, waiting, waiting…

And the whole soft furnishing department was waiting for the outcome of the Harrison curtain order. The order had been sent off to Clothworks on Tuesday 11th December, one week ahead of the Christmas deadline for sending and receiving orders. And all the staff were anticipating the arrival of the completed window dressings, then to be collected by the Steadmans and fitted at the Harrison's home in the Royal Crescent.

The curtains finally landed in the department via the loading bay goods lift, along with other completed orders, on the 8th January, ahead of schedule – Clothworks had gone the extra mile. Janet and Claire checked them in, while Samantha fluttered about checking their checking. Janet then notified the Steadmans who rang Mrs Harrison to arrange the fitting date.

The big day came. Friday 11th. An ash-grey day with a spitting of rain. The Steadmans arrived at just before 10am and collected the goods and other accessories they needed and drove over to the Harrisons. For their own protection, Janet had privately warned them of what might go wrong. They were a humble couple, excellent at their work, with a dedicated mindset, and therefore easily upset if accused of doing a bad job.

All the soft furnishing staff were present in the department and Samantha was at her work station, close to carpets and furniture. It was unusual to have this full attendance, which added to the sense that the day would be out of the ordinary. The department was quiet. No one wants to order new curtains in January. But the January sales were busily buzzing elsewhere in the store.

The morning slid into the afternoon, and stretched nerves began to shimmer in the atmosphere of the department. They had all adopted Marian's expression for the situation they just knew was going to go badly wrong, including Janet. They were all waiting for the shit to hit the fan. Only Samantha, from what Janet could see when she'd gone by her station to the ladies room earlier, seemed to be blissfully under the illusion that all would be well, as she happily chatted to one of the concession staff from Ercol. Clair, Gemma, and Kevin tried to look busy tidying sample curtains and pattern book stands. Marian was showing some new Berkeley designs to Milly. Janet was in her office going through the new stock sheets for the coming year. There were going to be some Zoffany fabrics which had been specially designed and printed for Masons at a good cost price, which would be quite a coup. Frasers and John Lewis would be sure to be jealous.

At 3.50pm, just after Kevin left to go to a dentist appointment, a deep booming voice splintered through the close low hum of voices from the cash area outside Janet's office. She shot to her feet and listened hard.

'I want to speak to the manager! Who are you, exactly? Don't you…How dare you…'

She quickly decided it must be Mr Harrison, the local MP himself. Who else could it be right now? His wife must have decided it was time to deploy him.

Janet rushed out of her office, banging the door accidentally against the wall. She pivoted on her heels and marched into the Berkeley Fabrics area. There was no one there. Then she saw everyone clustered together like an tight knot on the serving side of the nearest big bench.

A crimson-faced, small man in a suit was yelling at them from behind a disproportionately large belly for his stature from the opposite side of the bench. As Marian and Gemma swivelled their heads, having spotted Janet approaching, he glared in her direction, then resumed his barrage.

'Who is responsible for this farce? Who?' he shouted. 'The curtains are too short, ridiculously short, and those two bumbling half-wits back at the house don't know why!'

Janet approached the side of the bench, placing herself between Mr Harrison and the staff, stunned at the indignant outrage being directed at the wrong people.

'Mr Harrison,' said Marian, looking at him calmly. 'It was the interior designer who did the measuring. The Steadmans aren't to blame. Perhaps you'd better speak to Mr King, the store manager.'

Mr Harrison peered over the bench with his sharp beak of a nose at Marian, blatantly scrutinising the name badge on her white blouse with his beady eyes. 'Oh, you're the one who said we couldn't get the fabric, aren't you? My wife found you impertinent. You look like a right little tart, too.'

Everyone but Mr Harrison took an sharp intake of

breath.

'And as for the rest of you! You're just standing there like lemons, not saying anything! Useless! Don't you have tongues in your heads?' He glared at Milly, and she shrank back against Marian. 'I want an explanation, I want –'

'Mr Harrison!' Janet said, with a sudden stream of fury bubbling through her veins. Fury at this man. This obvious bully, thinking he could talk to her staff and Milly and Marian in this manner. With no respect for them as employees, and certainly no respect for them as women. And where had she seen this before? Well, it wasn't on! Not now. Not ever again.

Mr Harrison turned to stare at her, his balding head, shiny with venting his spleen.

'How dare you talk to my staff like this?' she said. 'And how dare you insult Ms Johnson here! This is not appropriate behaviour at all! Especially not for a public figure like yourself. I suggest you take your complaint to Mr King. I can escort you to his office. But first, I expect you to apologise to Ms Johnson here.'

'Excuse me?' Mr Harrison's eyes popped out of his head as he glared at Janet. 'And who exactly are *you*?'

'Janet Brewer, manager of the department.'

Mr Harrison drew his shoulders back and hitched up his trouser belt, bristling and squaring up to her like a rooster. 'Then you're the one to blame!'

'No, I am not. None of us is to blame. Ms Dixon-Wright did your measuring. She got it wrong.'

'This is a mockery! Those half-wits say there is nothing that can be done. That we'll have to begin all over again with a different fabric. My wife is beside herself! It's a complete cock-up! And I want to know who's going to fix it!'

'If you apologise to Ms Johnson here, and stop calling the Steadmans half-wits, I'll take you to Mr King. If you don't –'

'If I don't, then what? Mr Harrison sneered. 'The customer is always right, you know!'

Janet glowered at him. 'No, the customer is not always

right. In fact the customer can be very wrong, and you are a case in point.'

Gemma, Claire, Milly and Marian all gasped in unison.

Customers and staff in the linen department had stopped their activities and were watching the drama unfold in soft furnishing. The boiled sweet manager, Shirley, was standing as stationary as a flamingo in her pink suit in the adjoining aisle, eyes wide, mouth open.

'Are you going to apologise?' demanded Janet, her gaze locking onto Mr Harrison, while brushing away the blatant fact that this encounter had turned very ugly with the chances of resolution flickering around the zero mark.

'How dare you!' he shouted. 'This is preposterous!'

'Well, if you aren't going to apologise, you can leave.' Janet pointed to the aisle. 'Go on!'

She stepped up close to him. She saw his eyes flickering with a new uncertainty, but she'd had enough. Enough of being told what to do. Enough of being browbeaten. And she wasn't going to stand for it at work, especially with her staff who weren't used to dealing with this kind of aggression. But she was an old hand at it and she was the one who could stand up for them, even, she realised, in this moment, if it meant sacrificing her position at Masons.

So it's one last time, she thought, one last time where I can say 'my department'.

She pointed again and spat her words at him. 'Go on! Get off my department! Now!'

There was a frozen hush over the two departments. Mr Harrison scowled at Janet, snapped his mouth shut and spun around.

He stalked up to Shirley, who backed away, teetering on her heels.

'Where the hell is the store manager's office?' he barked at her.

Wordlessly, she pointed to the far corner of linens and watched him dart between the fixtures and fittings in the direction of her finger.

At the bench, Marian came up to Janet.

'Jesus, Janet, what have you done?' Marian muttered, watching Mr Harrison disappear through the door to Mr King's office. 'I mean, I appreciate your efforts, but…'

'But nothing. I have more serious things to worry about,' she whispered back. 'I might end up in prison. So what does this matter?' she said, casting her hands wide.

Marian shook her head.

'Now come on,' Janet said to Gemma and Claire. 'Try and look busy. I'm not going to have us standing around here like skittles.'

So while the linen department resumed play, Janet, Gemma, Claire, Marian and Milly also went back to their duties.

Five minutes later, Kevin returned from the dentists, soon miffed that he'd missed the goings on, and asking Gemma for a blow-by-blow account.

Ten minutes after that, the Steadmans came in, looking distinctly miserable, to return the offending curtains, which Claire stashed in the stock area to keep them out of sight. Janet spoke to the husband and wife fitting team in her office, giving them plenty of reassurances and explaining the whole thing would have to be put on hold. They left looking markedly relieved.

It was about twenty minutes after Mr Harrison had entered Mr King's office that the drama recommenced at 4.30pm, half an hour before closing time.

Janet was suggesting to Claire that it might be worth making a start on the cashing up when they both noticed Mr Harrison striding down the aisle, making a rapping noise with his highly polished shoes, and heading for the stairs. He paused after passing Janet, looked back at her with his beak of a nose, and smirked.

Janet shivered. What was coming next wasn't going to be pleasant, but surely it would wait until after closing time?

But that was not to be. And just a couple of minutes later, an emotive babble of high and low voices drifted through linens from the carpet department area towards soft furnishing like a toxic vapour, causing people to hold their breath.

Janet was silently joined by Claire, Gemma, Kevin, Marian, and Milly, as they formed a defensive cluster around the till.

The babble stopped suddenly. The linen department breathed into life again, but Janet and her allies waited. Something had kicked off.

When they saw Samantha stumbling through linens towards them and teetering on her beige high heels, they watched, spell-bound. When she drew nearer, Janet could see her blue eyes were clouded and swimmy with tears. She reached Janet and a single tear trickled down her powdered cheek and past her rose-pink lips. She was plucking at the bow at the neck of her chiffon blouse. It seemed the English rose had finally been knocked off her perch.

'He's given me the sack!' she groaned. 'I've never been given the sack before! I don't know what to do? What should I do? Do I go now? Right this minute?'

Janet caught hold of her hand to stop her tugging at her bow. 'Come into the office, Samantha,' she said. 'I'll get you a glass of water.'

Then Samantha's head twisted in the direction she'd come from. 'He's coming,' she whispered.

And sure enough Mr King bore down on them like an angry bull chasing a red flag as they stood huddled by the till. The staff and customers in linens tuned-in to listen once again.

'What are you all doing standing about like this? We don't pay you to stand about! Get on with some work!' A vein in his left temple was visibly pulsing as he flung his arms around.

Claire pulled away. But when she caught sight of the faces of her colleagues, she edged closer and they tightened their assembly.

Mr King clamped his stony eyes upon Janet. 'I've fired

Ms Dixon – whatever she's called – because of gross incompetence.' He jerked a fat thumb at Samantha. 'But as for you! Well, I can't have my staff being insolent to customers. It's an appalling example for a department manager to set! And in Masons, the customer *is* always right! So, I'm afraid I've got to be seen to do the necessary. You'll have to go too. Now, we need to make some kind of reparation to the Harrisons. We need to – '

'Does this mean Samantha and I go straight away?' interrupted Janet.

'Of course not! We'll have to fix the situation first, and I'm willing to be reasonable. You can both work out your notice. Now, I've assured Mr Harrison that we will make good on his order, that we will –'

'Who will?' Janet asked.

'What?'

'Who will make good on his order? Because, I for one, have had enough of this particular order, and I'm certainly not interested in helping a male chauvinist bigot like Mr Harrison. He insulted Ms Johnson here, and wouldn't apologise. But I expect you're probably not bothered about that, are you? After all, the customer is always right.'

Patrick King's mouth dropped open. His jowls quivered and frown lines crunched deep into his forehead. His hands tightened into fists. Rather than turn red with ire, like Mr Harrison, Patrick paled and his eyes bulged.

'How dare you!' he shouted, spattering out drops of saliva.

'How dare you,' Janet replied. 'And as for being a good example to Masons, I don't suppose raising a ruckus like you're doing here, during opening hours, is all that professional either.'

While Patrick King spluttered to find a retort, Janet turned to Samantha.

'Do you want to work out your notice?' she asked.

Samantha shook her head rapidly. 'No, I couldn't possibly work here now. It wouldn't be good for my nerves…'

'Right,' said Janet. 'Well, neither do I.' She looked hard at Samantha. 'Shall we leave together now, then?'

'Right now?'

'Right now.'

'I'll just go and get my things.' Samantha hurried away.

Mr King stared after her with his crag and slab face, then glared at Janet. 'So be it. And good riddance.'

Then he paced back to his office through a crowd of watching people who parted around him like the Red Sea.

After Janet had got her own belongings together from her office, she went to speak to her colleagues. They all looked so worried for her.

'Are you going to be alright, Mrs B?' Gemma asked, her brow furrowed with concern.

'I'm fine, Gemma. This place just isn't what I thought it was. I'll be fine. But you all look after each other, okay?'

'Come in and see us, won't you?' Claire said.

'You really showed him,' commented Kevin. 'And you were in the right.'

'You were so brave,' Milly said, her face flushed with sweat.

'What the hell are we going to do with the Harrison order now?' Marian asked, hands on hips.

Janet arched her eyebrows and smiled. 'Well, maybe you could go for the manager's job now, like you wanted, and sort it out. You're more than capable.'

'Oh Jeez,' sighed Marian.

Janet and Samantha descended the stairs, adopting a synchronised stepping rhythm, which felt surreal to Janet. It began to feel more reality-infused when they both wondered which exit they should leave by. The staff or the public?

'Why don't we leave through the main entrance onto the Promenade?' suggested Janet.

Samantha cracked a crooked smile and nodded.

'Will you wait for me in perfumery?' Janet asked. 'I've got

to go and get my coat from my locker.'

'I'll be at the Estée Lauder counter,' Samantha replied. 'There's a friend I should say goodbye to.'

As Janet marched off to enter the underbelly of the building for the last time, hearing her footsteps reverberate in the dim stairwells once again, she felt as if she was being sucked down into a mine shaft and would never more see the light of day. Passing the punched-in hole in the wall didn't help. The black hole. For the sinful. Not for Marian anymore, but for herself. It had been a warning of events to come to pass. It was where she'd been destined to end up when arrested for Frank's death, as she was sure to be. She'd already imagined being read her rights several times in the early hours of the morning as she lay awake thinking until her head became sore:

Janet Brewer. You are under arrest on suspicion of the killing of your husband, Frank Brewer, on the 5th December 1989. You do not have to say anything. But, it may harm your defence if you do not mention when questioned something which you later rely on in court. Anything you do say may be given in evidence.

Her only solace was that she'd extracted promises from Scott, Susan, Ann, and Cliff.

Ann would take Thomas to Winchcombe to live with her.

Scott and Susan would not bring Daniel to visit her in prison. It would be far too upsetting.

Scott would sell 9 Willow Lane, because there was no way she'd ever want to return to that house, and he'd take over her finances for the interim period of her confinement, whatever that turned out to be.

Scott would stay in touch with Florrie, Violet, Sarah and her family on her behalf.

Only Scott would visit her in prison and only when it was convenient for him to do so.

Susan would look after Scott.

And most importantly, Cliff would cease looking for

Vivien under the circumstances.

All settled, with no more to be said, she'd told them all.

And as for how she'd cope 'inside', well, she was as hard as nails, wasn't she? She'd get by.

A stale odour hit her nostrils when she opened the door to locker 149. It was the smell of her leather boots dried out from the morning's rain, together with the unavoidable smell of sweat. Stuffing her court shoes into the spare carrier she always kept folded in her handbag, she zipped on her chilled boots, snatched her black coat from its hanger, leaving it to rattle against the metal confines, and slammed shut her locker door. Suddenly desperate to get out, she rushed back to the stairwell and scurried up the steps like a black beetle escaping the teeth of a rodent, only letting out her breath when she made it into the retail gloss and glare. Then she headed for ground floor perfumery and the Estée Lauder counter.

Samantha was waiting for her surrounded by gleaming glass and chrome.

It occurred to Janet to wonder why they were adopting this camaraderie? They didn't even like each other. But maybe it was simply because they'd both been highly devoted to their jobs and had been treated with injustice by Mr King. After all, when it came to Samantha, he should have ensured she was properly trained to take measurements, decided Janet.

They both ambled through the revolving door onto the Promenade, Samantha pushing ahead of Janet, then they stood together in the falling rain, staring hard at the store façade. It was an extravaganza of shiny red and white sale banners with window displays of chic emaciated models strutting their stuff in frozen time. The store was almost ready to close its doors to the public for the day, but all too eager to open them again tomorrow.

'I was over the moon when I got that job,' sighed Samantha.

'Me too,' said Janet.

Samantha turned to look at Janet. Her blonde hair was plastered to her cheeks and her linen suit was blotted with raindrops. 'I'm so sorry. This really is all my fault. I should have listened to you. I should have gone out with the Steadmans to learn how to measure up properly.'

'Yes, you should. But you can still learn.' Janet hesitated. 'What will you do now?'

'Lick my wounds. Then go back to being freelance. I love working with fabrics and interiors, but I've under-estimated the measuring side of things and calculating fabric allowances. I'll have to learn.'

Janet grinned.

'What will you do?' Samantha asked.

'I haven't a clue. I just might end up in prison.'

Samantha hoisted her eyebrows high. 'What for?'

'Long story.' Janet felt a dragging sensation of inevitability. She was never one to shy away from the truth.

Samantha reached into her bag, drew out a card, and thrust it into Janet's hand. 'I know you probably won't want to, but just in case.'

Janet looked down at Samantha's freelance business card. You never know, she thought, and put it in her pocket.

She smiled, put out her hand, and they shook hands firmly like two business associates.

'I'm parked up near the gardens,' said Samantha.

'I'm in Portland Street.' Janet pointed in the opposite direction. 'See you around, then.' It was just something to say.

Samantha turned and Janet soon lost sight of her in the dazzle of shop fronts and the glimmer of wet pavement, then the darkness beyond.

Taking a last look at the store, she realised that she was out on the street in more ways than one, that it had been one year since she'd gone back to Masons as a widow, and that she'd given the store six years of faithful service. But it was all over now and so was her life for the immediate future.

When she approached 9 Willow Lane, twenty minutes later, and turned into the last bend in the road, what she saw in the flood of the street lamps didn't surprise her. It was that inevitability made manifest. A Ford Fiesta police car was parked outside her house. Close by was Cliff's black Rover.

So this is it, she thought. The talk with Dr Blake is done. The investigation has enough to go on, and I'm going to be arrested. And with the day I'm having, how perfectly apt. Everything crashing down all at once. Nothing will be left in the wreckage, not even Vivien. And look, they've even left me my drive for parking in.

Clutching her coat around her as she climbed from the car, she noticed Winnie's net curtain flick to the side, and she spotted her crinkled nose pressed against the glass. Typical, she thought, and she gave Winnie an exaggerated wave. The nose pulled back. She looked at the houses opposite, but they were curtained up for the night. That was good.

Standing in the rain outside her front door, she tried to put her house key in the lock but the blade kept missing the slot because her fingers were trembling so much.

But in the next second, it swung open, and Ann was standing there, looking flushed.

'Janet! You've been longer than usual. DCI Bridges and Cliff are here.'

'I know…the cars…'

Ann pulled her in and helped her take off her wet coat.

DCI Bridges stood up from where he was seated on the sofa and came towards her.

Janet backed away.

'Mrs Brewer. Janet, rather. I thought I'd come in person —'

Cliff came out of the kitchen with a pot of tea on a tray.

Tea? She thought. Tea! At a time like this!

'Jan, come and sit down,' Cliff said.

'I'd rather stand,' she said, her voice breaking, as she pinned her gaze to the policeman, still in his tweed suit and wool tie. She couldn't look anywhere else. Where were the handcuffs? Were they on the sofa out of sight?

'If I'm going to be arrested, I'd rather stand. Please…' she pleaded. 'Please can we get this over with?'

DCI Bridges's eyes widened. 'No, that's not what's happening here –'

'Jan, for God's sake, sit down,' Cliff ordered.

Ann had retreated to the entrance to the kitchen, grasping hold of the door jamb, as if, in her shock, she could gain some steadying perspective on the scene unfolding in front of her.

'Can we just get this over with? Can't we just go?' begged Janet. 'I can't stand any more of this. Please!'

DCI Bridges approached her again and took hold of her hand. He smiled warmly. 'Janet, it's not happening. You're not being arrested. The CPS, that's the Crown Prosecution Service, who've reviewed the evidence, have decided that it's not in the public interest to bring the case to court. So there isn't going to be an arrest. No arrest. No trial. It's all over, Janet. Do you understand?'

Janet heard his words, but they travelled to her through a sludgy soup of fear. Meaning was delayed as the words took longer to reach her. But she managed to arrange them in the right order and grasp their meaning. She groped forwards, with the detective letting go of her hand. More fissures in the granite. More raw exposure.

She lurched towards Cliff. 'Is this right?'

Cliff got hold of her arm and tugged her down onto the sofa. 'For God's sake, sit down, Jan. It's all over.'

'Really?'

'Really.' Cliff and DCI Bridges said together.

'We need something stronger than tea,' Ann said, breathing out heavily.

'Not for me, I'll be off now,' DCI Bridges said. 'I just wanted to tell you in person, Janet. I could have left it for your solicitor, Michael Armstrong, but I wanted to, well…'

She turned to look at him and saw the sincerity in his eyes.

'Thank you,' she said. 'Thank you so much.'

He was almost at the door when he turned around sharply. 'Oh, I almost forgot. Dr Blake wants to meet with you, Janet, at the surgery. Nothing to be alarmed about, but I promised I'd pass the message on. Now, have a good evening, won't you?'

And just like that he was gone. With the closing of her front door, and the growl and fading purr of an engine, the police were finally out of her life.

Chapter 26

'Ring Scott,' Ann urged Janet excitedly. 'Let him know.'

'Yes, and how about some takeaway to celebrate? Cod and chips anyone?' asked Cliff.

'And a bottle of wine,' added Ann. 'There's no sherry left. And we don't have anything else.'

Janet couldn't think straight. Thoughts and feelings were flapping around in her head like a flock of startled pheasants: the Harrison argument, the King argument, leaving Masons forever, shaking hands with Samantha, certain arrest, then no arrest. Why not?

'Why not?' she asked. 'Why is there no arrest? What do they mean not in the public interest? What's going on?'

'Jan, I'm going to explain about all that. But first, let's have something to eat. Maybe when you ring Scott he can come over with the supplies and be here when I explain.'

'I've walked out of Masons too.' She shook her head and felt tears brimming. Why was she crying so easily these days, when she didn't used to be able to cry at all? But without Masons as her focus, her life already felt so stretched and baggy, as if she was losing the substance of herself. 'Mr Harrison was rude and obnoxious to us all, Mr King was obnoxious…he sacked Samantha and me, but still expected me to sort out the wretched order while I worked out my notice. But I've had enough. And when I got back home, just then, I was certain I was going to be arrested.'

Tears streamed down her face. She made no attempt to wipe them away. 'I don't know what I'm going to do…'

'That bloody store isn't worth all this,' Ann said, shocking Janet with her vehemence.

'Well, at least you're not going to prison, Jan. Look on the bright side,' said Cliff.

She looked up at him through a split prism of tears. He was smiling at her.

'You always did have a warped sense of humour,' she said.

Cliff caught hold of her hands and pulled her up. 'Come on. Get changed out of your work things. Ring Scott. And we'll all have a good evening together. Small steps, Jan. Okay?'

'Small steps,' she murmured and did what she was told. Ann gave her a hug first, which Janet was finding more bearable these days, before rattling around in the kitchen in preparation for the takeout.

Scott was jubilant on the phone and he shouted the news to Susan, who came to the phone and told Janet how happy she was to hear it, and no, she didn't mind Scott coming over. He arrived 45 minutes later with four fish and chips portions and two bottles of Merlot.

With the wings of a drop-leaf table unfolded in the living room to accommodate the four diners, and the television turned down to a soporific burble for that sense of comfort which no one can actually name or explain, Janet, Ann, Cliff and Scott tucked into their feast, with Janet finding to her astonishment that she was really hungry.

It was with great discipline, which inevitably faltered now and again, as questions and thoughts crossed minds like ducks in a fairground shooting gallery, that they left discussions of the CPS outcome and the lesser issue of Janet leaving Masons, until after the washing up was done and they were all seated together with a glass of wine each.

The television was now switched off.

'So will you tell me why I haven't been arrested?' Janet asked Cliff. 'I thought it was sure to happen with Winnie's statement.'

'Yes, well perhaps it normally would have,' Cliff said, leaning forward in his chair to meet Janet's puzzled gaze. 'But the CPS don't just decide on whether there's enough evidence to aim for prosecution, they also consider whether it will be in the public interest. And there were other issues going on.'

'What issues?' asked Scott.

'For one thing, there's the fact that Frank was a policeman in the local force. If the CPS had agreed to take the case to court, the information about Frank's domestic abuse would have come out in the defence. The local papers might have got a hold of it. In fact, Michael Armstrong would have made sure of it. And the fact is that the police force is in good shape just now. They've regained public trust after some bad press in the past and they wouldn't welcome anything that might taint their image again.'

Janet nodded, taking it in. 'Yes, that makes some sense. But if a crime was seen to have been committed, they would have surely had to pursue it regardless.'

'Not if there was even more dirt to dish.' Cliff frowned. He put down his empty wine glass, but placed his hand over it when Ann offered him a top-up. 'Not if I'm driving.'

'Same here,' Scott said to Ann. 'But what kind of extra dirt?' he asked Cliff.

'Well, ever since Jan mentioned that signet ring of Frank's, it's been needling me. So I went to Money Spinners where Jan said she pawned it. It'd been sold, but from the manager's sales records, I was able to track the man who bought it to get a gander at it.'

'The eagle with the sword,' Janet said, wide-eyed. 'And you found it! But why did you want to see it?'

'In case it jogged my memory. In case I'd seen any other policemen wearing it back in the sixties or the seventies.'

Janet, Scott and Ann looked hard at him.

'You remember me saying there was a certain degree of breaching of standard procedures in the sixties? Using violence when making arrests and conducting interrogations?'

They nodded.

'Well, it got worse in the seventies. Actual corruption

going on. Serious stuff like policemen taking bribes and backhanders from criminals in return for warnings of planned police raids or arrests. Unauthorised disclosing of information. The falsifying of evidence against innocent men, and having charges against guilty criminals dropped. Even getting involved in drugs and sexual favours. A lot of this was in London and the Met, but this sort of thing spreads like a virus. So Operation Countryman was set up to independently investigate it between 1978 and 82 and many policemen were forced to resign, to retire, or to face charges. And they did discover a significant link between some police membership of certain Freemason lodges and the corruption. Police membership of the Freemasons was rife back then, in all departments. Most of it, no doubt innocent, but some of it undoubtedly not.'

'Did you have any idea this corruption was going on?' Scott asked.

'Hmm, well that's the problem. Like other colleagues of mine, I had an inkling, but after I'd moved to CID, I was largely operating outside of Frank's arena. It was pretty dodgy to be a whistle-blower back then. There could be a serious, internally-driven, personal backlash at that time, so you had to be very sure, with concrete evidence, *and* you had to be willing to risk your job. I wasn't. But that's where the ring comes in. When I saw Frank's ring, it reminded me of one or two police officers who I saw wearing one just like it on their little fingers when they were off duty back around that time. I think there is a connection. There may have been a fraternity that Frank was part of. A group dispensing their own kind of power and justice.'

'He went to the pub a lot back then,' Janet said. 'But he could have been going anywhere, meeting anyone. But why is any of this relevant to me?'

'Do you remember I stayed behind to talk to Armstrong for a few minutes?'

Janet nodded.

'I felt we needed some extra help on our side…in case

the defence of the domestic abuse wasn't strong enough to get you off. The idea of you being dragged even to the magistrate's court for a hearing just filled me with disgust when I thought of Frank and what you've been through. And solicitors can be pretty persuasive when they have some ammunition on their side. So Armstrong had the domestic abuse by a police officer on our side, but he could also have brought up the possibility of Frank being involved in illegal practices. Frank took early retirement after all, and there might well be a file on him. I believe there probably is. So they wouldn't want even the faintest sniff of corruption in the force being dredged up again before the public eye, just when the police are building up their reputations for the better.'

'But it's not right, Cliff. My getting off isn't fair and square like this...I want a clean slate...'

'Don't we all, Jan. But we seldom get one the way the world is.' Then his eyes softened. 'Jan, it was right and just that we looked after you. It was payback time. And Bridges was very happy about it. You've got to let it go now and move on. Can you do that?'

'It's the right result,' added Scott. 'God knows it is. And, yes, you've got to move on, Mum.'

Janet shook her head, desperately wondering how she was to do that without working at Masons. What would she do with her life instead?

'Promise, you'll try,' Ann said.

That Friday night, Janet wrestled with her sheets in bed but didn't wake, enabling Ann to get a full night's sleep. That was a measure of progress, but there was more to come a few days later with further revelations about Frank.

In the morning she was surprised to receive a huge bouquet of white roses and purple freesias delivered by Interflora. The card read, *'With kind regards from Michael Armstrong. Wishing you a happy future. Carpe diem!'*

'Seize the day?' observed Ann, frowning. 'Oh well, I

suppose he means get on with life, live it to the full.'

Janet was stunned by this gesture from the solicitor, which didn't seem to fit the brusque man she'd met at all. His manner had been stern and uncompromising, with no signs of sentiment. But she was warmed by his gift and was now grateful she'd had him on her side. She was beginning to realise that life wasn't black and white, but many shades of grey. And slates often bear the ghosts of previous chalk marks that can't be erased.

Later on that morning she phoned Sarah in Brighton with her news and the outpouring of relief from Sarah quite stunned her.

'Why are you so surprised?' Ann asked.

'Because she knows my history, but she doesn't really know me,' replied Janet.

'Maybe she likes you.'

'Already?'

'Yes, of course, Janet. You've got to start thinking more of yourself.'

More shades of grey, Janet thought.

It was far easier a task to pen a letter to Florrie and pop it in the post. But as Janet hurried back from the post box down the road, beneath a sky of tattered clouds, Winnie came out of her front door to intercept her.

Standing on her bowed legs by her gatepost and wearing her stiff yellow Mackintosh with her feet secreted into some enormous furry pink slippers, she drew herself up to the fullness of her short stature as Janet approached and demanded to know what the police car had been doing outside Janet's house last night.

'Are you going to be arrested or not?' she asked. 'After all, that's what you wanted. That's what you dragged me into it for. What you've made such a fuss over!'

'No, I'm not, Winnie. It seems it's over.'

Winnie wrinkled her pug nose. 'I see. A load of frigging fuss over nothing then. I told you not to bother. Pity, never mind.'

As Janet stared at Winnie, thinking how many times over the last 36 years she'd seen Winnie standing at this gate in this manner, before and after Charles, her long-suffering husband, to catch her neighbours, to dispense a dose of toxic gossip, or to pop around to their homes *just for a quick chat* to deliver more of the same.

And in this moment, Janet just knew she had to get away from this street. She was sick of the house, a house choked to the rafters with memories of Frank, which would take no painting over or flushing out with a change of décor. The memories would creep back in like a rank mould. Frank had always wanted to stay put, refusing to entertain moving to another area. But there was nothing to stop her now. There, she thought, that's one decision made and she hurried inside to talk to Ann about it.

She also decided now was the time to move the living room furniture around. So Saturday was spent shifting the television to the left of the fireplace instead of the right, adjusting the aerial in the loft, and moving the sofa to face the television at an angle against the wall adjoining the kitchen. The coffee table stayed put and the armchairs fitted in and around. As for how this felt, Janet was only partially satisfied, but it would do for now, she told Ann.

On Sunday, she and Ann drove to Safeway for lunch and the weekly shop, which was a routine they'd adopted during the time Ann had been staying. Drawn like iron filings to a magnet, they naturally discussed the Masons situation, with Ann finally getting Janet to agree that it was Mr King's mismanagement that had caused the fiasco, and Masons simply wasn't the same store with him at the helm.

'There's no point working there if he's the manager,' declared Ann. 'You're better off out of it.'

Then on a mentally spaced-out Monday morning, with Janet inevitably struggling not going in to work and worrying how the girls were doing, she made an appointment to see Dr Blake, as he'd requested through DCI Bridges. Dr Blake had forewarned the receptionists to accommodate her and an appointment was duly set for one o'clock the next day, between his morning and afternoon surgeries. Scott had asked to come too, so it was all set, with Janet racking her brains over what it could possibly be about.

Doctor Peter Blake was a short trim man, with a full head of silver hair, piercing eyes, and a neatly trimmed moustache. With an efficient and reserved manner, he'd suited Janet well over the years. He'd always asked about her unexplained bruising, which she'd tried to pass off as bumping into doors or tripping over something. Such fictional explanations she now knew were all too blatantly characteristic of domestic abuse victims, and they didn't fool doctors at all. And although he had sometimes pressed her, he'd also respected her wishes not to divulge the truth, with the proviso that she knew the door was always open. So what did he want to see her now for? she wondered, sitting opposite him with Scott by her side.

The doctor began to explain how he'd come home early from Tenerife when he'd found the police wanted to talk to him about Janet's confession, and as a result of that he wanted to talk to her with respect to Frank's state of health at the time of his death. He told her that as Frank's widow, he could share Frank's medical records with her, that he had the discretion to do so if it would help her come to terms with her husband's death, or to clarify the circumstances of his death.

But instead of listening further, because what possible difference could any of this make now, Janet stared through the slats of the consultation room's window blind into the car park beyond which was over-looked by bare trees. The stark branches seemed to claw at the sky, whilst a restless wind chased and harried leaves and litter around the tarmac. Why couldn't people simply dispose of their litter in the proper manner?

'…so you see, the pills were out of date.' Dr Blake's last few words snapped her back to attention.

'Sorry, what? Can you say that again?' she asked, her spine rigid and her eyes now riveted upon the GP.

'I'll start over because this is very important.'

Janet and Scott looked at each other, then back at Dr Blake.

'The police asked me why it was, when I arrived at the scene where Frank had died of cardiac arrest, that I didn't ask you as to the whereabouts of Frank's medication, because they understandably would class that as standard procedure. Well, you see, I already knew that he had no up-to-date medication because he hadn't renewed his prescription for approximately six months.'

'What difference does that make?' Scott asked.

'His regular prescription was for glyceryl trinitrate, which widens the arteries to help the heart pump blood around the body during an angina attack, reducing resistance, which eases the pain, while increasing the oxygen supply. An excellent drug. But it has a significantly short shelf life. It expires after eight weeks, possibly sooner if kept in a warm living room. After eight weeks it is totally ineffective. So even if Frank had managed to take a pill, it simply wouldn't have worked.'

'The pills I stopped him taking were out of date?' Janet's heart leapt into her throat and fluttered there. 'They wouldn't have had any effect?'

'Yes, that's exactly it.'

Janet felt a sagging in her body, and her heart sank back into its proper place, not heavily, but lightly – a new sensation. She let out a small moan, remembering the moment she'd thrown the bottle into the kitchen bin. 'I can't believe it. All this time, I thought…'

'But why didn't he renew his prescription? He must have known,' Scott asked incredulously.

'Oh, he knew. I warned him the last time I saw him about four months before he died, which brings me to another important point. His condition had actually worsened. I wanted to refer him to a cardiologist to look into the possibility of getting a stent fitted. It's a new cutting edge procedure where a tube is fitted into a blocked coronary artery to open it up. It's where the future lies for heart conditions like Frank's. But he didn't turn up for his appointment, and –'

'But I never knew any of this!' Janet said. 'He never told me!'

'I told him he should discuss it with you, Janet. That he should have you on board in the event of an operation. And later, I became suspicious that he was hiding his head in the sand because he never came back to see me. It's a common enough reaction. But perhaps most importantly, I warned him he couldn't afford to get all worked up because the medication wouldn't be as effective as in the past. He never got it renewed because at that point he stormed out. And as his GP there wasn't much else I could do. I did try phoning him, but he just put the phone down.'

'He'll have been furious,' Janet said quietly. 'He never had any patience with health matters. And he would have hated the idea of having to trust an operation.'

'So going back to the scene of his death, Janet. I didn't think about his medication because it was redundant in his case. And as his GP at the scene, I was able to write an accurate death certificate, and I reported it to the coroner because I hadn't seen Frank within fourteen days of his death. As far as I was concerned it was all straight forward and I assumed you had some knowledge of what his condition was. I had no idea that you'd been believing you could have prevented his death, because from a medical perspective it was due to his own self-neglect. Of course the police considered the out-of-date meds and the worsened heart condition were irrelevant to the case. But they are certainly not irrelevant to me. So I felt it was my moral duty to put you in the picture. I'm sure you realised for years that I suspected what sort of life you had with Frank and I do wish you'd confided in me, but the idea that you were punishing yourself for finally reacting in the way you did and my knowing what I did was just too much….' He tailed off, shaking his head.

Janet was silent, as her mind filled with realisations that swelled like balloons. No matter what she had done or didn't do, Frank had been a bomb waiting to go off at any time, especially when he next lost his temper and raised his own blood pressure. And because he hadn't told her, she'd been blaming herself. And he'd have loved that, wouldn't he? Leaving her with that guilt. Leaving her with unfinished business between them.

A small smile crept over her face and she turned to look at Scott. 'This makes all the difference.'

Scot nodded and shifted his attention to the doctor. 'I can't thank you enough, Doctor Blake – '

'Please call me John.'

'John, then. This means so much to Mum and me.'

'I hoped it would.'

Janet rose to her feet. She reached over to grasp the doctor's hand and shook it firmly – a cool, dry, steady hand – and she met his intense expression with her own. 'It means everything!'

Instead of being given a lift home by Scott, she decided to walk.

'Are you sure, Mum? It's quite a way and it looks like rain,' Scott said, glancing up at the sky.

But she was sure. And after she turned out of the car park of Charlton Surgery and began striding along Glenfall Way, through a tree-lined residential street of modern houses, and then Hartlebury Way with more of the same, she felt a lightness of being, so strange and unfamiliar, yet she knew it all the same. A sense of peace. A sense of having cast off and of sailing out. A sense of freedom. With her head held high, her pace picked up. She felt like skipping. She felt like running. And by the time she turned into Willow Lane her eyes were shining.

Chapter 27

'Do you still want me to stay with you?' Ann asked her later that night, after an episode of *Coronation Street*.

Janet shifted her scrutiny from her embroidery to Ann, who'd already commented on how much easier in herself she seemed after the doctor's revelation. 'Ann, I honestly can't thank you enough for keeping me company and for all your support. I don't know what I'd have done without you. I certainly wouldn't blame you for wanting to be back in your own home.'

'To be honest, I'm not all that bothered. It's been nice having company like this in the evenings, and of course I used to get out during the day to Masons, so it would be pretty lonely there now. Since Scott's been collecting my post for me, and since my son and daughter have this telephone number, staying here hasn't been a problem at all.' She hesitated. 'Maybe I could stay until you sell up?'

Janet smiled and touched Ann's knee. 'If you're happy to, I would love that. I can't stand being alone in this house anymore.'

'Then it's settled.'

The very next morning, Janet drove to McReath's estate agent in the high street where Susan worked. She'd checked with her the night before and Susan was taken aback but delighted to help her with her move.

'What sort of house would you like me to look for?' Susan said, flushed with excitement at her desk with her pen poised over her notebook.

'It'll have to be small, but something with a bit of character for change, and not on an estate,' Janet replied, thinking how surprised she'd been to find Florrie's cottage in

Cornwall so appealing. 'But still in the area.'

'Leave it with me!'

While Janet was busy with Susan discussing the sale of 9 Willow Lane, and how much it was likely to fetch being estimated at around £95,000, Ann, who'd accompanied Janet into town, was visiting the soft furnishing department of Masons to see how the girls and Kevin were getting on after the drama of just three working days earlier.

The two ladies met at Betty's Tiffin an hour later, and over a mug of coffee and a fruit scone each, Ann told Janet the news. The personnel manager, Kenneth Brown, had been appalled by the dismissals and was worried that the staff on soft furnishing couldn't cope without an acting department manager. He'd asked Marian if she would consider applying again as she was probably best placed to take over and she said she'd think about it. There'd been no sign of Mr King, but he was apparently in his office, and Shirley Appleton, manager of linens, hinted to Ann that there might just be repercussions after how he'd behaved in public. As for the Harrison order, Mrs Harrison had come in demanding her money back which had been duly refunded by the cash office with Mr King's authorisation. And she'd declared she'd be placing no more orders.

'They should be okay for a while,' Janet commented, thinking of her loyal former colleagues. 'Everything was up to date and they know their jobs really well.'

Ann nodded. 'Gemma seemed down though, and Marian was very quiet.'

'Did Marian have any obvious bruises on her face?'

Ann wrinkled her brow. 'Not that I noticed. Why?'

Janet explained that Marian still hadn't separated from the thug of a boyfriend who was undoubtedly hitting her. 'I gave her a Victim Support leaflet, but I doubt she's been in touch.'

'Well, you couldn't do much more than that.' Then Ann paused for a moment. 'Do you think you will miss Masons?'

'No, it's odd, I don't think I will actually. I'll miss the

interior design, but I feel so different about the place and I don't think I'd fit in there now. But I'll have to find something else to do because I can't really afford to retire yet. Maybe something part-time would do?'

Ann smiled. 'I can't tell you how much more relaxed you seem, Janet. It's lovely to see.'

But of course there was still one huge thing on Janet's mind which she yearned to resolve with all her heart, and she knew she would never stand a chance of future happiness without it. She had to find her daughter. Only this would truly heal her. All her instincts and senses told her that. It was the only thing that had ever really mattered. And now she felt more ready than ever before, as if the intervening years had counted for nothing, apart from the blessing of having had Scott. She had to find Vivien and for that she was relying upon Cliff. But she'd been tearing the days off her desk calendar with nothing much happening. He'd been waiting for government offices and agencies to get back to work after the Christmas holidays. The police's National Computer system had yielded nothing on Ruth and Leonard Matthews, who Violet had identified as the adoptive parents, so he'd now gone to Bristol to see if he could find Ruth's parents, Peter and Jean Cookson – to see if he could find anything of them in the suburb of Brislington where Violet had said they used to live. He had copies of the photograph taken by Ted in Western-super-Mare of Ruth, Jean and Vivien, and the one of Janet holding Vivien at Hope Lodge in Swindon. And he had a copy of Violet's letter.

He'd been keeping in touch with Janet by phone and giving her updates of his progress and he'd been delighted when she told him what the doctor had said.

'So are you off the hook now, Jan?'

'I think so,' she replied.

'You only think so?'

'Okay, I know so.'

'It's over?'

'It's over.'

But then he went quiet and she didn't hear from him very often over the next few weeks. When he did phone he was cagey in his responses.

'Yes, things are developing nicely.'

'What's happening though?'

'I don't want to go into details, Jan. I don't want to get your hopes up. Let me take care of things. Trust me.'

This was hard for Janet. She'd always taken care of her own life as best she could. She wasn't used to someone working on her behalf and she certainly wasn't used to trusting anyone. Liz, who she was still seeing, told her this lack of trust was perfectly natural, given her history. But still… and she kept imagining what might be happening.

The very worst possibility was that Cliff was getting nowhere, with the chances of finding Vivien looking bleaker by the day and him being too worried about letting her down. But if he had found Vivien's adoptive parents, why wasn't he telling her? What was he keeping from her? She started to pace her bedroom at night. Her bedside lamp began to echo her tension by flickering on and off as though the bulb was at crisis point, until Ann noticed and changed it for a new one.

Without having work to distract her, she became restless, despite energetic winter walks in the fields and woods beyond the garden, and despite spending more time with her grandson, Daniel. She and Ann drove to some of those Cotswold villages she'd never been to, but they weren't ideal viewing in the winter season. It was far better strolling down narrow sun-struck streets, bordered by glowing buttery cottages with their manicured hedges, with babbling streams and bobbing ducks to cross on quaint hump-backed bridges, in spring and summer, than in the dreary murk of a wet winter. The spitting rain and biting chill in the air simply drove them home, where the confined Janet grew as fidgety as a frustrated fly buzzing against a window pane.

But all this changed at last on the evening of Friday 22nd February, just over five weeks since she'd put the house on the market, when Cliff phoned to say he was coming over and he wanted Scott there too.

Scott arrived at just before seven o'clock and Cliff pulled up outside the house in his Rover at seven thirty as arranged. When he entered the living room in his navy blue anorak, ribbed jumper and cord trousers, he looked as far from the stereotype of a private detective as you can possibly get. He was certainly no Humphrey Bogart, and the only thing he had in common with Columbo was that his jacket was creased and rain-spattered.

'Nice to see the For Sale sign out there, Jan,' he commented as he slung his jacket over the banister.

'Never mind that, Cliff. What news have you got?' Her nerves were as tightly strung as piano wires. She had no idea how she was going to react to bad news, good news, or any shade of news between the deepest black and the brightest white.

'Let him get sat down first, Mum,' Scott said, sitting in his father's old easy chair. Cliff flopped down into the other chair and faced Janet and Ann who perched together on the edge of the sofa, legs tensed. Thomas put his head around the door, but retreated into the kitchen from where a thump of the cat flap confirmed his lack of interest.

'Okay. I want to ease into this,' began Cliff. 'So I'll tell you what progress I've made, then come to the outcome.'

Janet groaned.

Ann and Scott examined Cliff intently.

'As you know I went to Brislington in Bristol, where Violet said that Peter and Jean Cookson used to live – Vivien's adoptive grandparents.'

They all nodded.

'Through checking in the area telephone book I found they are still living there. So I got their address and telephone number and phoned them up. I told them I was a retired police officer trying to find someone for a friend and I believed they could help. Would it be alright to pay them a visit?'

Janet gasped, then noticed a twinkle in Cliff's bright eyes.

'They were happy to help and I met them at their home in Hardwick Close the following evening. Next it got tricky of course, but I told them the friend had given up her baby in a mother and baby home, called Hope Lodge, in Swindon in 1954, and I was trying to help find the child who would now be 36. That we were trying to find the child who her mother had named Vivien. That it was impossible to get anywhere through the usual channels that were obviously designed to protect privacy.'

'How did they react?' Scott asked.

'They were suspicious,' replied Cliff. 'Very guarded. It wasn't until I shared Violet's letter with them and showed them the pictures we have, that they began to believe the situation was for real and to be trusted. And it was all down to that rabbit!' He looked hard at Janet. 'If it wasn't for that rabbit, I don't think I'd have got anywhere, Jan. But Jean Cookson remembered Violet from the shop. She said she was a good woman. Her remembering Violet really helped, something I wasn't expecting. She was very moved by the letter. And then Violet's description of the rabbit in the letter, the colours and design, and then the fact that it was tucked up with baby Vivien in that photo taken by your father in the home before you gave her up, which they could see with their very own eyes, and also in the one taken in Western-super-Mare. All that did the trick, and they were finally convinced that our Vivien was their granddaughter, Rosemary, just as Violet had claimed.'

'That's wonderful!' exclaimed Ann, clapping her hands together.

Janet and Scott stared at one another in silence then turned back to Cliff.

'After that, it was a matter of giving them some key information. The date of Vivien's birth, the place of adoption, the agency. But they had no paperwork. All that was with their daughter, Ruth. And of course I had to steer the conversation around to seeing if they could open a line of communication between myself, on behalf of the birth mother, and their daughter and son-in-law.'

'What did they say?' Janet whispered.

'They said they would do it. Jean Cookson has a lot of sympathy for you, Jan.' Cliff looked earnestly at her. 'They both knew how impossible it was back then for single mothers. How painful it would have been to give up a child. They'd seen it happen in their own social circles.'

Tears began brimming in Janet's eyes. Tears of relief at not being judged harshly as she'd always felt she'd deserved, where she'd viewed her marriage to Frank a fitting punishment for her crime.

'What happened next?' Scott asked quietly.

'They told me they'd talk to their daughter, Ruth, and son-in-law, Leonard, to see if they thought Rosemary might want to meet her birth mother. So I had to leave them my number and walk away. It was hard, but I really couldn't press them for any more.'

Janet nodded. A tingling thrummed in her chest and she felt swimmy. But she couldn't move to put herself to rights. Her gaze remained fixed on Cliff and he smiled at her.

'One week later,' Cliff continued, 'the Cooksons phoned me with their daughter's address. And brace yourselves, it's in this area. Prestbury, to be exact.'

'What?' gasped Scott.

Janet's tingling surged through her, prickling her from head to foot. If Vivien's parents lived in the area, so might Vivien – or Rosemary – as she'd now have to call her.

'Apparently, it can happen,' Cliff carried on. 'An acquaintance I checked with in social services said that mothers-to-be usually made a point of travelling much further afield from their home town to have their baby, so it would be adopted in a different area and not likely to be seen afterwards with the new parents. The fact that you went to relatively nearby Swindon, Jan, was a stroke of luck in this case. And it was a logical place for Ruth and Leonard Mathews to adopt from. Then all they did was move from Bristol to Cheltenham, which is exactly what you and I did back then, Jan. They've been here for almost 25 years now –'

'Hang on! Have you met them?' Janet cried.

'Yes, and I'm getting to that.'

'Prestbury! That's only about four miles north of here,' Scott exclaimed 'All that time, and Vivien could have been living in the area. We could have passed her in the high street.'

'Right,' Cliff nodded. 'It's quite mind-blowing, isn't it?' He paused before getting back on track. 'So I met up with them, and showed them the letter and photos. Once again, it was the rabbit that really did it. Leonard was very suspicious until he saw the picture of Jan and the baby with the rabbit. Ruth was quite open-minded and trusting, probably because her mother was. She compared the baby picture with some they had of Rosemary and they looked identical. The rabbit had a long life apparently, until he unravelled just a little beyond mending. Turns out they named him Bobtail Bob. She said they'd told Rosemary she was adopted when she was twelve. She'd seemed to take it alright, but had been a difficult teenager.'

Janet winced. And how much of that had been because of finding out her own mother hadn't wanted to keep her? Not that it was like that, but Rosemary might have different ideas.

'They said they'd ask Rosemary if she wanted to meet you, Jan. But suggested that if she did, she'd better get a copy of her original birth certificate with you named as the birth mother. They'd given Rosemary her amended birth certificate and certificate of adoption years ago, with her new name and with Ruth and Leonard named as her parents. And when a couple of Acts were passed in 1975 and 1976, which allowed adopted adults access to their original birth certificate, Ruth had brought it up with Rosemary as an option. But she'd said she wasn't bothered and had never shown any interest in taking it further.'

'Then what did you do?' Scott asked, sitting forward and staring hard at Cliff.

'I gave them my contact details and left. And then I waited. Rosemary phoned me a week later to say she was interested and –'

'She is? She really is?' Janet asked, her voice rising to panic pitch.

Cliff smiled. 'She really is, Jan. I know, it's astonishing that we've got anywhere. But there it is. Rosemary seems like a nice girl too. Smart and savvy. So we met up in town where I showed her the photographs and Violet's letter. She really scrutinised them and because they are copies, I let her keep them. She asked me if I'd help her with the process, so we made a plan. She phoned Swindon's General Register Office and applied for access to her birth certificate and I drove her there to get it. She didn't want to wait to get it in the post. And she wanted to see the mother and baby home building too. Hope Lodge is a old folk's home now. Same name. I expect they thought it appropriate.'

Janet shuddered.

'So she has her birth certificate with you as her biological mother on it, and her original name. She's had a counselling session with a social worker to get her head around it and now she says she wants to meet you.'

'That's such fast work, Cliff,' Scott commented. 'And I don't think we'd have got anywhere without you either. Not with the laws as they are.'

'Just like that?' Janet asked, her mouth suddenly dry.

'Just like that. Rosemary Matthews wants to meet Janet Brewer, nee Turner.'

'Oh God, Janet,' Ann gasped. 'I can't believe this is really happening.'

'When? When does she want to meet me? And where? How are we going to do it?'

'I suggested a neutral place, which would be quiet with a

public lounge. She liked that idea and picked a hotel in Lower Slaughter – Oakbury Manor. She said she'd driven past it once or twice and thought it was a beautiful place.'

When Cliff said the name of the hotel, Janet drew a sharp intake of breath. It was where Samantha had claimed to have done extensive interior design, a fact which had no doubt blinded Patrick King to her supposed worth. How odd that Rosemary had picked this place? But she let it drift out of her head as a mere coincidence.

'Did she give you a picture of herself, so I'll recognise her?' Janet asked tentatively, desperate to know what her Vivien looked like now. What colour had her eyes become? Was she blonde, like Joe, or dark, like herself? Did she look like anyone on her side of the family or Joe's?

'No, she didn't want to,' Cliff replied. 'She seems to have this notion of keeping all that for when you meet. I can describe her if you like. She's –'

'No! Don't, Cliff. We'll do it the way she wants. I owe her that much.'

'Alright. Well, it's all set for 3rd March, next Sunday, at two o'clock. I'll escort Rosemary to the hotel. Perhaps Scott could give you a lift, Jan? Then Scott and I will go off for an hour or so, while you and Rosemary talk between yourselves. Does that sound okay?'

Cliff was beaming at her now, as were Scott and Ann. And once again, she couldn't believe this was actually happening. It was going to be such a long time until next Sunday. But she'd waited so long already, what was one more week?

Chapter 28

Over the following week, Janet was more grateful for distractions than at any other time in her life. The hours and days limped by. Thankfully, Susan kept her busy with four couples paying a visit to view her house. These ranged from the young, who vowed they'd make changes to the house, through to the middle-aged, who were happy with it the way it was. Susan's description in the advertisement was thorough and fair.

'9 Willow Lane, Charlton Kings, Cheltenham. A delightful and characterful 1930's semi-detached family house in a peaceful area with lovely views over the surrounding countryside to the rear. The accommodation offers small entrance hall and hallway, living room with bay window and regency-style marble fireplace, fully fitted kitchen/dining room, upstairs hall with three bedrooms (two large, one box room) and bathroom. The property has full central heating, under stairs storage space, off road parking and a garage, and the property has well-maintained and established front and back gardens with lawns and flower beds. 11mins from Cheltenham town centre by car, and a regular bus service operates. Easy access to many local amenities. Viewing by appointment with McReath's.'

Janet found it quite surreal how 35 years living in this house could be encapsulated in such favourable terms tailored to attract new owners. She reflected on what those walls had witnessed, and what they would go on to witness from different people's lives under its roof, absorbing more human trials and tribulations, but never able to tell of them.

As she dusted and vacuumed to make it spick and span for the visitors, she found herself saying goodbye to its nooks and crannies, the very sight of which spelled weariness to her. If further proof was needed that she should sell up, these feelings were it. Then after the preparations, she disappeared into town with Ann to leave Susan to her selling, who reported Winnie was having a good workout with her curtain twitching exercise. No surprise there. Those who viewed the house seemed very keen and Susan was expecting one or two offers to come in soon. This aspect of Janet's life was moving fast.

She also felt the need to pay a personal visit to Masons to see how the staff on soft furnishing were managing, surprised to find herself more concerned for their wellbeing than anything else.

It was a strange feeling to enter the store through the front entrance, to glide up the escalators just like a cosseted customer, then to find her feet pacing once more along the well-buffed aisle between linens and soft furnishing. And she was even wearing the same black winter coat and boots as they'd been handy by her front door; the new autumn colours that Ann had helped her choose to revamp her wardrobe hadn't quite become routine yet. But here she was on the department again. What used to be *her* department. Yet there was a sense of dissociation as if she wasn't seeing the *real* department at all – as if that authentic viewpoint was reserved for staff only and she was now an outsider. The very same space, yet seen through such a different lens.

She tried not to think about it and looked around. The first thing that caught her eye were the new Zoffany stock fabrics draped in a cascade arrangement at the very front perimeter of the department, and sporting festooned trellises and oriental birds, a perfect display for the forthcoming spring season. The second thing she noticed was Shirley Appleton making a beeline for her wearing a new peach suit and an oily pink smile.

'Janet! How lovely to see you!' she gushed in her syrupy voice. 'How are you? I think you were treated so unfairly, I really do! What are you doing with yourself these days?'

Janet had her answer ready. She'd rehearsed it. 'Oh, I'm

taking stock, Shirley, making a few life changes, selling my house, that kind of thing.' She made sure she used a low pitch to her voice at the end of her sentence to block further enquiry, as advised for assertiveness in one of her books.

Shirley smiled uncertainly. 'My, that sounds very adventurous.' Then she shifted her position so she was shoulder to shoulder with Janet. Lowering her head, she whispered, 'You know, they've kicked King out.'

Janet stiffened. 'Really?'

'Between you and me, I reported him for bad conduct when he was publically having a go at you and Samantha. There were so many witnesses. It was shocking behaviour. No excuse at all. There must have been other issues going on as well because they've moved him to Cardiff, and we've got a new lady store manager now, though it's early days to see how *she* works out. You know you could probably get your job back if you asked Kenneth.'

This pushed one of Janet's old buttons, and before she could stop herself she was responding as if she cared. 'But isn't Marian going for it?'

Shirley frowned. 'She's been doing it for a few weeks actually. But she's hardly appropriate management material for Masons.'

Janet flinched at the inferences. Just because Marian flirted a bit didn't mean she wasn't good at her job. She'd seen enough to know by now that Marian was pretty good, and she'd probably make a highly competent manager. But Shirley was old school and would hardly see Marian's good points. And the irony that she herself used to think like Shirley didn't escape her.

She peered over the department's displays and identified Milly at the desk in Berkeley Fabrics, Claire and Gemma standing by the benches, and Marian talking something through with them both. There was no sign of Kevin, so he must have been on a break or his day off.

Marian looked the part in her Eastex green and navy checked suit, which Janet remembered her wearing for her original interview on the 3rd of March last year, almost a year ago to the day. She wasn't wearing a low-cut blouse and her hemline was below the knee. With the lighter use of makeup and her hair caught back into a soft ponytail, she seemed to have gone through a personal transformation which Janet decided really suited her. But wasn't it a bit odd? Since when did Marian tow the line?

Janet murmured, 'See you later,' to Shirley, and she left her standing in the aisle like a remaining skittle in a bowling alley. She approached the benches, smiling.

Marian looked up and stared hard at her.

Janet froze when she saw the steely flash of hostility in those brown eyes, just before they became as blank as tarnished spoons. Now what? she wondered. Hadn't they come to a better understanding?

'Hello, how are you?' she asked Marian.

But Marian walked slowly by her without saying a word.

Janet felt a stab of pain in her chest at Marian's behaviour, but she didn't have long to wonder about it because Gemma and Claire clustered around her eager to hear her news and to share theirs. Even Milly came over to join in.

Gemma was finding Marian a good manager who listened well, but was getting tired of the customer service, so she was going to apply to the local college to do art and design. She'd dabbled with art for ages since school but said she had to get on with committing to it now, and she gave Janet her address and phone number to keep in touch. Janet's heart was warmed by this gesture.

Kevin and Gemma were going out together, but Kevin was angling for a job in the carpet department. One of the older men was retiring and Kevin believed better career prospects were to be found there. No doubt he was right, mused Janet.

After chatting to Claire, Janet could see she'd become the lynchpin of the department and was relishing it in just the same way as she herself had done. That sense of being able to handle anything that was thrown at you through such a detailed and professional understanding of what it took to make the department's cogwheels run smoothly and stay on course, with no wobbling or creaking. And this department really needed such a person. Janet felt proud of Claire and could see a new confidence which she instinctively knew would help her decide what to do about her troubled marriage. There was going to be someone new starting soon and Claire would no doubt be training them on the job. Nothing new there.

Milly was friendly and glowing towards Janet, just as she had been when they'd first met. And Janet was struck at how forgiving she was being. It was astonishing how her apologising to Milly was so obviously helping to heal their differences. How wonderful to have that kind of generous nature. Not weak at all. She knew that now. But special. And Milly was now doing Marian's former job for Berkeley Fabrics. Another lady with a lot more confidence.

And there was Samantha's work station, comprising of desk, chairs, and pattern books, for the higher end of the market, which had all now been moved to the soft furnishing department for any of the staff to use as design consultants with their customers. This had been at the insistence of the new lady store manager, Mrs Joy Hume. Janet liked the sound of her and nodded her approval. So many changes, both personal and departmental, in just a few weeks since she'd left. But that was retail for you; the wheels always kept turning.

Janet enjoyed everything about her visit apart from Marian's cold shoulder routine and she vowed to try and find out the cause at some future opportunity. After all, she'd got the job she'd wanted with more security for her daughter now. What could be wrong? Was she still with Rick, the thug? Had she gone to Victim Support?

But she put aside thinking about Marian because she was so soon to meet her very own daughter, Rosemary. She had to keep practicing calling her Rosemary to try to get the name Vivien out of her mind, but it was difficult. After Sunday in Lower Slaughter, she hoped this difficulty would end. And that was all she dared hope for, as the rest was simply unknown. She had to shove away all the questions that kept butting into her mind: Would Rosemary accept her? Would she understand why she had to give her up? Had she been happy? Was she happy now? What did she look like now? From a blue-eyed, blonde-haired baby to a 36 year old woman in the prime of her life. Would she see herself in her?

The drive to Oakbury Manor on Sunday the 3rd March, was a blur of winter fields and Janet was so nervous she couldn't even speak. She was wearing colour, as advised by Ann, and her hair had been lightened at the hairdressers to the rich chestnut brown that it had been in her youth. With the Paisley shawl wrap of reds, burnt oranges and jades, that Ann had given her for Christmas, worn over the shoulders of her new beige Dannimac trench coat, she looked like a very different Janet – a new Janet.

Scott drove them east from Charlton Kings. They bypassed Bourton on the Water, then turned left to Lower Slaughter, slowing down to negotiate the village of limestone storybook cottages and a watermill with a red chimney, all perched on both banks of the river Eye and connected via quaint footbridges. Named after Old English for a wet land, it was worthy of being in a victorian watercolour sketch. But it wasn't until they turned into the entrance to the stately home hotel at the far end of the village, and slid past its stone gateposts surmounted by lichen-encrusted finials, that Janet found her focus sharpening and her heart hammering.

As Scott pulled into the car park at exactly two o'clock with tires crunching on the gravel, she turned to him.

'I'm so jittery.'

'Of course you are. But you'll be fine, Mum. Honestly. Just take some deep breaths.'

Janet fiddled with her handbag while Scott noticed Cliff

ambling towards them. 'Here's Cliff, Mum, so Rosemary will be in the lounge now. I'll go to the pub with Cliff and leave you to it.' He looked hard at her and squeezed her hand. 'You'll be fine, Mum.'

She turned from his warm reassurance only to be enfolded in a hug from Cliff. 'She's waiting for you, Jan. Turn right from the foyer into the lounge. I've booked afternoon tea for you. It's all paid for. Just let the staff know when you want it. Take it gently and you'll be fine. We'll come back at about half three.'

She stood like a sentinel for a few seconds watching them stroll down the drive, then she pointed her body to the main entrance. Keeping her eyes averted from the ground floor windows of the manor, she mounted the stone steps, and with trembling hands she pushed her way through the revolving door. She looked around the foyer and spotted the entrance to the lounge on the right. The door was only slightly ajar and she could see nothing. With her heart now knocking against her ribcage and blood pulsing fast through her veins, she paused and took two deep breaths. She hesitated, with the flat of her hand just touching the door, feeling like a diver at the edge of a high board. Then swallowing hard, she relaxed her back and took the plunge.

Swinging open the door, she saw the small figure of a woman standing with her back to her and looking out of the window. Janet glanced around to see if there was anyone else present, automatically taking in the stone fireplace and its crackling flames, the overhead beams, and the blue and white ginger jar table lamps squatting on sleek, oak, side tables. The plush jacobean-patterned sofas and chairs were arranged in groups for family and friend gatherings, and coordinating damask curtains were puddled on the floor and swept back with tasselled tie backs. It was beautifully done out and there was no one else in the room.

At first the solitary figure was in silhouette, but as Janet got closer, she could make out the woman was wearing a teal raincoat, belted at the waist, with hair that was fluffed out over the collar.

'Rosemary?' Janet asked.

The woman turned on her heels and faced her with a glare that was as direct as a punch.

When Janet saw who it was, she reeled backwards, slack-jawed in amazement.

'Well, well, well. So it really is you, Janet. I wasn't certain. But now I know for sure. Now we both know. You know who your daughter is and I know who my mother is. And who would have thought it?'

The woman had red wavy hair, brown eyes, and lips the colour of garnets, and she was wearing a coat Janet had seen her wear before in C&A.

The woman was Marian.

PART FIVE

Chapter 29

'I bet you're so disappointed, aren't you?' Marian said sarcastically as she advanced upon Janet.

Janet fell backwards into a lounge chair that was so overstuffed she felt it was swallowing her up.

Marian stood over her. She leaned into Janet and pressed both her hands down onto the arms of the chair, pinning Janet into it. Her eyes sparked with anger. 'I bet you had such high hopes and now you've just got me! The little trollop from Berkeley Fabrics. That's what you've always thought of me as, isn't it? How awful for you!'

The bitterness in Marian's voice was as cold and vicious as an ice pick. And her Gloucestershire accent was in full force. Janet recognised it from their spat in Masons powder room.

She couldn't speak. All she could do was to stare into Marian's face, searching for a resemblance. Wasn't she supposed to know her own daughter? Wasn't she supposed to feel an immediate bond? Then the idea of a mistake grabbed hold of her and she found her voice.

'How can this be real? There must be a mistake. You're not called Rosemary. And...and what about the Johnson surname? Has Cliff made a mistake?'

Marian shook her head. 'No. Sorry, Janet. I'm afraid there's no mistake, despite you and me wanting there to be.' She released her hold on the chair, reached into her shoulder bag and flung a piece of paper at Janet. 'It's a copy of my original birth certificate with you on as my mother – Janet Turner. There's a blank box where the father's name goes.'

'I wanted them to put him on, but they couldn't unless he was there. He was Joe Fairlie of Ash Farm, Bishopsworth, Bristol. I've got the details for you. He was the love of my life.'

Marian went silent, walked to the window again and stared out at the sky which was clotted with grey cauliflower clouds.

Janet scrutinised the document. The names, the details. Everything was typed correctly.

Echoing her own thoughts, Marian broke her silence. 'Everything is right. All the documents. Everything. When Cliff showed me the photographs, I thought the one of you in the mother and baby home looked familiar. Then there was your name on the birth certificate, Janet Turner. Well I knew a Janet, and the woman in the picture could easily have been the woman I knew when she was young. When I saw you get out of the car just now, then I knew for sure.'

Is there any family likeness? wondered Janet, staring at Marian, who now turned around as if to be examined on cue. The brown eyes were like Violet's and Sarah's but she didn't have the long straight Davey nose, instead it was petite and nicely shaped. The full rosebud mouth was like Florrie's, but really that's all there was. And there was nothing of her own father, Albert, in her. So maybe she took after Joe's family?

'But what about your name? And what about your red hair?' Janet asked. 'They don't make any sense.'

'Well, they do to me! I dye my hair. I'm blonde underneath.' She roughly parted her hair with her fingers and stretched the sections apart. 'Do you want to check?'

Of course, Janet thought. She'd always known Marian's hair colour was out of a bottle, but she'd never assumed she was a natural blonde. And then she realised that both her Auntie Florrie and Joe had been natural blondes. She shook her head. 'Of course. I don't need to check. But most women want to be blondes. Why not you?'

Marian arched her brows. 'So now we're discussing hair colour? My, my, whatever next? For your information, I prefer being a redhead. They're seen as less ditzy than blondes and taken more seriously. And as for the name, my adopted name is Rosemary Marian Matthews. But I hated the Rosemary, so after I left school I decided to go by Marian, though Mum and Dad still call me Rosemary. Drives me nuts. Then I married Greg Johnson, a waste of bloody space he turned out to be. Three years later I got a divorce, but for Jessie's sake I kept the Johnson surname. So you see, that's how the names just don't connect. And how terribly confusing for you it must all be.' The fire of anger gleamed within the amber of her eyes again.

And her sarcasm burned Janet. But she recognised the glint of retaliation in those eyes, which she'd noticed before, close up in C&A, when Marian had been warning her about the Harrison situation. She'd connected with that look at the time, because it was one of her own. The pin-pricked pupils in the mirror after one of Frank's slaps, promising herself she would not be cowed by him. And this kind of recognition was more powerful than eye and hair colour. It counted for a great deal. So she decided she must accept Marian's ire and all the bitterness that was sure to come. If Marian was the daughter she gave away, and it had been proven that she was, then she would have to take it and make the very best of it. She wanted to and she needed to. She had to find a way of connecting with Marian, and instinctively she knew this first meeting as mother and daughter was crucial to both of them. And that if she didn't salvage something, there might never be another meeting because Marian would refuse. All these years she hadn't searched for her mother or father, so the risk of her turning her back again was high. Janet strove hard to lock her shock away for later absorption, together with her former expectations and romantic imaginings, to deal with the reality of what actually was – right now. And if nothing else, she'd always been practical.

'Okay, I see. That all makes sense with the names. But why didn't you tell Cliff your suspicions about knowing me?'

Marian tilted her chin up and looked hard at her. 'You were in control when you gave me away. I wanted to be in control of this.'

Janet pondered this for a moment and decided it was probably what she would have done herself in the same situation. 'That's fair enough, Marian. But now that we're here, why don't we take our coats off and have the tea that Cliff ordered so we can have a proper talk. I would love to explain what happened all those years ago.'

'You've got to be kidding! I'm not sitting down to clink china in this bloody place with the likes of you!'

Janet was still in the armchair, but felt the need to get closer to Marian, so she got up and approached her. Marian backed away.

'Okay, Marian. What is the likes of me? How do you really feel about me?'

She knew she was inviting condemnation, but it had to be expressed. And maybe she deserved it anyway?

'You're a cold, buttoned-up, vindictive, manipulating bitch. That's what you are! And you are a husband killer too!'

'Right, anything else?' Janet strove to contain her flushes of shame and the accusations stung her like darts.

'You're an interfering busybody, who should mind her own bloody business.'

Janet had a feeling she knew what this was about. 'Is this about Rick? Have you been to Victim Support yet?'

'Didn't I just tell you, you should mind your own business?' Marian yelled at her.

Janet gently caught hold of Marian's shoulders and looked into her face. 'Have you been?'

Marian held her gaze and Janet saw misery in her expression, and hard living in the creases around her eyes and mouth. Tears swelled in those eyes. Janet wanted to give her a hug, the kind of hug she'd been getting from others recently which had meant so much more than words, but Marian threw her off.

'Yes. Okay? Yes, I've been twice. And I know he's bad for me. I'm trying to break up with him. I've told him it's over, but he keeps coming around. He's very…very…persuasive.'

'Do you love him?'

'Not exactly...' She paused. 'I can't talk to you about this. This situation is just ridiculous.'

'Can you talk to your mother, Ruth, about this?'

'Are you joking? Everything in their lives is so bloody perfect. Mum and Dad would never understand. They've always lived in their own little world and they've never really understood me, or the world we *actually* live in. They thought it was a catastrophe when Greg and I didn't work out. They thought the idea of being a single mother was terrible. They think divorce is terrible. They even suggested that Jessie should live with them, like I wasn't up to it. 'For the stability,' they said. That's how much they thought of me. What would they understand about my relationship with Rick and the way he behaves?'

'They come from a generation that thought a single mother had to give her baby away for a better life – that's what happened to me. There was no alternative back then. No way of making it work. But I'm sure they are very good people. No, they probably won't understand domestic abuse – the power struggles going on, the hold over you. But the law is on your side nowadays.'

Marian brushed past her, jolting her shoulder. 'I'm going. This is stupid. I just wanted to see if it was you. That's all. You can't suddenly become a mother to me.' She shot Janet a look. 'And don't bother trying.'

'Please stay. I know I can't be a mother to you. But I can be a friend. At least I can try.' She clutched hold of Marian's arm. 'Please stay! Let me explain. I owe you that much, don't I? An explanation? Just an explanation. Then you can do what you like.'

Marian hesitated. She turned and looked hard at Janet.

Janet felt as if Marian's stark stare was boring into her very soul, such was the piercing quality to her unblinking expression. There was an uncompromising searching in it which Janet would have tried hard to hide from in the past to protect herself. But not now. Now was the time for giving and acceptance, and she instinctively knew she had to be completely open with Marian, even if she got hurt in the process. So feeling this, she returned Marian's gaze with a very new one of her own.

After a few more moments Marian's shoulders sagged and the hard set of her mouth softened a fraction. And much to Janet's surprise she said, 'Go and tell them we're ready for our fucking tea, then.'

They sat separately by the fireplace, Marian in a wing chair at an angle to Janet on a sofa. The waitress placed their tea tray down on the table between them, and the fire sparked when she used some tongs to add a fresh log to the fire. Then she left them alone, leaving the door slightly ajar.

'Let's get the sob story over with,' Marian said, hacking a fork into a slice of coffee and walnut cake. She slopped some tea from the pot into their cups and they both added sugar and milk.

Janet took a deep breath and began to tell Marian how she had first met Joe. And though Marian had copies of the photographs of both Joe, and Janet and the baby, Janet used the originals she'd brought with her to trigger her feelings and to tell her story for probably the very last time. But it was the most important time of all. Marian was quiet enough until something occurred to her, then she'd suddenly interrupt.

'Did you want to give me away?'

'No! Of course not. I loved you! You'll probably know from having Jessica just how strong the bond can be right from the start. It broke me when they took you away. I'd been hanging on to the hope that Joe would get in touch. I wanted him to know about you. If he'd known, I'm sure he'd have done the right thing. He'd have come back from America. But he didn't get in touch. Not one single letter. And never any address for him either. Then when you were born, there was no way I could have brought you up on my own. Not then. Single mothers simply couldn't support a child. They had no means, no job, and getting a home of their own was impossible. And they were socially ostracised.'

'Yes, I get all that. And Cliff explained that as the birth mother you had no way of being able to get in touch with me or find out who'd adopted me. It was me that had to do the searching.'

'Yes.'

'And from Violet's letter, it's clear that Joe did care about you.'

'Yes. I only found that out in the last few weeks. It means a great deal to me.'

'And later on, when it was classed as too late, your mother got rid of some letters that he finally sent.'

'Yes.'

'It's like a Mills and Boon story, isn't it? Star-crossed lovers with a love-child. And don't forget the violins.'

Janet flinched at Marian's cynicism. 'But that's how it was, Marian. We were both in love. I have no doubt about that.'

'And we have Bobtail Bob, the rabbit, to thank for everything.'

Janet ignored Marian's scathing tone. 'What happened to him eventually?'

'Buried in the garden, I think.' She bit her lip. 'I do remember that being upsetting.'

Janet nodded. 'You wouldn't let go of him at the home.'

Marian flashed her a look, but Janet couldn't read it.

After she'd told Marian everything up to Frank's death, realising she knew all about the circumstances of his death already, she wanted to tell her about the outcome of the confession and about Frank's pills being out of date, but she decided the right thing to do was to focus on Marian herself, so she asked her what her childhood had been like. Had she been happy?

Just at that moment a head appeared around the door. It was Cliff. He grinned. 'Do you need a bit longer?'

Janet looked at Marian, dreading that she'd take the

opportunity to shut down their talk and leave.

'Might as well get it all over with now,' Marian said, flopping back into her chair and twisting her legs together. She flicked her hair across her shoulder.

Cliff frowned. 'Right…well we'll have a coffee at the pub, then wait for you outside in the cars.'

'Thanks, Cliff,' Janet said, turning her attention immediately back to Marian, while Cliff withdrew. 'So, were you happy?'

Marian sighed. 'I suppose so, yeah, earlier on. I got everything I needed. In fact, they spoilt me really, and I was probably over-protected. I was a typical only child in that respect. And yes, they were good parents and I do love them. I do. But I always felt different to them and I didn't look anything like them, so when they told me I was adopted, it made a lot of sense. Of course, I wondered why I'd been given away, what had been wrong with me – '

'Nothing was wrong with you, you were –'

'Yes, they tried to explain that at the time, but at twelve you can't really take it in the way you can later as an adult. Anyway, after that, I suppose I rebelled more and they couldn't really cope with me as a teenager. It was like their sweet little girl had gone bad somehow. The succession of boyfriends with long hair and flairs, the smoking, the free love of the sixties, the house parties, the music, the bands. Of course I was on the pill, so nothing that they dreaded ever happened. But they seemed to disapprove of everything I wanted to do. I think they would have liked me to become a nurse or a teacher or something – a nice respectable job, whereas I fancied becoming a hairdresser. The compromise was me doing business and secretarial courses at the local tech, but then I ended up going into hotel reception work, which I loved, rather than a boring office job which they would probably have preferred. They saw hotel work as mixing with all sorts.'

She paused. 'Anyway, I met Greg when I was working at Ashton Hall; he was with a group of colleagues doing a working lunch. We hit it off straight away. But Mum and Dad didn't like his long hair and they didn't approve of his being a car salesman. They also thought he was too cheeky, which he actually was. But of course I liked him for that. Well, they turned out to be right about him. He was totally unreliable, didn't lift a finger to help with Jessie or around the house, and he went out with the lads to the local too often for my liking. We got divorced after three years, which Mum and Dad were kind of relieved about, and then it was all about Jessie's welfare. Greg's contributions or visits with Jessie were on and off, not reliable at all, and his mother wasn't interested, so I did need Mum and Dad to help me and they still do. They do plenty of babysitting and they collect her from school while I'm at work. And I really do appreciate it, but they always make me feel as if I'm falling short. And they'd never get Rick at all!'

'They've never met him?'

'God, no!'

'Is it the lovemaking you like?' The question was out before Janet could stop herself. What had previously been shut at the back of her mind from when she'd last seen Marian and Rick together outside the staff entrance to Masons, marched right up front into this mother-daughter reunion.

'Jesus, Janet!' Marian's jaw dropped.

Janet shook her head. 'I'm sorry. It's none of my business.'

'Is there something in this tea?' Marian stared down into the dregs of her empty cup.

Janet almost laughed at Marian's comical demonstration and her mouth twitched with a nervous smile.

'Actually, you may have a point, Janet. He is good in bed. The best I've ever had.'

If Marian was expecting Janet to be shocked, she was determined not to look it. After all, she'd read enough *Cosmopolitan* magazines to know the feminist attitudes of young women these days and what they felt they were entitled to – a vigorous sex life being one of those rights. She tried to put herself into Marian's place.

'Alright. And I can see how that counts for something. But he hits you. He's not great with Jessica. And he's a lout who mixes with other louts, isn't he?'

Marian was quiet. She stared into the fire's flames.

'Isn't he?'

Marian turned to face her. There were no tears threatening to fall talking about Rick this time, just a hard look in her eyes framed by a frown. 'Yes to all that. That's why I'm trying to end it, like I told you. I just have to stay firm and keep telling him it's over until he gets the message.'

'Okay, then.'

Marian sighed. 'Is there anything else? Because I'm thinking we're done here.' She shook out her coat and grabbed hold of her bag.

Janet seized the opportunity to explain that the case against her over Frank's death had been dropped, and that his medication had been redundant because it was out of date.

'Well, I'm pleased to know my birth mother isn't a husband killer after all.' Marian smirked. 'What a relief.'

'I know I've got no right to ask, but will you be careful with Rick. Lock your doors, that kind of thing.'

Marian groaned. 'Yes, yes…'

Janet reached into her bag and pulled out a piece of paper. She held it out to Marian. 'Joe's former address,' she said. 'Just so you have it.'

Marian snatched it out of her hand. 'Right.'

Janet decided to end their meeting by asking Marian about her new job. She was struck by the fact that in a strange way there could be some kind of benefit in she and Marian having known each other already, even if it was in a totally different capacity. They had a kind of bond through Masons, and she needed all the help she could get.

'How is the job going? Gemma and Claire seem to think you make a good manager.'

Marian tilted her head to one side, as if considering this new approach from Janet.

'That's good to know. It's okay. There's more to it than with Berkeley Fabrics. More complexities, but I like a challenge.'

'Yes, that fits. I'm sure you'll be up for it too. But can I ask why you've changed your appearance? With your hair tied back and so on?'

Marian scowled and Janet thought she wasn't going to explain, so she was surprised when she did.

'It's the new store manageress, Joy Hume.'

Marian went on to tell Janet that Joy was a very nice lady, who'd suggested she change her look. Marian had bristled at first, but Joy's argument had been persuasive. She told Marian, yes, she had a perfect right to dress how she wanted, but to consider that as she was obviously an intelligent young lady with a professional mindset, then she deserved to be taken seriously, and therefore toning down her fashion taste, by dropping her hemline and buttoning up her blouses, just for work, might be more advantageous.

Janet smiled. This new store manager must be quite something, she decided.

'Anyway, I could ask you the same thing,' Marian said, shrugging into her coat. 'What's going on with *your* new look? The hair, the colours. I mean that shawl you've got on doesn't belong to the Janet I know. What's with the after black look?

'I needed a change. I needed *to* change.'

'Marian nodded. 'Right. Well, anything's better than the black widow get-up.'

Then Janet remembered something else very important. It was so hard to fit everything in, but she had to try. She was pretty sure Marian might refuse to meet her again.

'Did Cliff tell you that you have a half-brother – Scott? He's outside if you want to meet him. He's your younger brother. He'd love to meet you. And his son is called Daniel. He's seven, around Jessica's age, I think.' Then she remembered Susan knowing Marian from their exercise class. 'You know Susan, Scott's wife, already, I think, from aerobics class?'

Marian's mouth tightened and she scowled. 'Yes, I know Susan. But I don't really want to meet anyone else today, Janet. I've had more than enough for one day. I don't know if I'll ever want to meet them.'

Janet nodded, feeling her heart twist with pain. She'd gone too far. 'Fair enough,' she managed to say, then paused to get control of herself. 'Thank you so much for coming today, Marian. It means a great deal.'

'Had to be done, I suppose.' Her tone had reverted to being frosty again, much to Janet's dismay.

As they made their way into reception together, a thought struck Janet. 'Why did you pick this place to meet?' she asked. 'Does it mean something to you?'

Marian strutted across reception towards the bar entrance.

Janet followed.

'This was where Samantha said she had a big commission to do the drapes. It seemed to impress big man King, so I wondered if it would impress me. I had a nosy around before you came, but I didn't look in here.' Marian peered around the door into the bar.

'And?'

'And it's possible she did the lounge and dining room, maybe even some of the bedrooms. And they are up to standard, I would say. But how do we really know she did them?'

They both stared around the bar area, Janet taking note of the plaster and oak beamed construction of the ceiling and walls, the massive tudor arch fireplace, the lattice windows with their red velvet curtains, and the copper-studded chairs to match. Then as her eyes came to rest upon a woman behind the bar drying some glasses, Marian drew a sharp intake of breath.

'Is that who I think it is?' she whispered to Janet. 'Bloody hell!'

Janet looked hard at the woman. The blonde hair tied loosely back, the beige suit, the chiffon scarf, and the same powder puff complexion as ever. It was the English rose, Samantha Dixon-Wright. And in the instance Janet recognised her,. Samantha spotted the two of them, with their heads craned around the door.

She dropped the glass she was cleaning and it shattered on the flagstone floor. Blushing as deep scarlet as a prized pedigree David Austin bloom, she darted to one side, then the other. But realising retreat was impossible she stood still with her shoulders hunched.

Janet and Marian walked slowly up to her.

'What are *you* doing here?' Marian asked incredulously.

Samantha's eyelashes fluttered, then she managed to look Marian in the eye. 'I'm working here part-time.' Her voice was small and childlike, as if she'd been caught doing something shameful.

Marian glanced sideways at Janet, wonder blazing forth from her raised brows and wide eyes.

'Not much work on the interior design front then,' observed Janet to Samantha, feeling somewhat sorry for her after their chat in the Promenade. 'I'm really not sure what I'll end up doing myself.'

'But you *did* do the furnishings here?' Marian asked Samantha.

Samantha's face hardened. 'Yes, of course I did. I'm only doing this because I know the manager, and he offered me this slot until I can get my business going again.' Then with a change of mood, she narrowed her eyes. 'What are you both doing here? Checking up on me?'

'Of course not,' Janet said. It was the truth from her side.

'I wasn't aware you even liked each other,' Samantha said.

Janet wondered what to do. Whether to reveal that Marian was her daughter or to hide the fact. For a few agonizing seconds, she instinctively knew she'd be dammed by Marian if she did and equally dammed if she didn't. It had to be Marian's choice.

'Can I tell her?' she asked Marian.

Marian shot her a look. 'No. I'll tell her.' She stiffened and glared at Janet and then at Samantha. 'I've just found out that Janet, here, is my biological mother. She gave me up for adoption as a baby.'

Samantha shrank back into the darkness behind the bar, eyes now as round as full moons.

'She wants forgiveness of course. But I don't know if I can give it. I don't know what I want. I don't know what I feel. What would you feel, Samantha?'

Samantha shook her head wordlessly.

Marian's tone spat venom and Janet collapsed inside. The fissures that had recently developed in the granite block inside her imploded, rendering her helpless, and floundering in flying shards and splinters.

Marian turned on her heels and marched out.

Samantha came around the bar. She grasped Janet's hand and squeezed it.

With tears spilling down her cheeks, Janet stared into Samantha's face, registering a genuine sympathy.

'Don't give up,' Samantha said. 'It's early days, she'll be confused. She needs some time. This happened in my family too. My older sister gave her baby away, but the reunion worked out well in the end. Don't give up.'

Chapter 30

Janet remembered Samantha's words during the following weeks. And as the trees budded and burst open their leaves in the spring sunshine and rains, the sheer shock of Rosemary being Marian being Vivien affected not only Janet, but also Ann, Scott, Susan, and Cliff, each with their own particular reactions and feelings which they naturally shared with one another.

When Marian had approached Cliff's car for a lift home, Scott had recognised her from Masons as the lady who'd been making his mother's life at work difficult. He'd hesitated, he told Janet afterwards, but decided that he must seize the chance to introduce himself. He held out his hand and identified himself as her half brother, and she had limply taken his hand and murmured, 'Hello.' This tiny gesture he deemed to be a positive thing, but Janet wasn't so sure.

Cliff had felt manipulated by Marian. She'd suspected all along who Janet was, but to suit her own designs had said nothing – not the kind of behaviour he could easily accept. But as soon as they'd driven away, Marian had explained why she'd needed to do it. So he kept his mouth shut on the subject and simply kept to the topic of where she wanted to go from here. She already had Janet's contact details, but did she want to see Janet again as her birth mother? She said she didn't know, she was all in a muddle. He asked if she wanted Janet to know her address. When she replied that Janet already knew it, he was confused. She told him she would contact Janet if she wanted to meet again, but for Janet to leave her alone otherwise. Like Scott, Cliff felt there were some signs of hope as he relayed this conversation to Janet. After all, Marian hadn't said flat out that she never wanted to see Janet again.

When Susan found out about Marian's identity, a woman she'd got to know a little from their aerobics class, she was full of ideas: 'Maybe I can have a word with her, tell her you're okay, Janet? Maybe I can try to be a sister-in-law and we can have Jessica meet Danny? That will probably be harmless enough to start with, don't you think?'

Janet shook her head, unable to contemplate any of these scenarios.

Ann scrutinised the pictures of baby Vivien to find a likeness to Marian, unable to believe in the legal evidence alone. When she did find a resemblance, and was finally forced to accept the truth, she was stunned into shame to think that Marian, the woman at work who Janet had called a slut, and who she herself had also treated badly, colluding with her friend's negative judgments, had been Janet's long lost daughter all along. But after expressing this to Janet, she could see Janet needed no promptings to be filled with a dreadful remorse, so she said little other than to reassure her that it would be bound to take time, while trying to get her own head around it. And in this vein, Janet often found her staring out of the kitchen window, deep in thought and shaking her head of silver hair.

As for Janet's relatives down south, Florrie and Sarah, who she'd informed of the situation, not having a clue as to Marian's stubborn character, chimed in with the 'give it time' advice and said that at least she'd found her daughter now. That was an amazing thing in itself, wasn't it?

But most affected of all was of course Janet. Since Frank's death she'd been subject to shifting tides which had been rocking her sense of who she was while she strived to make changes in her life and within herself. But the meeting with Marian had been a tidal wave. It had knocked her off her feet and swept her away in a frenzied foam, while she tried to keep her head above water, desperately reaching out for purchase on any rock close to the shore. At other times she felt slowed up in herself, as her thoughts rolled around like tangles of seaweed in sludge after the tidal wave had done its worst.

At first she'd stayed in bed in the mornings until around noon, exhausted by the recent tensions, unable to face her own reality, with no motivation to do anything about it anyway. Depression tried to suffocate any positive thinking that tried to breathe in her, and whenever she awoke from the blissful ignorance of sleep, she'd feel that wave ride through her again and again. She'd found her daughter, and that should have been a huge relief, but her daughter didn't want anything to do with her. And who could blame her after the way Janet had treated her in the past? She'd even wanted to throw Marian down that black hole in the staircase wall. Waking fresh to these realisations every morning was torture. Not only that, she was keenly aware that Marian, as well as potentially Jessica, were in danger from Rick's temper until Marian managed to properly end their relationship. Was she going to be able to do it?

But after airing her concerns to Cliff and Scott, who reiterated the ball was in Marian's court, she knew she had to stay out of it, and in the meantime, right now, her own life needed attending to. Her son, daughter-in-law, and her new friends kept gently nudging her to do just that, and they kept reminding her that Marian might change her mind about not wanting a relationship. There was always hope, they said, and that if she got herself well, then she'd be ready for when that time may come.

Slowly, taking this advice, she began to recover. She ate more of the food Ann prepared, then began doing her share of the cooking again. She went to town for a coffee and to shop. She met up with Liz. And she prepared the house for whenever Susan arranged a viewing. With Scott's help, she checked her finances. With no current work, money was tighter, but she had Frank's pension, a small life insurance payout, and she had some healthy savings of her own as a buffer. This meant she could take her time and find some kind of work that might suit her rather than consider paid work an urgent matter.

Somewhat ironically, at the end of April, she received a call from Kenneth Brown, personnel manager of Masons. He wanted to know if she would be interested in a part-time sales consultancy job on the furniture department, where the commission would be 5% on every sale. This was a tempting offer. He explained she should never have been forced into the position of walking out, so this was some way of making amends, and the store manager, Joy Hume, had keenly supported the idea. Janet considered the offer overnight, but decided that the least she could do for Marian was to stay away from the very building in which she worked as it might distress her.

Scott suggested to Janet that she enrol at the local college to do evening classes to formally update her secretarial skills, which these days would mean tackling word processing, spreadsheets and databases and maybe some accounting too. Janet thought it was a sensible plan. It would extend what she'd learned at Masons and would keep her mind occupied, so she signed up.

Cliff was keen on this idea too, because he was going to set up business at home as a professional private investigator, hopefully to specialise in missing persons, and would need a personal assistant. Would she be interested? She was moved by his proposition and asked if she could take some time during the course to think it over. Absolutely, he said.

And Liz had asked Janet if she'd consider becoming a Victim Support volunteer. With her own experiences to draw upon she would be able to support women victims of domestic abuse as well as those affected by other kinds of crimes. Liz was also sure she would make an excellent speaker for support groups. Janet said she would have to think about it, because for now it was Marian's own situation with Rick that she was preoccupied with, and besides, she just didn't feel up to it.

And that was the bottom line. She didn't really feel up to much at all, while these offers presented themselves like doors opening to a multitude of possible futures, after she'd firmly closed the Masons one. At one time all she'd wanted was a foot in the Masons door. But now she had more options than she'd ever dreamed of and didn't know which way to turn.

But life changes don't necessarily wait for you to be ready for them, and a big one came for Janet sooner than she was prepared for. After her drive and confidence had been seriously punctured in the aftermath of what she judged as having lost her daughter all over again, she was hardly in the frame of mind to go house hunting. However Susan sold 9 Willow Lane in the middle of May to a professional couple following some competition with another potential buyer. The final price to be paid for the house was to be £100,000, a fantastic result, Susan told Janet, but the couple wanted to be in the house by the 22nd June at the latest, so house hunt Janet must.

Rallying to the task, Janet gave Susan an idea of what she had in mind, namely something with cottage character and outside of Cheltenham. With Susan promptly doing a search, Janet visited a few properties Susan lined up for a viewing with Ann going along for the ride. They concentrated on rural locations towards the north of Cheltenham and checked out some houses for sale in Greet, Bishop's Cleeve, Gotherington and Taddington. But it was the fourth day's viewing that reaped rewards. The winning house was Jasmine Cottage, Gretton Road in Winchcombe, with Ann's own bungalow within walking distance and Cliff just up the road in Toddington.

But it wasn't so much the location as the actual cottage which managed to stir some feeling from Janet, reminding her as it did of Florrie's Riverside Cottage in Camelford. With a tiny front garden behind a box hedge, it was at the end of a row of attached houses, with a small parking space and a back garden sheltered by beech trees with fields beyond. Built of weathered Cotswold stone, the front was festooned with summer and winter flowering jasmine, and there were two downstairs rooms and a kitchen, with two bedrooms and a bathroom upstairs. Smaller than Janet's current house, what it lacked in space it made up for in character. This was emphasised by Susan and Janet agreed. It was just within Janet's price range, but the owner wanted a quick sale. In a picturesque road, close to the shops, it was sure to be snapped up soon, warned Susan.

With Ann pointing out features she liked, Janet absorbed the delights of the cottage: the light and bright low ceiling rooms with angles and nooks surmounted by dark beams; the exposed stone wall in the living room with a simple open fireplace topped by an oak beam mantel; the clever insertion of storage cupboards and shelving in alcoves to maximize all the available space; the terracotta tiled floor in the kitchen with a multi-coloured tiled splashback, while the window overlooked a garden packed with flowering shrubs and perennials, just perfect for Thomas. She decided she could use the small room downstairs for her sewing and as an office. Recently refurbished, the cottage was ready to move into, so Janet asked Susan to offer the owners the full asking price which they accepted two days later. When Janet gave Susan a big bunch of flowers to say thank you, she was touched by her blushing as pink as the roses in the bouquet.

Janet now felt as if her luck was changing and that she could breathe a new kind of air, fresh and clean compared to the previous year and her distinctly stale married life with Frank. Ann moved back to her bungalow, and after extensive packing and cleaning with many visits to the local tip to clear clutter like Frank's old chair, the Chinese rug Janet was sick of the sight of, and her old frilly housecoat she didn't feel right in anymore, Janet moved into her new home on the 14th June.

Back at Willow Lane, Winnie had watched the comings and goings and the removal men's activities with her customary bird of prey surveillance, but Janet decided to part on good terms and knocked on her door to say goodbye.

'Winchcombe, indeed!' commented Winnie, standing hunched on her stumpy legs. 'Going up in the world, are you?'

'I wouldn't say that, Winnie. I just need a fresh start.'

'Well I expect you'll miss me,' sighed Winnie. 'I thought we saw eye to eye, you and me. I don't know what happened. Pity, never mind.'

Janet shook Winnie's hand which felt like a claw trying to cling on to her. She pulled her hand away and wished Winnie well. Winnie sniffed and shut the door.

She hesitated before crossing the road to the Reynolds. This was the neighbouring family who Winnie believed were having marital problems, as evidenced perhaps by their lacklustre outdoor display at Christmas. She realised now she'd resented them for their fun festive seasons and zest for life, but Mrs Reynolds had always stopped to chat to her in the street, and Mr Reynolds had always been amiable enough, trying to tell her jokes she could never laugh at.

When she rang the bell, Mrs Reynolds answered. She was quite pretty, but always seemed to be in a bit of a mess with her hair falling out of a band or her jumper dusted in flour from relentless baking. She looked pale and surprised, but she smiled as she wiped her hands on her apron. 'You're off, then.'

'Yes. To Winchcombe.' She handed Mrs Reynolds a piece of paper with her new address on. 'I expect this will seem strange, as I know I've always been stand-offish, but if you ever fancy coming over for a visit, you'd be more than welcome.'

Mrs Reynolds blinked at her several times, then said, 'Have you got time for a cuppa?'

When Janet emerged an hour later, she knew far more than Winnie could ever hope to find out through her curtain twitching and most of it was sad, but also hopeful. Tony Reynolds had been tempted into an affair with a younger woman, and Alison Reynolds had been devastated by the betrayal. Finding the idea of forgiveness out of the question at the time – just before last Christmas – she'd wanted a divorce. But they were now going to marriage guidance together, exploring what may have gone wrong with their relationship, and were working on their family life. There would certainly be outdoor illuminations next Christmas, Alison assured Janet. Janet left feeling rueful that she and Alison might have been friends if her own circumstances with Frank had been different, but she was determined not to look back.

With a new found energy, she finally wrote to her old friend, Babs, who'd moved from Bristol to London, and whose address she'd managed to get from Bab's mother, Ivy, when she and Scott had visited on their trip down south. Getting in touch now felt like the right time and she told Babs everything that had happened in her life since marrying Frank in a very long letter. Babs's immediate reply was full of sympathy, but also positive urgings to 'get on with living her life now.' She also provided a long overdue update.

After she'd gone to London with her car mechanic husband, Ben, she trained as a hairdresser and now had her own salon, called Turning Heads, not to mention three kids into the bargain. She'd written to Janet's Bishopsworth address several times, but had received no replies. But it didn't matter, she said, they were back in touch and better late than never. Janet realised Mildred must have had a hand in this breakdown of communication once again, but she managed to shrug it off.

Most significantly, in her own eyes she decided to take the initiative with Marian. She had resisted the urge to send Marian a birthday card for the 2nd June in line with her instructions to leave her alone. But now Janet wrote her a letter giving her new address and telephone number and saying that she and Jessica were welcome to visit any time. She hoped her job was going well and if there was anything she could ever do for her, then please would she get in touch. She signed it, 'All the best, Janet', after ruminating on more heartfelt endearments which really didn't sound like her and which she was sure Marian would take exception to. She hoped for a reply, but didn't expect one, which proved an accurate prediction.

Nevertheless, as Janet settled into Jasmine Cottage with Thomas, who had alien territory to explore and claim, she felt her life entering a new phase with a fresh kind of freedom she'd never felt before, and she had her evening classes to look forward to. She'd believed that returning to Masons after Frank's death had been freedom at last, but how could it have been with the painful secrets she'd been haunted by and the coldness in her heart? Now was so much better. Family found and her sense of self recovered after lying dormant for so long. With increasing acceptance and forgiveness, she embraced her new life and hoped every night before she went to sleep that Marian would manage to break up with Rick and would come to visit.

Making frequent trips to antique shops and furniture stores, she treated herself to a few choice pieces more suitable for a cottage setting, and Ann bought her two stoneware jugs of local pottery as a housewarming present, which fitted in beautifully. With her cross stitch canvases gracing the walls and her embroidered cushions on her two new bijou sofas, she felt she now had a home she could call her own.

Only Ann gave her cause for concern. After Janet's move to Winchcombe, she and Ann met up in a local tea rooms once a week, and sometimes walked to each other's houses for a coffee, but Janet had noticed a change in Ann. She was frequently listless and sometimes irritable, the latter being especially out of character. It was clear that since Janet no longer needed her support, she was now having to come to terms with her retirement life back in her bungalow on her own again, and she didn't seem to be finding anything meaningful to do with her time. She picked at her food and her forehead seemed permanently dimpled with worry. Janet knew something was seriously wrong and asked her several times, but all Ann said was she just a bit run down. It was when Janet was expressing once again the wish that Marian would visit, that Ann lost her temper and the truth came out.

'Oh shut up, Janet,' she said, slamming her teacup down on its saucer and causing the heads of other customers in the café to swivel around and gawp. 'You're not the only woman in the world with daughter problems!' Then she promptly burst into tears.

Back at Jasmine Cottage, with some insistent probing from Janet, it was soon clear that Ann's daughter up in York was causing her much stress and unhappiness.

'She keeps calling me to ask her to lend her more money. I don't get any of it back and my savings are going down. I can't go on like this!' Ann wailed. 'My son won't lend her any and tells me I shouldn't either. I should learn to say no. But what can I do? She's my daughter!'

Talking it through, Janet found out that Ann's daughter, Jenny, had always been a Daddy's girl and had been spoilt by Bob, which Ann had resented and complained about. Ann had taken consolation in her relationship with her son, Richard, which was a loving one. Her relationship with Jenny had been one of animosity on Jenny's part and a lack of motherly feeling on Ann's. After Bob's death, ten years ago, Jenny began to make Ann feel guilty about this past lack of affection, making out she'd been a bad mother, and she'd recently managed to make Ann feel awful enough to keep giving her money to pay off her credit card debts, incurred by chasing after a lifestyle that was beyond her means as a clerical officer for the council. And as for ever being invited up to her daughter's for Christmas, well she'd lied about that to people. Jenny had never invited her. She'd been to Richard's a few times, up in Edinburgh, but he travelled a lot with his work and was enjoying his bachelor lifestyle, so Ann had spent quite a few Christmases on her own.

'You've got to say no to her,' urged Janet.

'But I'm not assertive, like you. I can't!'

'You can! You can ring her up and tell her there will be no more money. That you were a good mother. You did the best job you could.'

Ann stared at her with her mouth trembling. 'She'd never accept that!'

'You tell her that you need your savings and pension for your remaining years. That you and Bob worked hard for it. You've given her what you could, but there is no more you can do for her. Write it down and ring her if you can, but certainly have it by the phone for when she next rings you.'

Ann just kept shaking her head.

Janet squeezed Ann's hand. 'Promise, you'll try. Promise me. I can't bear seeing you taken advantage of and all upset like this. Say you'll try.'

Ann stopped shaking her head and looked miserably at Janet. 'I'll try.'

In mid July there was an important development concerning her own daughter. Susan phoned her with a proposal. The school holidays had begun and she'd had the idea of inviting Marian at their next aerobics class to have a get-together in Pittville Park on the following Sunday, which was promising to be fine weather. There would just be herself, Danny, Marian and Jessica. The kids could play on the swings, feed the ducks, and they could have ice cream.

'Something needs to happen, Janet,' she said. 'We get along quite well. She just might talk to me. What do you think?'

Janet's heart clenched painfully at the picture of this idyllic afternoon which she couldn't be included in. She also felt envious of Susan's influence. But surely any family contact was better than none? And she knew she should be grateful to Susan for suggesting it. The silence on the phone began to swell and press on her nerves.

'Janet? What do you think?'

Her voice caught in her throat like a prickly burr. 'Yes, Susan. Do it,' she rasped. 'And thank you.'

Two days later, Susan phoned to say Marian had said yes.

That Sunday Janet tried to keep her mind occupied by doing some weeding, but she kept picturing Susan and Marian and her grandchildren having a lovely time in the park without her. A warm breeze stirred the beech trees at the end of her garden, greedy bees laden with pollen buried themselves in the tubular flowers of foxgloves to harvest more, and there were some tinkling trills of classical piano music drifting Janet's way from a house further down – all creating a somnolent lazy summer day to relish.

But Janet was too on edge to appreciate it. She kept checking her watch and when five o'clock came and went, she downed her tools, went inside, and kept going to the phone to pick up the receiver, only to put it back down again without dialling. Luckily, she didn't have to wait long before discovering how the afternoon had gone because Susan called around in person at six.

Sitting in two deck chairs with the sun trying to work some balm into Janet's tensions, Susan explained to her it had gone quite well. They'd chatted about all sorts of things. Danny had been a little wary of Jessica at first, and Jessica had been shy, but after an ice cream each and then a few pushes on some swings with Susan and Marian, they had gone off together to investigate what adventures the play area had to offer. Susan and Marian had sat on a park bench to watch over them.

Marian did talk to Susan about how she felt about Janet, and much to Janet's surprise it wasn't as bad as she'd expected.

'She was glad you gave her the Victim Support leaflet,' Susan said, 'and it made her realise the behaviour pattern that was going on, that she wasn't to blame, and that she deserved better. So she's finished with Rick for good now. That's down to you, Janet.'

Janet couldn't speak, but her body relaxed with a sudden relief that Rick was out of Marian's life.

'As far as your potential relationship goes, she does have

trust issues. But she said she always has had ever since she was told she was adopted. She said she likes you far more than she used to, ever since that curtain order fiasco at work, and that you'd defended her being called a tart by the angry customer. But at the same time she also remembers your fights and how vicious you were with each other, so it's all a bit confusing.'

Janet nodded. 'It is. I don't expect many people have ever been in the position of having known their birth relative in a former capacity before finding out that all that time they were blood relatives.'

Susan grinned. 'You know, I can see similarities between you.'

'Really? What?' Janet felt mystified but was keen to clutch onto something they had in common.

'You're both feisty and stubborn, with a strong sense of right and wrong. You're both ambitious too.'

Janet thought hard and as objectively as she could. Then she smiled. 'Yes, you might well be right there, Susan.'

'So, she just needs more time, I think. But I have an idea.'

'Another one?'

'Why don't you have a little tea party in the garden next month, as a housewarming, and invite Marian and Jessica? Ann and Cliff can come, Scott, me, and Danny, and maybe someone else from Masons that Marian would like.'

Janet shuddered. The very picture of this in her mind's eye frightened her. All that social chit chat, all that small talk and ever so polite surface fluff, which she'd always hated and never been very good at. And as for hosting such a thing! But she drew a couple of deep breaths. After all, what did she have to lose?

'Maybe Milly would come?' she said.

But the next development that really rocked her, and which could lead to yet another door gaping wide in front of her, came from Cliff when he unexpectedly called to see her three days later at around five o clock, on his way home to

Toddington from town.

Wearing a light checked shirt and some chinos, and having acquired a summer tan along with a healthy gain in weight, Cliff looked like a different person to the stooped and gaunt man Janet had visited during that desperate time back in December, when she needed his advice about Frank's death, when Cliff was struggling with retirement and grieving for Angie. He looked fitter and happier now. Perhaps it was the new sense of purpose he'd acquired since Angie's death, Janet reflected. But whatever it was she was glad to see it and was pleased to call him her friend.

And the new Cliff was always full of surprises.

'I've got two significant pieces of news, Jan, both relating to Marian.'

They were sitting at the small dining table Janet had positioned by the front sitting room window which had a good view of the leafy road beyond. Looking into Cliff's piercing blue eyes beneath his bristling eyebrows, she tightened her spine. What now? she wondered. What on earth is it going to be now?

She squirmed in her seat in the glare of his gaze and her mouth went dry.

'It's okay, Jan. At least I think it is.'

'Just tell me, Cliff.'

'Okay…well I know we decided that the ball was in Marian's court regarding Rick, the boyfriend –'

'Yes, but Susan's talked to her in the park and says Marian's told her it's over.'

Cliff's eyebrows shot up. 'Right…well, it would seem so, yes. But let me tell you what I've been doing.'

'Okay.'

He looked sheepish now and she wondered what was coming. 'I've tailed him a few times, Jan. And I looked into whether he has a criminal record.'

Her mouth fell open. 'That was dangerous, wasn't it? To tail him?'

Cliff feigned a look of taking offence, then grinned. 'I'm a pro, Jan.'

'Sorry.'

'He has a bunch of mates he meets regularly at a few pubs in town. They get a bit gobby on the street after closing time. And I did spot him entering and leaving Marian's building a few times. Sometimes she was on the doorstep and they frequently parted acrimoniously, but the last time, a couple of months ago, she definitely told him it was over and not to come back. And as far as I can ascertain he hasn't been back.' He paused. 'And that's good, because he's got form.'

'What do you mean, form?'

'He's been arrested a few times for being drunk and disorderly, and he's done a couple of stretches in prison for actual bodily harm.'

Janet drew a sharp intake of breath.

'So we know he's a bad boy who now seems to be out of Marian's life.'

Right. So that's great.'

'It is. I just thought you should know what I've being doing behind your back.'

She smiled and her body released some of her tension. 'I should think so too!'

'But there's something else. The second piece of news. And this is the one I'm worried about.'

She shivered. Staring into Cliff's face, she just couldn't read it. Was this going to be good or bad?

'There's no easy way to say this, Jan, so I'll just come out with it.'

She nodded, her heart thudding a little faster.

'Marian phoned me a couple of days ago. She wants me to help her find Joe in America.'

Janet froze. Her pupils dilated and she couldn't break her eye contact with Cliff.

He reached for her hand. 'I told her I would only do it if you were happy with it,' he said gently. Then he paused. 'How do you feel about it, Jan?'

She felt as if she was swelling up and out like a character in a cartoon, while Cliff and the world around her were shrinking. A real Alice down the rabbit hole moment. All her senses were concentrated on Cliff's words, *she wants me to help her find Joe*, and her thoughts and feelings were like the white noise of a badly tuned television screen, with occasional flashes of a picture or sounds trying to come into focus: Joe wouldn't know anything about Marian; he would have a wife and family by now; it would come as a massive shock; he didn't even know she'd been pregnant; she'd waited and waited, but he never came back; *it won't be forever*, he'd said back in the summer of 53, but it had been; the red dress with the white spots and the dancing at The Palace; their initials carved in the ash tree; the letters he finally did send, too late, but he wished her well – was that all he wished?; the favourite love songs she'd listened to over the years that made her feel both his love all over again and the loss of it at the same time, certain phrasings charged with agony for the very ecstasy of love they celebrated; all this and more…

And then this: why did Marian want to know Joe and not her? Why was Marian choosing Joe over her? Was she so terrible a person?

Janet felt choked and tears came again when she thought she'd done all her crying. She began to sob, feeling utterly defeated. 'Why him and not me?' she cried.

Cliff came to her side of the table and put an arm around her. 'Jan, don't! Honestly, it might be a good sign. I think she just wants to know who both her parents are and to go on from there.' He squeezed her shoulders. 'Isn't that pretty natural?'

Janet managed to nod.

They talked on, Cliff trying his utmost to make her feel better and to get her to see the wisdom in agreeing to the search for Joe.

Janet wanted to move, to go and make them some coffee, but it was if a huge leaded finger was pressing down on her, forcing her to stay still. When she was finally able to go into the kitchen with Cliff following behind, she felt like a wooden mannequin all stiff in the joints.

Cliff switched the kettle on and spooned some instant coffee into a couple of mugs, while Janet stared out of the window.

Feeling the numbness that comes after a pouring out of feelings, she told him about Susan's idea of inviting Marian to a Sunday tea housewarming in the garden. She couldn't get her tongue around the word 'party', which seemed a farcical concept now.

'Brilliant idea! I'm sure she'll come to that.'

Janet turned to look at him, all bleary-eyed. 'Really?'

'Really! Let's set a date for it. And if by any chance it looks like rain, I'm sure we could get our hands on a little marquee.'

Janet stared numbly at the wall calendar with Cliff. He pointed to the 25th August. 'How about then?'

'Okay,' Janet murmured. 'Then it is. Do you want to ask her?'

'No, Jan. You send her an invite.'

'Alright, I'll do it.'

'And can I tell her it's okay with you for me to search for Joe?'

'Yes.'

The idea of denying Marian this was unthinkable to Janet. She'd just have to face whatever came of it. They both would.

'It probably won't take that long. There are no name changes to contend with and I have a detective mate in New York who I worked with a couple of times. He might be able to help, so I won't necessarily have to travel there.'

Janet nodded.

By the time Cliff gave Janet a hug goodbye on the doorstep of Jasmine Cottage, and she waved him off trying to pin a smile to her face, the day had been swallowed by the night.

Chapter 31

As Janet considered who to send invitations to for the garden-tea-housewarming, as she'd decided to call it, she began to feel a little brighter. And her mood was enhanced by an improvement in Ann.

'I did it!' said Ann, after sitting down at a table by the window in The Tea Kettle. This was their favourite vantage point from which to watch the passers-by in Winchcombe High Street, while they treated themselves to a tray bake.

Ann's face was beaming and Janet didn't have to ask what she meant. 'You told her to stop asking you for money?'

'Yes! And I didn't wait for her to ring me. I rang her.'

'Well done! How did she take it?'

'She was stunned at first and slammed the phone down. But two days later she rang to apologise. She actually apologised, Janet! I don't remember her ever doing that to me. She said she knew she had to rein her spending in, and then at the end of the conversation she said we should meet up more often. Maybe I could come up to York for a visit. I was so shocked, and to be honest, suspicious. I couldn't reply for a second or two, but then I agreed, yes, that would be very nice. We can see how it goes.'

'Great! And you didn't come across as too naïve about it,' Janet said. 'It'll be a chance to see if you can both reconcile.' She was happy for Ann, it was just what she needed. But she found herself wishing things could so easily turn around for herself and Marian.

When she told Ann about Susan's garden-tea-housewarming idea, she was all for it. And while they sipped tea and nibbled on their brownies, Ann helped her decide who to invite as Janet began drawing up her list.

Marian, Jessica, Cliff, Scott, Susan, and Daniel were all obvious choices, as well as Ann herself. But after that came more people who she'd become fond of, and in realising this, Janet surprised herself once again. Gemma, Claire, Kevin, Milly, and her former department manager, Ron, were added next, and after their recent conversations together, Samantha Dixon-Wright even made it onto the list. Liz from Victim Support was another, the Reynolds family from Willow Lane were added, and she remembered Marian's adopted parents, Ruth and Leonard Matthews, who she really wanted to meet some day if they were happy to do so. She wished it was practical to invite Florrie, Auntie Vi, and her cousin, Sarah, from down south, but she had to draw the line somewhere.

And here she halted, assailed by self-doubt. She frowned at the tall column of names, which was far more than she'd ever believed possible. 'Don't you think I'm getting carried away?' she said to Ann. 'This is supposed to be about Marian. These number might make it too formal?'

Ann thought for a moment. 'Yes, but if it's too small, she might feel under pressure. Maybe a larger gathering would mean she wasn't so much in the spotlight? And it is a good opportunity to show you like all these people. Just sending them an invite shows that, and of course they might not all be able to come. You can be doing it with Marian in mind, but you can be doing it for yourself too.'

Janet ruminated on this and decided Ann was right, and of course there were no guarantees that Marian would come anyway.

During the next two days she gathered the addresses together, needing to check the phone book for a few, then she sent the invitations out on some personalized stationery she'd ordered shortly after she'd first moved in – cream paper with a small black and white illustration of a cottage at the top, with her address and telephone number printed beneath. She urged those invited that if they couldn't come, they were more than welcome to visit any other time. Her hand shook as she wrote this because once again she was having to make herself vulnerable to being hurt. This new approach to life, for her own wellbeing and for the sake of others, was taking a good deal of practice.

Once she'd posted the invites she became twitchy every time she heard the latch click on the front gate which signalled the arrival of the postman. But replies by letter or phone soon dropped through the door or rang out to be answered.

Ron said he'd love to call and see her some time, but was away on holiday on the 25th of August.

Claire from work said she'd love to come, but was going to her eldest son's wedding on that day.

Ruth and Leonard Matthews said they thought it best to leave it this time, but would be happy to meet up with her soon. Maybe Janet could visit them in Prestbury, if Marian was okay with it, and they could show Janet some album pictures of Marian taken over the years. This generous offer warmed Janet's heart and gave her some hope like a sunbeam breaking through clouds.

Marian replied to say she'd try to make it, which was better than a no, Janet decided, forcing herself to be pragmatic about it, while everyone else she'd invited accepted.

So over the next two weeks she and Ann planned the food and beverages and did some home baking. When Monday the 19th August arrived, the weather forecast for that weekend predicted fine and sunny, so the heavens were aligning favourably for Janet's special garden-tea-housewarming to be held at two o'clock on Sunday the 25th.

After Cliff, Susan, Scott, and Ann had helped Janet set out two folding tables, which Cliff had borrowed from his local village hall, on the small patio in the back garden of Jasmine Cottage, and after the tables had been duly laid with platters of food and cutlery, with sparkling wine or juice to choose from, they all agreed it looked just like you might see in a *Country Living* magazine, but at the same time, suitably understated. A variety of sandwiches, sausage rolls, cheeses and biscuits were on offer, along with cakes and the quintessential Cornish cream tea comprising of scones, clotted cream and strawberry jam. There were cupcakes with sprinkles and marshmallows on sticks dipped in chocolate for the children who might come. Danny was first on the scene, and his fingertips had already slyly spider-crawled over a few of the cupcakes for which he'd received a suitable telling off from Susan and Scott.

The spread looked charming on blue and white checked cloths, weighted at the corners in case of a summer breeze. But the air didn't stir and the heat beat down on a day that felt to Janet like the last flush of summer before the onset of autumn. She'd chosen a dress from C&A, a store she was shopping in often now. The dress had a retro fifties feel, with short sleeves, a shirt collar and a flared skirt. Buttoned up the front with a belt, it was printed with a soft cream and white check, which was an effective contrast to her dark brown hair now worn in a bob instead of tied back. She felt comfortable in this dress and moderately optimistic, recognising this as very a new sensation.

Shortly after two, people began to arrive. A sign on the front door pointed them to the flagstone path which edged around the house to the back garden, and Janet managed to relax enough to be a reasonably confident hostess, as she greeted them, finding 'surface fluff' small talk topics actually very useful.

Gemma and Kevin seemed 'loved up', as Susan put it, and the two of them retreated to the bottom of the garden under the beech trees with their arms slung around one another.

Milly planted a red lipstick kiss on Janet's cheek, which caused Janet to stiffen for a moment, and then Milly bustled around the tables, handing an empty plate to anyone as soon as they arrived. She was wearing a floral dress bursting with pink roses and was sporting her usual gobstopper ruby ring. And as she busied herself, blinking furiously, Janet realised that Milly was nervous.

'Let me show you around the cottage, Milly,' she said. Milly was delighted with the offer and after entering through the back door into the kitchen with Janet, she began to relax, moving from room to room, listening to Janet describe what she'd done with the place. Her Spanish sun-crinkled eyes glowed in appreciation. When they came across Thomas curled up in Janet's bedroom, he deigned to allow Milly to stroke him and to call him Tommy Tiddler.

Next to arrive was Liz, who serenely sailed into the garden in a chintzy blue Laura Ashley dress, looking very much the part as Janet had anticipated she would, and she soon began chatting in earnest to Susan and Milly.

When Samantha arrived, she got a few frowns and puzzled looks from Gemma, Kevin, and Milly, but Janet went out of her way to welcome the interior designer who was determined to improve her skills and run her own business. She was wearing her hair loose and was dressed in a beige linen skirt and safari-style fitted blouse which showed off her generous curves. Very quiet at first, Liz soon had her winkled out of her shell and talking animatedly about her future plans.

Alison Reynolds turned up without Tony or the kids, or her apron. 'Sorry, I can't stay long,' she said to Janet. 'We're going over to my mother-in-law's for tea, but I wanted to wish you well. And I'm afraid there's some bad news to report about your next door neighbour, Winnie Parsons.'

Janet frowned, wondering what Winnie had been up to now.

'She had an accident yesterday. I went over to hers to give her a letter that had been put through our letterbox by mistake. She didn't answer, which I thought was odd as I knew she was in, so I went around the back and found her lying on the ground by the back door with a gash on her head. It looked like she'd tripped over the garden gnome she kept there. It was all in pieces like broken crockery with grey powder spilling out of it and she was lying there unconscious. The ambulance man said she must have tripped, then fallen sharply forward knocking her head hard on the wall.' She hesitated, looking directly at Janet. 'There was no pulse. She's dead, Janet. You weren't close, were you?'

Janet shuddered. 'No.'

It was all she could say. She was struck dumb by the irony, the sheer cosmic payback, that seemed to have been delivered by the spirit of Winnie's dead husband, Charles, contained within the gnome. He'd finally wreaked his revenge upon the wife that had tried so often to cause him a fatal accident. Would fate have something similar in line for herself? But she shook this off. There was no comparison at all. She was just being silly.

'Thanks for telling me, Alison,' she said, and she explained what the grey powder was.

Alison screwed up her nose. 'Crikey!'

By three o' clock, Janet was heavy-hearted about Marian not having come. She wanted to be alone with her feelings, but everyone seemed to be getting along so well and she felt she had to carry on for them.

But at ten past three, just as Janet was collecting empty plates from the tables on the patio, and shortly after Cliff had set off to the local shop for more juice, Marian came hurrying around the corner of the house clutching Jessica's hand.

'Sorry, I'm late,' she said, as she approached Janet. 'We got held up.'

'That's fine!' Janet said, putting down the pile of plates. 'I'm pleased you've come. And you both look lovely.'

Marian was wearing a sleeveless midi dress printed with a turquoise and green floral pattern and her red hair was worn loose on her shoulders. Janet was pleased to see that there appeared to be no bruises under her makeup. Jessica looked charming in a frilled denim dress and her golden brown hair had been curled into cute ringlets.

'This is Janet,' Marian said to Jessica.

Then she turned to Janet. 'Janet, this is Jessie.'

Janet took Jessica's hand and said, 'Very pleased to meet you, Jessie.'

Jessica stared into Janet's face, then she smiled. Her eyes were green, like Janet's own, and she had a scattering of freckles over her nose. 'Hello, Janet,' she said shyly.

Danny approached and tugged at Jessica's arm. 'You've got to come and see this den I've just built,' he said, and he led her to the bottom of the garden through the trees towards the back field, leaving Marian and Janet alone by the tables.

Scott followed the two children, saying he'd keep an eye on them, and Susan considerately kept her distance from Janet and Marian. Everyone else was deep in conversation, their chatter only broken by titters of laughter.

Marian stepped closer to Janet. She was biting her lip. 'I just had a row with Rick. I broke up with him, you know. Haven't seen him for ages, but then he turned up just as we were leaving. He won't let it go!'

Janet's heart clenched painfully at the knowledge that Rick was still in Marian's life. 'Cliff might have some idea what to do…'

'Yeah, maybe.' She hesitated. 'Listen, Janet. About me looking for Joe, I –'

'Marian!' a voice called out.

Marian twitched. 'Oh, God, no.' Her head swivelled in the direction the voice had come from.

'What?' Janet asked, feeling Marian's panic.

Right then a man strode around the corner of the house. His pace was fast and determined, but his tread was light, as if he was afraid of getting his shoes dirty. With his shoulder-length blonde hair and his tight jeans showing off the bulge of his crotch, Janet recognised Rick instantly. He strode right up to them and Marian stepped alongside Janet to face him. He drew himself up to his full height.

'What the fuck are you doing here?' he asked Marian.

The hard and blunt angles of his brow and jaw were tensed and the writhing inked dragons on his biceps breathed fire.

'It's none of your business, Rick. I've told you, we're finished, and what are you playing at following me here?'

'I'll follow you wherever the fuck I like.'

His cold blue eyes locked onto Janet and narrowed into slits as he looked her up and down. They came to rest on her face.

'I've seen you before. Once, maybe twice. Yeah, I know you.' He pointed a finger at her. 'I think you're the one from work that's been feeding her bullshit about abuse. She told me you were the one that gave her that stupid leaflet.'

He stood right in front of Janet and poked his finger into the hollow of her shoulder. 'This is all your fault, isn't it? All – your – fault.' For every word he thrust his finger into her.

'Stop it, Rick! You can't treat people like this. Get out of here!' Marian cried.

Shocked by the physical contact and the pain, Janet's old habits kicked in and she stood welded to the spot. If he was trying to frighten her, she wouldn't give him the satisfaction.

A vein throbbed in his temple as he stared her out.

Then he grabbed Marian's arm and squeezed it hard. 'Come on, we're going home. You drive your car and I'll follow you back in mine. Get the kid.'

Marian tried to shrug him off by twisting her body around.

The guests were rooted to their respective spots with their mouths gaping wide.

Janet struggled to see if she could make out Scott through the trees. With Cliff at the shop, he was the only one who might be able to help. But there was no sign of him. He must be with the children, she thought. But at least they aren't seeing this.

Marian finally managed to wrench herself out of Rick's grasp and stood shoulder to shoulder with Janet again, rubbing her red arm.

'If you don't come with me now, you'll be sorry.' His tone was horribly quiet and deliberate. 'You don't belong in a place like this. You belong with me. Do you hear me?' Then he shouted, 'Do You Hear Me?'

He plunged towards Marian, but Janet leapt in front of her and blocked him.

Clenching his fists he said, 'Get out of my way!'

'No.'

Glaring at Janet, his eyes tightened and his face flushed crimson. 'You fucking bitch. This is all down to you! So you can have it instead!'

And before she realised what he was doing, he'd snatched hold of a knife from one of the tables and lunged low at her.

He came in close. She saw the hate in his eyes. Boring into her. She smelled his sweat. And when he drew back, the knife had disappeared.

He looked down on her with his mouth twisting, as if he was working through a series of emotional responses to his actions. And then he was gone.

She stared down at herself.

The handle of a knife was sticking out of her lower abdomen, but she couldn't feel anything. How deep was it? What kind of knife was it? Did it matter? But what was important was it didn't belong there. She grasped hold of it with both hands and pulled it out. It was a sharp paring knife with a bone handle. She'd had if for years.

'No!' someone shouted. It sounded like Scott. 'Don't!'

The knife fell out of her hand and she heard it chink onto the concrete. She staggered backwards against Marian. Marian supported her shoulders as she slowly dropped to the ground. Lying on her back, she saw the solid saturated blue of a beautiful summer day. Then the pain cut in, and someone was screaming, someone was shouting, someone was running. Then Marian was pressing down on her with a tea towel where the knife had been. It hurt. Marian's hands were covered in blood. There was blood on her cheeks.

'Keep pressure on it!' someone shouted.

'Stay awake, Janet!' That was Marian.

'I've called for an ambulance!' That sounded like Susan.

'Where did the bastard go?' She knew that was Cliff shouting.

'He drove off. But I've got the license number!' answered Liz. She'd know Liz's voice anywhere. The voice that had talked so much sense, that had helped her see so much. That had helped her recover some of the person she used to be. The one she used to like, as well as move on to the new.

'I'll keep the children away,' cried Ann, her best friend, who'd stood by her when she didn't even deserve it.

Then these voices faded out and she heard another. *Pity. Never mind.* She cringed. Feeling cold now. It was her dead neighbour, Winnie, who'd liked to think they were kindred spirits, come to tell her that she too would not escape retribution. That she too would have to pay for wanting a husband dead. She too would die. *Pity. Never mind.*

Chapter 32

When she forced her eyelids to open, the beautiful blue of summer above had been replaced by a bright white, and her head felt as if it was resting in a cloud. It was a peaceful place she'd come to then. And there was a sea of green around her. But she heard creaking sounds, like a wobbly-wheeled shopping trolley makes as you push it along, and distant mutterings echoing off walls, which brought her back to earth. Forcing her eyes to focus, she saw the crisp turned down sheet of the bed she was lying in and the thin blue coverlet on top. Hospital. She was in hospital...and she began to remember snapshots of the garden-tea-housewarming, the screaming, the shouting, being on a stretcher and being bumped up into an ambulance, Marian, Rick, the knife, as she tried to put them in the correct sequence. And then everything had gone black.

She tried to speak now, to call out, but her mouth was so parched. The only sound she could make was a faint croak.

'Mum! You're awake!' A shadow leaned over her right side, and she saw it was Scott. He patted her hand, the hand that she now realised had an intravenous drip attached. 'You're going to be fine, Mum, just fine. You've had an operation, but it went very well. You're on a ward now and it's about eight thirty in the evening.'

She tried to smile, but her mouth wouldn't do what it was told.

Then a figure hovered over her left side. Red hair, pretty face, but as gaunt as a death mask. 'Janet, thank God you're alright. Thank God!' It was Marian, and she'd been crying judging from her puffy eyes. She was holding Janet's other hand and Janet gripped it. It felt good.

The sea of green parted and a nurse floated in and she

gave Janet a few sips of water. They trickled down Janet's throat like drops of dew in a desert.

'I'm Colleen,' the nurse smiled. 'You're nicely on the mend, Mrs Brewer. You'll soon be up and about now.'

Colleen was short and plump, but reassuringly wholesome as she bustled around the bed with indomitable vigour. She spoke with an Irish accent which was musically pleasant to Janet's ear. 'I'll be getting the doctor to explain things to you now.' She drew back the sea of green that had been surrounding the bed and disappeared out of sight.

When the surgeon arrived Janet was ready to listen, after having had her mind put at rest by Scott and Marian that everyone else was fine.

Jessica and Danny had been busy in their den in the back field while the stabbing took place, and afterwards Ann had kept them away from the hustle and bustle of the ambulance and police cars. The knife had departed the scene in a evidence bag and Rick had been arrested in The Dog and Gun in town. He was currently in custody and was expected to remain so. With all the witnesses and a statement from Marian down at the station as to the violence in their relationship, there was no question that he wouldn't go to prison for grievous bodily harm, having upped his own ante, so to speak. Blokes like him always do, Cliff had commented, who had appointed himself temporary guardian of Thomas the tabby.

The surgeon, a tall reed of a man with a hooked nose, spoke softly and plainly to Janet, while Scott and Marian smiled, nodded, or shook their heads and sighed as they took their cues from him during his narrative of Janet's abdominal stabbing and treatment.

'I'm Mr Waring,' he said. 'You're a lucky woman, Mrs Brewer, you –'

'Please, call me Janet. And I'll be changing my name back to Turner.'

The surgeon didn't flinch. Neither did Scott or Marian. But Janet had surprised herself with the certainty of this sudden decision.

'Janet, you're a lucky woman.' The doctor began again. 'The blade was short and didn't go in deep. It went in approximately three inches below your navel and to the left, angled down. All your vital organs are fine, and the blade missed your arteries, so although you had considerable blood loss through removing the knife at the scene, it could have been far worse. But part of your intestine and your bladder were punctured so we've surgically repaired these during the wound exploration. Scans haven't revealed any other problems.'

'Thank you so much.' She found her smile now, but she didn't feel lucky because she hated hospitals. The smell of disinfectant, the bed covers which seemed to pin people's feet down at the bottom, the helplessness you felt, and she'd never had a major operation before so she was bound to find more to hate in the next few days. 'How long will I be here?'

'Well, we'll have those stitches out in about three to four days, and we have to make sure the wound begins to heal well and doesn't get infected. We've put a surgical drain to collect fluid and blood from the area, and we have to keep an eye on your blood pressure and keep your fluids up…and you have a catheter just for now, but I'd say if you're lucky you might be out in seven to eight days. How does that sound?'

Terrible, she thought, and she had to stop herself from frowning, thinking of her so-called *luck*. 'That sounds alright,' she said.

'We'll soon have you up and about taking a shower, doing a bit of walking, and before you're discharged we'll want you to pass some water and some food. Okay?'

'Right, yes.'

There were a few more details from Mr Waring, but Janet didn't hear them. She stared out of the adjacent window. Although it was evening, there was still the shadow of a sunset pink in the sky. She was lucky to be alive; she knew that. She didn't have to join Winnie after all. Pity, never mind, she chanted to herself wryly. But being alive, even though she felt as weak as a new born kitten, and probably couldn't even stand up, all she wanted was to get out of hospital. She wanted to be free to think and feel. About her relationship with Marian — where was that at now? And about Cliff's imminent search for Joe — how long would it take and what would she feel if he found him? And about her own future as Janet Turner once again. What was the new Janet going to do in life? There was so much thinking to be done and she wanted to be at her new home to do it.

But her thoughts were tugged back into the present by a sob on her left from Marian. She turned her head and saw a face of pure misery. With her mascara having proved that it was not waterproof, as it no doubt had promised on the tube, the sooty blotches around Marian's swollen eyes, and her powder-pale pallor provided a dramatic contrast to her blood-red lipstick, rendering her a theatrically tragic look.

And Janet's heart went out to her. 'What's the matter, Marian?'

Marian leaned on the bed and buried her head in both hands. 'This is all my fault,' she said. 'I should have listened earlier to you about Rick. He could have killed you!'

'No, it's not – ' began Janet.

'Mum might just have saved your life,' Scott said on Janet's right. When Janet turned her head to look at him, a tight-lipped anger was evident on her son's drawn and tired face. It seemed her generous-spirited son and his goodwill towards Marian had reached an impasse.

'I know!' Marian said. 'Really, I know! I feel terrible about it. Just awful!'

Then her son and her daughter aired their feelings over her as she lay in her hospital bed without her able to get a word in.

'She's bloody lucky to be alive,' Scott said, glaring at Marian.

Janet hardly ever heard Scott swear, so she knew this new antagonism towards Marian was potentially serious.

'I know! But I've never known him to do anything like that before! I didn't know he was capable.'

Scott screwed his nose up. 'Oh, come on. He's a lout.'

'Well I know that now! But he honestly could be decent at times.'

'And having him around Jessica. I mean, come on.'

'He never behaved badly in front of Jessie or with her. I made sure of it!'

'But you were okay with him thumping you, is that it?'

'Of course not!' Marian hesitated. 'But he was always so sorry.'

'Oh, give me a break!'

'Scott, please don't talk to Marian like this. Please!' Janet begged.

'No, Mum. This needs to be said.' Then he scowled at Marian. 'You should have thought more of yourself than to go out with a scumbag like him.'

'Well, I know that *now*. And I'm working on my self-esteem. My counsellor at Victim Support suggested my parents weren't all that assertive and -'

'Oh, so now it's your parents fault.'

'Scott!' said Janet.

'It's alright, Janet. If Scott has something to say, let him say it.'

'She's been worrying on about you,' he retorted to Marian. 'About how you were. If you were okay. And fretting that you don't want anything to do with her.'

'It's been complicated with us having known each other already!' Marian replied.

Scott thumped the bed with his fist. 'Yes, but you could see that as a bonus, couldn't you? But oh no. It just couldn't be an advantage, could it? But why not? Why couldn't it be a case of you've seen each other's worst, now you get a chance to see each other's best?'

Marian and Janet stared at Scott, then looked at each other.

'Just think about it. Both of you.'

They nodded.

'You've got a point,' Marian said.

Then Janet had another thought. One derived from karma, or an eye for an eye, depending on your spiritual belief system. Nothing to do with Marian or Scott. To do with her and Frank and her stabbing. 'Maybe I had it coming?' she said.

'What?' Scott and Marian exclaimed in unison.

'I wanted Frank to die. Those pills might have been out of date, but I still kept them away from him. Maybe my being stabbed was payback?' A bit like Winnie's death, she thought.

'Oh, Mum. How long are you going to punish yourself? You've got to let it go! You heard what the doctor said. The pills were out of date. Dad's heart was in bad shape. He was like a time bomb waiting to go off,' Scott said. 'And you were none the wiser.'

'Janet, that's just ridiculous. He was a lout!' Marian exclaimed.

Then Scott and Marian both saw the irony, caught each other's eyes and grinned.

When Janet saw them smiling at each other, it was one of the most special moments of her life. Her son and daughter smiling at one another.

But there was an even more startlingly pleasurable moment to come very soon.

After Colleen scuttled down the ward to tell Scott and Marian that she needed to take Janet's blood pressure and they should be leaving now to let Janet get some rest, Marian pleaded for just five more minutes.

'You'll be getting me into trouble, mind,' muttered Colleen. But she went to another bed to take some vital signs from a motionless figure humped under some bed sheets.

Scott surprised Janet by leaving first. 'See you tomorrow, Mum,' he said, kissing her cheek. This new gesture of affection was something else she was unaccustomed to, but which hospital visits no doubt triggered, she decided.

'I'll see you outside,' he said to Marian over his shoulder.

Marian drew closer to Janet. Her face was softer and the tragic demeanour had gone, though the makeup looked exactly the same. 'Janet.'

'What?'

'Do you remember before Rick arrived, I was in the middle of asking you – '

'About looking for Joe.' Janet remembered all too well and steeled herself for what was to come. 'I'm okay about it, Marian. It's only natural you would want to find him.'

'No, that wasn't it.'

Janet raised her eyebrows. 'What was it then? What were you going to ask?'

'I wanted to know…I want to know, if we find him and if he wants to see me, if he wants to see us – will you come with me?'

And with shock giving way to an oscillating to and fro of disbelieve and happiness pulsing through her, as vital to her as her own blood flow which Colleen was now approaching her bedside to measure, there was only one word which Janet could manage to say.

'Yes.'

Chapter 33

Colleen said Janet was the worst patient she'd ever had. She wouldn't lie still, she wouldn't wait for assistance when getting out of bed and she was a terrible sleeper. She made a fuss when Colleen had to take a blood sample or give her a warfarin injection, she dragged her drips around as if they were stubborn dogs on leads, and she engaged in conversations with other patients about their rights. When Janet's stitches were out, when she was free of drains and tubes, and her digestion and waterworks were functioning normally, after seven long days Mr Waring was happy to discharge her. With instructions on surgical wound care and strict advice not to do any lifting, she was ready to go home.

'If I wasn't well enough to get out of here today, I'd have been crawling out on my hands and knees,' Janet said to Colleen as she packed up her belongings.

'To be sure, I'll be glad to see the back of you!' exclaimed Colleen, hands on hips.

But there was a soft side to the nurse and after a brief clasp of Janet's hand, she had some words of wisdom, an Irish proverb she said, which Janet puzzled over on the drive home with Scott.

'As you ramble through life, whatever be your goal, keep your eye upon the doughnut and not upon the hole,' Colleen had said in her sing song voice.

'Must mean look for the positive, see the glass as half full, be optimistic instead of pessimistic,' observed Scott, after he'd finished laughing.

'Well, I'll be doing that from now on!' replied Janet.

And as soon as she got home to Winchcombe she saw the evidence of the positive changes she'd managed to make, after letting light into the darkness of her past by opening herself up to others and to herself.

Colour was everywhere in the form of bright bunches of carnations, roses, and freesias, all springing forth from their vases throughout the living room of Jasmine Cottage. And there were Get Well cards from all the people she'd invited to the garden-tea-housewarming and more. There were cards from Dr Blake, DCI Bridges, and even her solicitor, the knobbly-browed Michael Armstrong. And two more, which meant so much, as they were from her family in the South – there were cards from Florrie in Cornwall and Sarah in Bournemouth.

'How did they all find out?' Janet asked Scott in astonishment, after scanning a handful of cards clutched between her fingers.

'The story of your attack was in the local papers,' he replied. 'And I've been getting phone calls too, so I thought it best to let Florrie and Sarah know what was going on.'

Feeling weakened by her exertion and overcome by the exhibition of kindness and caring around her she dropped into a sofa.

Never being one to be taken out of the equation, Thomas appeared through the kitchen doorway. He'd been brought home by Cliff early that morning, explained Scott. Thomas slinked up to her, head-butting her leg a few times. He allowed himself to be stroked and he even deigned to purr more quickly than usual as it was a special occasion. He was home again.

'Cup of tea?' Scott asked.

'Please.'

'Susan might pop over later. Is that okay?'

'Of course, it will be lovely to see her.' She hesitated. 'I was wrong about Susan, she's a special person. She's been an amazing help to me. Are you both alright?'

'Yes, Mum.' Then he looked at her. 'I think we've gone through most of our rough patches now. We're very different, even though we love each other, and sometimes we want different things in life, but we talk it through these

days and go for compromises.'
'Give and take.'
'Exactly.'

Janet's convalescence lasted for about six weeks. She had to keep the wound clean and dry and the district nurse called twice to check on her progress. Getting her strength back was gradual but steady as her muscles took their time to knit together again. And after driving too soon into Cheltenham to do some shopping, and feeling her abdomen to be suddenly very vulnerable with the need to physically shield it, she soon got the message that her overall recovery would take longer. Ann regularly popped around to vacuum and do a bit of housework and they walked together into town for a spot of lunch.

But there was of course a sense of waiting.

Waiting this time for Cliff to find Joe.

And Janet had asked Cliff, when he visited her in hospital, if he might be able to track down her brother, Norman, last heard of working in New England, and for which she had his first address in Massachusetts from Florrie.

'That should be easy,' he'd said. 'But Joe comes first?'

'Oh yes, Joe comes first.'

So while Cliff accessed his police contacts in New York, whom he'd worked with in the past on certain cases, to see if they could aid his search through their state and county networks, the weeks passed slowly.

With her injury, Janet had missed out on enrolling on her college courses so would have to pick them up next time around. To keep busy she decided to offer some help to Samantha for her interior design business, and to teach her how to work out all manner of fabric allowances and how to take accurate measurements. So after her shifts at Oakbury Manor, Samantha drove to Janet's house for her training. And she began to press upon Janet the need for a business partner. They would make a good team, she insisted. Janet said she'd think about it.

She also had to think about becoming Cliff's personal assistant, but she wanted those evening classes under her belt before she could feel confident about tackling his business needs. She did help him to design his new business card and came up with some promotional material he was pleased with.

She also had the great pleasure of visiting Marian's adoptive parents, Ruth and Leonard Matthews, at their home in Prestbury. Marian collected her one Sunday in early November from Winchcombe, in her red Ford Fiesta, and drove her to Prestbury with Jessica along for the ride. Up to this point, Marian had simply described Janet to Jessica, as Mummy's friend, whenever she'd asked who Janet was, with Marian never having gotten around to a proper explanation.

The Matthews were a quiet couple, and the décor in their house was all pastels and plains, with everything seemingly in just the right place. Conservatism and moderation was so evident in their behaviour and their environment that Janet could easily surmise how any extremes of behaviour or passionate feeling from Marian could have been hard for them to handle. But they were friendly and welcoming without a hint of judgment towards Janet, so the tweaking at her nerve endings soon subsided. She was also overcome with gratitude when Ruth described to Jessica that Janet was her mother's other mummy.

'Is that right?' Jessica asked Marian, wide-eyed.

'That's right,' replied Marian. 'Is that okay?'

'It's cool!' replied Jessica with her eyes shining. 'I get to have two Grandmas.'

And with that, the deed was done.

Over tea and scones, Ruth and Leonard said they were both behind Janet and Marian in their search for Joe and that it was quite exciting. That of course was an understatement, but Janet couldn't possibly have wanted more from them and their generosity was humbling.

Another topic of conversation concerned Marian having

changed her red hair to blonde in keeping with her natural colour. The softer shade complimented her brown eyes, and she had toned down her makeup saying the stronger shades were too brash now.

Ruth and Janet exchanged a look, prompting Marian to ask, 'What?'

Meanwhile the trees cast off their leaves and the daylight hours shortened as winter bedded in. The Cotswolds calendar in Janet's kitchen shifted into December with a snow scene of the aptly named, secluded village of Snowshill, while Janet and Marian became increasingly worried that finding Joe would never happen.

But finally, at the end of the first week of December, there was news. Cliff arranged for Marian to come over to Janet's on the Sunday as he had something for them both.

'It's a letter sent to me to give to you,' he said. 'It's from Joe.'

He reached into the inner pocket of his jacket and drew out an envelope and a piece of paper.

Sitting together on one of Janet's bijou sofas, Janet and Marian stared hard at what he held in his hand.

'And I've got Norman's whereabouts too, Janet. He's still in Massachusetts, still married, three children, still working in textiles. I've got his address and telephone number from the local sheriff's office, so you can ring him if you want.' He handed her the piece of paper.

'Just like that?' Janet asked, taking it from him.

'Just like that,' replied Cliff, grinning.

But both she and Marian had their eyes riveted upon the creased envelope with its airmail stamp, and its red, white and blue hatched edging, still in Cliff's hand – the letter from Joe. Marian had never met her father, and Janet hadn't seen him for 38 years, ever since he sailed out of her life on the 15th September 1953.

Cliff handed it to Marian. 'It's to both of you, as it says on the front, though he does have both your addresses. I've not opened it. And now I'm going to leave you alone to read it together.'

And saying that, he saw himself out of Jasmine Cottage with a feather-light tread, and he closed the front door so quietly behind him it was if he was departing a church hushed in prayer.

As Janet gazed at Marian she couldn't find any words. Neither could Marian.

A silence hung between them with an expectancy stretching tauter and tauter, almost to tearing point.

'You read it,' said Janet at last.

'No, you,' said Marian, trying to push it into Janet's hand.

'No, I want you to read it,' Janet insisted, gently pressing it back into Marian's hold.

Marian suddenly ripped it open like she was stripping off a plaster, unfolded the letter, and began to read.

Fairlie Farm
Northford Road
Wallingford
Connecticut

28th November 1991

Dear Janet and Marian,

There is so much to say but I'll try to keep it brief because I want to wait until I can hopefully talk to you both face to face. I'm so glad you've looked for me and found me. I've often thought of you both — my first love and my first child (a little girl, as it now turns out)

'He knew about you!' gasped Janet.

She took the letter off Marian to read these words for herself and was also struck by his neat handwriting, cursive in style, which she realised she'd never seen before. Then she handed the letter back and indicated for Marian to read on.

Janet, my mother told me just before she died about you becoming pregnant and how she and Dad had kept it from me. She said they hadn't done right by you. I was so shocked and angry with them, knowing that you'd probably have had to give our baby away. That should never have happened.

Janet felt the pain of that moment she'd handed over Vivien nudge at her again, but it didn't grasp hold of her and tighten its grip. And she knew this was because she had no need of it any longer.

After I first arrived over here I did try writing to you, Janet, and I sent letters to my parents for them to give to you – but they didn't do it and time passed. They told me you got married, so I stayed over here and worked the farm. It's called Fairlie farm and it's been my life. We do arable crops and fruit growing. I married a good woman and have two wonderful sons, but my wife, Stella, died ten years ago now. Since then I've often wondered about trying to find you, but I was nervous so much time had passed by and I didn't want to upset your lives. I'm sorry for this and I hope you can forgive me.

But hopefully we have now and the future.

'Do you forgive him, Janet?' asked Marian.
'Of course. Do you?'
'For sure!'

I want you both to come and visit me here. I'm going to send you tickets, Janet, and would love it if you would both come here to Connecticut for this Christmas.

'Christmas in Connecticut, Janet! Wouldn't that be amazing?' Marian jumped to her feet and began pacing Janet's sitting room. 'But how will I get the time off Masons?'

'Ask that new store manager of yours,' Janet said eagerly, tracking Marian's movements. 'Tell her you need compassionate leave and Christmas is dead in soft furnishings anyway.'

'Right. That might work. Good idea.' Then she paused. 'Anyway, there's no way I'm missing this chance.'

'Exactly!' Janet said. 'Finish the letter.'

You can stay for as little or as long as you like. I thought of enclosing a photograph of me and my boys, but I don't have ones of you, so thought we could leave that for when we meet at the airport. I'll be sure to know you, Janet.

'He must be 59 now,' Janet said. 'But I'm sure we'll recognise him. And he's right, that's a nicer way.'

I can't wait to see you both, and I've never forgotten you,

All my love,

Joe

XX

'Oh God, Janet! This is amazing! Isn't it amazing?' Marian said, her eyes wide and shining.

Janet couldn't sit still anymore either.

They both stood staring at each other. Janet saw the amber glow in Marian's eyes, the fiery spark, the sheer excitement.

And then they reached for one another. And they were hugging one another. And it was a heartfelt tight hug. Their very first. And Janet was able to mark the fact that she was finally holding her daughter in her arms once again after 37 years, and it felt so wonderful – so right.

After the tickets arrived a few days later, Janet couldn't help chanting out loud, 'Christmas in Connecticut', as she went about the house, and she knew that wherever Marian was, she'd be chanting it too. They were due to fly out on

Saturday 21st December, and Janet marked it on her calendar with a red felt-tip pen. She rang Florrie and Sarah with the good news, delighted to be able to share this with newly found members of her family. Marian discovered Janet was right about the new store manager, Joy Hume, who said four weeks was the maximum leave time Marian could have, but to go ahead. As for when they got there, they planned to stay with Joe for three weeks, then spend the last few days in Massachusetts, an adjoining northern state, visiting Janet's brother, Norman, who she managed to speak to on the phone. 'There's a lot of catching up to do, Sis,' he said.

So everything was arranged. Thomas was to go to Cliff's again, but Cliff told an anxious Janet that he and Thomas got along just fine. Thomas had yet another wilderness in Cliff's overgrown back garden to explore, and he'd be indulged with only the very best cat food, whatever that turns out to be, said Cliff. A relentless conundrum, commented Janet. And Ann wasn't going to miss out, which Janet had been worrying about, because Ann told her she was going to spend Christmas with her daughter, Jenny up in York. 'Hopefully we can build some bridges,' Ann said. Jessica was to spend the time with Ruth and Leonard Matthews. 'They adore her,' remarked Marian, 'and they'll spoil her rotten.' And Cliff was going to spend another Christmas day with Scott, Susan, and Daniel.

As the departure day approached, and on a mid-December morning, after she put the kettle on for her elevenses, Janet gazed out of the kitchen window in Jasmine Cottage. There was a faint glinting of crystal in the bare branches of the trees at the bottom of the frost-speckled garden, and the air was still. She remembered standing in her kitchen in Willow Lane, Charlton Kings, on a drizzly dark morning preparing to go back to work after Frank's death in the new year of 1990. Almost two years ago now. All she'd wanted was to go back to Masons and make sure Marian didn't usurp her there. Masons had been everything back then. She smiled at the memory. It had been such a different life – a cold embittered one, in which she'd trusted no one. Since then it seemed as if external changes had brought internal changes, and she'd become the Janet she'd been meant to be all along. She also smiled at the poinsettia on the windowsill. Marian had given it to her, not having any idea Janet hated them. But she'd accepted it gracefully and had kept it watered. Susan was going to look after it until she got back. This one was not destined for her rubbish bin. There were so many things she and Marian didn't know about each other. It was going to be an exciting journey of discovery.

Janet had never been on a plane before. She'd never even travelled abroad. So Marian, who'd been to sunny Spain a few times, suggested Janet should take the window seat on the Boeing 747 after they boarded. The sheer outer and inner scale of the plane astonished Janet, so many rows of seats for so many people, reducing human beings to the size of ants.

When the plane began accelerating down the runway and they were pressed back into their seats, Janet felt uneasy and realised she was tensing her legs as if she could defy gravity. But an hour later, when the plane hadn't dropped out of the sky and was cruising steadily at the required altitude, and when she could see the ruffled waves of the Atlantic far below, she relaxed and began to enjoy this new experience. And even better than that, she had her daughter by her side.

'Who would have thought it, Janet? Christmas in Connecticut with Joe,' said Marian.

Then she looked at Janet with some concern and squeezed her hand. 'Are you alright?'

Yes, I'm fine,' she replied and she smiled at Marian.

And for the first time in a very long time, this wasn't just her customary calculated response to shield herself and to keep out the world, this time it came from deep within. She really was fine.

ABOUT THE AUTHOR

Lynne was born in Durham City in 1962. After moving to the Scottish Borders in 1998 she rekindled her love of art, becoming an artist, tutor, and illustrator, before going on to study with the Open University as a mature student. Here, she gained a first class honours degree in the Humanities, with Literature and Art History, followed by a diploma in Creative Writing. Writing is a new passion, enabling her to put to good use her lifelong fascination with human nature. *After Black* is Lynne's second novel inspired by the retail world of the eighties.

On Turtle Beach, Lynne's debut novel, is set in the beautiful sea turtle conservation area of Dalyan in Turkey. The novel explores the relationship between two estranged sisters, following the death of their father, with secrets to unearth from the past before healing can begin. (Available from Amazon as paperback and ebook)

Lynne spends her time writing, blogging, painting and volunteering in social care. She is currently working on another novel provisionally entitled 'Rethinking Happy Ever After' along with a memoir, both of which are on the theme of midlife transition, together with a collection of short stories.

Thank you for taking the time to read **After Black**. *If you enjoyed it, please consider telling your friends and posting a short review. Reviews help independent authors by helping other readers to find their book, by boosting a book's visibility, and by providing useful feedback. It doesn't have to be long, just one or two sentences will do. Many thanks from Lynne.*

You can find Lynne at:

Head to Head, Heart to Heart: lynnefisher.wordpress.com

Facebook: facebook.com/lynnefisherheadtoheadhearttoheart
@lynnefisherheadtoheadhearttoheart

Twitter: twitter.com/writeartblog @writeartblog

Goodreads: Goodreads.com/author/show/16999979.Lynne_Fisher

Printed in Great Britain
by Amazon